MW01386176

THE YEAR 3107:

REIGN OF THE SUPREME

LAUREN LEE

The Year 3107: Reign of the Supreme

Copyright © 2010 by Lauren Lee

All rights reserved. Without limiting the rights under copyright reserved above, no part of this publication may be reproduced, stored in or introduced into a retrieval system, or transmitted, in any form, or by any means (electronic, mechanical, photocopying, recording, or otherwise) without the prior written permission of the copyright owner.

This is a work of fiction. Names, characters, places, brands, media, and incidents are either the product of the author's imagination or are used fictitiously. The author acknowledges the trademarked status and trademark owners of various products referenced in this work of fiction, which have been used without permission. The publication/use of these trademarks is not authorized, associated with, or sponsored by the trademark owners.

ISBN: 1461126630
ISBN -13: 978-1461126638

DEDICATION

In Loving Memory of Anna Linda Tarankov

Her lively and God-fearing spirit lives on in the souls she touched.

~

"Smile, Jesus loves you."

CONTENTS

ACKNOWLEDGMENTS

I want to express my utmost appreciation to those who supported me through this journey by offering comments and advice, reading and rereading, and helping with the designing, proofing, editing and publishing.

I would like to thank my mother and father for encouraging me while I was writing even though I know it took time away from them. I also want to thank my younger sisters, Jordan and Megan, who pushed me along when the writing blocks came.

Countless thanks to Katy Spraberry and Natalie Ware who helped me with editing and proofing. And lastly, I want to thank my many friends who gave me reassurance through the years.

Chapter 1
A FORBIDDEN HISTORY

Recorded 12.30.3107

Pull the panel back onto the wall. Tell no one of these contents. This recording is for your eyes only.

Verification that these contents will not be given to the Head Council
YES, I VERIFY
NO, I DO NOT VERIFY

You have chosen: Yes, I Verify – Listen closely

10.12.1492:	Columbus discovers the Americas.
2.5.1509:	The first cast iron gun is produced in England.
12.4.1681:	The French build the first bomb vessel.
3.19.1770:	The first tank is brought into existence.
5.9.1865:	The Gatling gun is patented.
1.31.1915:	Poison gas is created and used in World War I.
12.7.1941:	The United States enters into World War II as a direct result of Japan's attack on Pearl Harbor.
8.9.1945:	World War II ends with the United States dropping the atom bomb on Hiroshima and Nagasaki.
12.4.1960:	The Cold War and the Nuclear Arms Race perpetuate the idea of nuclear warfare.
6.7.1963:	The Soviet Union has enough nuclear power to destroy the world two times over. The United States has enough nuclear power to destroy the world ten times over.

7.4.1987: Operation SOL created. Genetic testing initiated. Selection process made priority.
9.11.2001: Terrorist Attack on the United States, ultimately resulting in the War on Terror.
7.4.2011: Operation SOL instigated; building commences.
2.27.2012: SOL construction completed. Archives are backed up. Selection process set in motion.
4.21.2012: Cloning technology used in military forces around the world.
12.12.2012: The world takes severe precautions against World War III.
3.7.2013: The United States sends CIA operatives to investigate the underground activities of North Korea, Iraq and Iran.
1.12.2015: The CIA submits Top Secret information to the Pentagon.
1.13.2015: The President of the United States, Blake Johnson, orders the acceleration of Operation SOL.
4.26.2017: Spies are discovered in the United States government.
5.31.2017: Emerging Japanese technology enables humans to extend their life spans up to 80 years. This technology increases the average life span from 80 years to 160 years.
6.2.2018: The world population exceeds 10 billion.
6.7.2018: The United States creates the National Anti-Replication of Hominids Council to push a worldwide ban on the use of cloning technology.
11.25.2018: Ninety percent of the world's nations sign an agreement to ban the use of cloning technology.
12.1.2018: Human clones sold on the black market.
12.26.2018: United States government suspects that the Pentagon may have been infiltrated by foreign operatives masquerading as personnel and staff.

Records from 12.27.2018 to 6.26.2021 are missing.

6.26.2021: The newly inaugurated President of the United States, John Lackey, is assassinated in the White House.
6.26.2021: North Korea launches a nuclear warhead on United States soil. The Vice President of the United States, Karen Tate, orders the implementation of Operation SOL.
6.27.2021: Ms. Tate urges the United States Congress to declare war on North Korea.
6.28.2021: Iraq launches a nuclear warhead on United States soil.
6.29.2021: Ms. Tate further urges the United States Congress to declare war on North Korea and Iraq as well.
6.30.2021: Pakistan launches a nuclear warhead on United States soil.
6.31.2021: Ms. Tate issues an executive order to launch nuclear warheads in the major cities of Iraq, North Korea, and Pakistan to completely devastate anything that once was living. It was executed.

8.27.2021: A World Council is assembled to determine if the United States acted unethically.
9.29.2021: It is decided that the United States government acted unethically, and all United States leaders are to be tried in a World War Crimes Court.
9.30.2021: A line is drawn and the world divides. The United States, Britain, Israel, Japan and China band together against Russia, Iran, Germany, Korea, France, Spain, Saudi Arabia, Afghanistan, and the list continues as other nations choose sides.
10.6.2021; 2:34 AM: World War III begins with the nuclear bombing of Washington D.C.
10.6.2021; 7:41 AM: World War III ends with nuclear annihilation – neither side is victorious.
10.7.2021: Total chaos dominates the survivors.
10.31.2022: All governments are overrun. Complete anarchy ensues.
4.16.2023 10:45 AM: Last transmission from the United States government received by the SOL.
4.16.2023 10:46 AM: Mankind, as it was known, exists no more.

From here world history ends, and our history begins.

I am Mary of Generation 43, an inhabitant of the SOL. My story commences in the year 3107. I write this account for those in the future who desire to know what happened in our past if fate brings this to them.

Only the genetically superior survived the deadly radiation from the War of Hell as it is referred to in our limited history lessons. When I say superior, I mean those that did not die within two years of being exposed. Darwin's theory has proven true in this world. Humans have evolved to live in the radiation and to become a part of the world our ancestors destroyed.

Men are not men anymore.

Men are the ravaging creatures who lurk behind the darkness and in the shadows and under the ominous blackness our ancestors would have called the sky. They prey on the living; they devour the dead. Some men have three hands or two heads. Other men have blood-red skin with yellow eyes. Yet, others have four eyes and many teeth. Men only mate because they still have that innate drive, but all other things human are long gone, forever embedded into the winds of time.

All they know is chaos. They know not love, happiness, anger, sadness, surprise, disgust or shame. They only know that the strongest and the most feared survive. They walk the ground like apes, using their knuckles to beat away at the rocks underneath them. They are bent over in a subhuman posture inhabiting the Earth and spoiling any good that once was or might come to be.

These men, if one could even call them such, are the demons from hell that were etched into the glory of what once were the Final Judgment sculptures on the Cathedrals of Medieval Europe. They snatch the souls of the condemned and viciously torture them as they enter forever into the fiery lake of sulfur. These are creatures that know no good and care not whether their victims suffer while they slowly devour them alive. Unrestrained men, courageous one might say, live a life without rules and decency, but in fact these men used to be human.

We had an event once when they had brought one down from the surface of the Earth. He was obviously dead. Afterwards, they told us he was only about nineteen years of age. They couldn't be certain because his bone structure had mutated. Based on their life spans, they estimated he had seen most of his years. They told us the life spans for males ranged one month to twenty-five years. They had him in a container to keep his radioactive body from the possibility of harming the precious SOL. They showed us how much damage the radiation has caused in the last 1085 years. His eyelids were hard and calloused. He had a full grown third leg and foot. He had no body hair; even his eyelashes were gone. His teeth still had bits of rotting flesh in them. His cheeks protruded like devil's horns. The bone beneath his forehead had been sunken by the blow of a fist.

I remember him so vividly. His peeling skin was a green-yellow color plastered with big reddish-black boils. His lips were hard, leathery, and curled back into what was left of his gums. His tongue was long, narrow and putrid green; his face, ashen.

He bled black blood as the scientists cut into his skull. I remember jumping in shock when I saw his cheek move. An eyelid opened on the side of his cheek and this white puss came slithering out. Rhome and Brent laughed at me, for I was the only one who jumped. I couldn't stop staring at his body. It was so misshapen and mutilated. His spine twisted too many times. His shoulder blades stuck out like vulture's wings. He had seven fingers on one hand and six on the other. It looked like he had been in many fights, and until the last one, had come out victorious.

His insides were gone. The meat from his arms and legs was gone too. The starchy white bones contrasted with his ashen, rotting skin and played hide and seek with the outer parts of his body. After the demonstration, I went back to my family quarters and threw up. It was too much to look at. I couldn't digest the fact that he used to be human, but as I said before, men are not men anymore.

The women are just as savage and just as grotesque. Our scientists tell us that the women are fatally seductive because that is the way they are able to survive. The men are bigger, stronger, and have more limbs to hold them down.

I have heard, though, that the men are stupid. The scientists captured their stupidity on tape multiple times over, and we had to watch it for one of our lessons. The women just lure the men into a position where they bite their necks and jam one of their long pointed fingers into their temples. After the male's lifeless body falls to the ground, the female feasts using her hardened nails ripping into the thing's thigh and pulling out the stringy strands of muscle and drabbling it over her long snaked tongues. But, this is how they survive. Seeing this, I couldn't watch anymore, but I heard Brent and Rhome making obscene jokes while the video was playing. I remember the scientist walked up to me during this recording and told me to watch. He said he had risked his life to go up to the surface and capture it in action. I lifted my eyes to the screen, and as he walked away, my eyes drifted back towards the chair in front of me. I was only five years old.

I now know why we had to watch this grotesque feast. They were conditioning us to fear the surface dwellers. This was to make sure we follow the rules; otherwise, we would end up with our thigh muscles strewn about in this thing's mouth. They told us it was to broaden our horizons; to teach us about the dangers we would have to defend ourselves against if we, as citizens of the SOL, were to ever again build a successful dwelling on the surface. To show us how important it is to always work in teams.

They told us that the surface dwellers don't attack in numbers. They roam alone like savage beasts, but one could easily take out one or two of us with ease. With their five to six strong limbs, they could crush us like twigs. They outnumber us in population as well. They tell us that most surface dwellers are sterile and are not able to reproduce. However, the dirty, disgusting things still live on.

I have seen images of the surface. The ground is littered with bones and bodies: few male, more female and many babies. Our research has shown that only twenty-four percent of babies live to see age three. When they turn three, they are on their own. Those who are on their own don't make it. Their mothers see them as aliens trying to steal their souls, that is, if they had souls. I'm not even sure God would forgive their actions.

I've seen many of these dead babies as they were brought down to be examined. They are not like our babies. Our babies are soft and innocent and angelic in nature or so I've been told. These babies are not human. They are these sickly and demon-looking children. Some are greenish-red and others are yellowish-black with multiple limbs and disfigured faces: these poor, poor creatures. These devilish appearing infants were still living beings who were mutilated, tortured and killed by the very thing that gave them life. Brent was making jokes about the poor baby, but his twin brother and my best friend, Michael, just looked at me with a sad countenance.

These creatures, like I said before, only live to see age twenty-five or so. Our scientists are still trying to figure out if it's because of the radiation causing their brains to falter or if it's because they are too old to defend themselves against the younger, stronger of their kind. But these are the genetically superior, and they do not die without a fight.

These humans evolved into these creatures that we now call Radiation Mutated Humans or RMH. The population of the RMH has been declining since the 2200s. They estimate that there are only about 1.4 million RMH left of the estimated billions they started out with.

Interestingly enough, the nuclear war and radiation only killed six billion humans either immediately or within two years of the war's end. We are hoping these RMH will die off soon, so our scientists will be able to go up to the surface for longer periods of time and try to restore what is left of our planet, or that is what they tell us.

I have been recruited to work on this project also. I have been assigned to work as a junior engineer, or a J-ENG, to build radioactive shields that will enable us to survive on the surface. These shields will provide us a biosphere and protect us from the sun's rays but will still enable us to feel the sunlight penetrate our cold skins, that is, if the sun decides to show itself again.

We have spent a great deal of time studying about the creatures who roam free on the surface of this planet. I formerly thought that this knowledge was to aid in our future attempt to repopulate the planet's surface, the true purpose of the SOL, but now things are not as they seem.

We have been manipulated and used to advance an ancient motive, one created in the first century since the SOL has been in existence, one not to benefit the SOL but the Head Council.

There is need for change, but I don't know who I can trust. If this finds you and you don't want to know anymore, then quit reading and hide this somewhere safe. Give it to someone else, so they might decide for themselves. Otherwise, remember the things I am about to record.

The one who enlightened me with her words from the past said these things:

"I broke the rules, so please break the rules also.

Do not turn this over to the Head Council or you will lose something much more valuable than your life: something that is infinite in its range, something that life itself cannot live without, and yet the Head Council has kept it from the SOL.

So many beautiful things and other horrible things that might make you want to go back to your normal life, but they are worth knowing.

Knowledge is infinite and should be sought after every moment of every waking day. It eludes me time and time again as I can only grasp at the little I have captured. I am letting it survive here in this record, and I hope it passes from me to you with the same vividness and voracity that I possessed when it entrapped my mind. In essence, it has captured me, and I pray and hope that it captures you as well.

There are many images that I have gazed upon and want you to experience the same gaze as well. There are words here that you will not understand, but just read and listen to my voice. Try to imagine the glory of these images and the reasons why the Head Council would keep you from such. I could not find any reasons, so this is why I am now writing this account. In case I am exiled from the SOL, you and others can know this truth.

I cannot speak of fires because I was not supposed to have read about them, but that is our little secret.

I have read of fires, and how they used to provide warmth to the soul. I wish that one day I will be able to sit around a fire and be warmed. Something so marvelous and something so forbidden is in existence somewhere on this Earth. A consuming creature that destroys anything in its path, yet it can create the purest of metals and yield the power of life with its flame. The images of fire are captivating. The flaming arms seem like they are reaching to grow, pulling back to safety and then jutting out again. Its head grows stronger and bigger as it fuels its body with the subordinates it steps on. It consumes and consumes until there is nothing left, and then it slowly dies an agonizing and painful death. Flickering and crackling and popping until the bright red and orange that once lured in its adorers is now a pile of ash buried within the smoke that teases it. Fire is a captured beast and once released it will scar the face of those who captured it. My desire to learn is like fire. I want to learn until there is nothing left to learn. I do realize that when I die, my knowledge will probably die with me. Knowing this, I will endure the same agonizing and painful death while the winds of time will forever mock my useless attempt to keep the fire going.

Don't let this happen to you. You must keep that fire going. First, learn of your heritage, where your family has been and the culture that embodies your ancestors' spirits. Second, read the books from the Library of History and follow the pieces I have hidden in attempt to keep them from the Head Council. Third, do what you must to give this incredible knowledge to those you can trust. "

I give you the same challenge.

I have learned of my heritage. I did not know what heritage was until I saw pictures of people like me but living a different way of life. I did not know we were different, but we are in our ancestor's pasts. We are now all the same except for the one I learned from and me. We are different; we know what they do not want us to know.

I have read about rebellion and resistance movements when those in charge need to be overthrown. I have read of diplomatic solutions to a nation's problems, but here in the SOL, they scare you into submission with the threat of leaving you on the surface with the RMH if you decide to speak up on what you really want to know.

They say our SOL is a republic, but we vote the way they want us to vote. Our leaders are chosen at birth and brought up in the ways of the old SOL. The SOL is ignorant and afraid to question.

I record all of this now because I fear I will be found out either sooner or later. You will probably never hear my name because the Head Council will erase my records as they erased the records of the one before me. I will have never existed, but my bones will be buried under the soil of the surface.

You are living a shallow life. I believe it's better to know who you are and die than to live a lie. If you do not agree, hide this away from you and leave it for someone else to find. If you agree, keep reading.

They have kept so many secrets from us. I will not underestimate the Head Council anymore. Its power is great, and its reputation is strong. It has kept us alive for the past 1085 years with the same methods it used in the beginning, or so they say. I know that the clergyman has lied to us; the doctor has lied to us, so why wouldn't the Head Council lie to us also?

I have read the Bible, and I have read medical journals. I was not supposed to, but I did. Our clergyman and health professional, or HP, tell the people of the SOL things they need to hear to get their job done, to reinforce the assumed rules of the Head Council. They are charged to protect us, but I see differently.

Our clergyman tells us that God wants us to be diligent in the ways of the SOL, to better our lives through our works in the SOL, with the SOL and beyond the SOL meaning the surface SOL. We have to save the SOL by doing what we are told. Our faith in the SOL should keep us going and give us happiness. Yet, I found faith when I opened the pages of the Bible and read its words through my own eyes. The SOL is never mentioned in the Bible, but the individual soul is affluently addressed. The SOL is ignorant and afraid to question, but the soul wants to break free and be saved from the lie its living.

The soul is one's own, the very being and fiber of their person. It is something to be treasured and kept and not thrown away to be greedily eaten by the Head Council. A person is a soul, not the SOL. A person should do everything to save their soul. Our clergyman has misled us, but I have found him out.

They don't let us think for ourselves; they don't let us learn the things we want to learn. They have kept everything so hidden, and have forbidden such knowledge from us. If given the chance to learn, we wouldn't know where to start except for our given field because that's all we know.

Everyone speaks in acronyms when on the job because it's faster and more efficient. We are an advanced society in comparison to the old world with far less people. We have succeeded to survive, but now it is no longer just about survival. We need the beauty of life to be breathed back into the SOL and into the destiny of the people who live here.

Someone is coming. I must hide this for now.

Recorded 11.21.3109

It has been almost two years since I last recorded because it has been very dangerous for me. I will start where I left off and tell you what lies ahead.

When I broke the rules, I found out that words can have meaning in them and that their life cannot be sucked out of them if used in their wholeness. Michael long ago has noticed that I began declining in my use of short phrases, and he began to copy me. I fear that he will be suspected of breaking the rules. He is my best friend and husband, and he would not betray me.

On the other hand, I take pleasure in speaking with someone else. Life moves more slowly when I am with him now. I can enjoy it more because I can hear his deep soothing voice make the sounds of each word as he speaks instead of harsh letters said side by side. I know the words behind the letters now. GD is our greeting to those we pass when walking in the halls; it means Good Day. The DQ is the dining quarters. LQ is our living quarters. The HC and the LC represent our government system consisting of the Head Council and the Lower Councils. They have ingrained into our minds that speaking in this way saves several minutes in each day by using letters instead of words and helps us to focus more on the task at hand. If we are all to survive together, we must all perform at the best of our abilities as our ancestors were bred to be the best.

Intelligence and curiosity races through our veins, but the Head Council steers us in the direction we are allowed to go.

I would be as everyone else if it hadn't been for that one fateful evening, but I'll speak of that later on.

Unlike the RMH, I, along with the others I live with, know when I was born. I came to life on April 12, 3086. I live in an underground society protected for now from the radiation that haunts the Earth nine hundred feet above. I hope you will break free just as I have.

Our scientists tell us that we have only another hundred years before the radiation gets to us as it seeps through the ground. We are constantly moving deeper into the Earth's crust, and with each foot, the hope within us seems to dwindle. We all can see it, but the Head Council pushes onward not caring about our wellbeing.

Our archives, the archives everyone is allowed to read, tell us that our saviors knew something horrible was going to happen, and in the year 2011, began to build this sanctuary. They called it, the Shield of Life, or the SOL. On June 26, 2021, one hundred healthy newborn babies (Fifty male, fifty female) were born, created with only the best of human DNA placed inside surrogates. After their births, they were placed in the SOL with the top five scientists, professors, clergymen, doctors and engineers along with several women aged 25-35 to aid in the raising of the children. They were saved to enable the human race to go on.

We have survived.

As the years went on, they were taught to read and apply what they had read. In short, these one hundred ten year olds were the smartest humans ever to walk the Earth, and they were all gathered in one place and for one reason.

The last transmission sent to the SOL was by the United States Secretary of State, Justin Greensmith. I hacked into the archives and witnessed his bloody face as he breathed his last, "They've overtaken…there is nothing but..." and then his lifeless body slid down the screen and fell to the floor. A more human-like RMH had pierced his back with a broken chair leg and stood where Mr. Greensmith had been standing. He banged on the screen with a fist and a growl. When he had finished amusing himself, he took the microphone and beat Mr. Greensmith's head into the ground. There was blood spatter across the screen, and then the following images suggest that he began to mutilate Mr. Greensmith's body.

Mr. Greensmith's soul lives on in my memory.

Our twenty-five elders at the time decided to lock the elevator that went to the surface to let nothing down or up. After the first one hundred grew and provided the SOL with the next generation, the Head Council decided to keep knowledge in its place among specific fields. The SOL thus became a stratified society, each person an expert in their field.

We each are tested at a very young age to see what we are to become. At three years old, I knew I was to become nothing but an engineer. We need each other to survive. I know nothing about anything else except engineering. There are several others like me, but many of our population become engineers or scientists. We only have one clergyman and one historian, and only a small percent become HPs. Being an engineer, I was not supposed to venture into the Library of History exactly one year, eleven months, twenty-two days, and eleven hours ago, but I snuck into this forbidden sanctuary anyway, when no eye could perceive me.

I violated the code that binds us all to each other, but I needed to know why I had to wear this white and black outfit, why I was not allowed up to the surface, why everyone had a certain job they had to do, why we had to keep digging and why I had to work with our senior engineers to design a living place another fifty feet into the Earth's crust and yet at the same time help design a living place on the surface. I needed answers. I thirsted for an expanded knowledge, and I found my living water in the forbidden Library of History.

I have taught myself the ancient languages Spanish, Latin, and French, and I am working on Chinese. These are dead languages but are beautiful when spoken. La belleza en palabras es revitalizada por un paso muerto del idioma de los labios. I know I can never speak them outside this secret place, but they bring me great joy. Speaking these dead languages makes me feel like I am enlivening these ancient cultures.

I envision what it would be like to witness the building of the wonders of the world: the Great Pyramid of Khufu and the Great Wall of China, brick by brick, stone by stone. The heritage of the world being stuffed into history's timeline all with advanced architecture of the time. I wish I could go back in time and watch as Mount Rushmore was being carved out of the rock. The details of engraving four men's faces on the mountainside to forever witness the actions of the world's inhabitants. Their eyes have seen the destruction of the world and the creation of a hell that now haunts the humans who live below it.

I wondered what it would be like to see the empire state building having its power given to it with every drop of sweat and grueling labor hour with which it was created. I can only imagine the awe of the people in that time witnessing the construction of the Eiffel Tower and the Statue of Liberty. I wonder if these great symbols of the people's will and heart still exist up on the surface. I have dreams that I'm walking in a fire storm with nothing but death around me, and as I come over a mountain of ash, I see the Lady's face with her hand gallantly stretched upwards defying the physics of erosion and rebelling against the atrophy of time. I want to see them, but I know if I went to the surface, I would die, not of the radiation, but of the RMH.

I was disgusted at some things of the old world too. I wished I had never read those things. I read about these "crimes" committed man against man, man against child, woman against man, woman against child and the list continues. How can a brother kill his brother?

The tablets tell me that the most heinous crimes are committed for a thing called power. We were taught about wars but we were not taught that a war could be between two people. I have never heard the word "fight" in all my life. We were taught that by ourselves, we are weak, but united together, we are strong. This is why we had disagreements that could always be reconciled for the good of all.

I see why the SOL has no such thing as money. I have learned through my readings that more money a person had, the more important they became: how ridiculous a world where paper determined a life an individual could live. Then I realized that this SOL held a similar principle: how ridiculous a world where a few determined a life the people could live?

I wish I could live in the old world for at least one day, to see the people there and their ways of life. I want to witness their values and belief systems. I want to be able to access knowledge freely and be able to learn anything I desire without fear of punishment. They had so much. And yet, they could not put their greed aside.

They wanted more and more until they destroyed the Earth and each other. Everything was there. They just had to reach out their hand and grab it; the opportunities were endless, and ironically enough, therein lies the problem.

I know why their civilization collapsed.

The mindset of the old world was me, me, and me. What makes me happy now? Our mindset of the SOL is SOL, SOL, and SOL. What can we do to help the SOL advance in the future?

Each mindset is flawed because they are both in the extreme. The old world never really planned for the future; patience was not a key aspect of living. To wait for something was not accepted in any facet of life. We wait all the time here. We wait to eat, and we wait to learn. The SOL is still waiting to learn. In time, they will, and when they do, it will be a glorious day.

Our society is flawed. Our society contradicts itself much like the society of the old. We say advancement is key to our survival, but the Head Council keeps most of history from us. We say patience will keep us calm through problems that arise from our work, yet our work-lives are so fast-paced that we use acronyms for everything. We say family is important, but we are the SOL, the entity we have pledged our undying loyalty to.

The one thing I do admire about the people of the old world is that they weren't afraid to resist the tyranny that constrained them. They fought and died for their rights and their freedoms.

I wish a new day here could bring with it the possibilities of the old world. Every day is a new beginning. A new direction could be taken. Here, if I tried to start a new beginning, it would be all discovered, for there is one who is always watching. I do not yet know how to evade him, but I must think quickly. If this account finds you, then I was successful, and the one before me did not die in vain.

I wish you could see the images of the old world, but you are constrained to this account. Do not let this account be found by the Head Council. It is the hope that some may seek. Do not take away their hope, for their hope is like a new day filled with light and angelic wisps of faith.

My hope began when I embarked on dreams of the sun and its dawns and sunsets.

I can see the sun's golden rays drifting and sifting through the royal purple and lavender fluffs of God's pillows. The golden dust falling from the sky tints the white waves of the ocean with an opulent touch. The majestic sky demands its reflection from the sea below. Then you witness such a potent ruler disappear and leave behind a darkness. All is lost until you realize that he still graces us through the moon, visible only because it is a reflection of his might and supreme status. The sun must hide himself for us to see the glory of the night sky, the trailing underside of his cloak pierced with shimmering diamonds. He's telling us that he will be back and begin for us a new day.

These dreams give me hope that the God who created all these things can once again create the same beautiful world that mankind took away.

But I have gone to the surface, and he does not show himself. A dark and diamond-less night fills the air. All around is blackness except for the lights that we bring up from our underground sanctuary, if such an ironic word can be spoken about this place. However, I believe that once again, he will push through the barrier that the men of the old world put up with the war, and let his life-giving light shine through exposing the Earth and the RMH to his mighty heat and fiery appearance.

The old world seemed so full of opposing, yet mutual relationships with man and Earth. Maybe a building still stands with its face towards the ocean breeze, or maybe a telephone pole still marks the way to the west, still standing to forever fulfill its obligation of connecting peoples of distant lands. Maybe roads still intertwine with the grass, rolling over hills and winding up and down mountains.

I want to sit atop a mountain and look out over the land and see the wonder and beauty that has escaped our lives. The rising giver of life in the east slowly climbing the cliffs until its warmth touches the peaks first. These things I can only imagine.

The overly clean and stringent stench that stalks the SOL drowns any imagination that tries to live here.

I believe we are kept from knowledge such as this so that we are able to focus more on our tasks and assignments. Yes, we do have recreational time, but it is encouraged that it be spent with the family. When I became twenty years of age, I was assigned a room to myself, and then that was the time I had to sneak away to the Library of History. It was by pure luck and chance, or it might have even been fate, that I was given a room that shared a wall with the third floor of the Library of History. I married at age twenty-two along with the rest of Generation 43 of the SOL, and now share a couple's quarters with my husband which is still my single quarters due to a miracle that was set before me.

Before I was married, I feared I would not be able to sneak back to the Library of History once I became a wife. Because of that, I did not want to marry. I wanted to be the Historian, but in light of recent events that I will speak of later, our Historian is filled with corruption.

Our Historian sits atop the SOL and observes what is happening and dictates into the computer what he observes to record our history. He is never allowed to tell his spouse or offspring what he does to keep bias off the records. He is to leave when personal conversations are going on around him unless it is with his immediate family. He starts formally teaching the next historian when his offspring, his pupil, is of age twenty-five. At birth the son or daughter of the Historian is nursed and grows up in the Library of History. His only social connections exist when he enters the DQ or tags along with the Historian to the Council Meetings. He must follow the protocols of the SOL, but he is given the freedom of living in the Library of History or up above the SOL or in a LQ with his family. When the historian turns seventy, he is allowed to leave his job and pursue another, continue to help the current Historian or retire to what I like to call the Blessed Peace or the Floor of Rest. It is where those who are aged seventy-five and above can go to live out the rest of their lives if they so choose, but most stay in their respective fields and continue to teach the new generation.

The Historian is the only individual in the SOL who is allowed to go to the Floor of Rest so early in life or change fields. If he goes to the Floor of Rest, he may never speak of what is in the Library of History or what he has recorded about the dwellers of the SOL. However, his pupil must have read every book in the Library of History and fully understand his responsibilities before the current Historian is allowed to leave.

As I was saying earlier, I wanted the Historian's job. Right now, the Historian is Hunter. He is forty-eight, part of Generation 42. His father left the Historian's job and is now studying in the science fields. Hunter's teacher and grandfather, Matthew of Generation 40 retired this morning and only a few hours later, Hunter approached me. Because of the ultimatum he gave me, I made this recording for you. Once again I will speak of that later on.

Hunter, along with the HC of the SOL, lie to the SOL, keep knowledge from them, and limit their true potential because they are afraid of what would happen if the SOL was given slack in its leash.

I wonder how they can keep so many books, so much knowledge from us. How can they sleep at night knowing that they hold mankind's history? How can they be so selfish?

I was not given the opportunity to have this job. I want to be able to control my own life. I know these words are slander to the very basis of the SOL, but I want to know more, learn more, and live more.

Yes of course, there are Libraries that are available to the rest of the SOL, but to access them, technically speaking, a compelling interest in the SOL or the advancement of the SOL's ambitions needs to be present.

To get information on the structure of the SOL, I would have to go into the Library of Engineering, identify myself, submit my request to the Council of Engineering, and then they would gather the materials that I needed to do my research. I would not be able to gather information from any other Library because I am an engineer and nothing else.

I have read about bureaucracies and the red tape in the Library of History; I wonder if the first dwellers here modeled this system after a bureaucracy. Why can't I just go into the Library myself and get what I need? This is another reason why I just snuck in after the hour of sleep. I just needed to know what they were keeping behind those large, locked, and closed doors.

When I first crawled into the Library of History, no words could describe the overwhelming feeling that overcame me. I don't know if it was the rush in knowing I was breaking rules or if I had found my true calling in this life.

As I inhaled, I took in my surroundings. There were so many books! Real books with paper and bindings flooded the walls, and yet there were even more stored on tablets, stored in the research tables. As I exhaled, reality set in. I was standing in a forbidden place.

I knew that if I was to tell anyone about this, I would die by being sent to the surface. I devised a plan to sneak one or two books back with me every night.

I remember it was my first night in my new assigned LQ almost two years ago, and my blood was boiling, my face flushed and my muscles twitching. I don't even remember what had made me so angry. All I remember is that I threw my holographic generator into the back wall and noticed the metal wall panel had come loose.

I cautiously approached the wall and slipped my fingers in the slight opening between the panel and the wall and gently pulled. Curiosity got the best of me; I should have called for a maintenance bot, but I decided instead to explore. The panel wasn't even attached, and it fell off. Before me a crawl space appeared. I grabbed my light pin and entered. I shined the light all around and found a tablet on the floor of the crawl space. I picked it up and brushed the concrete pebbles from its surface. It was old, not like the tablets we use now.

I activated the memory and a silent message filled the screen:

PULL THE PANEL BACK ONTO THE WALL AND TELL NO ONE OF THESE CONTENTS.
THIS RECORDING IS FOR YOUR EYES ONLY.

A sense of importance and urgency filled me to where I instinctively did what it told me to do.

As I lay in the small space between the walls, I tried to figure out how to get the contents of the tablet to come out. I tried speaking to it, which is how our tablets work. I tried activating it again, but the same message appeared. Finally, I touched the screen, and it made me verify I would not give this over to the Head Council. I touched the "Yes, I verify" section of the screen. It told me to listen closely.

A woman's strong voice filled the tiny crawl space:

"My name is Ana. I am part of Generation 39 of the SOL. I know I will not be alive within the next few days, as I have been found out. This recording is to tell you the beauty of what I have learned. The Head Council is deceiving you. Beyond the next wall is the Library of History. Explore it, but do not get caught. They will send you to the surface, as I was sentenced to not only an hour ago. I am going to give this to one of my followers and he will place it in this little sanctuary. The Historian cannot see you here as I did not give away many of my positions of secret entrance. I challenge you to find the knowledge worth dying for beyond the wall in front of you."

Then a long list of information filled the screen. At the end, a man's voice said:

"Ana was sent to the surface on August 1, 3030. She was never seen again. The same day, her existence was erased from the SOL's records. Don't let her death be in vain."

I listened to these voices long forgotten, placed the tablet down and gently lifted my eyes to the wall in front of me.

Why would someone give their life for the mystery beyond the wall? Life is valuable and short, why would someone die for some-thing, not even someone? What was so much more important than life itself? Why would that man risk his life too? Why didn't he get sent to the surface as well? Who was this man?

He would have to be in his hundreds if he was part of Gen39. Dare I find him? He would have to be on the Floor of Rest if he were still alive. Maybe he is; maybe I should find him and speak with him before I venture onwards through the black wall daunting before me. Should I risk searching for him? Maybe this was a trap to see if anyone would respond to Ana's pleas and they too would be sent to the surface for questioning the Head Council's authority. Would I be sent to the surface as well? What if he has already been sent to his death too? What if he has already died and the knowledge of Ana died with him?

Inundated with my continuous strings of answerless questions, I slowly closed and opened my eyes and once again saw the wall that separated me from this blissful knowledge Ana spoke of. It called to me to open up this long forgotten joy and master and once again at least try to bring it to the people of the SOL.

I cautiously stretched out my hand and gently placed it on the wall. I turned out my light. I closed my eyes, breathed deep and felt my heart beat within my chest: bum, bum…bum, bum...bum, bum...

I felt my heart beat as it began to beat faster… bum,bum..bum,bum. .bum,bum..bum,bum…I thought of the things I was about to witness and unveil.

I made up my mind. My fingertips pressed on the wall as I held my breath. The wall began to open like a door. There was no sound, yet a muggy aroma filled the tiny space. As soon as my eyes could perceive what was in front of me, this overwhelming sense of peace and belonging overtook my body, my mind, and my spirit.

Now, I ask you to follow in my footsteps: put your hand up on the wall in front of you and gently...push it open.

Chapter 2
A NEW BEGINNING

On December 28, 3107, Mary of Generation 43 entered into a forbidden place in silent darkness.

As she outstretched her arm to pull herself through, her mouth remained ajar. She gracefully stood up with her back erect and her arms helplessly fallen by her sides. She gazed about her novel surroundings thinking of nothing but the pure mass and quantity of the ancient knowledge that now enraptured her. Her slender leg made the first move as it took a step forward. It was as if Mary was in a trance following a sweet and alluring voice to come hither.

She placed her hand on the grained banister that led to the floors above and below her. She stepped closer and guided her other hand to the banister. With a deep breath, she leaned over the railing. On her tiptoes, she longed for more. She looked down, around, and up in amazement of all the bounded books that surrounded her. She slowly released the captive air she held within her lungs.

Turning around, she placed her hand on the books' spines and began to walk away from her secret entrance as her fingers lightly passed by each written entity. With each step she took, she could only imagine the far off places and knowledge she could acquire from the pages of the books lying un-opened upon the endless shelves that painted the walls.

She walked to the edge of the first step of the overwhelming staircase that enveloped the east wall. She dared herself to go on.

Upon reaching the bottom floor, there were only research tables and flat open spaces. She cautiously looked around to make sure no one was there and tiptoed up to the first table's surface. It sensed her and began to light up. The floor alongside the table began to become mirror-like.

"Hello, what would you like to research?" The table spoke to her.

Mary stood frozen with her eyes darting back and forth. No one seemed to be in the Library of History. She debated staying and researching this new found resource or going back to the safety of her quarters. Curiosity got the best of her again. She mustered her courage and stepped on to the mirrored floor. Immediately, the table's surface slid up and faced her. Underneath the table's surface laid interactive gloves and glasses. Mary looked around and quickly snatched the apparatus.

As she slid the glasses on, her world became new. She looked down at her feet and it seemed as if she were standing in mid-air. Nothing surrounded her: a vast openness filled the space. The table's screen lit up in front of her posing the same question: "what would you like to research?"

"What is the SOL?" Mary asked because that is all she could think of at the time. The screen's light fell across her face, and her blue eyes glowed intensely.

"The SOL is a learning community, built to enable the human race to go on. World War III left the planet's surface inhabitable for humans; however, some remain living there. The SOL provides its inhabitants, collectively known as the SOL, a place of refuge and survival. There has never been a crime committed here. We grow our own food with synthetic water and sunlight. In the year 2772, Jacob Smith developed the oxygenator, or the OXY, which artificially transforms carbon dioxide into oxygen gas. In the year 2895, the Head Council approved to the SOL's pleas to return to the surface and allowed the SOL to start building a surface dwelling, or SD.

The Head Council rules the SOL with the advice of the Historian and the Lower Councils. There are five lower councils: The LC of Science, the LC of Engineering, the LC of Health, the LC of Professing, and the LC of Religion. The Head Council consists of six individuals who must be twenty-five years of age, and they serve for twenty-five years or more and are able to go to the Floor of Rest at age seventy-five if they choose. These individuals must have come from one of the Lower Councils. The Lower Councils must also consist of five individuals; however they report to the Head Council whereas the Head Council reports to no one.

At a young age, the SOL's inhabitants learn that the SOL is their fortitude and sanctuary and therefore they must honor and respect the SOL by giving their best to maintain and expand it.

However, the population of the SOL is three hundred humans. The goal of the SOL is to eventually repopulate the planet Earth's surface. Before it was time for repopulation, the SOL had grown to be unsanitary because it had become overcrowded. As a result, the Head Council created a law in the year 2500: Couples are to be married at the New Year when the generation will become twenty-two and made to have one child in the year when the woman is twenty-five."

"Stop!" Mary thought that was all fascinating, but it was said in such a monotone voice that it became annoying to her.

"What would you like to research?" the screen asked her again.

Her blood rushed to cheeks as she realized she had the world at her fingertips. Greed almost overtook her as she opened her mouth again to speak, but then she thought back to why she standing in the Library of History, and said, "Ana of Generation 39."

A woman made of pure gold came forth out of the screen, and with a soft and gentle, monotone voice said, "I'm sorry. There is no record of Ana of Generation 39. What would you like to research?"

"Shield of Life year 3030," Mary dictated to the golden woman.

The woman began walking towards Mary with her high shoulders pulled back unwavering. Mary watched as the golden statue-like woman neared her and gasped as she walked through her. Mary spun around as the woman disappeared into the nothingness. Looking back towards the screen that shone out like a light in a diamond-filled mine, Mary held her breath, afraid of what would happen next. Would she be caught? What if this table is a trap? What if she too would be sent to the surface to die? The woman interrupted her thoughts as she appeared behind Mary with a tablet.

"Here are your requested subjects of research," the woman said as she extended the tablet towards Mary. Her eerie black eyes stared blankly at Mary with her body straight as the maintenance bots that run the SOL.

Mary grabbed for the tablet, but her hands grasped at nothing.

The woman threw it upwards, and it split into hundreds, maybe even thousands of different files. "If you define your search, I will assist you."

Mary was surrounded by file tablets. Ignoring the woman, she grabbed one as it floated near her.

As soon as she touched it, her surroundings transformed into what seemed like a LQ. She looked around and saw a man sitting at the edge of his sleeping cot staring at a blank wall with silent tears sliding down the side of his face.

"Why is he leaking water from his eyes?" Mary asked.

"Rephrase your question," the woman said.

"There, that man. What is he doing?" Mary asked as she pointed to him.

"Crying; expressing a state of sadness; creating excess liquid from his tear ducts," the woman droned on in her monotone voice.

"Why?" Mary asked now intrigued.

The woman's head twitched. "I'm sorry, that data is no longer available."

"What's this man's name?" Mary asked.

"Benjamin of Generation 39," the woman answered.

"Where is his wife?" Mary asked.

The woman's head twitched. "I'm sorry, that data is no longer available."

"How old is he here?" Mary asked as she stepped towards the heartbreaking image of the crying man.

"Benjamin of Generation 39 was 44 years of age in the year 3030," the woman replied.

"He must have been married by then and had children. Where is his wife? Where are his children?" Mary deduced and asked again, this time looking at the woman.

The woman's head twitched. "I'm sorry, that data is no longer available."

"Take me back." Mary's surroundings transformed back into the nothingness with the same file tablets floating in the air.

"I want to see the Head Council meetings on 8.1.3030," Mary ordered as the woman stared straight ahead.

The woman touched a floating file tablet, and Mary's surroundings transformed once again. This time she was standing in the Head Council's meeting quarters.

"What time is this?" Mary demanded to know.

"0600," the woman answered.

"Take me to the time of day when they sentence a woman," Mary said as she looked around the meeting quarters in awe.

The woman's head twitched, "I'm sorry, that data is no longer available."

"Take me to the containment center when it was occupied during 3030," Mary said snapping her thoughts back to her investigation.

The woman's head twitched, "I'm sorry, that is an unavailable request."

"When was Benjamin of Generation 39 married?" Mary asked again.

The woman's head twitched, "I'm sorry, that data is no longer available."

"Why is that data no longer available?" Mary asked as she felt her pulse quicken.

The woman answered, "You do not have access to that explanation."

"How do I get access to that information?" Mary quickly asked before the woman finished speaking.

The woman's head twitched, "I'm sorry, that data is no longer available."

Mary shoved her face in her hands and exhaled a heavy huff. Disgusted, she clenched her teeth and then planted her hands into her hips. She shook her head blindly to floor trying to think of every question to use in bargaining with this stoic hologram. With every loophole she tried, there was a barrier between her and the truth.

"Where is Benjamin of Generation 39 right now?" Mary asked as she tried to exhale slowly.

"Benjamin of Generation 39's location is unknown," the woman answered.

"Take me to the SOL on 8.1.3030," Mary commanded throwing out her attempt to calm herself.

There she stood in the DQ, watching as machines dispensed the peoples' food. There was laughter and chit chat. Mary gleaned the scene looking for Benjamin of Generation 39. She could not find him. As she came to the conclusion that he was not in the DQ, the laughter died down and the chit chat hushed. She looked at a man sitting down and watched as his eyes rolled back into head just as everyone else began to have the same symptom.

"What is happening?" Mary asked concerned and afraid.

The woman's head twitched, "I'm sorry, that data is no longer available." Then as soon as the DQ appeared, it vanished.

"Go back. I want to see what happened next," Mary said as she tried pulling back the image from the gray nothingness.

The woman's head twitched, "I'm sorry, that data is no longer available."

"Take me to Benjamin of Generation 39's offspring," Mary ordered.

"Define your search please," the woman requested.

"Take me to Benjamin of Generation 39's Generation 43 offspring," Mary clarified.

The nothingness morphed into a LQ. Mary walked around to the side of the sleeping cot where a man slept. She could not see his face because of the darkness of the room.

"Is this happening right now?" Mary asked.

"Affirmative," the woman answered.

"Am I able to wake him?" Mary asked.

"Negative," the woman answered.

"What is his name?" Mary asked as she knelt in front of his increasingly familiar face. She reached out to him just as the woman answered her.

"Michael of Generation 43."

Eyes opened wide, she fell backwards. "Michael?" she whispered.

"Please define your request more concisely."

Slowly crawling back to her feet, her eyes never left the sleeping cot that held the man she longed to be with.

"Can he see me? Hear me? Feel me?" she asked softly.

"Negative. Negative. Negative," the woman replied.

Mary gently brushed his hair watching him as he slept. "Does he know about Benjamin of Gen39?" she finally asked.

"Negative."

"Why doesn't he?" Mary asked as she looked up sharply.

The woman's head twitched, "I'm sorry, that data is no longer available."

"Is there any data that is still available?" Mary passionately exclaimed in exasperation as she threw her hands in the air and faced the golden statuette.

"Please define your request more concisely," the woman requested.

After a long sigh and a short growl of frustration, Mary thought of something that would change the rest of her life. She slowly turned and asked the woman, “How do you know what is happening right now in Michael’s LQ?”

“I’m sorry; you do not have access to that information.”

“Who has access to that information?” Mary asked stepping closer to her.

“I’m sorry; you do not have access to that information.”

“Is the Historian seeing into our LQ?” Mary asked as her stomach wrenched into a tight ball of nerves.

“I’m sorry; you do not have access to that information.”

“Does the Head Council know about this?” Mary asked as she stood eye to eye with the hologram.

“I’m sorry; you do not have access to that information,” the woman answered staring blankly back in to Mary’s eyes.

“Is there anywhere that cannot be seen by the Historian?” Mary screamed at her.

“I’m sorry; you do not have access to that information,” the hologram repeated.

“But I do,” a man’s voice boldly said in the background.

Mary froze. She turned around, but saw no one. “Who said that?” she asked in a shaky voice.

“Please verify access information,” the woman said in her unusually feminine monotone voice.

“I did,” the bold, base voice replied to Mary.

Mary could not discern who was speaking. No one else was in Michael’s LQ.

“Incorrect verification of access information,” the woman said.

“Take me back now!” Mary shrieked. The woman took her to the gray nothingness with the floating file tablets. There stood an elderly man who looked at her with blazing green eyes. His full head of white hair hovered above his eyes; his skin pulled taunt around his face, yet his mouth had the appearance of a small smile.

“You are not supposed to be in here.” He looked at the tablets floating around as Mary stood frozen in fear. “Ah, I see you’ve been researching the year 3030. I remember that year. I was only a young adult, just an infant in my studies, but my grandfather made me remember that year. Why do you, a Gen43,” he said with an unsure tone, “want to know about the year 3030?”

“Please define your request more concisely,” the woman said thinking the man was talking to her.

“Melinda, deactivate,” the old man ordered. With that command, the golden woman bowed her golden head and disappeared. “I was talking to you, young woman.”

“I…I…I don’t know,” Mary answered.

“What’s your name?” the old man asked her.

“Deactivate!” Mary yelled at him, yet the old man remained and chuckled.

"I'm not a computer hologram. I walked in and saw you researching. New users have a hard time discerning the real from the projected images. Now I know my grandson has only one son and not a daughter. So, I have come to the conclusion that you do not belong in here."

"What are you going to do to me?" Mary asked as she drew away from him.

"Nothing."

"Thank you!" She whispered as she pulled off the glasses and gloves, and the nothingness disappeared into the first floor of the Library of History. She placed the apparatus back into the nook of the table and the table's surface slid back down. Mary stepped off of the floor and it transformed back into its metal façade. She looked across at another table and the old man waved to her.

"How did you get in here?" he asked.

"Through the front door; it was unlocked," she said as she bit her lip knowing that was the most ridiculous answer she could have ever come up with.

"Well, I would say to go back to your LQ using the third floor passageway," he answered as he motioned upwards with his eyebrows.

She looked at him. "You know?"

"I know all things." He looked deep into her eyes, and Mary thought she witnessed wisdom in physical form. She walked backwards toward the stairs. "Be lucky you ran into me and not someone else." She tripped over the first step and fell down. He approached her and put forth his hand. She took it, and he pulled her up.

"Did you know Ana of Generation…," Mary began to ask.

"Quiet! Do not speak of her. She was put to death for the things she found out, and the entire SOL was tortured. I fear it will be far worse for you and those you love. I will erase the computer's memory of your research done today. Next time, do not be so brave. Ana did not use secrecy, and it cost her, her life. I wanted the people of the SOL to know what she knew, but I knew better than to go against the Head Council without a plan," he began, but then he saw her blue eyes as she looked up to him. "I saw you researching Michael of Generation 43. Why do you want to research him?"

"He is Benjamin of Gen39's great grandson," Mary answered.

"Yes, he is. How do you know about Benjamin of Generation 39?"

"I researched him."

"He did not…" He hung his head in shame and reluctantly whispered, "I've said too much. For your own safety, do not come back here until you are ready. You are so much younger than…" He urged her up the stairs.

"Ana?" Mary finished his sentence for him.

"Please watch what you say for now," the old man pleaded.

"What do you mean 'until I am ready'?" Mary asked.

"Just go," the old man said as he ushered her toward the stairs.

"What were you going to say about Benjamin of Gen39?" Mary asked.

"Nothing, please go," he urged her on.

"Why does Michael not know about him?" Mary asked.

"No one knows about Benjamin." He urged her up another stair.

"Why did the computer say his location is unknown?" Mary asked as stood her ground.

"It is too much to explain." He urged her on to the third stair.

"Was he married to Ana…?" Mary asked as she stared into his green all-knowing eyes.

The old man sighed, "Yes."

"I need to find him," Mary implored.

"Then find him, but exercise caution. The Historian sees everything."

She looked at him blankly. "Why is he allowed to do that?" she asked.

"Because he is supposed to know everything."

"Does the Head Council know about this?" Mary asked softly.

"Yes, they mandated that command to him. Now go!" he ordered her.

"When did they do that?" Mary stood where she was.

"A long time ago," he quickly whispered in a hushed voice.

"When?" Mary pressed further.

"Decades maybe even centuries before today. Now go!" His voice bellowed through the empty library.

She turned and darted up the stairs, and when she got to the top of the stairs, she turned around and looked at the old man.

"What did Ana find out that cost her, her life?" she asked as her brows bunched.

"I cannot help you any longer. You must choose your own path: to either live with the SOL and forget this ever happened or find out what happened and risk your life and the well-being of the SOL. If you succeed in a greater way than Ana, you might be able to pick up where Ana left off." He paused and looked with sorrow at Mary. "You are so much younger. I did not think this day would come so soon in your life. Make your decision wisely."

"This day? Were you expecting me?" Mary asked as she took a step backwards.

"Like I told you before, I know all things," he said and sadly smiled.

"Who are you?" Mary curiously asked.

"I am Matthew, Generation 40, Historian," he replied. "Who are you?"

"I am Mary of Generation 43, Engineer."

He nodded his head, and then said, "Mary, go before someone else sees you."

"Thank you," she whispered. He nodded again and shooed her away with a wave of his hand.

She ran up to the third floor and back down the aisle toward her secret passageway. She pulled the wall back, and before she entered, stopped and gazed at the books that lined the seemingly unending wall. Impulsively, she made her decision, grabbed the closest book to her secret entrance, and entered into the darkness.

Sitting with her knees to her chest and the stolen book in her arms, she leaned her head back against the wall. She felt around for her light pin and knocked it onto the old tablet. Turning it on, she opened the old book and began to read.

Hours passed, and Mary opened her eyes to darkness. She tried getting up but bumped her head against the concrete that was only a few inches above. Rubbing her head, and feeling the book beneath her leg, she remembered she was still in the wall. Climbing out, her eyes adjusted to the lighter darkness in her LQ. A loud banging was presenting itself at her door.

At this, Mary's eyes opened fully, and she put the panel back into its place. Running to the door and being short of breath from the adrenaline rushing through her blood, she pushed the button, and it slid open.

Michael stood in the doorway. "Come on, let's go!" His muscular body showed through his tight uniform. His jet black hair shone in the light of the SOL, and his blue eyes happily danced at the sight of Mary.

"Go where?" she asked as her black wavy hair stuck to the sweat on her face.

"Mary, we have to go to the surface today," he reminded her.

"Right. Give me a moment," she told him.

"You know what will happen if we're late. Are you alright?" Michael asked as she shut the door. She ran to the mirror, brushed her hair and tied it up. Sliding into the bath quarters, BQ, she swished some mouth cleaning compound, swallowed and ran back to the door. She breathed in deeply and slowly let it out. Her heart still raced.

"Alright, I'm ready. Let's go!" Mary exclaimed as she opened the door and walked out.

They hurriedly ran to the transporter.

"You look tired," Michael whispered to her as they passed some fellow SOL mates.

"I didn't sleep well," Mary said shortly.

"That's not good. You're going to need your energy up on the surface," Michael said.

"Are you caught up on your surface abbreviations?" Mary asked changing the subject.

"Yeah, I studied them during my recreation time on Sunday."

"You spent your forty minutes of recreation time studying?" Mary asked in disbelief.

"Yes, you did the same," Michael said as he leaned down closer to her.

"Oh yes, now I remember," Mary sadly said closing her eyes.

"So you're so tired that you are now forgetting what you did two days ago?" Michael said shaking his head.

"I guess so," Mary sighed.

"What were you doing?" Michael asked.

Mary burned with the desire to tell Michael what she had found out, but the old man's words whispered back to her: *I fear it will be far worse for you and those you love.*

"I just couldn't sleep," Mary lied as they stood waiting for the transporter. Michael's brow bunched, and he slowly slid his eyes over to witness Mary's slightly quivering hand.

They stepped onto the glass floor and the transporter whipped them down to Level One. "Well you need to get more sleep Mary; otherwise, you'll make mistakes and the LC won't want you on the surface team."

"I know Michael," Mary said with a fluster.

"Don't get mad Mary; I just want you with me." Michael stopped and grabbed Mary's hand. "If anything's going on, I'm here. I'll always be here. I just want you to be alright."

"I'm fine, Michael," Mary answered. "I'm not going anywhere. You'll always be with me. Don't worry; I'm fine. Now let's go before we're late." She turned to leave.

Michael let her hand drop, stood in a passing moment of bewilderment, and then followed behind this perplexing woman. Upon arriving to the SPR or surface preparatory room, they had to split up into their respective fields.

Michael hurriedly slid into the back row of the scientists already gathered and now reviewing the chemical analysis schedule of today's work session. The head scientist, John, who served as a LC member, looked with a countenance of annoyance upon Michael, briefly walked up alongside him and whispered out of the corner of his mouth, "I'll let this one slide, but next time, you will not be going to the surface with us." The stench of his breath filled Michael's nostrils.

"Yes John. Thank you, John." Michael straightened up and assumed the body language of a scientist: his back straight and head slightly elevated and tilted to the side with his hands neatly folded behind his back, walking with a sophisticated saunter.

He began to walk around the holographic images placed around the floor and in the air quietly observing them and taking notes and making improvement suggestions via his brain interface system or BIS: a small two-piece head apparatus. One part was round and fit right about the left ear and a small wire connected it to the second part that was elongated in shape and was placed on the nape of the neck. With the BIS connected to the centralized reporting database, Michael frequently had to eliminate some of his processed brain data because his thoughts were not completely of the chemical analysis reports situated in front of him.

***

Mary snuck into the SPR-E or the Surface Preparatory Room-Engineering. She too was late; everyone already had on their interface equipment and was looking at the schematics or BPs of the SD, surface dwelling, modifying the SBs, surface bots, to meet the day's building requirements, and altering the building parameters to encompass the entire work area. The head engineer, Amanda, slowly made her way to Mary. With each coming step, Mary's heart began to race a little faster maybe because she knew she was late or because she felt guilty for sneaking into the Library of History last night. Tiny beads of sweat began to form on her brow, and her hands became cold and clammy.

It's because I'm late, she thought. *It has to be because I'm late.*

"GD Mary. You decided to join us; your decision not to would have been unwise," Amanda said cocking an eyebrow at Mary and slowly folded her long arms in front of her chest. Her tall stature, fair, clear and healthy skin, and pin-tucked blonde hair all perfectly played up to the perfection the HC demanded.

"I didn't sleep well, but I'm here and ready to work," Mary replied ignoring the implied threat Amanda gave her.

"Well that makes sense; you look horrible. Maybe you should go to the HP today," Amanda retorted with no genuine concern in her voice as her brown eyes intently glared at Mary.

"I'm fine. I don't need to see the HP," Mary said ignoring the implied insult. "Thank you for your concern," she said with a sarcastic undertone after a few moments of awkward silence.

"You look ill. Go to the HP. You won't be coming to the surface with us today," Amanda said with a half-smile, half-sneer. "That's an affirmative order, J-ENG."

"I'm fine. I just..." Mary started.

"Go!" Amanda interrupted and pointed her elongated and bony finger towards the door.

Mary dropped her equipment on the table and walked towards the door, never once losing eye contact with Amanda. She got to the SPR-E entrance and the door slid open. Mary stood there glaring at Amanda, and Amanda glared back.

Amanda mouthed the words, "Because I can."

Mary sharply looked away and took a solid step taking her outside the SPR-E. She stiffly walked down the hallway with her hands balled into tight fists. Her jaw clenched itself tight as the veins in her neck began to bulge. She got to the transporter and wanted to scream out, but remembered that the

Historian sees everything and instead said with a growl set low in the back of her throat, "Take me to Level Two."

The transporter floor slid Mary onto Level Two, and Mary briskly walked to the HP office. At the door, she had to log in with her hand print and body scan. The door did not open, because her body scan came back negative for health problems. Mary then shrugged and went back to her LQ during work time.

Apparently I look ill. Amanda said I wasn't going to the surface today, so why should I go back to the SPR-E? I'm tired, and I'm going to sleep to work better tomorrow, Mary reasoned with herself.

Her LQ door slid open, and she went straight to her sleeping cot, laid down and fell asleep.

Michael finished his pre-review of the day's analysis and went through his de-briefing on the surface equipment. White and black, just like the other uniforms of the SOL, were the colors of the surface equipment. He had a PS&G, protective suit and goggles, an OXY mask and SBGs, surface boots and gloves. The elevator, the sole way to the surface, opened its doors, wide and inviting to the alien looking SOL members. Beside the doors, there were atom guns for each member to have on the surface. These small grey guns fit perfectly in the side holder on the surface pants.

John stepped inside the elevator and said, "Everyone is to be on frequency 0.00313 the entire time we are on the surface." He tapped on his head covering and said, "0.00313" to make sure the BIS was on that frequency. "Computer, run a check to make sure everyone in the SPR-S is on frequency 0.00313."

"Affirmative check," the computer responded.

Alright, I'll take the first group, John said to everyone through his BIS. Michael stepped forward and was trying his hardest to not think of other things besides his work for the day. The elevator zipped them to the surface and opened its doors to darkness and a barely visible, abandoned work station.

John sauntered to the power grid, plugged in the alternate power source and flipped the on switch. They walked outside the work station, and there stood large light poles with a half built surface dwelling encompassing it. The large glass like sphere loomed against the darkness and the light shot several hundred feet in the air.

S-Group One, you will be assigned to figure out the formula to mass produce the OXY for the SD, John ordered. *Do not go outside the SD*, he said afterwards. *I know it was part of your de-briefing, but every year, we have someone who does. No one has been hurt yet, but there's always that chance. You have been warned.* He turned and went back down the elevator to bring up Group Two.

In a mass, S-Group One moved over to the table of schematics for the OXY. Weston, one of the head scientists but not quite in the LC, turned on the holographic projector, and they began to discuss the various alternatives of how best to mass produce the OXY for the SD in complete silence using their BIS. They could not make noise in abundance or it would attract the RMH. The sphere had a cloaking device which hid the light from the outside, so the RMH would not know they have returned to the surface, or so they were told.

S-Group Two shortly arrived thereafter and began to create a formula for organic matter synthesis using the atoms in the air on the surface. S-Group Three picked up where they left off several weeks earlier at the liquid creation site to provide the SD with all the water they would need without depending on other resources such as the one found in the SOL.

The engineers began to arrive. E-Group One arrived. E-Group Two arrived with the construction bots. E-Group Three was the last group to surface. Michael noticed that Mary was not present in any of the three E-Groups.

Michael, we need your attention here, Weston said through the BIS. Michael had forgotten they were all thinking collectively together and others could see his thoughts in processed form.

I'm here. Now what if we added a synthesized compound maybe some UH to the second stage in the process? Do you think that would make the OXY produce more O_2 from the original formula? Michael suggested in a scholarly manner while his eyes intently gazed upon the holographic image.

I'm not sure. Let's put it into the simulator and see. All eyes watched the holographic container as Weston changed the formula via his BIS. The material inside the container instead turned to flame and exploded the surrounding area. *I'll run an analysis to see what reacted with what and see how we can expand upon Michael's idea so that the matter doesn't combust in the next simulation,* Weston said with an insulting glare towards Michael. Almost immediately everyone could see the report running in the vision of their left eye. Michael saw his glare and ignored it.

It looks like H was over produced within the formula and caused a small nuclear bomb, Rhome said.

What if we added UHE_2, so the E would absorb the excess H? Michael inserted in to the data stream of processed thoughts.

I'll insert it, Weston said. The next thing they saw was a dark liquid seeping from the lid of the container. *I suggest starting over.*

From scratch? Rhome asked. *That is weeks' worth of work.*

Affirmative, Weston responded.

But we only go to the surface a couple of times a month. All of the equipment is here. This will be a huge setback, Rhome argued.

I am the H-SCI. You are a J-SCI. I know what is best for the SOL. Do not question my authority, Weston said as he puffed his chest and glared at Michael and Rhome who stood side by side.

What if we added UHE_2 and NX_4 in order to keep the air inside the container warm enough to stay in gaseous form? Michael asked knowing that this time it would work because of all the research he had done on Sunday during his recreation time. Just at that moment, John entered into the Group One's BIS frequency.

That is a good hypothesis Michael. Let's see if it works. Aw, I see you originally came up with the addition of UH. I like your thought process. I'm interested in how you came up with this. We will talk later in the DQ, John said. *Weston, where is this simulation?*

Right here, John. Weston's eyes were downcast fixed upon the projector's base. The container began making a mass production of O_2. A smile crossed Michael's face.

Congratulations Michael. Now, all of you run tests to make sure it is the maximum amount we can create and that there is nothing erroneous with the product, John ordered. As he turned to leave, he gave Michael a big smile and a pat on the shoulder. He walked away in a sophisticated saunter with his head slightly elevated and his hands neatly folded behind his back.

Weston's eyes burned with hatred, but his years of experience allowed him to master the BIS, thus preventing the others from seeing his thoughts.

The elevator ride back down to the SOL at the end of the work day was unbelievably silent.

I think Michael led us through a great progress today, Rhome said to the other Group One members to try and have a short conversation as the elevator neared the first level of the SOL.

"*Agreed*", "*Yes*", and "*Affirmative*" were the responses of the Group One members except for one, who silently leaned back into the corner with his arms folded, legs crossed and face scowled. He twitched his head to turn his BIS off and silence the cheer for his star subordinate.

Michael eagerly took off his PS&G and SBG and started off toward the door; however, John caught up with him and asked him to join him in the DQ with the other LC members. Weston, who was following Michael out, overheard the invitation and sunk back even farther while a green haze began to overcome his brown eyes.

***

Mary woke with a start: loose pieces of hair plastered to her face, bloodshot eyes, and beads of sweat softly lay on her moist skin, tense hands gripping the sleeping blanket and chest heaving. Her eyes began to look around as she tried to quiet her breathing.

Her dream was so vivid that she felt she was actually living it. Fire surrounded her in the black darkness while she stood on the surface unprotected, but it was not hot, and she was not burning. However, everyone else around her felt the fire's burning pain. She saw her mother and father and Michael, Brent, and Rhome and her best friends, Katy and Violet, boiling in agony and watched as their skin melted away and as their bodies crumpled into ash, but she noticed they never died. They stayed in constant agony, yelling out in insufferable pain and anguish.

She tried to save them by pulling them out, but anywhere she grabbed, their arms, their hands, their legs, their torsos, would just slip through her grasp. She tried to run for help, but all around her was darkness and she got further away from the dense flames, the cries of misery got louder. They screamed out, "Don't leave us to die!"

Not knowing where to run, she ran back to them, and as she got closer to the first writhing body, it looked up. Katy called out, "Mary! I can see you. Save me!" Her face looked like that of hot tar and plaster. "I don't know how!" Mary said in exasperation. She reached down to her and touched her bloody face, but Katy kept saying, "Save me! Save me!" Then the others joined in: "Save us, Mary! Save us!"

Then she looked up and saw another figure like her who was not burning. He stood with his arms folded and his feet firmly grounded in the flames that worshipped his body. Dark shadows fell across his face, and his sneer would be enough to scare a child. At this daunting appearance, Mary stood up and faced the shadowed man. The cries in the background got louder, and the figure began to eerily snicker.

"Help me save them!" Mary screamed over the cries.

"They are not worth saving," the dark figure replied in a hard tone.

"Yes, they are!" Mary yelled back in disbelief at the man's unwillingness to help.

"Show me then Mary!" The man yelled back in a booming voice that rattled the ground. Afterwards, he turned around and nonchalantly walked away.

Mary called after him with tears welling up in her eyes, "What am I supposed to do? Help me! What am I supposed to show you? They are my family and friends. How are they not worth saving? Someone help me! Someone please! Help. Please help me." She fell to the ground weeping helplessly, reaching towards her mother who was still screaming in pain. Her mother reached towards her through the flames. Mary felt their fingers touch but then watched in horror as her mother's fingers slowly deteriorated into blackened bones.

Mary put her hand up to her head and it felt warm to the touch. She walked over to the mirror in her LQ, put a hand on either side of it and leaned in. *You went into the LOH and read that stupid book last night, and now you are having dreams with fire, death and crying. Mary, you need to get those memories out of your head. Why did Ana pursue this when it leads to nothing good? Why did she die for books that give you bad dreams?* Her thoughts were interrupted when a knock came at her LQ door. "Open," she said, and the door slid open.

"GD Mary. Oh, you don't look well at all," Katy said to her as she moved to make the light come on in the room. "Did you see the HP?" Her brown hair pulled tight on her head made her cheeks look high and pointy.

"Yes, my pre-body scan came back negative."

"Maybe you should go again. I came by to see if you wanted to go to the DQ with Vi and me?"

"It's already time for us to go to the DQ?" Mary asked as she shook her head to rid herself of the dream.

"Yes, the bell just rang. You got back fast. We just finished our work."

"Don't tell, but I actually didn't go to work today."

"Why not?" Katy asked with a gasp as her blue eyes glowed in the white lights of the SOL.

"I'll tell you why while we walk to the DQ." With that, Mary ushered her out.

"You need to pull your hair back. It's falling down," Katy whispered to her friend.

"Thank you Katy," Mary said while she eagerly looked around for Michael.

"So what happened?" Katy asked.

"Amanda told me I looked ill and that I was not going to the surface. So, I thought why should I go back to the SPR-E and do nothing but make sure the room stays empty when I could catch up on sleep in my LQ."

"She said you weren't going to the surface because you looked ill?" Katy asked with her mouth ajar.

"Yes," Mary responded with a smirk.

"Did she get a HP's report on you to order that?"

"No, I haven't been to the HP in years except to get my DNA rejuvenation sequence," Mary said as she crossed her arms.

"She didn't even ask to see a report?" Katy asked with her eyes wide.

"No. I guess I will have to work harder to satisfy the job performance requirements," Mary said rolling her eyes.

"But Mary, you are the best J-ENG there is in Gen43. How could you work harder?" Katy said with a sigh.

"I don't know. Every time I'm assigned to Amanda, I don't get to help out with anything big, and I've been assigned to her for the past twelve years," Mary said with another sigh.

Awkward silence filled the small space between them as they walked down the hallway until Katy said, "I'm still assigned to DQ&LQ BI."

"Bot Improvement?" Mary looked at her friend in disbelief.

"Yes," Katy responded with her eyes downcast.

"Well you keep the SOL in tip top shape. What would we do if we had to rely on ourselves to take care of ourselves?" Mary asked sincerely.

"I just don't know Mary," Katy said with a sad smile.

"You'll be fine Katy. Our promotion date is coming up," Mary said optimistically.

"Yes. That's right. In thirty-two days. Hopefully I'll be promoted to engineer and assigned to a project other than BI which is where all the incompetent engineers go," Katy said as she put her forehead on her hands.

"Katy. You made junior engineer when I did; they just needed someone of a higher caliber to supervise all the other incompetent engineers," Mary whispered to her friend.

Katy looked up and smiled. "I guess you're right."

"I'm always right," Mary said with a grin and a shrug of her shoulder. They both began to laugh a hushed laugh as they stepped into the DQ.

Most of the SOL had already arrived to eat. Mary spotted Michael sitting with John and some other LC members and figured she would catch up with him after DQ hours. He acknowledged her with a nod of his head and went back to his intent listening of John's words.

"Mary. The marriage ceremonies: what do you think of them?" Katy randomly asked interrupting Mary and Michael's speechless communication.

"Katy. My thoughts on the marriage ceremonies: I think they shouldn't be forced, but I can see why the SOL does it that way," Mary answered.

"And why is that?" Katy asked.

"To keep a fifty year old something from reproducing with a fifteen year old something, and it keeps everyone in groups and defined generations. It's just easier to keep track of people that way. If everyone marries at twenty-two and everyone has a child at twenty-five, they are all the same age, and it prevents overpopulation. Sooner or later though, they are going to have to raise the child limit to two because we are on the verge of becoming under populated," Mary explained.

"How do they know they will have an even number of males and females?" Katy asked.

"Michael said they predetermine what sex the child will be through DNA manipulation, and he also speculates they manipulate personality genes as well," Mary said and then stiffened because she just remembered the Historian can see and hear anything that goes on in the SOL.

"What? So my personality configured like a blasted program when I was a fetus?" Katy asked as her forehead bunched in disgust.

"I don't know for sure, but don't tell anyone. It could get me and Michael in trouble. It's so that you are compatible with at least one other person of the opposite sex and same sex to ensure no one is an outsider or loner and everyone has at least one probable partner for the marriage ceremonies," Mary whispered to her friend.

"Well, I guess that makes sense. What do they do with anomalies like Brent and Michael?"

"That's why we have Jenna, Violet's sister. She's a full nine months younger than us but considered a Gen43," Mary said as she gulped down some of the white mush they had eaten every day. "The doctors were surprised that Ashley of Gen42 had twins, so they had to correct the problem by forcing another couple of Gen42 have another female child. It just so happened that Violet was the first-born of Gen43; therefore, her parents were the first available to have another child."

"You know a lot for an engineer," Katy said in amazement.

"All I can say is that it's good to have connections to other fields," Mary said as she glanced quickly over at Michael.

"Are you going to pick Michael for the marriage ceremonies coming up in a few days?" Katy asked in a know-it-all manner as she noticed the several times Mary had glanced over at Michael.

"Yes. I know he'll pick me as well," Mary said smiling.

"Well apparently, seeing that you and he were literally made for each other," Katy sarcastically said.

Mary laughed and then she straightened up and seriously said in a hushed voice, "Not a word to anyone else."

"I understand," Katy said nodding.

"What about you? Are you going to pick Rhome?" Mary asked.

"Yes. I think I could also pick Blake too. And Brent. And Shawn," Katy said as she scanned the DQ.

Mary laughed, "Slow down there young single one."

Katy looked at Mary with her eyes dancing and laughed, "I'm just ready for a change. This life right now is so mundane."

Mary thought back to her night in the LOH. "I agree. I'm ready for a change as well."

"GD Mary, Katy," Violet said as her blue-gray eyes sparkled from the reflection of the starch white floor. "May I join you?"

"Yes. Sit down. We were just talking about the marriage ceremonies," Katy informed.

"Ah yes. The marriage ceremonies: have you figured out which male you are going to pick?" Violet asked Mary.

"Yes. I have, but you should change your question to state 'males' for Katy," Mary responded.

Katy rolled her eyes in a joking manner, "Just keeping my options open. What about you, Violet? Any possible partners?"

"Probably Brent," Violet said as she began to eat.

Katy and Mary looked at each other with big smiles. Katy said, "Then I will only pick three males."

Violet looked up. "Why? Were you going to pick Brent as well?"

"Yes," Katy said smiling at her friend.

"Go ahead. I can pick Blake or Shawn too," Violet said with a forced smile. Mary and Katy busted out laughing.

"You were going to pick Blake and Shawn too, weren't you?" Violet said.

Katy could barely speak, "Yes. Wait, if you were going to pick another male, who would it be? Rhome?"

Violet sighed and looked to the ceiling, "Yes. Either him or Michael, but we all know he is going to pick you Mary, so why waste one of our three picks on him."

"I agree with Violet. Michael was my second pick, but why bother?" Katy said.

"I'm interested to know who Mary's other picks are going to be," Violet said with a sly smile.

"Honestly, I will only pick Michael, but I am good friends with Rhome, Blake, Brent and Shawn, so probably one of them." Mary said looking around at her friends sitting in the DQ, and then they all started giggling like the young girls they once were.

Katy, as she gasped for air, said, "Best friends think alike." Then she thought, *No wonder we are all friends and gravitate towards the same males: we were all programmed that way before we were born.*

The young women settled down, smiled at each other and finished eating.

"Katy and I are going to the RQ, did you want to come with us?" Violet asked Mary as they exited the DQ.

"The recreation quarters? No, not tonight. I'm still tired. I think I'm going to try to sleep some more tonight, but thank you."

"Alright. Maybe next time, then?" Violet asked as Katy and she began walking towards the level transporter.

"Yes. I'll see you tomorrow Katy and Vi," Mary called after them as the transporter whipped them away. "Now to either sleep or get caught up on work," she said to herself.

"Yes because someone wasn't at work today," Michael said in a deep voice as he came up behind her.

"Michael, you startled me! Don't say that too loudly please," Mary said looking around in a whisper.

"It was a whisper," Michael said.

"You need your hearing checked. Go to the HP," Mary ordered as she pointed toward the transporter.

"Maybe later, but I need to tell you something. John and the others offered me a LC member position at promotion day. I accepted it," Michael said as his blue eyes shone and his smile lit up his face.

"Michael! That's wonderful! I'm so happy for you! You are so young, though. What did you do to get the offer?"

"John was on the surface with us today, and I figured out how to mass produce the OXY for the SD. Apparently, he was impressed because I was a J-SCI and able to do so."

"I am so proud of you!" Mary looked at Michael with a sincere smile and loving eyes. "What would the SOL do without you?"

Michael's shoulders slumped ever so slightly. He wanted to hug her so badly. "I guess they would keep on going like they always have."

"But you have just figured out how they can have a better quality of life! This is important!"

"I guess I did do a pretty good job," Michael said smiling down at her with eyes filled with pride.

Mary smiled at him, and a few seconds went by. "I have to go to the LOE to catch up on some work I didn't get done today," Mary said sheepishly.

"I will go with you to the Library of Engineering," he said matter of factly. With that, they started towards the transporter to take them to Level One.

Upon arriving at the gigantic library doors, Mary scanned her access card, hand and eye and announced she was there with a guest, Michael of Gen43 who then scanned his science access card, hand and eye. Then the doors slid open and they walked inside. Mary walked over to a research pod.

"Commence new search. SD-E/BD&BP. Record to LQ134 for further review. Allow all controls there. MaryGen43 assigned. Check retrieval and settings."

"Affirmative, retrieval and settings are as you inputted. LC of E approved. You may return to LQ134 for further review," the pod responded to her and then deactivated itself.

"Alright let's go," Mary said to Michael.

"That's it? We have to stay in our library to run simulations in the lab."

"I guess engineers are just more…innovative," Mary said jokingly.

They exited the LOE and went back to Mary's LQ.

"I believe we should celebrate your LC member offer and acceptance!" Mary excitedly said as they walked into the room.

"By doing what?" Michael asked while stroking Mary's long, black hair. Thinking to himself, he answered his own question which led to a sheepish grin that suddenly appeared on his face.

"Well, I have saved up some RQ tokens. I was thinking we could go to the RQ and I could let you beat me at a game of Dodge the RMH," Mary said as she leaned on the wall.

"Or we could stay here and let you finish catching up on your work," Michael said following suit.

"That's not celebrating! That's everyday life," Mary said naively not understanding why he wanted to stay in her LQ.

"Well to celebrate, what if we just stayed here and talked?" Michael said as he let her hair fall out of his hands.

"I'd be alright with that," Mary responded as she went to her sleeping cot and pressed a button which automatically turned it into a sitting couch. "And that way I get to save my RQ tokens."

"So you can use them when?" Michael asked with a laugh.

"I'll find time," Mary said confidently.

"Yes, of course, and I'm sure this entire day's work you missed would take up all of them," Michael said.

"Don't say that, you don't know who is listening," Mary said as she sat down.

"Mary, we're in your LQ. No one can hear or see us," Michael said as he looked around to the blank walls.

"Sometimes I think they can," Mary said remembering back to the night before when she virtually walked into Michael's room in real time.

"Paranoid. One day you miss in the past twenty-one years of your life and you think they are coming to get you." He walked over and gave her a big hug. "It's going to be alright. I'm here, and I will protect you," he said pulling her up.

He moved his hands up her back and laid them to rest cradling her face. He gazed deeply into her jeweled blue eyes. "You worry too much." He smiled.

She smiled and kept her thoughts to herself. She thought *I have to act like I don't know about the Historian's eye in every room of the SOL. I have to sneak back in the LOH and find out the places where he can't see.* Then her thoughts began to drift towards Michael. *I want to kiss you, Michael, but I know it's against the rules. We've kissed before in our LQ, and we haven't been reprimanded. Maybe no one was watching at that time, but everything is recorded. Maybe others are doing it too, and it really doesn't matter. Maybe…*

"You look lost in your thoughts," Michael said. "What are you thinking about?"

She realized her face was still being cradled in Michael's strong hands. "I was thinking about you."

He smiled, leaned down and kissed her ever so gently on the forehead. "That's for your thoughts, and this is for you." He kissed her again, this time on her soft and silken lips. He felt like he should kiss her again but in a different way. He did not know how. All he knew was what he heard some of the older men talk about during recreation time at the card tables.

"Now it's my turn to ask, what are you thinking about? You look lost in your thoughts," Mary asked.

"I was thinking about how to kiss you," he said as he stroked her face.

"How to kiss me? You just did!" Mary exclaimed.

"Well, you know, in a better way," Michael said sheepishly.

"Michael, I love your kisses. There cannot be a better way." She went up on her tip toes, so that she was face to face with him, grasped his hair, and tenderly kissed his bottom lip. He wrapped his arms around her, thus beginning a long night of shared kisses.

Mary was about to fall asleep in Michael's arms on the sitting couch when Michael suddenly acted like he was going to say something.

"What is it?" she asked.

"I…" He paused because he couldn't find the words. "I wish we had more time like this."

"We can," Mary said.

"How?" Michael asked.

"It's more a matter of when."

"Oh, the marriage ceremonies," he said as if he had read her mind. "But we are still going to have this life filled with work for the SOL. We work all the time and we even choose or sometimes are forced to work during some or all of our recreation times. I want to spend hours like this with you, just me and you and at times, our friends. We work twelve hours a day, not including the hours of pre-research it takes to do our jobs. The marriage ceremonies will let us live together, but we still don't get any more time with each other. You are my best friend, and I hardly know anything about you. You are my best friend because we grew up with each other, and we've always just stuck together."

"Do you want to know me?" Mary asked with a serious countenance.

"Yes," Michael said.

"I am Mary of Gen43. I am a J-ENG," Mary said jokingly.

"Not that. I already know that; I want to know you. I don't know if that even makes sense."

"Hold on one moment." Mary walked over to her LQ research pod and searched BIS and inputted for two. Immediately, two BIS headpieces appeared on her table. She grabbed them, toggled with them, and walked back to Michael. "This will make it easier."

"What frequency?" he asked.

"I already set it," she responded.

Can you see my thoughts? Mary asked.

Yes. He responded.

I encrypted the interface, so hopefully no one can see our thoughts but us. You said you want to know me, well, I want more, Mary said.

What? What do you mean? Are you referring to me? Michael asked.

No, it's not that. I just want more in my life. I feel like I'm caged. I feel like I do the same mundane thing every day. I felt like there is nothing to live for, but then I found something. It's very dangerous, and I could be sent to the surface if anyone found out, but I felt alive with it in my mind and in my hands, Mary explained.

What is it? Michael asked.

I can't tell you. I don't know what I would do if you were harmed or even killed because of me, Mary said.

The HC wouldn't do that. They've never done that, Michael reasoned.

Yes, they will because they have, Mary said.

How do you know that? Michael asked.

Because of the thing I found. Do you ever think there is more that the HC is hiding? Mary asked.

Is this a theory or a hypothesis not yet proven? Michael asked in response.

Theory and I know because of the thing I found, Mary replied.

What is this thing? Michael asked again.

I can't tell you, Michael. Just always remember me if something happens, Mary thought to Michael as she remembered Ana of Generation 39.

Nothing will happen. We are in a BIS conversation; no one can hear us; this conversation isn't being recorded; just tell me, Michael pleaded as he looked into her eyes.

I don't know if he can see this, Mary said.

Who? Who can see this? Michael asked.

The … Mary caught her thought before it was released. *Please just don't ask anymore. I won't tell you for your own safety.*

I wanted to be the one to protect you, but it looks like you are the one protecting me.

I love you, Michael. If I ever needed anything, I know you would always be there for me. You are so smart and talented and positive. I am picking only you.

As am I Mary.

Tell me about you, Mary said as she grabbed his hand.

I like a strong-will. I dislike when people complain. I think things should be different around here. Maybe once I get on the LC, I'll work my way up to HC and make those changes, Michael said.

What sort of changes? Mary asked.

For one, I want more time for myself, my family, and my loved ones like you. We are just like the bots that take care of the SOL. I did some research, and I figured out that most of the radiation on the surface should be gone by now. It's in the ground, but it wouldn't have moved 900 feet into the crust by this time. So for the past 400 years we've been moving farther and farther down for no reason. We are working just to be working. We are constantly progressing towards what? No one knows or cares. It's a job and that's why we are here: to do that job. I wondered if anyone else found out the same thing I found out: it is basic science: the half-life of each radioactive element, throw in some formulas and any amateur scientist could figure out that the radiation should have been gone at least a century ago. We have been working on the SD for as long as I can remember and of course there are no dates on the records that I can see. I think the HC is stalling for some reason and just giving us miniscule work and treating it as something big. For example: today on the surface, we as in a team of five, were told to mass produce the OXY. I already knew how because I had researched it during my half hour of recreation time on Sunday. I just decided to waste time and act like I had to work through it. One person could have done that, and the rest could have been working on something worthwhile like taking samples of Earth's atmosphere and hypothesizing solutions to make it pure again, Michael replied.

I thought you said the radiation was gone.

It is, but the air is still polluted. I believe it wouldn't be good for you to breathe, but you wouldn't mutate into an RMH, which leads me to another subject: the RMH. How are they still alive? When I get to be on the LC, I want to lead a team of investigative scientists to the surface to find out how they are still alive. According to my calculations and the information the SOL provides us, they should all be dead by now. They should have died out centuries ago, Michael said.

That's interesting. You might be too curious for your own good.

Look who's talking: Miss I-won't-tell-you-for-fear-of-someone-hurting-you, Michael said as he smiled and kissed her hand.

Mary rolled her eyes, but smiled at Michael and kissed his forehead. *I love you too much.*

Mary, you know I wouldn't tell anyone.

I know but if I was to be found out and they found out you knew and did nothing, they would send you to the surface as well, Mary reasoned.

At least we'd be together.

Yes, together to die.

Michael kissed Mary a soft and gentle kiss. *I think we'd figure out a way to survive and make our own life.* Mary smiled at this as he continued. *I love you more than life itself. My heart will always live with you.* He told her as he whispered the words, "I love you."

They lay in each other's arms thinking sweet thoughts to the other, feeling closer than they ever had before as they gently lulled themselves to sleep.

***

Mary's eyes slowly opened to the image of Michael's face: peaceful and dreaming. She disconnected her BIS. *Dreams are private thoughts,* she thought.

She quietly snuck back to her hole in the wall and consciously made the decision to find out what Ana of Gen39 gave her life for, even if it meant she had to give hers too. Sliding onto the third floor of the LOH, she replaced the first book she had borrowed, and went to see if anyone occupied the LOH at this hour of sleep.

Mary stealthily moved down to the first floor of the LOH and returned to the search engine hidden in the table and activated it. She had to find out if the Historian could see their thoughts while on the BIS. Melinda, the golden woman, came forth out of the screen.

"Hello, what would you like to research?" Melinda stood there straight as a pin with her hands folded and placed on her stomach and her eyes staring straight into the nothingness past Mary.

"LQ134: the last twenty-four hours."

She walked through Mary off into the nothingness and returned a few seconds later.

"Here are your requested subjects of research," she said while extending a tablet.

Mary took it and threw it into the air. She grabbed the file titled 23:00. Her surroundings transformed into her LQ. She watched as she walked back to Michael with the BIS devices. She couldn't hear anything. "Melinda, decipher the thought processes on the BIS between Mary and Michael."

"Unable to process request," Melinda responded as her golden hue glittered in the lights of the LQ.

"Why are you unable to process my request?" Mary asked.

"There is a barrier preventing the deciphering of the thought process," Melinda answered.

"Run a diagnosis, find the error and fix the problem," Mary ordered.

"Affirmative." Melinda's head twitched to the side, and then again. She stood with her head titled down and to the side for a few moments. Then she straightened up again and said, "Error fixed and able to process request."

Mary could see her and Michael's thoughts through lots of static but it was still understandable. Her encryption was not enough. "Melinda, how do I block a file to where only I can research it?"

Melinda's head twitched, "I'm sorry, you do not have access to that information."

"I am Matthew, Historian of Generation 40," Mary said, hoping that the program relied too much on the SOL doing what they were supposed to do instead of breaking into the LOH and researching forbidden subjects.

"Please enter your security number," Melinda said as her hand swiped the area in front of Mary and a number pad appeared in the air.

Mary didn't know what to enter. She began to think back to her only encounter with Matthew. Then with some hesitation, she entered 3030 into the pad.

"Welcome Matthew. What would you like to research?"

"I need to block several files to where only Mary of Generation 43 can access it."

Melinda walked in to the nothingness and came back holding a tablet. "Here are your suggested subjects of research."

Mary then analyzed her request: *If I restrict access so only I can view this file, then that creates a pointed finger at me.*

"I would like to research how I can delete certain files and remove any trace of their existence."

Melinda walked back into the nothingness and reappeared with another tablet. "Here are your suggested subjects of research."

Mary threw the tablet up and it blossomed into program files. She touched the one that read: Delete restricted information.

The nothingness transformed to holographic images of report listings written in some code unfamiliar to Mary.

Mary said, "Convert this code to JT-C format."

Melinda responded, "Please enter the pass code." She swiped her hand in the air and the number pad appeared again. Mary inputted 3030. "I'm sorry, that is incorrect. Please enter the pass code."

Mary started to panic. *What could it be?* She took a deep breath and let it out slowly. *There is no turning back now. Think, what could it be?* Mary thought back to her conversation with Matthew. Finally she entered the number 3011, the year Gen40s were born.

Melinda at once said in her smooth and overly feminine voice, "The coding can now be converted to JT-C format." The code began to change as a blue wave of light grazed past the floating program changing it into a code Mary could read.

Let's see what we have here, Mary thought as she began to read the coding. *I must rearrange the sequencing and make the seconds appear longer to cover the time I want deleted. Then I must delete the file and erase the entire coding of the file's program. After that, let's see, I need to do a virtual cleansing of the system and set a time clock to get back to my LQ before it starts recording again.*

"Who created this program?" Mary asked.

"The Head Council of Generation 27," Melinda responded.

"That's interesting," Mary said under her breath. "Why did they create this program?" Mary asked Melinda.

Melinda's head twitched and she responded, "I'm sorry, that data in no longer available."

"Did someone delete that also?" Mary asked with a sigh hearing the all too familiar words.

Melinda's head twitched and she responded, "I'm sorry, that data is no longer available."

"The answer to that question I believe is Yes," Mary responded with a rising uncomfortable feeling that she was living in a place worse than anything she could imagine.

She opened up the day's files and embedded a string of JT-C coding that lengthened the timing of a second by .021 seconds to cover the thirty minutes of the day where she had said and thought things she did not want the Historian to see. She then grabbed the program from the air that contained her BIS conversation with Michael and deleted it. She also opened up some parts of her DQ conversation with Katy and Violet and deleted those as well. Mary thought, *Am I really deleting files from history? Am I doing the very thing that erased Ana's record from the SOL?* She tried to talk herself out of the guilt that started to creep in. *Ana died for something, and if I'm going to find out what it is, I have to protect myself. I have to protect those I love and who love me.* She thought of Michael, Katy, Violet, Brent, and Rhome: her friends and support group. *Please don't let me get caught. What am I going to do if we are all sent to the surface? What would I do? How would they still love me? How would they forgive me?*

Mary created a temporary program that acted like a nanite and virtually chopped the deleted files into tiny little pieces. Then she ran a cleansing macro, to virtually wash all the pieces down the drain and out to nowhere. *I did it. I'm going to find what Ana gave her life for. I'll set this time clock for thirty seconds. That will give me time to grab another book and sneak back to Michael before he wakes up.* She set it, started counting, took off the interfacing devices, ran up the stairs, grabbed a book on her way in to the secret passageway, left it in the wall, and slid back into Michael's arms. *Twenty-seven. Twenty-eight. The BIS!* Mary quickly put back on the BIS that connected her to Michael's thoughts, closed her eyes and hoped no one reviewed those few seconds too closely.

Her mind settled down and her heart beat dropped. She looked at Michael's sleeping face and took a deep breath. She caressed his hair and the side of his face bringing forth a smile on his lips.

GD Mary, Michael said to her through his thoughts.

Go back to sleep Michael. We have almost another hour before we have to go to the SPR, Mary told him.

He leaned towards her face and kissed her forehead. *Alright, Mary.*

Mary closed her eyes. *I need some sleep.*

Maybe you should go see the HP, Michael said.

Mary forgot about her still connected BIS. *I'm not ill. I just keep having trouble sleeping.*

Even though, the HP might be able to help, Michael suggested. *Go see Brent.*

Alright, Michael. I'll go tomorrow after work hours. Now go back to sleep, Mary said.

Michael smiled at her through the darkness, closed his eyes, and after a while, his deep breathing took over signaling he was asleep. Mary followed soon after.

The wake-up call came too soon. Mary felt as if she had just fallen asleep, which wasn't too short of the truth. Her dream of the surface fire had returned to her in the short time she had fallen asleep.

"I will see you in a few minutes," Michael said as he got up, kissed her cheek, and walked out towards his LQ.

The dark circles under his eyes were a dead giveaway that we had been up all night conversing, Mary thought. She walked to her BQ, undressed, and started the G-L converter. The air in the room began to turn to liquid and blasted on her body, and as soon as it hit her body, it converted back to air. Mary turned around and around until she felt clean, then turned the G-L converter off. She gazed at herself in the mirror thinking, *I do this every single morning. What keeps me going?* The air was dark with the dirt from her body, so she pushed the ventilation button. The vents opened overhead and swept the air to the surface. She reached for her towel that hung on the wall and gently dried any remaining water that still clung to her skin.

I am so tired. I need sleep. I need something to keep me awake. What if I fall asleep on the surface? That is, if Amanda lets me work on the surface today. I might just take another day off and catch up on sleep again. Wait, no. That will look too suspicious. A knock came at the door.

"Computer, who is at the door?" Mary asked.

"Michael of Generation 43," the computer responded in a voice Mary had come to know.

"Tell him I will be out in a few minutes," Mary said as she reached for her cleaned uniform.

A holographic image of a colorful Melinda appeared on Mary's door facing Michael. "She will be out in a few minutes." Michael sighed deeply. *She's been acting so strange. She's late and tired. She needs to go see the HP.*

Mary finished putting on her uniform and tying up her hair. Staring at herself through her mirror, she didn't recognize the person she was becoming. Her old self had been carefree, always striving to be the best engineer of Generation 43 to help the SOL live back on the surface. She had always just gone about her life like there was nothing more.

Now, she felt like she needed something more. She wanted something more. She was something more. She is something more. She just didn't know what that something more was.

A knock came again. Mary reluctantly left herself in the mirror and walked outside her LQ.

"Mary, I'm worried about you. You really need to see the HP," Michael said voicing his concern.

"I told you I would go after I get done with the surface work today," Mary told him.

Michael nodded in approval, but he felt like he had opened another door to Mary's soul by asking to know her, maybe one that was too deep for him to understand.

They walked to the transporter in silence. Rhome came briskly walking up to them. "Hold."

"GD Rhome," Mary and Michael said in unison.

"GD Michael, Mary." He stepped inside. The transporter took them to Level One. Rhome turned to Mary as they began walking to the SPR. "Did you hear that Michael got an offer to sit on the LC?"

"Yes. I am very proud of him," Mary answered.

"Yes. I am too," Rhome said as he patted Michael on the back.

"Well, Rhome. I'll put in a good word for you too. I couldn't have gotten to where I did without you," Michael said.

'You knew what went wrong. You are just too modest to say anything," Rhome rebutted.

Michael took a short, quick breath. "No. No, I didn't. You were the one who ran the analysis and found the mistake."

"Alright, Michael. If that's what you want to say," Rhome said as he shrugged his shoulders.

Mary smiled and glanced at Michael and Rhome; they both had smiles on their faces as well. Michael and Rhome entered the SPR-S, and Mary took a deep breath as she stepped into the SPR-E.

"You still don't look well," Amanda said as she walked in.

"GD Amanda. I am fine. The HP report came back negative." Mary walked over to the computer and accessed her report. "Feel free to review it. I am going to go debrief myself on the BPs."

Amanda's nostrils flared a little, and she reviewed Mary's HP report as Mary entered the lab.

"GD Mary. Amanda said you were ill. Are you well now?" Blake asked.

"The HP report came back negative. I feel fine. What are we working on?" Mary asked.

"The BPs for the LQBs," Blake responded as he looked back into the holographic schematics pit.

"There are so many inefficiencies here," Mary said as she glanced over the layout. She began making marks all over the holographic blueprint, cutting down layouts and condensing runways for the bots. She then changed the image to display the BPs for the surface SOL. She rearranged the layouts for the LQ to optimize space and reworked the plumbing to decrease the amount of material they would have to use. She also replaced all the OXY locations to maximize its full potential. "See, this layout is much more efficient while still maintaining a high level of effectiveness and standard of living."

"I'm impressed, Mary," Blake said as he looked over her work. "I never would have thought to do all these things."

Amanda came up behind him. "Negative, Blake of Generation 43. We all work together. No one is better than anyone else. Mary would not have been able to make those mediocre changes if you hadn't laid out the basis."

"Amanda, you laid out the basis with help from BI," Blake responded. "And these changes are more than mediocre. They will save us so much time and material."

Amanda's face flustered. "The HC will have to approve it." She saved the work and sent it to the HC. "Now we wait. I would suggest you get debriefed on your surface equipment."

As they walked toward the surface gear, Mary said to Blake, "Thank you for supporting me."

"You're welcome, Mary. I think the changes you made will definitely put you up for a LC nomination." He smiled at her.

Mary lightly laughed, "I doubt it if Amanda has any say in it."

"I've noticed she doesn't like you very much. What happened between you?" Blake asked.

"It was a year or two ago. She had proposed an advancement to the computer system that runs the SOL to the LC which had been my idea in the first place. I was there with her when she proposed it, but I was the one who knew all about it. So they asked her to explain, and when she couldn't, she looked to me. I said nothing, because she took my idea. She looked like a fool in front of the LC, and she has not liked me ever since."

"Did you ever submit the advancement idea to the LC?" Blake asked.

"No, I don't want it to look like I took her idea or have the issue opened because I don't know what would happen to her," Mary replied.

"But the SOL could benefit from it?" Blake inquired turning to look his friend in the eye.

"Yes, but there is more at stake here than just the SOL," Mary said.

"What? What are you talking about?" Blake asked now seriously focusing his blue eyes on Mary, waiting for her response.

Mary just put her finger to her mouth and pointed to the holographic instructor debriefing their team on their project for the day.

"...attach your BIS and keep it on frequency .00045601. E-Group One: Gen43: Mary, Blake, Rachel, Andrew. Gen 42: Mark. E-Group Two: Gen 43: Josh..."

Mary began walking towards the elevator with her group.

"Mary. Connect your BIS," Mark commanded her.

S-Group One was already on the surface, when E-Group One arrived. Mary spotted Michael.

We have just received a rejection on the changes Mary made to the BPs. I looked over them, Mary. In my opinion, I thought they were excellent; however, the HC knows best as they have more experience and knowledge about the advancement of the SOL as a whole. I'm sure their reasoning is sound, Mark said to everyone through his BIS.

Are we able to see their reasoning? Blake inquired.

Negative, Mark responded.

Then how are we supposed to confirm their reasoning is sound? Rachel asked. She too had seen Mary's changes and was looking forward to the reduced time it would take to build the surface dwelling.

Mary stood silently by, observing her friends as they supported her changes, seeing if they too thought the HC was corrupt.

They are the HC. They know best, Mark responded. *We will build according to the old BPs.* Everyone seemed to accept that assertion and began their duties.

***

Mary sat idly in her LQ. She wasn't going to the DQ to eat. She was thinking. Her hands softly clasped. Her feet firmly planted to the floor. Her elbows perched on her thighs. Her back slightly slouched. Her head was down with her gaze burning a hole in the floor. Mary sat on her sleeping cot. Yes, she was tired, but more important matters were swimming around in her head.

How am I going to outsmart the HC?

How am I going to keep off the Historian's radar and all-seeing eye?

How am I going to keep from dying in vain?

How am I going to protect my friends and family?

How am I going to get the knowledge I need?

What is my plan?

What is my strategy?

Where is Benjamin of Generation 39?

What does Matthew of Generation 40 have to do with all of this?

How am I going to access the different resources I need?

Am I going to be able to sneak back into the LOH every time I have to delete something?

Will I delete it in time?

If I get sent to the surface, how will I survive?

Who will support me even if it means a surface sentence?

What is the HC hiding?

For what did Ana die?

For what am I risking my life?

How will I find it?

These questions raced through Mary's mind.

She had no answers.

She breathed deeply and slowly let her inhaled air out in one fell swoop.

What am I going to do?

She walked over to her mirror and braced herself against the wall. Staring into her own eyes, she began to realize she was not as strong as she thought she was. *I am only human. I am nothing without the SOL. The SOL? What is the SOL? The SOL is a learning community,* she sarcastically thought to herself remembering back to her first encounter with the LOH research database. *Research database?* She thought back to the advancement she created a long time ago. She had never recorded it; it was in her mind, and she had to recall it from memory.

The objective of the advancement was to be able to access the library from any pod. What if I tweaked the coding and allowed myself access to the LOH from anywhere in the SOL? How would I erase my presence during or after my entry? What if I made myself invisible to the Historian? An idea sparked in Mary's mind. She quickly turned around, and went into her passageway. There she sat in the dark, re-reading through Ana's discoveries, but the more she read, the more she found missing files, important missing files. *What is it Ana? Why did they sentence you to death? What did you find out about them?* Mary hopelessly turned off the tablet and leaned back against the wall. *There's only one way to see if my advancement works.* She quietly snuck into the LOH. She covertly examined her surroundings, grabbed another book and put back the other one she had just read. She began to tiptoe down the stairs towards the research pods. No one was around. She sneakily stepped onto the mirrored floor.

"Hello, what would you like to research?" the table asked her.

"I need to see the program's coding," Mary told Melinda as she came forth from the screen.

Melinda's head twitched, "I'm sorry, you do not have access to that information."

"I am Matthew, Historian of Generation 40," Mary said and entered 3030 into the number pad.

"Welcome Matthew. What would you like to research?" Melinda asked.

"I need to view the program's coding," Mary repeated.

The nothingness, in which Mary stood, transformed into walls upon walls of coding in moving streams. "Convert to JT-C format." The coding changed with a blue wave of light.

"I now need to simultaneously view the event log of Mary of Generation 43. Convert to JT-C format," she ordered Melinda.

Let's see what we have. Here am I going through normal daily activities a month ago and sixteen weeks ago. She highlighted the coding with her fingers and moved it to a blank wall. She inputted various random factors to make it seem more real. She also inputted environmental factors in case someone was sitting in the DQ where she had sat. She coded herself to move to a vacant spot. She located her tracking number: 0000238, and erased her locational data, and inputted her new program. She smirked. "Melinda, locate subject 238."

A holographic image projected and there she saw herself sitting at the DQ with Michael, Katy, Violet, Rachel, and the rest of her close friends. She smiled a pleased smile, but then it hazed in and out with the image of her standing in the Library of History.

"Melinda. How does the system know that I am still here?" Mary asked turning to face Melinda.

"CPU1200 tracks the inhabitants of the SOL through their transmitter," Melinda responded.

"What transmitter? Where?" Mary asked in a frantic.

"It is located on the inner side of the right thigh," Melinda said.

Mary felt her leg, pushed into the meaty tissue of her thigh and felt something deep within her skin. She sensed her heart drop to her stomach. "Deactivate subject 238 transmitter. Is it deactivated?" Mary asked in a panic.

Melinda's head twitched. "Negative."

"How do you deactivate a subject's transmitter?" Mary asked.

"The transmitter is attached to the femoral artery. When the blood quits moving past it, the transmitter deactivates. Disposal of the vessel of which it is attached deactivates the transmitter."

"When was this process started, and how did they get these inside of us?" Mary asked.

"This process was started in the year 3030; the HC prepared a routine DNA-B check for all inhabitants of the SOL, and the HP injected every person while they were unconscious. Later when the next generation was born, the HC ordered the HP to put them in the infants."

"Did the HC receive transmitters? Did the Historian receive a transmitter?" Mary asked.

"Negative. Negative," Melinda responded to both of Mary's questions.

"Oh Ana, you've made my mission so much more difficult now," Mary whispered to herself. *I have to mask this somehow until I figure out a way to remove it without dying.* "Melinda, what is the frequency of subject 238's transmitter."

"The frequency of subject 238's transmitter is 0.00000000000000000031287654O1."

"Repeat," Mary said as she got lost in the zeros that fronted the transmission frequency.

"The frequency of subject 238's transmitter is 0.00000000000000000031287654O1."

Mary entered the transmission frequency in her coded program to tag the fake Mary instead of herself.

"Melinda, locate subject 238."

The projection was less hazy and the image of her in the Library of History was too faint to see with the untrained eye. *That's not good enough.* "Melinda, is there a damper or mask I can install?"

"Negative."

"I will just have to create one then," Mary said with the sound of uncertainty creeping through her voice. *There is no turning back now. I have to keep pressing forward and hope no one walks in right now. Everyone should still be in the DQ.* Mary stared blankly at the wall of coding that stood in front of her. *I am an engineer. I should know how to design this coding. Beat the system. I can do it. I can do it. I can do it.* Mary's train of thought trailed off as the daunting appearance of the code surrounded her and the tiny sliver of hard material attached to a major artery in her leg intensified her fear of being caught.

She had to remove it. Somehow, she had to remove it. Mary kept telling herself this. *The HP put it in there, he can take it out. Now, who do I know that is an*

HP? I know a junior HP: Michael's twin brother, Brent. Mary thought she had figured it out, but then another dark thought crossed her mind. *If I do that, then I'll be endangering Brent. How to keep him from knowing anything?*

"Melinda, what was used to erase the SOL's memory in the year 3030?"

"The precipitate of Na_3Yi and KRe was mixed with the DQ food. After twenty-four hours at the next designed DQ time, Ar_2O was released in the air. The chemicals mixed and erased the SOL's memory of the previous 72 hours. The HP then went into each person's memory bank and deleted any memory of Ana of Generation 39. Then the memories were deleted."

"How do you perform a memory deletion procedure?" Mary asked.

"A memory extraction is performed by having the inhabitant fall asleep. This is when the HP will keep him or her asleep and project his or her memories onto a wall via a specialized brain interface system, or SBIS. The HP will then dig deeper or guide the dreams until they become memories displayed on the wall. With an ES280, he highlights the person or thing he wants deleted in the inhabitant's memory and pushes the black button. This provides a blank in the inhabitant's memory by smoothing that part of the brain so he or she no longer remembers that person or thing," Melinda explained.

"Where is this specialized brain interface system?"

"The specialized brain interface system is located on Level Four of the Library of History."

"Oh great," Mary said thinking she's got it made. She'll just prance down the halls of the SOL carrying a SBIS to the HP. "Well, that's what I'm going to have to do."

With this new found confidence in her plan, she got to work creating her mask. She was dragging pieces of coding, creating new pieces, modifying others, until she had created a mask that surrounded everyone within a five foot radius of her transmitter.

She saved her newly created locational coding as coding program 749012.

"Melinda, locate subject 238."

A holographic image projected and there she saw herself sitting at the DQ with Michael, Katy, Violet, Rachel, and the rest of her close friends. Everyone was getting ready to leave. The projection had flickers in it, but just enough to show where she was. *This is good enough for now. Just until I get to Brent and have him remove this transmitter. Now, I need to cover all this up.*

She re-created her locational data and used it as a superficial coding on top of her newly created program. "Melinda, locate subject 238." The projection stayed the same. *I beat the coding; now to beat the system.* "Melinda, locate access data."

A whoosh of walls of coding flew by Mary's face and gradually slowed to a stop. "I need to create a new user account."

Melinda highlighted the section. Mary inputted herself as Omega 7 password 2023, allowed herself full access, and forged the Head Council's approval by copying the signature file from Matthew's account. She canceled the notification that would be sent to the Historian and the members of the Head Council. She inputted her advancement into her account allowing her access from any device that could connect to any library. She also coded her account where it automatically calculated the time she was in the research database, deleted any recording, and expanded the time to cover the period: a virtual flush.

Now, where should I hide this wondrous creation? Mary thought to herself. She decided to hide it under the detail-level files of cow milk processing. *They will never find it there. I don't even know what cow milk processing is though I'm pretty sure it has nothing to do with information coding,* she chuckled as she thought. Mary was smiling ear to ear now. "Melinda, sign Mathew off."

Melinda's head twitched, "Hello, what would you like to research."

"I am Omega 7." She entered her password, 2023.

"Hello Omega 7. What would you like to research?" Melinda asked.

"Locate Benjamin of Generation 39," Mary said.

Melinda's head twitched, "Unable to process request."

"Am I not allowed all access?" Mary asked as she sighed and hung her head.

"Negative; Benjamin of Generation 39's records were erased 2/5/3050, 05:30 hours."

"What?" Mary said in disbelief looking up.

"Benjamin of Generation 39's records…"

"I know. Shut up."

"..were erased 2/5/3050, 05:30 hours."

Mary rolled her eyes, but then thought she heard something. "Sign off Omega 7," Mary whispered.

Melinda's head twitched, "Hello, what would you like to research?"

Mary put the research apparatus back in the research table and went back to her passageway. She turned and looked down at the research floor; no one was there. "Erased," she whispered with a confused countenance. "Oh wait, the SBIS, on Level Four." Looking around cautiously, she went up to the fourth floor, located it, and turned to go back down to the third floor, but something caught her eye. It was a stairway that led into the ceiling.

Mary wanted to climb it, and just as she put her foot on the first step she heard noises, more like people talking, coming from above that were getting louder. Stepping back in fear, she turned and flew down the stairs, heart racing, with thoughts of dread starting to emerge on her terrified face. She tried to control her breathing as she neared the passageway. She felt like she couldn't get enough air into her lungs, and began to feel faint. She got to the doorway of escape, habitually grabbed another book, and crawled into her passageway in the dark. She rolled over on her back, and slowed down her breathing and heartbeat. *So close,* she thought, but she was safe with the SBIS and two new books.

She had never felt that way before, and it was exhilarating. She began to smile. She sat up, turned on her light pin and began to read.

One hour passed, and she had finished reading the two books. She sat with her head leaned back against the wall. "Why were his records erased?" She thought, *Only one person who I think I can trust would know the answer to that question. Matthew said, 'No one knew who Benjamin of Generation 39 was'. What did he mean by that? His records were erased nearly twenty years after Ana was sentenced. Why wait so long to send him to the surface as well? Maybe he deleted himself and is living somewhere else? No, how would he survive this long without his DNA rejuvenators?* She grabbed the tablet that sat next to her. "Locate nearest engineering pod. Access LOH, Omega 7." She entered 2023, and Melinda appeared on her screen. "It works."

"Hello Omega 7. What would you like to research?" Melinda asked as her small holographic frame stood on the screen of the tablet.

"I need to review the files of Benjamin of Generation 39 from year 3030 to year 3050," Mary told her.

After scanning and re-scanning the files, Mary said in desperation, "He just had a normal routine life; then he just disappears? I need to find out what happened to him, and what he did to be erased." Mary began recalling facts about his life: "He was a scientist. He was married to Ana. They had a son, who had a son, who had a son who is Michael." A light bulb went off in Mary's head. "Melinda, track Michael of Generation 43's DNA throughout the SOL. Show all related matches."

Melinda threw up a tablet into the air and the files dispersed around Mary's face. There was no file labeled Benjamin of Generation 39, but one was labeled "Unknown Survivor". One of Mary's eyebrows cocked, and she pulled that file.

For the first time in the SOL's history, a survivor was found on the surface on 2/5/3050. He was badly burned from the radiation and found with what looked like RMH attack marks. He had broken English and could not speak very well. The SOL took him in and labeled him "Subject Unknown Survivor."

That was all the file said. Mary thought to herself: *Interesting; they deleted everything even past records of Ana, but they leave Benjamin's records and just make him disappear, put him on the surface and maybe the SOL found him, didn't recognize him, brought him down, and the HC renamed him Unknown Survivor?.... That makes no sense. Why not just slip the SOL something to erase their memory of Benjamin of Generation 39? Something is going on, but I will start with this Unknown Survivor.*

"Melinda, locate Subject Unknown Survivor," Mary said.

"Subject Unknown Survivor is on the Floor of Rest," Melinda responded.

"Melinda, sign off Omega 7."

Melinda's head twitched, "Hello, what would…"

Mary deactivated the tablet. "First let's get this transmitter deactivated."

Tablet under arm and SBIS in her work bag, Mary withdrew from her inner-wall sanctum and headed towards the transporter to take her to the HP.

"GD Mary!" Katy said as she walked past the DQ.

"GD Katy."

"I didn't see you in the DQ today. Were you at the HP?" Katy asked.

"No, why does everyone think I'm ill?" Mary asked sharply looking at her friend.

"You just don't look like your normal self." Then she whispered, "Is everything alright with you?"

"Yes, Katy. I have just been not sleeping well," Mary said.

"The HP can give you a DNA-B to at least keep you working at your best," Katy suggested.

"Katy, DNA-Bs gives a boost to your DNA, not to your cells." Mary stopped dead in her tracks. "DNA-Bs and DNA-Rs?" *DNA boosters and DNA rejuvenators do very little to nothing for the health of your cells. What book was I reading? The Japanese Art of Life? It talked about the technology they developed to expand life spans. We don't live that long. What are they giving us?*

"Are you sure you're feeling well?" Katy asked, jerking Mary from her thoughts.

"Yes, Katy. I feel fine. I have somewhere I need to go. I'll speak with you tomorrow," Mary said.

Katy waved as Mary began running towards the transporter.

"She needs to see the HP," Katy whispered to herself under her breath.

Chapter 3

RALLY OF THE SOUL

Once inside the transporter, Mary sighed to herself. Her taunt jaw line, cocked eyebrow, crossed arms and leaning stance displayed the look of betrayal she felt in her heart.

The floor slid her out onto Level Two, and she swiftly walked to the HP. Walking up to the door, the body scanner dropped from the ceiling. *I can't be scanned or they will know something is not right with my file and locational data,* Mary thought to herself as she jumped out of the way. With her hand creeping alongside the wall, she accessed the computer and signed in as Omega 7. "Override scan and open HP door."

The body scanner went back to which it came, and the door slid open. Mary snuck in and headed towards the junior HP offices. She knocked on Brent's door. The door slid open revealing Brent's smiling face. He looked almost exactly like his brother: the same square jaw line and muscular body, the same jet black hair and blue eyes, and the same six foot stature and tanned skin.

"GD Mary. I didn't know anyone was coming in. The body scanner must be malfunctioning. Come on in. What seems to be the matter?" Brent asked.

"I need to talk to you," Mary said as the door slid shut behind her.

"Well, I'm an HP. I am here to listen." Brent said with an all too well rehearsed smile on his face as his arms crossed.

"Do you trust me?" Mary said in a serious tone with a firm stance.

"Mary, the SOL trusts each other," Brent said as he uncrossed his arms and placed them on his hips.

"Would you give your life for me?" Mary asked him.

"Of course, Mary. You would do the same for me," Brent responded. "My brother loves you. I love you."

"Then do you trust me?" Mary asked.

"Yes," Brent said in a confident manner. "What's going on?"

"I need to access your computer," Mary said.

"Alright. It's by the door," Brent said pointing. "What is this about?"

Mary took steps backwards keeping her eyes locked with Brent's. She finally turned and walked over to the wall. She turned and looked over her shoulder. With a serious face, she told him, "Don't tell anyone about this."

"I won't," Brent said as he smiled.

She turned and faced the computer. "Sign on Omega 7."

Melinda stepped forth, "Welcome Omega 7. What would you like to research?"

Brent ran over to Mary. "What is this? What did you get yourself into? I don't think we are supposed to know about this."

"We aren't. Melinda run coding program 749012 on Brent of Generation 43, subject 234."

Melinda's head twitched, "Affirmative. Coding program 749012 is now active on subject 234 file."

Mary turned to Brent. "They can't see us now, but they still know where you are."

"Who are you talking about?" Brent asked as he walked around the golden Melinda.

"I'll explain later." Mary said in a hushed voice. "Either you are all in, or I'll leave and you will not say a word to anyone."

Brent inhaled cautiously and stood in silence locking eyes with Mary. "Does Michael know?"

"No. You are the first because I need you to do something for me," Mary said.

"I'm just a J-HP, Mary. What can I do?" Brent asked as he came around and stood facing her.

"I have a transmitter in my leg. We all do. I need you to remove mine," Mary told him.

"A transmitter? I've never heard of or seen one in someone's leg," Brent said shaking his head and walked back over to his desk. Mary followed him.

"Trust me, it's there." She took his hand and placed it on her leg. She pushed her fingers on top of his.

"I feel something," he said as he pulled his hand away. He averted his eyes. "Let's take a closer look. I'm going to need you to lie down on the table."

Brent put on his user interface equipment and hooked up a wireless projector to Mary's leg. Mary turned and faced the wall. Brent was virtually digging through her leg tissue looking for her transmitter. "Mary, I'm not seeing anything."

"It's right here!" Mary said as she pushed in on her leg.

"It's not showing up in your leg; therefore it's not there," Brent argued.

"Melinda, locate transmitter in subject 238 on the projection screen," Mary ordered the computer. Melinda's head twitched and the projection blurred as it ventured through muscle, tissue, and veins at an extremely fast pace. It finally came to a stop inside her artery. "There it is. I need you to remove it," Mary said to Brent in a demanding tone.

"What? So, it is there. It looks like it is attached to the inside of the femoral artery. If I try to remove it, you could die. Is there any other way to deactivate it?"

"Melinda, is there no other way to deactivate it?" Mary asked to answer Brent's question.

Melinda's head twitched. "To deactivate the transmitter, no motion must surround its .01 cm diameter."

"Mary, I can't remove it. It looks like it's attached to the artery wall," Brent repeated.

Mary stared at the wall. *I need this removed. I can't accomplish anything if they know where I am, if they always know where I am.* "What if you stopped my heart and brought me back to life?" Mary asked Brent still staring at the wall.

"Mary, that's insane, and besides you could still exsanguinate." Brent looked at her with a hint of fright in his blue eyes.

"Do you trust me?" Mary asked.

"Mary, I'm an HP. This is illogical. This is too much risk," he said but then saw the determined look in her eyes. "What is it transmitting?" he sighed.

"My location within in the SOL," Mary answered.

"Why do you want to stay hidden?" Brent asked.

"I'll explain later. I need you to remove this. Find a way. You are the best HP of Generation 43. Find a way. I will wait here patiently," Mary said to him as she laid her head back and closed her eyes.

"Mary I can't do that. I'm not even on the LC or HC. I'm not that good. The SOL works together," Brent said exasperated, seriously doubting his own confidence.

"Sometimes the purpose of your life is unknown, but then, when it becomes perfectly clear, you know what you must do," Mary said with her eyes still closed. "I know my purpose. I know what I must do. I need you to help me."

Brent just stared at her as she lay so calmly on the table with her hands folded on her stomach, which slowly rose and fell with her calm breathing. "You could die, Mary."

"I know what I must do. I trust you will not let that happen," Mary responded.

At this, Brent took a deep breath and a spark within him flamed. "Alright Mary, I will find a way."

"Melinda lock door to HPQ13. Allow all research databases under subject 234," Mary said as a smile crossed by her lips.

Melinda's head twitched and she turned and faced Brent. "Hello, what would you like to research?"

"I need to research this transmitter: how it works, how it is attached, the possible entry ways to remove it, Mary of Generation 43's body scans and vitals, and technology for evasive surgery,' Brent said as he breathed hesitantly. He turned at looked at Mary who now looked as if she was sleeping, turned back to the files Melinda was holding. "I am the best of Generation 43. I can do this," he said to himself.

"I know you can," Mary said.

Brent smiled, "I know I can too."

Several hours passed. Brent woke up Mary who had fallen asleep. "I've found a way. There is a technology I didn't even know about. It takes a needle and it works its way up the artery, and then it attracts the laser that I point at the artery and it heats up whatever it touches. As I was studying the transmitter, I found it only can withstand temperatures up to 110 degrees Fahrenheit. It will cause a lot of pain because I will basically be burning a hole in the side of your artery. I will have to cut into your leg first though, before I turn on the laser. Then the problem comes, removing the transmitter from inside the artery, because then it would be free flowing in the artery. Through the hole I burn in your leg, I would have to pull it out with some medical tweezers. Then I will quickly have to switch from needle to clamp and clamp the hole in your artery and sear it." Brent told her seemingly in one breath.

"Will I exsanguinate?" Mary asked.

"I am going to slow your heart, so the blood flow won't be as fast. I'm also going to strap you down so you don't move. I will have vitals going the entire time, and I have some synthesized blood that matches your blood type just in case," Brent explained.

"Thank you Brent for helping me," Mary said.

"I hope you are not mistaken in putting your trust in me," Brent whispered as he injected the anesthetic.

"I am not," Mary said as the drug he gave her started to take effect.

Brent injected the drug to slow her heart. He placed the needle right above her knee. It injected itself into her artery and used her body scan to follow the artery up to the location of the transmitter, as Brent strapped her down. The light turned red which Brent could see through her skin.

He breathed deeply and sliced through her leg to the artery. He saw a tiny sliver of the artery that blocked the light that came from within. He used the clamps to hold her leg open. He breathed deeply again. He adjusted the nodule on her knee to narrow the light's shine and change the shape to a long rectangle. He turned on the laser, and watched as it reached 115 degrees. Tweezers in one hand, he reached in, grabbed the transmitter and with the clamp in the other hand, seared the artery. He looked up and was shocked to see that her vitals were not at all in bad shape. He attached the medical connector, and it sewed up her leg not missing a single vein, tissue, or muscle strand. He retracted the needle and put it aside. He injected DNA-R into both the tissue above the knee and her thigh. He removed the medical connector once it finished, and set it aside. Melinda was still standing in the corner.

He picked up the transmitter with the tweezers. *She said we all have these in us.* He looked down at his own leg. He placed it in a small jar and put it inside his safe. He did not want to wake Mary yet because he had to think.

Where is it transmitting its information?

Why did Mary want it out of her?

What is going on?

He looked over to her as she still lay strapped down.

What is she hiding, or what did she find out? He asked himself as he began to take off her constraints. He injected some adrenaline in her neck, and she came to.

She smiled a weak smile, "I knew you could do it."

"Your leg is going to be sore for a few days. There shouldn't be any bad side effects. Here are some DNA-Rs to help strengthen your leg."

"You know, DNA-Rs do nothing to help heal cells. They just strengthen the DNA inside live and healthy ones. They make your eyes brighter or your hair more healthy looking."

Brent looked at her. He had never thought of that, but she was right. "They told us they make you live longer."

"When you die, your DNA still lives on, but your cells' functions die with you."

Right again, he thought. *Why have I never thought of this either?*

"Read this book. It's called The Japanese Art of Life," Mary said as she handed him a tablet. "I recorded a summary of the file to this tablet. Make sure no one finds it."

Brent, eager to learn more, activated the tablet right away. "I want to know the technology behind longer life spans."

Mary patiently waited for him to finish reading.

"I'm speechless. I don't even know what to say. Where did you find this? Where did you get this?"

"I found it in the Library of History," Mary responded while rubbing the SBIS in her hand behind her back. "Can you replicate the technology right now?"

"Not right now, but I sure can try. Come back tomorrow, and I'll give you a progress report," Brent said.

"Do you ever leave this office?" Mary asked.

"Not usually," Brent said with a grin.

"Don't leave this office until you figure out how to replicate it. I'm going to put a mask on your file. Don't record anything in the computer. I'll keep

Melinda activated for you. Use her as a resource. I've created a program where it will erase any research that you do," Mary said.

"But Mary, the SOL could benefit from this. Why can't I tell anyone about this?" Brent asked.

Mary jumped off the table and stood pin straight glaring at him while a sudden surge of pain seared through her leg, but she did not let her pain show through her face. "Because I found it in the Library of History," she said with a cold undertone. "If the HC finds out what I've done and what you've done to help me, they will send us to the surface unprotected just like they did with Ana of Generation 39 whose records were consequentially erased. Do you understand why you can't tell anyone?" Mary clenched the SBIS in her hand.

"Mary, they would never send anyone to the surface," Brent said all too calmly.

"They have, and they will. You will endanger everything I've worked for and the plan I have to set us all free. Then and only then can we benefit from our past and not constrain our future," Mary said pleading with him to understand.

"What plan?" he asked.

"I'll explain later." There were a few moments where Brent stared at Mary deciding whether or not he was going to go along with this. She didn't really have a plan. She was still trying to figure out a way to find out what the HC was doing.

He breathed deeply. "Alright Mary, I will not tell anyone, and I will stay here until I figure this out."

"Thank you," Mary said as she turned to Melinda. "Melinda run dual controls, one here in HPQ13 and the other with Omega 7. Have you set my parameters?"

"Affirmative," Melinda responded.

"I will stay with you if you need me to help you," Mary offered.

"Maybe, it looks like I'll need some chemicals from the Library of Science," Brent said reviewing the tablet.

"Make a list of everything you think you'll need, and I'll go get them," she said.

He handed her a list. Before she left, he asked, "What if someone comes in?" looking at Melinda.

"No one will come in. Everyone is sleeping," Mary said. To ease his still nervous face, she spoke again, "Just say, 'Melinda deactivate.'" Melinda bowed her head and disappeared. "Melinda reactivate."

Melinda appeared again, "Welcome Omega 7. What would you like to research?"

Mary gave Brent a look that said 'see-it's-that-easy'. "I'll be right back." With that, Mary left HPQ13 and headed towards the Library of Science.

***

They worked until it was almost time for everyone to wake. Head on his hand, Brent glanced up at Mary who was still going strong. He rubbed his eye with his palm.

"Mary, I'm so tired. I don't think I can go much longer without getting some sleep," Brent said.

"It doesn't look like you have to. Mary said holding up a bottle of clear liquid. Melinda, scan substance and compare it to the substance described in The Japanese Art of Life."

Melinda put up her hand towards the bottle and looked off into the corner of the room. Suddenly she dropped her hand and displayed a projection of the results of the comparison.

Mary sighed a sigh of relief. She turned her head towards Brent who all of the sudden was now very interested in the results. "After a hundred eighty-five attempts, we have succeeded." She entered the final formula into her tablet.

Brent looked at her, and asked, "What are you doing?"

She finished recording, grabbed a syringe and drew some of the serum out of the bottle. "Wish me luck."

Brent jumped up from the chair from which he was sitting. "Mary, you don't know how much, and you don't know the side effects."

"Actually I do. I read it in the book but didn't mention it in the summary because I know you are a good person, and you would try to give it to your patients." While she was telling Brent her hidden secret, she injected herself in the leg. "In a few hours, I will be strong and healthy with no scars," Mary said as she put down the bottle and grabbed another syringe. She walked up really close to him as his face displayed utter shock. "And you won't remember anything that happened here," Mary said as she injected him with Thioxilline, a drug that makes people fall asleep very quickly. He stumbled back into the chair.

"I trusted you," he said as his eyesight began to blur and his breathing began to slow.

"I'm sorry, Brent. I need you to not know anything for your own safety. Thank you for all your help," Mary whispered to him as he drifted off.

She attached the SBIS and projected his inner most thoughts, his dreams, onto the wall. Then she went to work searching and finding the memories of the past thirteen hours.

"Violet?" Mary asked after witnessing a memory that took place after their time in the DQ. Mary laughed to herself. "I know who she will be picking after all." She left that memory alone.

After selecting all of those memories that included their forbidden research and surgery, she decided not to completely delete them. She instead saved all of his memories in her Omega 7 account and coded it to where if she was found out, the data would be sent to subject 234 on a secure data stream of which she encrypted.

She removed the SBIS and kissed his forehead. "I'm sorry Brent, but you will have a very painful headache when you wake up." She gave him a small dose of their new creation to help him with the pain.

She signed off Omega 7 and left the HP. As she walked down the corridor with the SBIS, the bottle of life and syringe hidden within her small work bag, she couldn't help but feel the guilt of betraying someone's trust well up inside her stomach, and sink to the depths of her toes.

"GD Mary," a fellow SOL inhabitant said to her.

"GD Tara," Mary said as she entered the transporter.

"Are you ready for another day of advancing the SOL to excellence?" Tara asked, her brown eyes shining in pure blissful ignorance.

"Affirmative," Mary said in a monotone voice with her eyes straight ahead. She was biting the inside of her lip. She didn't know if it was from the guilt or the fact that she wanted to yell at Tara at the top of her lungs that the superficial work they do is to mask some veiled motive of the HC.

The floor slid them out to Level One.

"What is your assignment on the surface?" Tara asked.

"I'm working on the BPs of the SD," Mary responded.

"Oh, I'm working on the mass production of the OXY. The other work day, Michael really impressed John with his accomplishment," Tara said excitedly.

"I heard. What a great day for the SOL!" Mary exclaimed half-heartedly.

"Mary," someone said behind her in a hushed yell. Looking back, she saw Michael walking up towards her.

"GD Michael. We were just talking about you and your great accomplishment the other day with the OXY," Tara said cheerfully.

"Thank you Tara. Rhome also contributed quite a bit," Michael said as he glanced back towards Mary whose eyes were downcast. An awkward silence filled the small space between them.

"I need to get to the SPR-S before I'm late," Tara said as she got the hint that Michael needed to talk with Mary.

"We'll be along in a minute," Mary said to her as she turned and left.

"Where were you?" Michael asked.

"I can't tell you." Mary looked at him with her big, blue eyes. "I'm sorry. I can't tell you," she said again as she saw his face wanting to rebuke what she just said.

"Did you go to the HP?" Michael asked.

"My body scan came back negative," Mary lied.

"Mary, I'm just worried about you," Michael told her as he noticed her averted eyes.

"Don't be. Let's go before we are late," Mary said calmly as she turned to go. Michael stepped into sync with her and they approached the SPR door. Mary half smiled at Michael and turned to enter her SPR.

"Good luck today, Mary," Michael said as he watched her enter the SPR-E.

"You too, Michael," Mary softly responded.

As soon as Mary stepped inside the SPR-E, Amanda growled, "Mary. You are late again."

Mary ignored her and kept looking straight ahead as she walked by into the SPR to be debriefed. She had other things on her mind than being on time to another pointless work day.

"Mary, I know you're upset from yesterday," Amanda said, "but that is not an excuse for showing up late." Mary had completely forgotten about what happened yesterday which flowed through to the confused look she had on her face.

Amanda filled in the blanks. "The HC rejected your proposal." Then she smiled and haughtily said, "Now you know what it feels like."

In response, Mary coolly said, "I don't know what you're talking about. I made a suggestion and the HC thought the original plans were better for the SOL. I didn't make a proposal and when asked about it, not know what I was talking about." She smiled and gave Amanda an innocent look and walked off to put on her surface equipment.

Amanda followed her in and whispered hotly in her ear, "I am the H-ENG. You treat me with respect or I will report you to the LC."

Mary swiftly turned to face her. "You don't respect me, why should I respect you? You have no regard for me, my ideas, my well-being, or my progress. After ten years of this type of treatment, it causes a person to resent you. I love what I do because I'm good at it, and I genuinely love solving near impossible problems. You hinder my abilities to move forward; you are the reason I haven't been able to propose anything to the HC. Everything I do has to be approved by you. You either reject it or take it for yourself. My attitude of disrespect is just a manifestation of your leadership, Senior Engineer. I come in late, so there's just that less amount of time I have to spend talking with you. I leave quickly because I want to get away from you. How am I supposed to respect someone who despises me for no apparent reason?"

Amanda stood there speechless. Everyone around them stood there speechless. Amanda's jaw clenched and her nostrils flared. She became aware everyone had heard what Mary had told her. Her hands balled into fists.

"If you will agree to it, I think we should start over. I will respect you if you respect me," Mary suggested in a whisper.

Amanda nodded in agreement, turned around and walked out towards the hallway.

The rest of the junior engineers smiled while they put on their surface equipment in silence.

***

"GD Michael," John enthusiastically said when Michael entered the SPR-S.

"GD John," Michael said matching the same enthusiasm John possessed that morning.

"Today, I'm putting you on an assignment with some of the other LC members."

"Thank you John. I'm honored. What is our assignment?" Michael asked in the most professional tone he could muster.

"You will be working on filtering the air on the planet, in order for the Earth to be reborn. This is an exciting opportunity for you Michael. I requested you to be put on this assignment. Don't disappoint me," John said as he smiled a threatening smile while he put his hand on Michael's shoulder.

Michael looked him dead in the eye. "You made the right decision. I will not disappoint you or the SOL."

"Right answer," John said as he patted his shoulder. "I suggest you go to the debriefing room."

Michael nodded and whispered to him, "Thank you for this opportunity John."

"You deserve it," John said with a half-cocked smile.

Michael mimicked his smile and then proceeded to walk away to the debriefing room. His mission was to figure out why the HC said the air was still toxic because of the radiation.

"GD Michael. I heard about your new work team. Good luck. It won't be the same without you," Rhome whispered to him as Michael came beside him. They were both staring straight ahead.

"It's just for one assignment." There was a slight pause in between their dialogue.

Rhome sighed a little, "John said I wasn't proficient enough for the SD. He is moving me to CD."

"Chemical Defenses would be good for you Rhome. You are always thinking of ways to defend ourselves in case the RMH attack," Michael said smiling at his friend.

Rhome half-heartedly smiled back. "But it's not the same as being on the SD team. I just get to work here all day, in the SPR-S with some SPR-E reject to come up with better weapons."

"You aren't rejects. You are being utilized better to suit your best abilities."

"Think about this, Michael. There hasn't been a surface attack for as long as we can remember. What good is it to create a weapon to defend against nothing?"

Michael couldn't formulate an answer. That question was just one more question he would seek to answer. He stepped forward into the transporter and watched his friend stare at them as the doors closed.

Up on the surface, Michael's mind raced. They were all connected via BIS.

Michael, we haven't had your input, John said to him.

I think we should take a sample from different spaces of air and dirt of the surrounding area, bring it back down to the SOL, study it and figure out why it is taking so long for the radiation to absorb into the ground, Michael responded confidently.

How do you suggest we do that? Robert asked him. He was the head of the LC.

Michael looked down.

Let us see your thought processes, Robert demanded.

Michael pressed the side of the BIS attached to his head. He glanced over to S-Group One and saw Weston glaring at him.

Focus. We bring up the bot that digs deep, BOTID 76, and have it roll outside of the SD and take a sample of one hundred feet of dirt. We transport it to the laboratory. We take air containers and with a group of us armed with our atom guns, ride out on our hover trains to 350 miles away from the SD and take a sample of air and dirt, come back and analyze it.

What is the reason for going that far away from the SD? Robert inquired.

To see if the air is the same as it is around the SD. We've been working on the SD for years and years, maybe even centuries. Maybe we've been putting off some sort of chemical that increases or idles the radioactive life, Michael responded.

I don't think so, but it could be. I believe it is enough of a good hypothesis, that I'd be interested in proving or disproving. I will pass your suggestion along to the HC to get approval, Robert said as he pulled out a black tablet and connected it to his BIS.

Within five minutes, the HC responded. 'REJECTED ACTION' flashed in everyone's left eye through their BIS.

The HC has rejected Michael's form of action. We will just use what they already had us doing in the first place.

Which is what? Michael thought just remembering they could all still see his thought processes and turned it back to the original setting. John glared at him.

Fill in your boy, Robert said to John.

Yes Robert, John smiled at Robert and then sent a piercing glance at Michael. *We are taking samples via the SD casing, and analyzing the results on the surface so that we do not endanger the SOL.*

Endanger the SOL from what? Michael asked.

From the harmful gases in the air up here, John replied.

If it's in a container, how would it get out? Michael asked.

You never know, John said and abruptly turned around and walked over to the rest of the team. Michael followed a little after him.

E-Group One arrived on the surface. They had the construction bots with them this time. The day slaved on, until it was time to go back to the SOL and get ready to go to the DQ.

"GD Michael," Weston said as he came up behind Michael.

"GD Weston," Michael said as he looked over his shoulder. He finished placing his PS&Gs on the wall, and turned around.

"How did your day go with the LC team?" Weston asked with a sincere overtone, but deep hidden inside him, there laid a growing seed of envy.

"We made a lot of progress," Michael said not believing his own words.

"Good for you," Weston said. Then he crossed his arms and shifted his weight to both feet that were firmly planted in the floor. "Will you be joining us again tomorrow?"

"I don't know, Weston. Maybe, maybe not."

"Just let me know," Weston said as he walked away.

Exiting the SPR-S, Michael saw Mary swiftly walking down the corridor towards the transporter.

"Mary," he called after her.

She didn't hear him and stepped inside the transporter. Mary's mind was on other things. The glass door slid up and the floor slid out to leave Mary on Level Four. The holographic receptionist smiled. *Interesting, it's Melinda in color again.*

"Hello..." The hologram's head twitched. "I'm sorry. I am unable to recognize you. Please place your hand on the biometric scanner."

"I don't think so." Mary said in a cool manner knowing that if she did, it would contradict her locational data program she entered for herself. "Sign on Omega 7."

The hologram's head twitched, "Welcome Omega 7. What would you like to research?"

"I need to override access control to Floor of Rest. Open the door."

"Affirmative."

"Sign off Omega 7."

"Hello, please enter," the hologram said as she smiled and outstretched her arm towards the open door to the Floor of Rest.

Mary had all this power and no one knew, or at least not anymore. Her guilt from the morning began to creep up her spine again. She walked boldly through the big frosted glass door and began looking around for someone who was older than the rest and maybe who had scars from the surface. Instead, she spotted her grandmother, and walked over to her.

"GD Jane," Mary softly said.

"GD Mary!" her grandmother said as she stood up and gave her a hug.

"What are you doing, Jane?" Mary asked as she noticed the tablets strewn about her.

"Oh, when you get ready to come to the Floor of Rest, you have to submit your life's work in an indexed form to the HC, before you are actually allowed to 'rest'," Jane replied with a sigh.

"I didn't know that," Mary responded.

"I didn't either until they told me," Jane said with a chuckle. "It's a good refresher and memory bath for my old brain. It makes me believe I'm relieving the old days."

"You don't have an old brain, Grandmother," Mary retorted.

"I'm seventy-eight. It's a lot older than yours!" Jane laughed. "Now what are you doing here?" she asked with her brown eyes tired from a lifetime of working.

"I need to find the Unknown Survivor. I want to ask him some questions. Do you know who I am talking about?" Mary asked.

"Alright Mary," she said as her eyebrow cocked. "I believe he is over there sitting in the corner." She pointed at an old man in the corner. His eyes were closed and his head was down on his chest. "He is much older than anyone here or it just might be the damage the surface radiation caused. You are working on the surface aren't you?"

"Yes, Jane," Mary said.

"Please wear your protective suit," her grandmother pleaded.

"I have to. It's required along with other safety precautions," Mary said matter-of-factly.

"Do you know what generation he is from?" Mary said referring back to the Unknown Survivor.

"Negative. I don't know how he survived up there either. How did his kind live through all the radiation throughout the years? Did you find another survivor?" Jane asked.

"Negative. I was researching and came across his file. It's very short, nothing much in it. I am just curious and want to know more," Mary told her.

"He doesn't speak. I think he's a mute. The radiation must have damaged his mind," Jane added.

"That's too bad. I really wanted to know more about him and where he came from." Mary and Jane didn't notice, but he looked up at Mary, smiled a wishful smile and closed his eyes again.

"I don't think he writes or records anything either. I've never seen him do anything. I think that's why his file is so short. He's never left the Floor of Rest since he's been here."

"How long has he been here?" Mary asked.

"Before I was born, I believe. I don't know how old he is, but he has to be older than me," Jane said redundantly.

"Well, I don't mean to keep you from your…life…indexing," Mary said as she searched for a word to describe what Jane was doing.

"Oh," Jane giggled. "They call it historical data preservation or HDP."

"Right," Mary said with a smile.

"I'll just be sitting here for the next few years compiling my life's work. Feel free to go over there and sit with him. No one ever goes near him. They are afraid he is putting off radiation," Jane said implying she didn't want her to stay there more than she has to.

"Alright Jane, I won't stay there long," Mary said noticing the implication while she thought: *He has been sitting there since the year 3050 with no one to talk to? How can people be so dumb? Radiation only comes from actual chemicals and atoms, not from people. Once again I am disappointed in the inhabitants of the SOL.*

Jane sat back down and watched as her granddaughter approached the Unknown Survivor.

Mary approached this man whose grey hair appeared as a halo around his balding head. What was left of the muscle on his legs hung off his bones instead of clinging to them and pulling them tight into a healthy shape. Legs spread open: he slumped in his chair with his hands hopelessly fallen into his lap, and his head slightly tilted downwards and to the side. His arms were weak and decrepit as was the rest of his body. His eyes were closed and his mouth was open, mouthing words only his mind and memory could decipher.

Her grandmother had told her that he was much, much older.

She stood there gazing upon him wondering how to wake him. A few moments later she tapped on his shoulder, and he opened his eyes. His eyes were dull and lifeless, grey and wanting to die.

"GD. Are you the Unknown Survivor?" Mary asked in a whisper.

He stared blankly back in response.

She sat down on the table in front of him. "I've been told you don't talk. If I say something right, can you blink at me?"

He blinked back at her.

"Great." Mary smiled.

He smiled back at her.

Mary leaned in close. "Are you Benjamin of Generation 39?" She said barely audible, but he read her lips.

His head lifted a little and he stared cautiously at her.

Mary waited for his blink. When he didn't respond, she asked another question, "Where did you come from? Are there others like us? Are there humans that survived the radiation?" Just then, she noticed he was wearing a clear BIS, barely visible to the naked eye. Her head cocked and her eyes stared at him right above his left ear.

He nodded to someone unseen; then he blinked.

"What did I say that was right? Are you Benjamin of Generation 39?"

He blinked again.

"How did you get on the surface? Were you sentenced too?"

At this, his eyes lifted and became wider. He shook his head ever so lightly.

"I wish you could talk," Mary said as she slumped. Then she stiffened and grabbed her work bag. "I have something that will lengthen your life and make you be able to talk again." She smiled at him.

"I want to die," he said in a soft, hoarse voice. He motioned to her to come closer. She leaned in closer. "They took her away from me, and they erased her memory. I've lived 121 years with that stuff in your bag. I quit taking it because I want to die," he whispered in her ear.

"How did you know about the Japanese Art of Life? Did you know what Ana was doing? I found your tablet in the passageway."

He gave her a confused look. "I don't know what passageway you are talking about, but yes, I knew what Ana was doing. She told me to stay here. I did what I had to do and then went to the surface to see if I could find her."

"Did you?"

"I didn't get very far, but I believed with all her knowledge, she found a way to survive. She took a bottle of that stuff with her. She might still be alive," he said with wishful thinking knowing she probably died the day she was left on the surface. From his still dull and wrinkled eyes, a tear slid down his old cheek.

"I am finishing what Ana started," Mary said to him in a whisper.

At this, he said nothing, but his eyes came to life one last time. He reached into his robe and pulled out an old tablet like the one she had discovered in the crawlspace. Mary gently wrapped her fingers around the tablet and as he still held on, he barely whispered, "So, you are the one."

She looked deep into eyes now blue, crystal blue. He smiled a weak smile. A fire lit in his eyes. Then it was gone.

His hand dropped suddenly from the tablet, and he died in silent victory.

Mary jumped back in shock as she fell back over the table. This was the first time she ever witnessed death in person. She was lying on the floor, tablet in hand, just looking at him.

He just sat there, eyes open but down trodden just as his chest began to sink. He withered within his chair. She quickly hid the tablet within her work bag as all the Floor of Rest inhabitants came to gather around the dead Unknown Survivor. Two ceremonial bots came and took him away as Gen 40 followed to pay him their last respects.

Mary's grandmother came up behind her and whispered in her ear, "He was old, much older than anyone here. It was his time to go. Don't be startled dear. Go back down to Floor One and do some research. Maybe your generation will get us back to the surface. I think he was waiting to see that day come, poor old man. I hope he gave you something to work with."

Mary nodded with a frightened look on her face, turned, kissed her grandmother on the cheek and walked briskly away towards the transporter. She looked back as the frosted door was sliding shut and saw as the lights dimmed, a fire being lit in the back room.

She closed her eyes tight and entered the transporter. "Level Three," she said with panic in her voice.

So this is what it feels like to be alone, Mary thought as the transporter whisked her back to the floor below.

She didn't wait for the floor to slide her out onto Level Three. She leaped out of the transporter and began running to her LQ.

"Mary!" Michael called after her as she passed by him heading to the DQ. Katy and Violet were standing by him.

"She needs to go to the HP," Katy and Violet said in unison.

"Was that Mary?" Brent asked as he came up to them.

"Yes. She's been acting strange all day," Michael said.

"Maybe she should come see me, but maybe tomorrow. I fell asleep in my HPQ last night, and now I have this horrible headache," Brent said as he held his forehead between his thumb and middle finger. "I think some food will make it go away, or at least I'm hoping."

"I'm going to go see what's wrong with her," Michael said. He ordered another food plate and walked down the hallway towards LQ134.

"Mary, open the door," Michael insisted.

From within, he very faintly heard, "Computer, open door."

The door slid open and Michael saw Mary lying down on her sleeping cot huddled in a ball.

"I brought you some food," Michael said as he placed the plates down on her counter and the door slid shut behind him.

"Thank you, Michael."

"Mary, what's going on?" he asked her as he kneeled down next to her. He untied her hair and let it hang long. Stroking her head, he said, "You can tell me anything." He noticed her hair was sleeker and softer than usual.

"Michael, the HC is behind something, and I think I'm so close to figuring it out, but then something happened today that is going to keep me from going any farther."

"The HC is not behind anything. They just know what's best for the SOL," Michael said trying to believe the words he just spoke.

"Michael, they are. I'm just asking you to trust in me. Our life here isn't what it seems. They have created this illusion of progress in the SOL. We are all being fooled."

"Mary, I heard about the HC rejecting your suggestion, but you just have to trust they know what's best. Just because they reject something of yours doesn't mean they are holding you or the SOL back. They rejected my hypothesis today."

"Why? What reason did they give?" Mary said looking at him.

"They didn't give a reason," Michael said as he shrugged his shoulders.

"Then how do you know they aren't advancing a hidden motive?"

"Mary, that hidden motive is to help the SOL," Michael said hesitantly as he didn't really know the answer to that question.

Mary gave him a sarcastic look in response.

"All I'm saying Mary, is that there's a lot that I don't know and you don't know and there is a lot that the HC knows."

"Why don't we know more? Why do they limit our access to the libraries? Why do they track us with biometrics? Why do they interconnect our brains and see our thoughts?"

"They can't see our thoughts."

"How do you know they can't?" Mary asked knowing full well they can.

Michael stared blankly at Mary. "I don't know," he said after a few moments.

"Think with that big, smart, intelligent brain and open your eyes to all the phony events that take place. Make your own decision, but don't mock me for mine," Mary challenged.

"Mary. There's a lot I want to know, but I know I'm not allowed right now: the key words being right now. You must have patience. Everything will come to light in due time."

"Please leave me alone right now: the key words being right now," Mary said as she turned away from him and faced her hidden secret passageway in the wall.

Michael left without a word and walked back towards the DQ with one food plate filled of white mush.

Mary took off her body suit uniform and examined her leg. She didn't even see a scar. Her body felt revitalized. She put back on her uniform and sat down on her sleeping cot.

She put her work bag in her lap. As she stared at the work bag, she thought back to its contents.

If Benjamin of Generation 39 didn't put the tablet in the wall, then who did? She grabbed her work bag again, and pulled out the tablet he gave her. This tablet was a little bigger than the one she had hid in the passageway. It was a little bigger than her hand as a whole. Her thoughts jumped to how both Ana and Benjamin recorded their discoveries. She pulled out a new tablet and began recording everything she had read and gave her readers the same challenge she was given only a few days ago.

A knock at the door ended her thoughts.

Chapter 4
THE OMNIPOTENT EYE

"Computer, who is at the door?" Mary asked stuffing the tablet back into her work bag.

"It is Travis, HC member," the computer responded.

"Oh no!" Mary whispered to herself. She looked at the door, looked at her work bag and then looked at the wall. She ran to the wall with her bag and threw it in the passageway and replaced the wall panel. She went over to the door and opened it.

"GD Travis. May I help you with something?" she asked innocently.

"Affirmative: come with me," he said with his hands behind his back.

"Will it be long? I haven't eaten yet," Mary said as she pointed to her countertop.

"Negative, please come," he said with a slight narrowing of the eyes. "But first you need to compose yourself," he disgustingly said. Mary remembered Michael stroking her hair. She closed the door and retied it. She took a deep breath and calmed her nerves. She heard another pounding at the door. "Mary of Generation 43, come with me." She went to the door and opened it.

As soon as she stepped out, two bots entered her room.

"What are they doing?" Mary asked.

"Never mind them. Follow me," Travis said as he turned and began walking towards the transporter.

"Level Zero," Travis said in a deep voice to the transporter.

The glass doors closed just as Michael, Katy and Violet were exiting the DQ. They saw her. Michael took a step towards her, but she was gone. He turned to his friends and said, "Something is going on. Come on, let's go to her room."

As soon as they got there, two bots came out empty handed, the door was closing but Michael slid in and opened it for everyone else.

"So they tore through this place," Violet said in amazement.

"It looks like they were looking for something," Katy suggested.

"Look at this," Brent said as he popped his head in.

Violet responded, "I know. What is going to happen to Mary? What did she do?"

"I don't know," Katy said.

Michael looked around at the thrashed room. "Maybe she was right," he said to himself.

"I didn't know we had a Level Zero," Mary casually said.

Travis stood there legs shoulder width apart, hands behind his back staring straight ahead. "I know," he arrogantly muttered.

The floor slid them out onto Level Zero which was a small platform with large doors that covered the entire wall. Travis told her to wait there and had his body scanned. The doors opened, and they walked through into a circular room with several doors all around.

"Where are we?" Mary asked with uncertainty.

Leaving her question unanswered, he ushered her forward to a narrow hallway that led into another room. There sat a patient bed with the HP HC member, Owen, who held a syringe filled with some blue substance.

Mary slowed her walking as she saw him. Behind him there sat the other members of the HC and the Historians, Hunter and Matthew. When Hunter saw her, his eyes glowed and his eyebrows jumped. He had to catch his breath. Matthew noticed his body language and looked at Mary. *She is very beautiful; maybe her beauty will help save her,* he thought.

Travis took his place among the other HC members.

"Please be seated Mary of Generation 43," Owen said as he put his hand on the patient bed.

Mary stood as she was and looked up at Matthew and then scanned the others.

"I want to know why I am here," Mary demanded.

"You are here because you are supposed to be dead," Owen told her. "Your transmitter deactivated. It only deactivates when you die."

"What transmitter? What are you talking about?" Mary asked acting like she didn't have a clue to what was going on.

"When you were born, we inserted a transmitter into your leg. It stopped transmitting your locational data exactly 18 hours 32 minutes and 26 seconds ago," Owen responded.

"Why would you do that? Why just me?" Mary asked acting like she was surprised to hear that while trying to buy some time to think of a good excuse and her escape plan, but the one thought she could muster was: *You idiot; why didn't you think of this happening?*

"It's not just you, Mary of Generation 43. Every inhabitant of the SOL has one. It is so the Historian can make sure everyone is where they are supposed to be," Travis said as he looked to Hunter.

"I'm not sitting there with you holding that syringe anywhere near me."

Owen walked forward towards her, "You will sit down on the patient bed."

"I will not. What is that?" Mary asked demanding to know what was in his hand.

"It is none of your concern," Owen told her.

"It is. You are holding a blue substance in a syringe, asking me to sit down on the HP bed. If you think that is not a concern of mine, then you greatly underestimate me," Mary said rather quickly trying to get her logic through to his head.

"SIT DOWN MARY OF GENERATION 43!!" Travis yelled in a deep, booming voice.

Mary jumped in shock, and then once the echo cleared the room, she just shook her head at him. The HC members stood up. Mary backed up against the wall as they started coming towards her. She saw the whites of Owen's eyes and turned away, waiting for something miraculous to happen to save her.

"Look at her. She is so frightened and pathetic. Leave her be. I will take her to our laboratory and perform the procedures myself. I am the only one here that has been through this before." The voice was so familiar to Mary; she opened her eyes and looked. There Matthew stood with his eyes brilliantly staring down every HC member there.

"You are right, Matthew. You and Hunter take her to your laboratory. We will leave her in your hands," Travis said.

Mary noticed their minds were all connected via BIS. *Why are they speaking aloud their plans, when they can see each other's thoughts.* That thought passed by rather quickly as a new thought took place. *Now here comes the test of whether or not I can trust the Historians. Matthew just saved my life. What about Hunter?*

Travis took her arm and led her to Matthew. "Follow him," he demanded. "Pathetic," he whispered. "She didn't even try to run," he said to the others. They all laughed a quiet laugh. Mary peered over her shoulder, but walked behind Matthew down a back hallway to another transporter.

"Where is your laboratory?" Mary asked Matthew.

"On Level Five," Hunter responded for Matthew.

"I didn't know we had a Level Zero or Five," Mary said to herself. They entered the transporter. There were no controls on this transporter. Matthew and Hunter didn't even have to tell it where to drop them off. There was only one stop: Level Five.

The glass floor slid them out into a large room that looked like nothing Mary had ever seen before. A big circle in the floor with railing lining the shape presented itself at the other end of the room. Near the transporter sat user interface equipment and several research pods and what looked like an HP office off in the corner. Matthew led her to that corner.

"Please sit down Mary of Generation 43," Matthew asked in a gentle voice.

She cautiously sat at the end of the bed with her back to the wall. Hunter began walking behind her and she followed him with her eyes just as his brown and dark eyes were glued to her.

"Please lay down Mary," Matthew again asked in the same gentle voice.

"What are you going to do with me?" Mary asked exchanging glances between Hunter and Matthew.

"The HC wants us to study you to find out why your transmitter deactivated and then erase your memory. Your friends' memories are in the process of being erased as we speak," Matthew answered. "Please lay down Mary."

"Why?" Mary asked as she cautiously lied down.

"They saw Travis get you and the bots destroy your LQ," Hunter piped in.

"What were they looking for?" Mary asked.

Hunter looked at Matthew with uncertainty; Matthew was too busy mixing a formula to notice.

Mary noticed this and asked, "What are you making?"

"A formula to put you to sleep and ease the headache after we examine you and erase some of your memories," Matthew said bluntly. "There it is done." He turned and rubbed his hands together. "Hunter, stay with her while I go get the SBIS."

Mary's heart sank. It was sitting in her passageway. *He will know I have been back. What is he going to do to me? They will see everything when they dig into my memories. They will send me to the surface for sure.* She closed her eyes and then sensed someone's face was too close to her hers. She opened her eyes and her body jumped. Hunter leaned in close with his elbow by her head. He examined her face.

"What are you doing?" Mary asked.

"I'm studying your beauty. You are much more beautiful in person than on the CPU1200."

Mary turned her face away. "What are you talking about? CPU1200? I've never seen you before."

"I know, but I've seen you," he charmingly uttered.

Mary felt a chill race up her spine and a hard ball of nerves settle in her stomach. "What do you mean?"

He leaned in closer and slowly whispered in her ear in a god-like tone. "I can see everything."

"Why are you telling me this?" she whispered back.

"Because you won't remember it in a few moments," he snickered as he stroked the top of her head. She pulled her shoulders up and let out the breath she was holding.

"Hunter!" Matthew hollered as he reentered their laboratory. "She is already frightened. There is no need to frighten her more."

"Matthew, I'm just telling her it will be alright," Hunter said in an innocent voice as he straightened.

"Hunter, I believe I can handle this on my own from here. Your son needs your help on Level One of the LOH. Go to him," Matthew ordered.

"I want to stay here and examine her..." he looked back at Mary. "Beautiful mind," he continued as he placed his hand on one of her slender legs.

"Go!" Matthew said again. "The future of the SOL rests with your ability to teach your son. That is more important than this."

Hunter began to walk away as his hand slid down the rest of her leg. Mary closed her eyes tight and bit the inside of her lip.

As soon as Hunter had left, Matthew came up to her and said in a hushed voice, "You stupid, stupid girl. I told you to be careful."

"I ran my locational data and it showed me in two places at once. I didn't think..."

"That's right, you didn't think. The HC knows every corner of this SOL inside and out. Don't tell anyone what I'm doing. Don't let anyone know. I am not going to erase your memory, but be careful. Act as if you know nothing about what has happened. I know where you were last night. I'm going to reinsert a transmitter that will transmit the locational data that you created in your program. I also modified the program you created to adjust for variances such as if you are talking with someone in the hallway, it will stop with your location because Hunter would see the person talking with themselves if I didn't. You must blend in with the crowd. No more strange tangents. You must be discreet and subtle. Do not be fooled by anyone or anything."

He filled the syringe and placed it in her neck. "Replace the SBIS as soon as you can, but do not get caught. I don't know if I can save you once again. They wanted to examine you and do away with you, but I reminded them we still needed you for reproduction purposes. You have that excuse until your twenty-fifth year of life. I will watch over you, but I cannot help you anymore. You are on your own."

"Benjamin of Generation 39 died today," Mary whispered as the drug began to take effect.

"I know. He was my friend and mentor," he reminisced. Then with a change of heart he whispered back to her, "I will do the same for you as I have done for him," but she was already asleep.

Matthew began the procedure to reinsert his modified transmitter into her leg.

Mary woke up in her LQ, hair plastered to her face, hands balled into fists. She dreamed about the fire again. The room seemed to spin as she struggled to sit up. Too disoriented, she just lay back down and stared at the ceiling. She remembered what Matthew had told her.

Then she remembered back even further. He had risked his life to save her. She now knew she could trust him. Did her passageway still contain all that she had put in there before Travis came to take her? Did Matthew remove it? She struggled to sit up again eager to see.

Then all of the sudden in her left eye, she could faintly make out the words: *Mary, everything is still where it is though I replaced the SBIS. I will guide you on what you need to know. You still have access as Omega 7. Don't worry; I have made sure no one will find your account. Go back to sleep, you still have a little more than two hours before the wake-up call.*

Mary blinked several times, finally trusted her eyes, and without wanting to, fell back asleep.

***

The wake-up call came and Mary's head throbbed with each pulse of sound that radiated throughout the SOL. Her vision blurred as she sat up.

"I feel horrible," Mary said to herself in a groggy voice as she put her hand to her head. She tried shaking her head, but her brain felt like it slipping around within her skull. She blinked very slowly, and her LQ took shape. She looked around first at the counter, then her door, then her mirror, then her entrance into the BQ, then the blank wall, and she remembered what lay behind the bottom right panel. She looked back up to the ceiling and blinked a few more times.

Today is the marriage ceremonies. Get up, and put on your uniform. Her left eye flashed.

Who is this? she thought.

This is Matthew, Historian of the SOL.

This has to be a trick, she thought again not knowing it was set where he could see all her thoughts.

This is no trick. This is what I did for Benjamin of Generation 39, and now his actions in the past will enable what Ana discovered to live on.

Why don't you just tell me what Ana found out?

I'm not going to tell you because that is the journey you have to take. You must know the past in order to understand the present and better prepare for the future, for I fear there will be a war in your time. I am confined here, but I can see you. This way I know where you are and can guide you through in order to help you not be discovered. If only Ana had this same advantage as you, she might have survived.

So can you see me while I'm in the BQ? Mary asked and then blushed.

I will deactivate my BIS for ten minutes from the time you enter. I will respect your privacy. Anytime you want me to deactivate, tell me and for how long. This is the only way for you to contact me without anyone knowing about it. So if you ask me to deactivate, I will no longer be with you until I reactivate. Now, you will be late for the ceremonies. Get up and put on your uniform.

Mary inhaled deeply and slid out of bed. *I'm going into the BQ.* She entered and her left eye shocked her.

"Ow, what was that?" she screamed as the pain sent her to her knees. She waited for a response, but none came. She strained her neck to the right and tried to feel for the BIS. After a few minutes of searching, she felt something in her hair, and ran to her BQ mirror and tried parting her hair to see it. Finally she made out a small, flat, and transparent BIS strategically placed so that it was hidden under her hair. It felt like it had been drilled into her head.

Her head pounded.

She turned on the G-L converter, and remembered she had a little less than ten minutes to get clean and dressed again. Her dirty uniform fell from her body as she stepped in front of the G-L converter. She began turning in circles until she felt clean and stepped out. Her clean uniform popped out of the wall. She picked it up, and as it dangled from her hand, she wondered, "Why do I do this every day? I wear an envelope that keeps your body warm every day." She pulled it up and then zipped the front. The zipper melted into the rest of the uniform, and the uniform sealed itself tight against her body. "Here's to another day," she said sarcastically.

A knock came at the door. She tied up her hair and walked outside to see Michael. "GD Michael. You waited for me?"

"Today is the big day," he replied.

"I know. I can't wait," Mary responded to his reply and then thought: *And yet, we are still wearing our everyday uniforms.*

"Mary, I..." Michael began to say, then stopped and looked around realizing they were in the hallway.

She interrupted, "I know, me too." She breathed deep. "Let's go." Michael smiled which brought out a smile on Mary's face as they walked to the RQ to join the congregated mass to either observe or participate in the marriage ceremonies.

Another shock to Mary's left eye sent her hand to her face and made her stumble backwards a bit.

"Are you alright, Mary?" Michael whispered.

"Yes, I'm fine. I just woke up with a really bad headache," she said as she rubbed her temple.

"I woke up with a headache too, but by the looks of it, yours is worse than mine."

Mary realized that he had his memory tampered with as Matthew had told her it would be.

Benjamin got used to the shock. Don't worry; you will too. Mary read in her left eye.

Matthew, what am I going to do? Tonight we will be moved to a couple quarters. The passageway is in my single quarters. How did Ana get into the LOH?

She found another passageway that was filled up after she was discovered. The one you found was the one Benjamin of Generation 39 used once Ana was sentenced and he was moved back to a single quarters.

How am I going to…?

Don't worry; I will guide you. Have a little faith in me. You will still be in your single quarters until you become with child. At that time, you will be moved to a couple quarters. That has always been protocol, but only those who have lived before you know it. I have secretly arranged for you and Michael to live in your single quarters, so you can still have access to the books in the Library of History and your work bag in the passageway.

Michael interrupted. "Mary, what are you thinking about?"

You are going to have to learn to go through your life without displaying the traditional BIS symptoms. You are going to have to learn to read what I am saying to you and live your life simultaneously.

"What did you say, Michael?" Mary asked as she noticed his lips moving when she looked past the words in her left eye.

"The headache must be bad if you can't understand what I'm saying. Maybe you should see the HP."

"Not today. Today is about you and me," Mary responded with confidence. *And the rest of Generation 43,* she added in her mind.

All of the sudden with a loud applause, the ceremonies commenced. All of Generation 43 stood in the middle of the circle with all the older generations sitting around them, watching them, seeing who would pair up with whom.

I am here. I am sitting behind the HC members.

They actually came forth from their cave for this, Mary thought sarcastically.

Oh yes, marriage ceremonies enable the race to go on in a moral manner according to our clergyman.

"Inhabitants of the SOL please be seated as Generation 43 comes forth to choose their life-long mate," Travis bellowed in his deep voice.

The bots came and separated out each Generation 43 member by gender. The males lined up against the row of pods to select their mate. The females lined up against another row of pods to select their mate. They were standing back to back. Mary placed her hand on the pod, and it identified her as subject 238. It brought up her most compatible matches with Michael numbered first. She half-heartedly smiled because, one, she knew Michael was for her and the other because the SOL had predestined them to be that way.

The SOL did not predestine you and Michael to be compatible. Matthew interrupted when he read her thoughts.

We were born that way? Mary inquired of her guide.

No, someone else predestined you and Michael to be compatible as you and your friends. That is all I will tell you. Pick your husband, Matthew ordered.

Mary instinctively obeyed, touched the screen and pressed 'submit responses'.

Who predestined us? Mary asked.

You will find out in due time, Matthew responded.

You are almost as frustrating as Melinda, Mary told him.

The screen changed and asked her the question: Do you forfeit your other selections?

She pressed "Yes" without hesitation.

You really love this Michael? Matthew asked reading her thoughts.

I keep forgetting you can see every thought that goes through my mind. Is there a way to only display thoughts I want you to see?

Unfortunately, no. It's a very old BIS that hasn't been upgraded. I only still use those because they are no longer traced by the Historian or the HC. Our conversations are completely invisible.

Mary looked down the row to her friend, Katy. She saw her peering over her shoulder at Rhome, who was doing the same. She felt Michael's hand in hers. They both looked over their shoulders and smiled at each other.

"We have received the selections!" Travis' voice boomed. The bots came and took the pods away, and Michael's hand dropped suddenly and everyone looked straight ahead. A projection came on the front wall, and none other but Melinda appeared. She was not gold, and she was not in color. She was pure white with her feminine features in color such as her red lips and black eyelashes.

Melinda is the computer system that runs the SOL. Anywhere that links to her database, she can appear, Matthew thought to her.

That's why I was able to access the LOH research database from anywhere in the SOL.

Yes, but I will leave you alone with your thoughts. I will connect again tomorrow at 1030 hours, or thirty minutes after you begin your work day.

We start at 0600; we don't start at 1000.

Tomorrow you do. Try not to act as if your eye hurts.

An overwhelming shock pulsed in Mary's eye as she saw Matthew ever so slightly twitch his head. Her hands balled then released to absorb the pain.

Travis was calling out all the matches. Mary wasn't listening until she heard her name.

"Mary of Generation 43, Engineer....and....Michael of Generation 43, Scientist."

There was some applause as they first looked at each other, then nodded to the observers and to the HC.

His listing went on.

"Violet of Generation 43, Engineer...and...Brent of Generation 43, Health Professional."

Applause filled the RQ. Mary laughed inside as she remembered back to their conversation in the DQ and what she had witnessed when she was sorting through Brent's memories. Then a ball of guilt hit her stomach, and she quit smiling.

"Katy of Generation 43, Engineer...and...Rhome of Generation 43, Scientist."

More applause. Michael smiled. Katy and Rhome looked at each other with glee.

"Rachel of Generation 43, Engineer...and...Blake of Generation 43, Engineer."

Michael and Mary and the rest of those in the RQ applauded.

"Andrew of Generation 43, Engineer...and...Deborah of Generation 43, Scientist."

The applause had become constant.

"Tara of Generation 43, Scientist...and...Josh of Generation 43, Scientist."

Tara and Josh nodded their heads.

"Jenna of Generation 43, Scientist...and...Shawn of Generation 43, Scientist."

Mary saw Violet's shoulders tighten with excitement. Katy was thinking about the conversation she and Mary had about her and her friends' genetic and personality predisposition.

Travis ended with the listing with the two sons of the Historian and the Clergyman. "Amy of Generation 43, Scientist...and...Eric of Generation 43, Historian. Denise of Generation 43, Health Professional...and...Paul of Generation 43, Clergyman."

The SOL stood up and applauded as did the HC and Historians.

"I now cede this ceremony to our Clergyman, Peter," Travis said as he stepped aside and applauded as Peter took the stage.

Hands folded in front, head upright and neck stiff, he began to speak in his old and scratchy voice, "Inhabitants of the SOL, we are gathered here to witness the union of these young males and females to be wed together in order for the human race to go on. They will love each other, work with each other, live with each other, and raise Generation 44 in due time to meet and exceed the standards of the SOL. They will obey the HC just as all of you have done. These, the members of Generation 43," he said as he reached his arms towards the mass in front of him, "will give us yet another opportunity to return to the surface and repopulate the Earth with their offspring. This is the SOL's mission and why our ancestors saved us from the War of Hell 1085 long years ago. Remember this mission and work hard to build our surface dwelling so that our next Generations can live on God's planet and not inside of it. Remember this mission and do as you are told. Remember this mission and always wake to a brighter and more auspicious day."

Everyone clapped as Peter sat back down and Travis walked back up to the stage. "You are wed. Please stand next to your spouse and a bot will assist you shortly."

Mary looked to Michael who was already looking at her. His warm smile was contagious. A bot came up to them, "Please follow me." It led them back to LQ134. "LQ134 will be your couple quarters until more room is available. You do not have to report to work today, but you must report to work tomorrow at 1000 hours. Please stay in your LQ. If you need food, I will bring it to you. My identification tag is 01212." Then it rolled off down the corridor.

They entered the LQ, and Mary whispered to Michael, "What are we supposed to do for twelve hours? We cannot leave."

"I don't know," Michael replied. They just looked at each other, smiling, with no idea what to do with the free time they were just given. "I know you have a headache. Maybe you should lie down."

He stepped towards her. She stepped towards the sleeping cot. "Maybe I should, and you too. I know you have a headache too," she said as she sat down. Michael sat down next to her. Mary's head was still hurting and her vision still had blurry edges. She blinked a couple of times. Michael's hand instinctively went to take down her hair. Her locks bounced about just below her shoulders. Mary looked at him and asked with her eyes why he loves her hair so much.

He answered as if he read her thoughts, "I love your hair because it's unique and it's hidden. It's a hidden, unique phenomenon. It's unlike anyone else's."

Mary smiled. She loved feeling special, something that is rarely felt in the SOL. His fingers grazed the length of her hair.

"I love you more than life itself," he whispered as he caressed her face. "My heart lives with you." This was the only phrase he could utter.

"As mine does with you," Mary whispered back as she leaned towards him. He kissed her forehead, then her cheeks, then her sweet, soft lips.

***

The wakeup call at 0900 came all too soon for Generation 43.

"GD Mary of Generation 43," Michael whispered to her as they lay in each other's arms, smiling from ear to ear.

"GD Michael," Mary said as her cheeks became full of color. She giggled.

"I don't want to work today," Michael whispered again.

"I want to stay here," Mary whispered back agreeing with him.

She felt his warm hands skimming her back underneath the body heat conservation or BHC blanket. He felt her warm breath upon his chest.

"I say we exchange our RQ tokens for another twelve hours of no work," Michael suggested.

Mary smiled and hugged him tight, kissing him until she made her way up to his lips. "I think that is a great idea," she said softly. Michael slid out of bed and immediately shivered. "It's cold out here," he said as he stepped in his uniform and pulled it up to his waist. He jogged over to the computer in the wall, and exchanged their RQ tokens for half hours off. He turned and looked at Mary. "We really never went to the RQ much." He began to saunter back to the bed. "It took twenty-four tokens for today and we still have eighteen left for the each of us."

"I don't care. I'm just glad I get to spend another whole work day with you," she said as she kissed him.

"I'm hungry, though, Mary," Michael said. "What was that bot's id tag again?"

"I think it was 01212," Mary responded.

"Computer, locate bot 01212 and have him bring us two food plates from the DQ,"

"Locating…command sent," the computer responded. "It will arrive in forty-five seconds."

"I'm actually not that hungry, Michael."

"What? How can you not be? You haven't eaten in almost two days."

"I know. I know I should eat," Mary said thinking back to the Japanese Art of Life serum she had hidden her passageway.

"Please," Michael begged her as the bot opened the door, set the plates on the countertops and left. He brought her a plate and sat down with his. Then he decided he was too cold and fully put on his uniform.

Mary looked at the white goop she had eaten once every day since she was born. "I've never asked, but what is this stuff?"

"I'm not sure. I think it's just a mix of vitamins and protein and all the stuff your body needs in a day. I won't go into the full list because I know that would probably bore you," he said as he smiled at her.

"You don't bore me, Michael. I love learning new things," she said as she playfully toyed with her food.

"I know," Michael murmured as he ate his white goop.

She grinned at his eating style and began to dig into hers.

All of the sudden, a shock pulsated through her head and she froze.

"What's wrong, Mary?"

"Nothing. I just got a cold chill," Mary said as she pulled the BHC blanket up closer to her chin.

I decided to take the work day off to spend time with Michael. Please contact me tomorrow at 0700.

Mary, I need to tell you something. Your transmitter is still emitting your location with the program you created as I told it to. You have to tell me these things in advance so I can protect you. What is your password to get into Omega 7?

2023, Mary responded. The panic became evident on her face.

"Are you alright, Mary?" Michael asked. "You look like you just saw an RMH come at you."

"Yes, I'm fine, Michael. I need to excuse myself to the BQ." She carefully rolled out of bed as to not spill her food. "Oh, it is cold out here. I've never known for it to be this cold."

"I can tell," Michael said as his cheeks turned pink. Then he responded to her other statement, "It's because you've always worn a uniform except in the BQ which heats up when motion is detected."

Mary smiled sarcastically, "You know everything, don't you?" She put on her uniform and walked into the BQ. Michael's eyes never left her until she disappeared behind the door.

What else do you need? Mary thought to Matthew.

Nothing. I already changed your locational data to say you will be in your room until 0600 tomorrow. You must tell me where you are going in advance, so I can make it look like you are either where you say you are or somewhere else. As soon as Michael enters the BQ, grab your work bag from the passageway and give yourself another dose of Jumyoo.

What is Jumyoo?

Jumyoo is the serum you created with Brent two days ago. I can tell it's working, because there was no scar on your leg and you look younger already. The more you take it in your younger years, the longer the effects will last: the effects being your lengthened life span. With that one dose, you have probably added five to seven years to your life.

Why do you want me to take another dose so soon?

Because you were bred to lead the SOL, and you are going to have to stay alive to do so. Take Jumyoo and don't get killed by an RMH when they put you on the surface.

When they put me on the surface? Mary jumped.

It will happen, but only when we are ready and the second phase of the plan is set into motion.

What plan is this?

The plan Ana, Benjamin and I created long ago before your grandparents were born: the plan that will free the SOL from the control of the HC.

What does this plan entail?

You will find out for yourself soon enough. I will disconnect now and reactivate your transmitter at 0700 tomorrow.

*Wait...*she thought, but it was too late. The pain that Mary felt was a little more bearable this time. She turned on the G-L converter, and just stood in the G-L tank shoulders slouched, head down, gaze fixed, thinking about this plan that had already cost a life.

"How do I fit into this? Was it planned or was it by accident?" Mary asked aloud to herself.

"Did you say something?" Michael asked through the BQ door.

"No, I was just trying to sing," Mary said trying to come up with some excuse.

"What's singing?" Michael asked as he got up and came to the BQ door.

"You know, like this," she sang to him. "I was experimenting with the bot's vocal mechanisms about eight years ago, and I found out what singing was."

"It's soothing," he said to her as he leaned in the doorway.

"That's why I sing. It calms me down," Mary sighed as she leaned on the wall of the open G-L tank.

"Why do you need to be calmed down? Are you mad at something?"

"No. I'm just thinking," Mary responded thinking about this plan she was to fit into.

"Mary, we have the day to ourselves. Quit thinking for twelve more hours. Then you can think tomorrow." He smiled at her and reached into the G-L converter to brush his hand against her cheek.

She took his strong hand and pulled him in as his smile grew bigger.

***

Mary and Michael lay on the sleeping cot head to head whispering their inner most goals and dreams to each other.

"I had a dream once that frightened me," Mary confided.

"What was it about?" Michael asked as he pushed a piece of her hair behind her ear.

"Fire on the surface. A fire unlike I have ever seen. It wasn't small like the ones we use to build the bots. It was everywhere and seemed angry. I was standing in it, but it wasn't burning me. It was burning everyone else. Then this dark figure came up and started laughing. He said he wouldn't help me save them unless I showed him why he should. I saw my mother's body turn into ash as she was still screaming and alive. That dream has haunted me for the last several days. I don't know what it means."

"I'm sorry, Mary. It's just a dream." Then seeing the discomfort on her face, he added, "Maybe it means you will be the one to figure out how we can go back to the surface, repopulate the Earth and save the SOL from burning up in this cage we are living in."

Mary smirked. "Maybe. It was just so real and vivid. I woke up and actually thought all my loved ones were burning somewhere."

"Mary, you have a vivid imagination because you are so good at what you do. You can see things before they are built and make corrections before the BPs are done. I can see why this dream is so vivid for you."

"But Michael, I have this same dream every night, the exact same dream."

"Maybe you're trying to tell yourself something," Michael suggested.

"But what?"

"I don't know. Maybe you need to find the reason why we should all be saved from the fire or find the key to why you are not burning with the rest of us and give that to us so that we won't burn either." He looked deep into her eyes and kissed her forehead. "Or maybe you know you have to do something to gain some sort of sense of purpose, but you don't know what it is yet."

Mary's brow bunched. Michael made sense and she began to think about all the different possibilities. Michael took her hand and smoothed out her brow. "Mary, I love you. You will figure it out in time. You are so smart." He kissed her forehead again.

"I love you too Michael. Thank you for helping me sort this dream out," Mary whispered to her husband.

"I had dream once about a fire," Michael said to her as he held her close.

"What happened?"

"I am walking towards my LQ when the corridor becomes enveloped in flames, not the little flames that we have in the lab but this huge fire like the one you described: uncontrollable. Everyone bursts out of their LQ and runs to me for help. I lead them to the transporter, and tell them to go to the surface. I am the last one to take the transporter, but the fire encases me and pulls me further and further into it. I'm not burning like yours, but I am in pain because I saw that your LQ door is not open like the rest. I fight my way to you, and when I get to the door, I wake up. I never get to see inside."

Mary just stared at him not knowing what to say. "Do you think it's weird that we both had dreams of fire?"

"I don't know. I haven't talked to anyone else about their dreams. Maybe the SOL dreams of fire. Maybe we are the only ones," Michael hypothesized.

Mary smiled. "We have different views of the fire. What could that mean?"

"We are both trying to figure out the same sense of purpose, but from different approaches," he replied with uncertainty. Mary chuckled, put her hand on the back of his neck, and pulled his face closer to hers.

"You are so philosophical, and I love you for it."

He smiled, but his eyes showed his confusion. "What does philosophical mean?"

"It means deep thinking," Mary said not really knowing the true meaning of the word.

"Where did you learn that from?" Michael asked impressed with her vocabulary.

"Oh, I…" Mary found herself too comfortable and panicked. Then she remembered Matthew told her to have a little faith him. *Maybe he will erase this conversation,* she thought. "I found it in that thing I was telling you about a few nights ago."

Michael just smiled, but his eyes were suspicious. "What is this thing?" he whispered so low that Mary had to read his lips to understand what he was saying to her.

"I told you I can't tell you," Mary whispered back with a seductive smile.

Michael pulled her closer. The warmth of her body against his compelled him to forget about the subject of their dialogue.

***

Mary pretended to fall asleep, and waited until Michael was asleep. She slid out of his arms and her bare feet lightly touched the floor. She grabbed her uniform at the end of the bed and slipped into it. With light feet, she tiptoed to her passageway. Gently slipping inside, she replaced the wall panel, and turned on her light pin.

She grabbed her workbag and emptied the contents into her lap. Picking up the bottle of Jumyoo and the syringe, she gave herself another dose. The tablet from Benjamin of Generation 39 lay in her lap looking up at her. She scooped it up and activated it.

An old man's voice, scratchy, groggy and filled with sadness quietly whispered:

"If you are hearing this, then I am gone, and you are the one I have been waiting for to fulfill Ana's work. I recorded this as my brain ages, so I might jump around for I am about to explain the last decades. The year today is 3105. Ana found a way into the Library of History when we were thirty-eight years of age in the year 3024. Six years later, she was discovered and sent to the surface. This I believe you already know. There are three of us who planned you and your friends into existence: I, Benjamin of Generation 39, my wife, Ana of Generation 39 and our helper and enabler, Matthew of Generation 40. Just as the SOL was bred to enable mankind to survive, we bred you through superior genetic technology to enable man's spirit and voracity to thrive.

We made you all unique, each to bring a different skill to our plan. You will be the leader as we created you to absorb knowledge more quickly and apply it faster than anyone in the SOL. We made you to be a woman as you are the mother of life. Your mate is your support and guide. We made him to be a man to protect you on the surface. Yes, I know what you are thinking. You will go to the surface. We made you to be too curious for your own good. You will be caught eventually, but Matthew will watch over you and make sure you are not caught until all the pieces are in place. Until that time, there are passageways all over that Matthew has encoded to be invisible to the bots and to the Historian. I hope you are reading this in one of the passageways you found to enter into the Library of History.

Have you ever wondered why your mate and your male friends look stronger than the others? We bred them to create muscle faster. We created the females to be fertile, as they will be the ones to repopulate the surface. Each one of your friends are your friends because we manipulated their personalities. Each of you is born with extra capacity in your brains to absorb information through a BIS. Matthew will begin to send you information found in the Library of History and you will remember everything. You will be able to apply what he's given you within nanoseconds. This we believe will enable your survival while on the surface alone. Yes, you will be alone for a short while. You have to stay alive. We have equipped your genes to withstand more blood loss than the above average human and still be able to carry out normal functions. Your genes enable you to run faster. You are stronger, but you don't know your own strength. I assume you already know of the Jumyoo. If not, contact Matthew. With this, you will live a long time. It rejuvenates you, and you feel younger every day. Start taking it now as it affects your old age. You will inform the next generation of the knowledge you know and will come to know. Your brain cannot become old like mine. The Jumyoo can allow you to go days without food and water, and it can allow you to go days without sleep all the while your body will still function normally. Jumyoo also has healing attributes. Sleep and eat! If you don't, it just counters the effects of the medicine. You trade life for life. Sleep and eat!

You have sought me out, so I know there is no turning back for you. Do not let Ana's death be vain. Please follow out her mission. Save the SOL from the lie it's living.

We created ten to carry out our mission, but you are just the beginning. If you reproduce with the mate we created for you, your offspring will be more than you and your mate alone. Keep your breed pure; they will lead the new people.

As you have this record, you have either received it from Matthew or me. If I gave it to you, you probably already know that I wanted to die. I stayed behind in the SOL for twenty years to finish our plans as Ana asked me to three months before she was discovered. The plan was then for me to go find her and start a new dwelling on the surface so that all of you would then have somewhere to at least start your mission. The plan failed in this case. It took a longer time for me alone to figure out the genetic codes and manipulations. I am a scientist, but I needed her engineering expertise to help me. It took twenty years for me to plan you and your friends. I then went to look for her, and Matthew erased my records as he was supposed to, but I couldn't find her and came back. I fought off a small RMH, but it left me mutilated and scarred. The SOL found me and labeled me the Unknown Survivor. I have stayed on the Floor of Rest waiting for you to find me. When I knew the time was coming, I stopped taking the Jumyoo. My mate gone, my body mutilated, my friends long passed, I sat alone ever so often speaking with Matthew through my BIS. I waited for you and this day to come. Honor us; trust us that there is a better way to live. The Head Council is intentionally holding the SOL's progress to a slowing halt. They are intentionally cloning the RMH to keep the SOL underground. They are power-driven, and greedily hunger for it. They can control what happens if it is within their domain. The SOL has been their domain for over a millennium. They have become tyrants, and the SOL needs a new way of life. They need someone to save them from their meaningless lives. Your mission is to recruit your friends and slowly let them know the plan by giving them clues to where to find their own missions. I myself do not know where Ana hid them, so you must first find them. Utilize Matthew as he can help. Ana formulated this plan before I knew what she was doing and I believe before Matthew knew as well. You must find them and have the right person open them. The people you can trust are the ones we created: six engineers, each with a different specialty, three scientists, who together, are unstoppable, and an HP, whose innovation will lead you to new heights and make sure everyone stays alive when you all begin to build the new surface. You will also be the Historian as Matthew, by that time, will have given you every single thread of information that can be found in the Library of History. It will be up to you to spread that to your offspring. Be warned! If they do not have the excess capacity, they will die because their brains cannot handle a massive influx of information sent so quickly. In essence, their brains will be electrocuted.

Ana's mission for you is hidden somewhere in the SOL. I have given you what I think to be her mission. This is my record for you, to aid you in accomplishing what you were created to accomplish. I pray you well, and I hope you do not fail. Otherwise, it will have all been in vain."

Mary lowered the tablet, and whispered to herself, "Otherwise, it will have all been in vain." Closing her eyes, she took a deep breath. *Sleep and eat!* The old man's words raced through her mind. She slipped out of the passageway and into the darkness. She slid into Michael's strong arms once again. She stroked the side of his face, kissed his bottom lip, witnessed his smile, and then forced herself to sleep.

Mary and Michael woke with a start as the wake-up call loudly sounded. Mary woke with sweat on her body and her brow.

"Are you ok, Mary?" Michael asked.

"Yes, I…I just had that dream again," Mary said as she slowed her breathing.

He pulled her close and rubbed her back. "It's just a dream. We are all here, alive and well." Mary settled down. "You go to the G-L converter first. I'll wait."

"Thank you, Michael." Mary kissed him, daintily got out of the sleeping cot and walked to the BQ.

While standing in the G-L tank, she rolled her head around straining to loosen the tight muscles that burrowed into her neck. She stretched out her legs and back. They were so tight. She closed her eyes, and with her hands, tried to massage the tension out of her muscles. It was to no avail. She stepped out still tense as ever. She reluctantly received her uniform from the wall and slipped into it.

"Your turn," she murmured as she entered the LQ.

Michael hopped out of bed, and began running to the BQ. He grabbed her since she was in the way, kissed her, spun her around and entered the BQ. Mary beamed. For that one second, her tension vanished.

She quietly tiptoed back to her passageway and entered quickly. She gave herself another dose of Jumyoo to see if it relieved her discomfort. She heard the G-L converter turn off and she hastily made her way back to the sleeping cot. Her heart beat increased. *My mission is to find my mission and find my friends' missions as well without knowing where to look and knowing that the Historian can see every move I make.* She breathed deeply. *I can do this. Think like Ana. I'm caged, with no one to trust. Where would I go? Where would I hide something that I hoped wouldn't be found for generations to come?*

"Ready to go?" Michael asked as he exited the BQ interrupting her thoughts.

"Yes," Mary answered.

"Are you alright?" Michael asked noticing the somewhat worried yet determined look on her face.

"Yes," Mary replied. She walked to the door, but then suddenly Michael grabbed her arm, turned her around and kissed her passionately. "What was that for?" she asked as she bit his lip.

"Because you are captivating," he sweetly whispered to her. She genuinely smiled, and softly returned the kiss he had just given her.

An unexpected and loud bang came at the door. "Mary, you had better come to work today!" Amanda bellowed through the door. Mary rolled her eyes at the sound of her voice.

She whispered to her husband, "I thought she agreed that we would start over."

At that, Michael opened the door and firmly said to Amanda, "GD Amanda. If you have something to say to my wife, then say it, but say it with respect and treat her with dignity because every member of the SOL deserves it. We all work together to bring about our mission equally. Therefore, if you ever come bang on our door again, I will report your actions to the LC-E and make it my business that you are reprimanded."

Amanda stepped forward and stared him down. Michael held his stance. Her eyes drifted to Mary, who stood there looking at her with a confused expression mounted in her eyes.

Amanda haughtily mumbled to Michael, "We'll see about that, J-SCI." She slowly turned and walked towards the transporter. Michael looked back at Mary who came forth and hugged him.

"I'm so sorry if she does something to make you lose your LC member offer," Mary quietly whispered to Michael.

Michael took her hands and kissed them. "It will be alright." He let her hands drop. "I say we make our way to the SPR," he said with a fake smile. Mary laughed a little as they began to walk towards the transporter.

"GD Mary, Michael!" Rhome exclaimed upon seeing them in the transporter. Michael held it for him.

"GD Rhome. Where's Katy?" Mary asked.

"I gave her my RQ tokens, so she could have the day off again." Then he whispered in a low voice, "She doesn't like what she does, but I keep telling her she's the best one at it. That is the reason why they are keeping her there."

Mary's heart sank as she felt the overwhelming despair that her friend was feeling.

Rhome went on as the transporter slid them out onto Level One, "I only found out because I overheard two LC-E members' conversation. They want her to take over the entire BI sector within the next ten years. I thought that was great news, but Katy doesn't want it. She wants to work on the surface."

"Believe me, it's not that great," Mary whispered back. "I would like to be in charge of something big. Tell her I think it is a great opportunity for her."

"I will. She admires your example, Mary."

Mary smiled, "I admire her too. She is a hard worker and diligent in her tasks."

Michael and Rhome split off to go into the SPR-S, while Mary stood at the doors of the SPR-E and sighed before entering.

"GD Mary. You are on time today," Amanda said with a cold sneer.

"You're correct. I have been on time every day except the previous two in the last twelve years."

"You were not working under me when you were eight," Amanda replied with disgust.

"I was. I came up with the advanced BPs for the DQBI, and instead of approving them, you took them for yourself and received a promotion the following year. I remember that year very well."

"You don't know what you are talking about. I did what I was supposed to do," Amanda mumbled.

Mary looked at her blankly and then walked off towards the debriefing room as a numbing shock hurdled through her left eye.

You just missed the fight of a lifetime, Mary thought sarcastically.

Oh, and who with? Matthew thought to her playing along with her sarcasm.

It doesn't matter. I read Benjamin's last recording dated 3105. He said the HC was cloning RMH? He said our missions are hidden from us. Do you know where they are? How am I supposed to find them? Why is the HC keeping us from progressing? Is it true? Are they power hungry? What are they doing? Are you really going to fill my brain with information from the LOH through this BIS? Where are we supposed to go after we are sentenced to the surface? What is up here? All I see on the surface is nothing but dirt and blackness and bones. What am I supposed to do? Am I supposed to rebuild the old world, just me and my superhuman friends?

Stop, with the questions. Yes, with every other generation the HC undoes the previous generation's work. They completely erase all of their records of work. In essence every other generation starts over. Your offspring will be working on what Gen42 started. Yes, I will give you the information you need, but it is a delicate process and will take time for me to master. I cannot damage your brain; it is needed if we are to free the SOL.

Mary stepped into the elevator tuning to both frequencies. She asked Matthew, *How is this working? I'm wearing two BIS.*

We made your brain more capable of handling it along with the others. I placed my BIS slightly higher than a traditional BIS, so both fit on your head. You will see my thoughts behind the other processes. You will have to learn to read simultaneously my thoughts and the thoughts of your group.

The elevator doors slid open. Mary walked out into the brightly lit SD skeleton.

How am I supposed to find the missions?

I don't know where Ana hid them, but I have been looking for several decades trying to locate a general area of where they could be.

Her head became warm to the touch and her eyes blinked rapidly. Her hands balled into fists as her breathing quickened. The muscles in her neck tightened as Matthew sent her his findings through her BIS.

Rachel came alongside her, *Mary. Are you alright?* She thought to her. Mary's head twitched to the left, as she found she couldn't breathe out.

She whispered inside her protective suit the silent words that were filling her brain.

Rachel, I'm fine. She focused past her group connection and told Matthew, *Stop. I.* Her vision blurred, and as her knees hit the ground, she lowered her head closing her eyes. Rachel was calling Mark over through her BIS. Mark tried communicating to Mary through his BIS, but when she wasn't responding.

He started yelling, "MARY! MARY!!"

Mary faintly heard her name. It sounded as if it was coming from a far off distance, muffled. She lifted her head. She all the sudden became perfectly normal. She stood up without even having to help herself with her hands.

I'm fine, Mark and Rachel. My head hurt from the elevator ride, she processed her thoughts to them. Behind the data screen, she saw Matthew apologizing and saying it was too much at once.

At least Mary knew where to start her search. Matthew had sent her sixty years of research within a few seconds.

Mark responded to her, *Turn your BIS off for a second. Go to the BPs, review them and then turn your BIS back on. Maybe after your marriage ceremony, you got out the habit of wearing a BIS.*

Mary nodded, but laughed inside. She twitched her head, and turned it off.

Why can't I turn my BIS with you off? She asked Matthew as she walked over to the BPs of the SD floating in the makeshift chamber.

I said it is an older technology. You are a receiver. I am the initiator. Only I can turn our BIS on or off. I think you start your search for your mission in the…

In the right wall of the DQ, Mary responded. *I am a receiver. I received all the information you sent to me. That wall shares a wall with the LOH. I know there is a passageway somewhere. How will I search for it?*

You will go after DQ hours. I will provide for you. I will make it seem as if you are in your LQ, and you are free to roam. Caution: don't talk to anyone, Matthew warned.

What if someone sees me? Or talks to me? Mary asked.

You will have to go to the Library of Science, and recreate one of Ana's inventions. She made me fix it to my memory, so that I could help you. I'll send you the instructions, more slowly this time, Matthew said.

Mary received the instructions. *What is this supposed to do? From what I received, it seems I have to drink the concoction, but what does it do to me?*

It will make you give off a hormone that makes people ignore you. If they can't smell you, their brains don't associate you with someone they know. Alternatively, if they see you, just lower your head and don't make eye contact. Your face and body will be blurry to them, and they will walk on by. You'll be in your uniform and everyone in the SOL looks the same in that uniform. If they don't see your eyes, they won't know it's you, Matthew explained.

But I know I can recognize someone from behind and when I am walking toward them, without seeing their eyes.

This creation makes you invisible to them. It cripples their senses. Well, actually it distorts their senses.

When should I go make this? Mary asked.

After you eat in ten hours, Matthew ordered.

Mary focused on the BPs situated in front of her.

I saw your suggested BPs. They looked like they would save about twenty years in construction and thousands of units in materials. The HC didn't even look at it. They don't look at anyone's suggestions unless they are at their annual meeting with the SOL's LC, when they have to keep up with appearances, Matthew told her.

They don't want the SOL to advance.

No, they don't. That is why the SOL needs you, Matthew said.

Mary mindlessly worked on the original BPs for the SD. She looked past the BPs and off into the far distance. *Maybe Ana is still alive,* she thought remembering back to the few last words of Benjamin of Generation 39. *Maybe she's waiting for me.*

I don't think she is still alive. With the Jumyoo, it is possible, but Benjamin went to look for her. She was nowhere to be found.

She reconnected her group BIS. She immediately saw the processed data flow in a stream in her left eye. They were working on the G-L converter systems. She thought of yesterday with Michael, then remembered Matthew could see all her thoughts. She went back to thinking about the G-L converter systems.

Meanwhile in the SPR-S, Michael strolled in with the usual form of a scientist.

"GD Michael," John said with a bright smile. "The LC liked your suggestion the other day. It was too bad you didn't come to work yesterday, but the LC forgives you. They are willing to give you another chance to show them what I saw last week."

"Thank you John," Michael replied with a nod. Weston overheard their conversation and angrily turned away to lead his group to the surface.

"One more thing, Michael," John said as Michael began to move towards the debriefing room. "Why were you absent yesterday when you knew how much the LC needed to see you perform?"

"I wanted to spend another day with my wife," Michael said innocently.

"Your wife comes second. The SOL comes first. If you want to be an LC member, you will have to remember that. You are lucky because the other LC members do not think that highly of you," John told him out of the side of his mouth.

"My wife has shown me more respect and attention than the SOL," Michael said bluntly to him. "Why should I put the SOL first when everything I do must make a good impression and reflection upon you? You have no concern for me. Last week you told me you would report me to the LC for tardiness, once in thirteen years. Now, when I make a good discovery, you want to show me off to the rest of your LC members."

John stood in shock. He was rendered speechless of such a backlash from his diligent inferior who had never said a word such as this before.

Michael had never before felt such adrenaline rush through his body. He had never before talked back to a superior. Now he had done it twice, both times that began in defense of his wife. He needed to protect her. He desired to see her safe.

"Michael, you had better make me look good today or it will be the end of your field in science," John told him as he took a step closer to Michael.

"All I know is science, and I'm good at it, better than anyone here. If you really wanted to see the SOL progress, you wouldn't threaten me." Michael was testing him; his eyes piercing John's.

"You're right," John replied after a few moments of silence. "Please go into the debriefing room and prepare to go to the SD," John continued in an almost monotone voice.

Michael nodded, assumed the body language of a scientist and strolled into the debriefing room, this time with his chest a little more puffed than usual.

***

"Mary, are you alright? I heard about your incident on the surface," Violet asked as she saw Mary approach the DQ.

"Yes, I'm fine. I…" Mary said when Violet cut her off.

"You need to see the HP," Violet firmly suggested. "Go see Brent," she ordered.

"I'm fine, Violet. Thank you for your concern, but I'm fine," Mary reassured her.

"GD Mary. Rachel just finished telling me what happened on the surface. Are you alright?" Katy said as she bounded up to her two friends.

"Yes, Katy, I'm fine," Mary said again.

"Maybe you should see the HP," Katy suggested.

"I already suggested that to her, Katy. She says she fine," Violet told her.

"Well, alright. I'm hungry. Let's go eat," Katy said as she nodded toward a table. They followed her inside and got the white goop they called food.

"So Katy, enjoy your day off?" Mary asked.

"Yes, I got to sleep…all day," she answered.

"That's nice," Mary said.

"You should know," Violet said smiling at her.

"Yes I do," Mary said as she cocked an eyebrow.

They all smiled and looked down to eat, except Mary who glanced over at the right wall of the DQ.

Not now, Matthew told her.

How many have died for the SOL? Mary asked as she stirred the white goop in front of her. Silence greeted her on the other end. *Matthew, how many have died for the SOL?* She asked again as she swallowed and looked up at Katy.

Too many. Matthew finally answered. *A long time ago, many generations before mine, a man lived and went public with his discovery of the things in the Library of History. Instead of erasing the minds of those who heard him, the Head Council tortured him and left him to die on the surface. They threatened the people with the same fate if they were to ever again tell of what they heard. A few did and they were exiled to the surface. Eventually, everyone knew, but no one stood up for the things they learned. Fear overtook their hearts, and rationalization murdered their hope. They justified not speaking out because it was better here, they said. There is light in the SOL and civilized humans all around them. 'The luxuries of technology and advancement outweigh the need for life's meaning,' they shouted. With that, only the curious ones remembered and told their children. Thus the next generation grew not knowing who the man was that spoke against the Head Council. The lucky ones who were told of his actions were ignorant enough to think it was just a story and subsequently disregarded it as such. He was the last before Ana who found the Library of History by a touch of luck guided by fate.*

So is it fate or luck that I came to be? Mary asked as she answered Katy's question, "I think you should learn as much as you can while you can and then put it to good use."

Katy sighed deeply and responded, "But I don't want to be in BI."

Violet consoled her, "Katy, you're the best there is. Just take it and run with it."

Mostly fate, and with a tad bit of luck, we will keep you alive and well to train the next generation, Matthew responded.

Mary smiled. "Yes, just take it and run with it," she said more to herself than to Katy.

***

All was dark, and Mary rolled out from underneath Michael's arms and snuck away. Down to the Library of Science, she tip-toed through the eerily silent corridors of the SOL.

Walking up to the huge doors that halted every non-scientist at its doorstep, opened wide for Mary. Slipping in, she quickly made ten more bottles of Jumyoo and then painstakingly pieced together the hormone imbalancer that Ana created so long ago.

Why do I need to drink this if no one is awake? Mary asked Matthew.

Because the effects last days upon days. We might need you to be invisible during the day to others. Here at night, everyone is asleep, and they can't see you walk into the Library of Science to make this concoction, Matthew reasoned.

Won't that look suspicious? Mary asked.

No, you will just be one of the others. Don't do anything to draw attention to yourself.

Am I really supposed to drink this? Mary asked Matthew as she held up the green-brown slightly translucent liquid.

Yes, Matthew responded. *A forewarning: it will hurt,* he continued just as Mary brought it to her lips. She breathed deeply, closed her eyes, and then gulped it down.

Slamming the glass beaker on the table, she grabbed her throat and fell to her knees. Her arms writhed in burning pain as her heart beat increased. Her neck tensed and her face numbed. Her fingers tightened and her spine twisted. She gulped for air as her lungs collapsed within her chest.

It's all in your head, Matthew told her. *Just breathe,* he coached.

Gasping for air, Mary's vision began to blur and her head spun.

Breathe, Matthew told her again.

Falling over, her head hit the cold stone floor, and suddenly when Mary thought death would overcome her, she breathed. She maneuvered her hand to help her sit up. She looked around and everything was in clear view. She stood up and felt perfectly fine.

I don't ever want to do that again, Mary said to herself. *I can stand the shock from the BIS and I can do the data transfers to my brain, but this I will not do again,* Mary announced to Matthew.

We shall see, he responded. *Now go to the DQ.*

Mary nodded and boldly walked to the transporter in the dark silence. Once inside, she walked over to the wall and began feeling for any weakness beneath the metal panels. Tapping on the walls, she strained to listen for hollow points. A bot rolled in seeking out the cause for the noise. Mary froze, held her breath and remembered the bots use heat and body scans to identify members of the SOL as it rolled up to her.

I am reprogramming it to view you as a part of the wall. Keep looking, Matthew ordered.

Mary let out the breath she was holding and slowly slid down the wall away from the bot still tapping, hoping she could find something.

As she neared the end of the wall, she let out a sigh of despair and tapped on the last panel with her head upwards praying this was it.

The sound she heard sounded like the others, but there was something different about the "tap" noise it made. It sounded as if there was another wall behind it: two sheets of metal back to back pasted to the DQ wall.

Reading her thoughts, Matthew answered her, *Take the panel off and see.*

Mary dug her nails into the tiny seam that separated the panels. A shock pulsated through her hand.

She pulled away, holding her hand. "What was that?" she whispered.

I assume it was the protective programming shield, Ana put in place over all the secret entrances into the Library of History, Matthew informed her.

Can you disable them?

I'm not sure. Let me try now that I know where one is.

Mary waited in silence staring at the wall panel that could hold the mission she was born to achieve.

Try to open it now, Matthew told her.

Mary approached the wall, dug her fingernails behind the panels and gently lifted up. A holographic wall panel appeared as she pulled the top panel away and began to disintegrate as a black hole emerged in its place.

I found it, Matthew.

Matthew smiled. *Is there anything in there?*

Yes. There are ten tablets. Mary reached in and picked one up. It looked as old as the one she found in the passageway in her LQ. She stuffed all of them into her workbag, and turned to replace the panel.

Go back to your LQ, take another dose of Jumyoo, and then read the tablets until the wake-up call. Make sure your husband does not know where you have been, Matthew told her.

Mary obediently nodded and snuck away to her LQ. She stopped cold at the opened door. Michael was there staring at her.

Does he know who I am? Can he sense me? Mary asked her mentor and all knowing, all seeing eye.

If he can see your face, then yes, otherwise, no. He cannot smell you or sense your presence. The hormone imbalance blurs others' vision when they look at you, but he has genetically superior eyesight as one of the mutations we gave him for his purpose on the surface, Matthew informed her.

"Mary? What are you doing?" Michael whispered to her through the darkness.

"I don't know, Michael. I woke up in the hallway," Mary lied to her husband as she slipped in and closed the door behind them.

"Mary, what are you doing?" he asked again.

"I told you," Mary said as she went and placed her workbag on the counter. Michael followed her and picked it up.

"Michael, put that down," Mary ordered him.

"What did you do?" he asked Mary again.

What should I do? Mary begged for help.

I was afraid this would happen. Hold off on telling him for a little while longer. I am running code to place the both of you back in the sleeping cot asleep. I'll tell you when you can tell him, Matthew responded.

"Nothing, Michael. I woke up in the hallway. I'm tired, and I need to sleep before tomorrow's work day," she answered as she pulled her workbag away from him. Walking over to the sleeping cot with the workbag securely held in her arms, Michael grabbed her shoulder.

"Mary, what is going on? I need to know where you go at night. Do you really think that I can't feel you slip away in the darkness? What are you doing?" Michael intensified his grip as he turned her to face him.

"Michael, I told you I can't tell you," Mary said in a hushed voice.

"Mary, tell me," Michael ordered. At her silence, he went on, "How am I supposed to protect you, love you, be with you, if you can't tell me what's going on?"

"Michael, I love you and that is the reason why I cannot tell you. If anything ever happened to you because of me, I do not know what I would become," she said gently.

Michael placed both of his hands on her shoulders and looked her straight in her eyes. "What have you done that would put you and me in harm's way?"

"Michael, stop. Please, stop," Mary said as three little tears slid down her face.

You have until the wake-up call to tell him. Matthew's message came through. *He still loves you.* He added reassuringly.

Michael loosened his grip, kissed her forehead, hugged her in his strong arms, and whispered to her, "You know when the time comes to tell me, I will still be here."

"I know," Mary whispered back. He let her go, and walked back over to the sleeping cot, laid down away from her and fell into a restless sleep. Mary lay facing the opposite wall as Michael and hugged her workbag as tightly as she could.

Should I tell him, Matthew? This is the first night he has not held me as I slept.

He will understand in due time. Sacrifices must be made. He will have to learn. Right now, you are sacrificing happiness for a greater joy to come.

I can't sleep, Matthew. I feel as if I have betrayed him and his trust in me. I want to tell him, but like I told him before, if something happened to him because of me, I don't know what I would do.

One day, Mary, you will have to face that fear. He will go to the surface because of you, Matthew said as he sensed her anxiety. *I can't monitor him without a modified transmitter. Take him to the passage way now. I will meet you and we can do the procedure.*

Mary rolled over and whispered to her husband, "Michael, are you awake?"

"Yes, Mary."

"Get up. You want to know. I will show you. Do not say a word," Mary ordered as he turned and faced her.

"Where are we going?"

"I said not a word," Mary told him as she walked around the sleeping cot towards him. She took his hand and pulled him over to the secret passageway. Pulling off the panel, she told him to follow her.

They stepped out into the Library of History. Michael pulled Mary back behind him when he saw Matthew. "I showed her how to get here. She knows nothing of this place," he boldly told the man who stood in front of him protecting Mary from whatever punishment that may befall such violators of the SOL's laws.

"Michael, do not worry. I am the one who has been guiding Mary," Matthew said in a hushed voice. "Now follow me," as he turned to walk up the flight of stairs. Mary came out from behind Michael and smiled as she went first.

They came to the stairs that led into the ceiling. "Where are we?" Michael asked in whisper.

Matthew walked up the stairs and disappeared into the ceiling. Mary followed. Michael looked around and ducked as he got closer to the solid wood, but then realized it was just a holographic image and moved right past it. Mary was waiting for him at the top. She looked over the railing and saw holographic images of everyone and everywhere in the SOL. She whispered to Michael, "I told you, they could see and hear everything. We are not free, Michael. We are not even in control of our own lives. We are slaves, and we do not even know we are slaves."

"Michael, Mary, come," Matthew called to them over in his HP corner. Michael lingered a little while longer with his eyes intently gazing down over the railing.

Matthew motioned him to lie down on the HP bed.

Mary explained as she saw the confusion in his eyes. "You have a transmitter in your leg that tells the HC and the Historian where you are at all times. It also allows them to look into your life and see a recording of what is happening or has happened around you. Everything is stored in the Library of History. If it senses no motion, it deactivates. The only way that happens is if you remove it or are dead. If you remove it, the HC will know you know about it and will punish you accordingly. Matthew modified my transmitter to where he can manipulate the recordings to make it seem like I am somewhere else when I am actually not. He can manipulate conversations that I have with others, so that the Historian cannot hear something he is not supposed to hear. You and I and others in the SOL were bred to lead the SOL to freedom. We are genetically superior to withstand the surface. We have been genetically altered to be the best and to work together to create something so much better than what we have here. There will be hardship and sacrifice. We will be sent to the surface. We will leave our memory here with the SOL and they will choose to leave with us or fight against us. There is a war coming, Michael. It's time to choose for yourself what side you are on," she said as she intensified her gaze into his eyes.

"What war, Mary?" Michael asked as he looked first at her then at Matthew.

"The HC is growing the RMH population to keep us from ever going to the surface again. They are power-hungry enough to kill anyone who goes against them. There were others who did so and were exiled on the surface to be murdered by the RMH. Our mission is to go to the surface and create a sanctuary for those living here. I went to find Ana of Generation39's plans for us tonight, and I was successful. They are here in this workbag," she said lifting her bag.

"Mary it sounds like a losing war. The surface is barren now. The SOL has everything. Who would want to live on the surface as it is now?"

"Who would want to live on the surface as it will become? What will happen then?"

Michael got her point. He looked to the ground in contemplation and placed his hands on his hips. After some moments in silence, he finally said, "What is my part in this, this master plan?'

"I can find out," Mary said as she emptied her workbag on the HP bed. Michael approached.

"What is all this?" He asked holding up a bottle of Jumyoo.

"That is Jumyoo. It extends your life span, can heal you, and can let you live without food, water and sleep for many days. The Japanese created it in the twenty-first century."

"Who are the Japanese?"

"They are an ancient people of the old world," Mary hurriedly explained as she was searching through the aged tablets.

"The HC rid the SOL of knowledge such as this to make sure nothing would ever inhibit their control of the inhabitants here. They control everything, and everyone goes along because they don't know any better. Would it help to tell you that for generations beyond of what I can remember have been doing the same exact work? Not the same type of work, but the same work. The HC does not want the SOL to progress. The HC wants power and wants to be the sole source of dependence for the members of the SOL. Now is the time to change that: now because of what was done in the past and now because of you and the other chosen ones," Matthew urged him.

"It's a losing war, Mary. So far, it's just you and Matthew and me. What are we going to accomplish with just us? Even if there are five more of us, what are we going to do? The RMH above us and the HC below us, we have nowhere to go," Michael rationalized.

"We are the best Michael. We were bred to be that way. We all have a part in making something better for all of us. We can't stop believing in that something. We have to try and give it everything we have. We at least owe that to the ones who died for us to live," Mary justified to him.

"We have four hours until the wake up call, Michael. Past that time, I can no longer help you," Matthew told him.

After several moments of silence, Michael slowly and softly said, "Alright, I'll do it," as he looked into Mary's eyes. He took a deep breath and laid down on the bed.

Matthew injected him in the neck. Michael kept his gaze into Mary's eyes, as he began to fall asleep.

"Was I right to tell him?" Mary asked Matthew once Michael was unconscious.

"He needed to find out sooner or later," Matthew said as he started the procedure. "Just like the rest of you," he continued. "Read the tablets to me," he said looking at her.

Mary picked up the tablet that lay on the top of the pile and activated it. Ana's voice filled the small corner.

"If you have found these tablets, then we are one step closer to freeing our people. For five years, I have been seeking out new knowledge and uncovering truths I don't want to believe. The HC is not growing the RMH population, they are..."

Matthew snatched the tablet from Mary and deactivated it.

"What are you doing?" she asked.

"It will be faster if I download and transfer the data via BIS," he answered as he uneasily held the tablet. "I'll just do that for all of them."

"But don't you want to know as well?" Mary asked him.

"I do, but the wake-up call is coming soon. I am almost finished with his procedure. We need to get him back to your LQ," Matthew responded after a few seconds of silence.

Mary cautiously looked at him. "Did someone threaten you, Matthew?" He finished the procedure without answering her.

Finally he replied, "Negative, no one threatened me. Now, let's get him back to your LQ," he said as he lifted Michael's arm and placed it around his neck. Mary joined in and after a half hour, they finally had him back in the sleeping cot.

"Mary, I will send those tablets to you," Matthew said as he turned to enter the secret passageway. Mary watched him disappear into the darkness wondering if she could trust he would send her all of the tablets' contents. She replaced the wall panel.

Mary, you can trust me. Have faith in me. I will not leave you, Mary read in her left eye. She turned her thoughts to Michael. She kissed him on the forehead and lay down beside him. "My heart lives with you," she whispered to him. He smiled and kissed her back.

Falling asleep, she began to dream of fire.

***

Michael's eyes gradually opened at the sound of the wake-up call, and the beautiful vision of his wife came into view. He smiled at her as his head pounded.

"You went through this?"

"Yes. The day of the marriage ceremonies," Mary responded. Michael chuckled a little, and she continued, "I asked Matthew to give you a BIS as well so he communicate with you."

"A permanent one?" he asked.

"Yes. It's right here," she said touching the BIS on the back of his head. "He will turn them on in an half hour, and you will feel a pain in your eye when he does. This is an old BIS, so it is no longer recorded by the HC and Historian. It will keep our conversations secret," Mary explained.

"Why must everything about you, Mary of Generation 43, be a secret?" he asked smiling as he glided his fingers through her soft hair.

Mary helped him up and helped him into the BQ. She calmly walked over the passageway and got out the Jumyoo. She gave herself a dose and walked in on Michael and gave him a dose too. "This is the Jumyoo," she told him as she injected him. "It'll make you feel better today," she smirked and kissed him.

She walked out of the BQ, grinning from ear to ear. *No more secrets*, she thought.

Michael and Mary stepped outside their LQ and audaciously began the new day. They had both received one tablet earlier through their BIS. They knew about the clones. They knew what the HC was doing with them. They knew they needed to bring the SOL's technology with them when they left. They knew they needed to spread out copies of the history they had found and the plans of the HC around the SOL so that others may find it and follow them.

Stepping off of the transporter they both glanced at each other not saying a word. They were all communicating through the mind. They were one. Mary went to the SPR-E and Michael entered the SPR-S.

Mary walked right past Amanda, and she did not recognize her. Mary kept her eyes down and no one knew she was there except Rachel and Blake.

Five more tablets came to her throughout the work day. Looking up from the last transmission, she breathed deeply and stared at her friends sitting across from her at the DQ table.

"What is it, Mary?" Katy asked.

Mary kept her silence.

"Brent do you think you could look at Mary even without a positive body scan?" Violet asked her husband.

"I'm not sure. I would have to check the HP policies," he responded to her in a whisper.

"I feel ill, Brent. Do you think we can go now?" Mary asked.

"Sure, let's go," Brent said as he stood up from the table.

Michael looked at them as they left the table. He had gotten the same message from Matthew as Mary.

"Michael, aren't you worried that something is wrong with Mary?" Violet asked him because his face seemed so calm.

"No Violet, she will be fine. She hasn't been taking well to sleep the last few days," he answered.

Mary's body scan came back positive, and Brent didn't have to consult the HP policies.

"Let's take a look here," he said as he pulled up her scan on the projector as she stood beside him.

"I think there is a glitch in the system. Everything looks great, Mary. I believe that you are the healthiest person in the SOL. I don't know why you are feeling ill. I can't explain it," he said as he sighed.

"Brent, I don't feel ill. Someone manipulated the scanner. I'm not going to ask if you trust me again, because I already know the answer," she said as she walked over the computer in wall and accessed the LOH research database. "Put on the BIS," she ordered him.

"What are you doing, Mary?" Brent asked unsure of what was happening as he put on the BIS Mary handed him.

"You will see. This way is just easier, faster and safer," she said in a hushed voice. She went up to him and pulled out a syringe and filled it with Thioxilline.

"Alright Mary, what are you doing?" Brent asked as he stood up and stepped back from her.

"You have to be asleep when I transfer all of this information to you otherwise you could die. Please lie down on the bed, and calm your nerves," she explained.

He cautiously approached the bed and laid down. Closing his eyes, he said, "I trust you."

"I know, Brent. That is why you must know what I know," she said as she injected him with Thioxilline. As he began to fall into a deep slumber, Mary pulled out a modified transmitter made for Brent and began the procedure. She commanded Melinda to start the data transfer to his BIS. His head began to ever so slightly shake.

"Slow the transfer to 200b/s," she ordered Melinda.

Mary finished the procedure. Then she pulled out a bottle of Jumyoo, left it in Brent's safe, and put a protective programming shield around the safe itself. She watched as the safe disappeared into the wall.

Brent came to and his head pounded. Mary injected him with a dose of Jumyoo. "This will help with the pain," she said.

"Is that the Jumyoo?" Brent asked.

"Yes," Mary replied as she placed it on his desk.

Brent looked at her. "Mary, why did you erase my memory when I helped you remove the transmitter?" Brent asked her with a hurt in the back of his eyes.

"I didn't want you to be hurt because of me. I couldn't tell you everything because I did not yet know everything. I wanted to keep you safe," she said as the guilt she suppressed began to rise again in her spine.

He looked at her, and said nothing.

"I'm sorry I broke the trust between us," Mary said looking to the ground.

Brent sat up and gave her a hug. "It is not broken," he whispered in her ear.

"Do you know what you must do?" Mary asked him.

"I do," Brent said. "How did you know I would go along?"

"Because you were bred to," Mary answered as she cleaned up the space and deactivated Melinda. "Matthew will be contacting you shortly. When he does, you will feel a horrible pain in your left eye. Do not let anyone see your reaction to the pain. This is a temporary BIS. We will have to create a plan where Matthew is able to make it permanent. The permanent BIS records everything your brain thinks or tells your body to do or sees just in case the HC decides to erase your memory, you'll have a backup," Mary smiled.

"What if the HC gets a hold of the backup?" Brent asked.

"It is an unrecorded technology. It would take months to tap back into it, and even then, they could only see from that present point forward. They couldn't see anything from the past. Matthew is monitoring the BIS. We can trust him. He saved my life. He wants the same thing as us," Mary explained.

"What will we tell the others?" Brent asked.

"For now, we will tell them that I was exhausted and needed a DNA-R and DNA-B sequence," Mary said matter-of-factly.

"Alright. Let's go," Brent said as he led her out of his office.

The end of the work day came. Mary sat down on the sleeping cot next to Michael and placed her hand on his chest.

"Are you alright, Mary?" Michael asked opening his eyes from his restful nap.

"Vi now has been brought into our knowledge," she replied looking straight ahead.

Michael nodded, "That's good."

"What if we are dooming all of our friends to the same fate as those before us? Like you said before, we have sided on the losing side of the war..."

Michael cut her off, "Mary, we are bred to be superior. I believe it is enough to survive so that others can follow." He looked into her eyes. She knew. She smiled a little smile, and lay down next to him. Closing her eyes, he held her close against his chest, and she fell asleep to the soothing rhythm of his heartbeat. She slept all night without dreaming, the first time in a long time.

The wakeup call came only a few hours later. "Did you receive three units of information?" Michael asked to her.

"I received six," Mary responded rubbing her head and laying her head back on his chest.

Mary, take three hours off this day. You will discover more today than in the past months. You will have to see it with your own eyes, so that I can transfer it to the others, Matthew told her.

"Matthew wants me to use my tokens to take three hours off today," she told Michael.

"Let me know what you find out," Michael replied as he got up and left.

Where am I going Matthew? Mary asked as she entered her RQ token information into the computer.

Go to the transporter, and don't make eye contact with anyone, he told her, and she instinctively obeyed. The transporter automatically took her to Level Base which was below Level Zero. The doors opened to her.

Walk inside, Matthew ordered.

She tentatively stepped inside the darkness. *I can't see anything,* she said squinting.

I will give you light, Matthew told her as the lights slowly came on one at a time. Mary jumped back in shock at the first image she witnessed. A RMH wrapped in a cylindrical container growing with a black metal plate engraved with the name, DAMINGIN, over its head, was situated in the center of the large room elevated amongst all the other growing RMH.

"How many are there?" Mary asked breathlessly as she walked around the one labeled DAMINGIN gliding her hand on the glass.

There have been over three million produced in the last six generations. Now, here, there are 400,000 RMH being produced, he informed her.

Mary held in the breath she had taken, and repeated the number, "Four hundred thousand."

Don't worry, Mary. We can still win, He encouraged her.

There are only ten of us!! There are four hundred thousand here alone not including the ones that have already been put on the surface and reproduced since then, Mary told him.

Mary, they cannot reproduce. They are clones of RMH. When they tried recreating the RMH, the internal reproductive organs could not be replicated due to the massive genetic mutation the RMH have. It could not be applied to the human genetic code that is used to clone the RMH, Matthew said.

It is so real looking though. Was this an actual RMH when its DNA was extracted? Mary asked.

Yes, they killed over a million RMH for this project through the years trying to find good DNA to replicate. This one fought back and killed a human scientist. It took the longest to die. They decided its genes were good enough to lead them. It is the only one that is named. Damingin is the only one that knows it and the others are clones. All the clones have the same pheromone. They are all programmed with their life purpose: to kill anything that doesn't smell like them, Matthew said.

Why did they kill so many RMH? They have the genetic material of one RMH. Why not just replicate it for all of them? Why create genocide just to have them all reborn? Mary asked.

I don't know. There is more to this than I can see or figure out, Matthew responded.

You are the Historian. Shouldn't you know? Mary cautiously asked.

I am the Historian; that is correct, yes, but I felt the Head Council did not trust me with the entire truth. They told me the clones were for scientific study and research, so that we may have a defense against them for when we return to the surface. They cut off my eyes in this level some sixty years ago. I did research on my own, and forced the last member of that Head Council to tell me something as he lay dying in his LQ. What I have told you is what I found out that day. That is all I know. Matthew paused in his brain thought process. *Remember that face, Mary. Damingin, I fear, will be the one who you will have to kill when you are on the surface.*

Why don't I just kill him here? You can cover for me just like you have been doing. The hormone imbalancer is already in my system, Mary argued.

If he dies right now, Mary, the Head Council would be notified and they would know something is not right, and I fear I would not be able to help you anymore, Matthew explained. *And besides, clones are meant to be reborn. It would not do any good.*

Mary placed her hand on the glass, and looked up at the almost fully grown RMH. "Is there any good left in this world?" she whispered to herself.

There is, Mary, and it starts with you. Matthew encouragingly said.

All the sudden, the RMH opened its eyes and stared at Mary as she jumped back. It pulled its hand up to the glass with a forceful pulse and with its nails scratched it. It bared its teeth and narrowed its eyes. She heard a growl coming from within the container. Mary boldly approached this poor creature, and put her hand to his.

"Many think you are not worth saving, but one day, I will show you that you are," Mary whispered to him through the glass. He began to pound on the glass and little cracks started to appear. Mary stepped back as a bottle of syringe labeled Thioxilline began to empty into Daminigin's tubes that connected him to the container. He began to shake his head ever so slightly and close his eyes. As soon as he was unconscious, Mary turned and ran out of Level Base.

"Level One!" she shouted to the transporter. She walked uncomfortably to the SPR-E and entered with her head down. *Tell Michael and the others what I found,* she ordered Matthew. The SPR-E was empty. Everyone had gone to the surface.

The data is in the process of being sent, Matthew informed her. Putting on her surface gear, she realized she no longer smiled.

I'm not a warrior, Matthew. What am I supposed to do? There are who knows how many of these RMH clones living on the surface. How am I supposed to survive until the others come? How are we supposed to survive until the SOL joins us? How is the SOL supposed to survive when there is no one else to follow?

Mary, you were bred to be a warrior. You will have to make the production of clones stop and ensure it cannot be restarted in order for you and the others to be successful, Matthew told her.

Mary nodded to herself as the big transporter doors opened to the workspace on the surface. She took a deep breath through her OXY mask and stepped out. Amanda walked up to her and told her the frequency. She didn't seem to recognize her.

Michael looked up from his work and over to her with concern in his eyes. He had gotten the message. Mary looked back at him, turned and walked toward her group.

The end of the work day came, and all ten had been told the truth about the Head Council. Mary, Michael, Violet, Brent, Katy, Rhome, Rachel, Blake, Jenna and Shawn sat in the DQ silently eating their white goop as chatter surrounded them, but they didn't hear it. All they heard was silence, lost in their own thoughts. They wondered how they would stop such a growing empire. Individually they would fail, and even together, there was not much chance of success. They could only talk to each other if Matthew connected them. Their brains could only handle two or three connections at a time. They couldn't even collaborate amongst themselves efficiently or effectively.

They all had the deep and aching feeling in the bottom of their gut: it was far too gone, the goodness of the world soaked into the soil of the surface and in the walls of the SOL. They were bred to bring it back, but how was the question, a very difficult and almost impossible question to answer.

They were outnumbered: an unknown hundreds of thousands or maybe even millions to ten. They were conflicted: die here from old age or die fighting there on the surface?

They were stuck.

Chapter 5
EVIL SPEAKS

"CPU1200 record conversation and allow my commentary. Date: 11.19.3109. There she is. Mary, the most beautiful woman in the SOL, stands next to her husband. She turns, faces him and places her hands on her perfect hips. They gaze at each other for a moment. He smiles, and her eyes dance. I know he is looking at her perfect body and imagining her as his," Hunter sneered.

'We're going to be late,' he says with a sigh and strokes her pristine cheek.

She rolls her eyes playfully and his smile grows bigger.

'It's just to the DQ,' she protests.

'But if we don't get there in time, all of the good stuff will be gone,' he sarcastically argues back.

"She slowly grins and lightly brushes by him into the hallway. They lock eyes once again. I had to watch him take her at the marriage ceremonies. Her, who should be mine, is his. He doesn't deserve her. I watch them and wish I was him. I wish I could put my hands in her hair and kiss her gently on her silken lips. I want to feel the warmth of her breath on my neck and feel her hands rummaging down my back. I long every night to hold her in my arms and envision her perfect arched eyebrows and her smooth baby soft skin under the glow of the LQ's dimmed blue night lights. He will never love her as I do, and she doesn't even remember me. I have watched over her every night since she was a little girl, and she doesn't even remember me. She looked into my eyes, and she didn't even remember me. She met me again, and my grandfather erased her memory. She can't remember me. She won't remember me," Hunter growled as he paced back and forth looking down at the holographic images.

'GD Michael. GD Mary,' Sara says as she walked by.

'GD Sara,' they say in unison.

"Michael steps out of the hallway and gently wraps his slithering hand around her waist and lays it to rest on the small of her back. She closes her door and smiles up at him once again. I wonder if she would smile the same amount at me in a lifetime as many times she smiles at him in a day. Mary has this gaze that will turn any man's attention towards her. She's captivating: her alluring eyes, her full lips, and her perfect nose; she keeps my focus day after day."

'Did you hear about John's plans for the SD?' Michael asks.

'No,' Mary replies as they head to the DQ.

"He doesn't deserve her; I do. Their conversation is involving static. I will try to recover what they are saying. CPU1200 follow subjects 234 and 238."

"John already has a team building the..." was the only phrase he could pull out of the static he began to hear.

"CPU1200 stop recording conversation and upload subject 238's file." Hunter gave up trying to figure out what they were saying. "I just need to see her."

"Hunter, how goes the history-making?" Matthew said as he came up the stairs. Hunter hurriedly changed the image on the floor to the DQ as his grandfather came walking towards him.

"Very well, Grandfather." He spun around and walked to the edge of the dome that supports the Earth from falling in upon the SOL.

"Hunter, in a place of work, you will refer to me by my name."

"I apologize, Matthew."

"I need you to stop what you're doing. We need to talk about some things," Matthew said as he took in a deep breath.

"Let me turn off the CPU1200." He removed his head and hand interface equipment. "What do we need to discuss?"

"You have just turned of age forty-six and I, ninety-six. I have taught you everything I know. When I retire, though, I will record my last memoirs of Historian and you will read them thoroughly."

"Yes Matthew."

"I have helped you, aided you and advised you in all the areas of responsibility that the Historian holds. I know you have read every text in the Library of History. I do not doubt your knowledge, Hunter." Matthew sighed and deeply inhaled as if there was more he wanted to say, but regrettably decided to say nothing more. His tired eyes watched Hunter and his fidgety behavior. An awkward pause filled the space that hovered above the SOL.

"Thank you, sir." Hunter finally uttered. Another awkward pause as Matthew stared at his grandson with an ache in his heart.

"Do you feel you can take on the responsibilities of the Historian without my help from this time forward?"

"I believe I can," Hunter responded with pride.

"Do you know you can?" Matthew asked again.

"I know I can," Hunter repeated with a look of confusion in his eyes.

"Are you sure?" Matthew asked yet again.

"Grandfather, are you doubtful of my abilities?" Hunter asked insulted.

A screaming silent "YES" filled Matthew's lungs and traveled up into mouth and onto the tip of his tongue, but he simply could not utter the words. He had failed the SOL. He could not raise, he could not teach, he could not provide the SOL with a Historian worthy enough to be entrusted with the responsibility of Historian. Old age and age beyond his years had conquered him. Years of study and years of endless sleep drew on his last energies. He slowly shook his head. He decided he would leave his last memoirs for his great grandson to read when he was to become the Historian.

"Then I will choose a day at 0800 when I will inform the Head Council of my retirement." He turned to walk away, and Hunter grinned. "Hunter, I almost forgot. You will need to be present as they commit you to the responsibilities of the Historian."

"I will be there. Matthew, thank you for teaching me all you know," Hunter said with a slight bow.

"Thank you Hunter for learning with a willing heart. This job is the most important job in the SOL. You have all the power. You will be the most trusted advisor to the Council to make decisions that do not repeat history. No one supervises your work without compelling reason based on corruption. Hunter, this job is yours and will be yours alone. You will see, as I have seen, things that may not be right under the law but may be right to the person and what beliefs that person holds. You have the power to judge the future of that individual. I have chosen to be a silent observer, not interfering in the lives of those in the SOL and let them make the history while I only recorded what I witnessed. My predecessor chose to inform the Council of every infraction he witnessed; he caused them grief. He put someone on the surface. She never had a chance. Sometimes, I think they didn't want the SOL to know what they were doing behind closed doors. Use your own judgment, but remember to be unbiased and fair in all your dealings. Once you start to play favorites, well…just know that you have been warned."

"Thank you, Matthew. I will not disappoint you."

"If you disappoint me, Hunter, then you disappoint the SOL also," Matthew said as he turned to leave.

"I won't," Hunter called after him.

"I hope not," Matthew said to himself as he began to walk away with his back erect and hands gently folded in front looking over the railing into the all the lives of the underground dwellers. When he got to the other side, he slowly rotated and stared at his grandson. "Your job is to protect the people of the SOL. You are to love them as free-willed beings."

"I do," Hunter affirmed.

In your heart, you do not. Matthew thought as he descended into the SOL.

As Hunter watched his grandfather leave, images began to flash in Hunter's mind, all of Mary, not of his wife, not of his child, but of Mary. He said her name softly, "Mary." He put on his interface equipment and the floor projected Mary's identification picture and her basic information: Mary – Generation 43; Birthdate – 04/12/3086; Height – 5'5"; Weight – 124 lbs; Occupation – Engineer.

He stared at subject 238. Her eyes called to him.

"CPU1200 open subject 238 file."

The floor flooded with lists of dates of recordings, pictures, important medical files, uploads, entrances, exits, and interactions with those living in the SOL.

"Mary, I know everything about you. Let us see what you last recorded. Well, the last date you recorded anything was on 12.30.3107. Ah, let's see."

Mary's voice filled the room: 'Part I: The Sacred Record...10.12.1492...Columbus discovered the Americas. 2.5.1509...'

"Mary, you aren't supposed to know much of this information because it is only found in the Library of History. That's where you go at night. I respected you at night, but now I see you sneak away and invade my domain. A year you've been fooling me. How could I not catch this? I watch over you. I protect you. I keep you safe. I record your actions so that the future may know you. I keep you alive. I'm making you immortal. You sly unfaithful witch; you deceived me! CPU1200 find subject 238."

"There you are, you lying coward!"

But as he watched her, the anger within him quickly simmered. She gracefully stood up from the DQ table and eloquently pushed the disposal button. Her food disappeared from the table. She pushed Michael's disposal button, and they walked out, her laughing at one of Michael's stories. They headed to Level One, the floor where the libraries' entrances are located. The brightly lit hallways put a glistening effect on Mary's pulled up hair. They approached the transporter and stepped inside.

***

"Mary, what are we doing?" Michael asked her as he sent a message to Matthew to cover their conversation again.

"We are going to the Library of Science to make some more Jumyoo. Remember, we are the best of Gen43, and thus, we must ensure we free our people," Mary explained as they stepped out of the transporter and turned to go down the other hallway toward the libraries.

"Mary, it's been almost a year since I found out about what was going on. We've…"

"Michael," Mary cut him off and continued, "Everything is in place and soon we will have to follow through with our part of the plan. I have done everything I needed to do, and I fear my time is coming when I will be put on the surface."

Michael's face fell. "Remember when we used to sneak away after DQ hour?"

"Yes," Mary grinned and looked over at him.

"Well, I gladly woke up the next morning having only slept for a few hours."

"Michael, why are you bringing this up?" Mary asked with a little laugh.

"I don't want you to go, and if you must, then I'm going with you," he said in a low voice as he grabbed her arm and whisked her around to face him.

"Michael, that wasn't part of the plan," she whispered to him and smiled at a passerby. "I…" Mary's mind raced back to her long gone teacher and enlightener, and how her name had no record in the SOL.

"You, what?"

"Nothing," she quickly responded and averted her eyes.

"Mary, don't lie to me," Michael said as he found her eyes.

"I'm scared, Michael, but I'm committed to this and willing to do what I must so that our plan is optimized for the highest chance of success. For that to happen, I have to go first, and you have to stay behind and finish what you must do," Mary said as water began to well in the back of her eyes.

Mary glanced at the locked door of the Library of History. A look of unsatisfaction passed on her face for a brief second, but Hunter witnessed her longing of more as he tried to figure out what they were saying.

"Oh Mary," Michael said as he brought his hand up to her face as if he was going to brush away the fallen strand of hair from her face. Then he noticed the Historian's camera situated above the door of the Library of Medicine, and let his hand fall.

"Michael, we all must make sacrifices. To me, if I die, I know it won't be in vain because I have ten others who are all working towards the same goal. I have faith we will be successful, and that's all we have is our faith," Mary whispered to him.

Michael smiled a soft entrancing smile. "I know," he responded.

Mary stood before the giant scholarly doors of the Library of Science, and they gazed at each other for one silent moment, and then he whispered, "I love you."

Hunter pounded his fist on the rail as that last phrase was uttered through the static in his headpiece, but no one could hear the resounding gong that pierced the silence in the space about the SOL. "No! I love her!"

A smile slowly appeared on Mary's face, her soft silken lips parted as she slowly whispered the words, "I love you too".

At this, Hunter sank to his knees and fiercely hit the holographic ground image of Mary over and over with such vengeance. "Love me! Mary! Love me!"

She gave him a smile back. "Let's get this plan rolling," she whispered to him.

He smiled back and silently turned to go into the Library of Science wishing to himself that at the very least he would be the first to go to the surface instead of his only love.

You are going to have to let her go. Very soon, I'm afraid, Matthew told him as he read his thoughts.

***

Bent over and breathing deeply, Hunter's body began to stiffen. He slowly stood up, and the hand interface, broke from the beating the floor received, fell off. He slowly turned around and leaned over the railing and whispered, "Mary. You are such a beautiful woman, yet you break the rules. You have all these things: beautiful body, beautiful voice, beautiful mind that wanders, all these things are alluring; you are irresistible. I hear her laugh as they enter the Library of Science: her rich ringing of the voice forever imprinted in my memory. I hear great emotion as she implies her desire to want more. Smart girl, never saying aloud that which she does, but she does not know of all the historian's cameras placed in every room, every respected corner of the SOL. She does not know that I can see her everywhere she goes, everything she does, and hear every thought."

He gladly forced himself to think of her and only her. He wanted her.

"CPU1200 play recording dated 4.31.3107 2003 hours. Mary, the steam covers you, but your singing rises from the sound of the G-L converter. I need you, Mary. I see all that you do; you keep no secrets from me. This is why you need me: to keep you safe from the others. Mary, your name, it draws me closer to your soul. CPU1200 pause recording and present image on holographic projector," Hunter ordered the computer.

He slowly stepped in front of subject 238 and tried to kiss her translucent lips, but without the hand interface, it was useless. "Mary, tell me you love me." Her blank eyes returned no response. The projector could not replicate the dancing stars found in the eyes of subject 238. "Oh, Mary. You will come to know me," he vowed to her. "CPU1200 erase commentary from this session."

Chapter 6
THE BETRAYAL

Mary lay wide awake in Michael's arms thinking about the processed thought data Matthew had just sent her. She recorded the last half of her record she was leaving behind through her BIS, and Matthew secured it. A tear slid from her eye, down her check and landed in Michael's hand.

Today was the day. Everything is in place. An overwhelming urge to throw up seized Mary's stomach.

I am brave. I am strong. I can and will survive, Mary thought to herself. "I'm so afraid," she whispered to the darkness. Turning to face her husband, she tunneled into his chest trying to capture this moment of warmth. His hands tightened on her back.

"Is it today?" he asked in a soft, yet hard tone.

"Yes," she quietly replied.

"How will it happen?" he asked through his teeth.

"Today while I'm working on the surface, they will take me and try me for violations made to the SOL's code. They will sentence me, and then they will send me to the surface after the work day. Everyone will be present," she whispered. "They will erase me from the SOL's history. They will erase your memories of me."

"I will never forget you, Mary. My heart lives with you," Michael insisted. "Brent will not erase our memories. That is the plan."

"Yes, so it is. Matthew is stepping down from Historian today. That was not part of the plan," Mary said in a low voice.

"What?" Michael's eyes narrowed. "He's not responding to me."

"He is not responding to me either," Mary said.

"Why is he doing that?" Michael asked. "He cannot cover our tracks if he is on the Floor of Rest."

"He has been nothing but good to us. He must have his reasons for doing so," Mary defended him. "He told me a long time ago to just have a little faith in him."

Michael smiled a sad smile and kissed his wife tenderly on the lips. "I love you," he told her as his sea blue eyes glossed over. She wrapped her arms around his head and passionately kissed him back.

The wake-up call came suddenly. They didn't want to leave the warmth and comfort of their sleeping cot, but they each knew they must go through with the day ahead. Michael went to the passageway in the wall and gave Mary a dose of Jumyoo. The bottle was almost empty.

"Take the rest and give yourself another dose when the time comes," he told her.

"I know. Thanks," she said as she took it from him and stared back at the ground.

He looked up, took a deep breath and kneeled in front of her. "Mary," he said as he gently lifted her chin. "I will come for you. I will find you. I will protect you. I will fight for you," he promised.

"I know you will. You were bred to do so," she replied.

"Mary, I love you more than life itself. I would die for you as long as my heart lives with you," he told her.

"You will always live with me, Michael," she said as tears fell.

Michael stood her up and took her in his strong embrace. "I will come for you. I will find you. I will protect you. I will fight for you," he repeated as a soft whisper into her black hair.

***

Mary mindlessly went about configuring the railings for the SD. She had mastered the modern BIS. She could send only the thoughts she wanted the others to see.

Today, she was not sending out any thoughts. Matthew hadn't spoken to her since his last transmission that morning. Rachel and the others received the same transmission. She looked at Mary and walked over to her. Rachel glanced at her work, patted Mary on the back and told her good job. They were all disconnected from each other. Mary couldn't even tell if the others knew that Matthew was stepping down as Historian.

Four hours into the workday, and still nothing. A sinking feeling kept itself in the center of Mary's gut. The others' hands ever so slightly shook and their minds were not entirely on their tasks at hand.

Finally six hours later, Travis led a group of HC members to the surface and called for Mary of Generation 43 to join them. Mary longingly looked to Michael, turned away from him and boldly walked to them. She followed them to Level Zero, and walked the familiar path into the HC room.

They took their place in their respective seating and the only door leading out closed and locked itself. Mary stood before the Head Council members, and noticed Matthew was not among their ranks.

"Mary of Generation 43, you have been charged with treason," Travis said. "Do you have anything to say about this matter?"

Mary remained silent.

"Speaking would greatly help you right now," Owen curtly told her.

"I would like to face my accuser," Mary requested as she stared down the members.

Hunter stood up slowly with his shoulders pulled back and his back erect. He smirked.

"Mary you are so smart, but you did not know I see everything," he said with slick whip of his tongue.

Mary stood silently.

"He found this recording," Travis said as Mary's recorded voice filled the room speaking of the forbidden records.

Mary closed her eyes and looked to the ground thinking back a year ago when she recorded that part. Matthew hadn't begun helping her yet.

"Why did you do it?" Council member Faith asked interrupting her thoughts.

She paused and then spoke. "People have fought and died for this record. The people of the SOL need something more than this life that they are living. They need someone to take them by their hand and lead them to something better. They need someone to tell them they are living a lie. They need someone to save them from you!" Mary answered.

"And that someone was going to be you?" Owen asked with a chuckle.

"I know about…" Mary started, but then was interrupted when Matthew entered.

"She knows about the erasing of the work done by past generations," he cut her off as they all looked at him. "She knows about everything," he told them as he leaned in on the long table they sat behind. At this, all of their heads snapped back to face her.

"Matthew, you were to watch her and help her locate all of Ana's records and destroy them. You were not supposed to let her find out about everything. You were supposed to ultimately give us reason to destroy the ones she, who has been erased, and Benjamin created," Faith told him. "You were not supposed to jeopardize our dealings by letting her find out about all of this, and then give her opportunities to tell the others!"

"My apologizes, Faith. It was the only way for her to not suspect me. And as you can see, she did not fail us," Matthew said as he turned to look at Mary.

"You just wanted to use me then dispose of me? I trusted you!" Mary said.

"As was your folly," Matthew said again as he stood erect and took his place next to his grandson behind the table. "We cannot erase your memory because of the vast amount of knowledge you now possess. Doing so would probably kill you or leave you as a vegetable, and we cannot have our hands dirty with the killing of you ourselves."

Mary stood silently.

"You must be embarrassed and ashamed," Faith said with a horrible grin that stretched across her face.

"I'm not ashamed. I'm not embarrassed. We spend all our time waiting for something to happen just so you can take away our hope."

"That's what slaves do," Travis growled. Mary shot him a deadly glare. "That's right, Mary of Generation 43, you are a slave. You are here to do as we say, do as we want, and do as we desire. Slaves, who do not follow our laws, rules, and edicts, then must be punished and made an example out of. And as you know from others in the past, you will gain your freedom but with a fatal cost. We made sure it would be that way."

"Of course, who would follow you by choice? You are tyrants! You will never be true leaders of the SOL!" Mary yelled at them and threw her work tablet at Travis.

"We find your audacity quite appalling," he said as he rubbed his head and picked up the tablet off the floor.

"I find your disregard for the value of human life appalling," Mary retorted, and then shot Matthew a dirty glance.

A sharp pain in her left eye presented itself.

I trusted you, Mary told him.

I have to play this role. It is all part of the plan.

The plan to kill me, she retorted.

No, Mary. Listen. If I don't, they will kill me, and our plan will never go through. I told you that when it was time, you would be sent to the surface, but I didn't tell you why and how. I needed them to believe your sincerity in thinking I had turned on you. Don't worry. I will be here for you. You and your friends will lead the SOL to freedom, Matthew explained.

Yes, freedom meaning death. You are going to kill my friends just as you have done to me. To eradicate every possibility of Ana's plan succeeding, Mary seethed.

Have a little faith in me. I saved your life on multiple occasions, and not once have you thanked me. I could have let you die, but there is too much at stake. And Mary, I care for you just as I do all of the SOL. You are genetically superior. You will live. You will survive. I will follow out our plan. I know the Head Council members will attempt to kill me, and I will make them believe they have, he explained again.

The Head Council was now deciding a time to send her to the surface and whether or not to make it public.

"If she has told anyone, then we need to make it public," Hunter told them. "Let's put her in the incarceration center until we decide what to do," he suggested after a few moments of debate. They all nodded in agreement, and then he looked toward Mary and smiled a wicked little smile.

What seemed like hours later, Mary finally heard footsteps coming towards her from within her containment cell. Hunter appeared in front of it with his arms crossed and legs confidently planted.

"You know, I am the most powerful one here," he began. "And I can make this all go away. I can make the SOL know what we are doing, and I can sway the Head Council members to see things your way."

"I know you Hunter of Generation 42. Those are empty lies, and you are full of disgusting obsessions," Mary said with a monotone voice as she stared at the wall.

His eyes grew bigger and his lips quivered. "I am offering you everything you ever wanted!" he yelled at her.

"And what must I do for you to bestow these gifts?" Mary asked as she cocked an eyebrow.

"To satisfy a desire of mine," he told her as his fingers slid up her arm.

"Get away from me!" she screamed. "You sicken me! You will never touch me again!" she got up and ran to the other side of the cell. He followed her and wrestled her to the ground.

"We shall see about that!" he said as he bit her ear.

Mary screamed over and over for someone to help her. Matthew walked in suddenly and yelled in a booming voice, "HUNTER!" He yanked him up by his neck and threw him against the wall. "She is still a member of this SOL, and you will treat her with dignity and respect." He stood between them and stared him down until he walked away.

"You have chosen death!" Hunter pointed at Mary as she lay on the ground, her ear bleeding. Their eyes locked, and then he swiftly turned and walked out of the incarceration center. Matthew helped Mary stand up.

"Did he hurt you?" he asked as he wiped the blood from her ear.

"No, I'll be fine," she replied.

"Take the Jumyoo," he mouthed to her with a nod of his head.

Mary instinctively obeyed and injected herself with a dose of Jumyoo. She was going to tell him something, but he pointed to his BIS.

Matthew, I'm afraid. I don't know if I can do this, Mary confided in him.

You must. You can. You will, he told her. *I will help you, and remember you were bred to do so.*

Do I really know everything? Mary asked him remembering back hours ago to her trial.

No. You only know as much as me. He winked at her, and held her chin in his hand. Abruptly, it looked as if something hit him like a thought passed by that he had never thought of before. Then as suddenly as he had come, he left without a word.

That was the last transmission Mary received from Matthew that work day. It seemed as if they weren't going to leave her on the surface until the next day.

She closed her eyes and lay on the sleeping cot. Calming her breathing, she tried to sleep, but she found it difficult to sleep by herself. Her eyes shifted under her eyelids. There were too many thoughts racing through her mind. Finally with her hands folded on her lap and her hair spread about her head as a halo, she relaxed herself and fell asleep.

At the start of the new work day, the wake-up call came once. Then, unusually, it came again. A soothing almost perfect female voice followed, "Members of the SOL: today is a special day. We will all be gathering on Level One. Please form a straight shoulder to shoulder line against the right wall of the Level One corridor in twenty-five minutes. Additional instructions will be communicated then. There will be unbearable consequences if these instructions are not carried out as ordered."

Mary's body was covered in sweat. She dreamed of fires again. Her mouth was pasty and dry.

"Why are they worth saving?" she asked herself as she awoke.

Travis and two bots appeared at her containment cell. "It's time, Mary of Generation 43," he said as his eyes portrayed nothing but wickedness.

She walked to the thick glass door and stared him down. He opened the door, and she stepped out onto the bot. It strapped her hands down and followed Travis hovering behind his every step. He walked out of the incarceration center into the round room then to the transporter.

"Level One!" Travis bellowed. Then he turned to Mary, and asked, "You are going to die, you know. Is it worth it?"

"I am genetically superior. I will live. And I believe that anything is worth being free," she responded in a greater tone looking straight ahead. "You fail to realize the strength of those who desire and seek it."

The transporter floor slid them out to Level One where all the SOL was gathered shoulder to shoulder along the right wall of the corridor.

A heavy weight set itself deep into Michael's stomach as he watched his wife, chained to a bot, make her way to the SPR-E room. His thoughts were barely interrupted as the female voice filled the corridor, "Please make your way to your appropriate SPR, and put on your assigned surface equipment. Turn your BIS frequency to .01 and enter the surface transporters in an orderly fashion." Mary recognized the voice to be Melinda's voice. It had the same monotone rhythm to it.

Michael felt a hand on his shoulder, and heard his brother's voice, "Remember, everything will work out in the end."

"I know. It's just hard to believe it right now," he whispered behind him.

They all ended up on the surface with the SD lights blaring down on them. Huddled in a mass, they all stood and faced the hover craft carrying HC members, Faith and Travis, Historians, Matthew and Hunter, and the sentenced, Mary of Generation 39.

Travis began in a bold voice, "Members of the SOL, I, Travis of Generation 41, have been a member of your HC for the past two generations. I have not led you astray from our mission. We have brought before you on this day a traitor amongst you. Mary of Generation 43 has violated the code that binds us all together by breaking into the Library of History and Science to gain unauthorized knowledge. She has broken the rules and accepted exile as the only consequence. If you do the same, then you will be forced to accept exile as your only consequence as well."

He turned around and began to move away into the darkness, when a voice yelled out from behind him, "She should be allowed her last words!" He stopped as the roar of support grew louder.

He whispered into her ear, "If you tell them anything, their minds will be erased and so will your record of existence."

"Is that a threat?" she loudly whispered so that others could hear her. Travis balled his hand into a fist beneath the craft console. Mary stared him down, and then turned to her fellow SOL mates.

She began in a loud voice, speaking clearly into the BIS phone. "We are all just human in the end. We live and we die. But it's up to you how you want to live and what you want to be remembered for when you die. As I live, I have chosen to be free from the slavery the HC has forced upon us, and when I die, I have chosen to be remembered for standing up for what is right." She paused for a moment of emphasis. "I do not want to die afraid, but I do not want to die a slave always wanting more. You may think I'm insane," she said looking at the HC members, "to think I would embrace death for freedom, but I would rather live and die in a moment of freedom than live a hundred years as a slave for you. I am not alone. One day, others will rise and will know what crippled independence you bring upon them. They will fight back and destroy your plans to destroy them. I promise you that."

Travis snarled at her. Voices rose up from the crowd: "How are we slaves?" "How will they destroy us?"

Travis pushed the accelerator.

"You are all slaves because they are creating a…" Faith punched her in the stomach as the gigantic SD door closed behind them.

"You really are a traitor," she told her through her teeth.

Mary gasped for a breath of air as she fell to her knees. Matthew took her by the arm and helped her to stand again.

"What are you doing?" Travis asked him.

"She is a member of the SOL until we leave her on her own. She should be treated with respect and dignity," he responded as he shot his grandson a piercing glance.

Hunter took over the console by shoving aside Travis and made the hover craft fly out the two hundred miles to the drop spot. "Here, Matthew, throw her off," Hunter said as he turned to face him.

Matthew took her hand and led her to the step down.

Hunter grabbed her arm, and whispered in her ear, "Remember the deal I made you. I am still willing to grant that to you if you do as I wish," as his hand slithered around the back of her neck. Matthew overheard this and shook his head in disbelief that his grandson would do such a thing.

Mary spit in his face as her response, and growled, "You will never have the pleasure." Hunter slowly wiped her spit off of his cheek, and let his hard grip on her arm go.

Everything will be alright, Matthew told her as Travis approached her from behind and gave her a hard shove off the hover craft.

***

Matthew stood staring off into the darkness at the place they left Mary. He knew she was too far out there to go back for her now. They could see the illumination of the SD getting closer. All of the sudden, Travis slowed the hover craft until it halted to a stop.

"What's going on?" Matthew asked as the halt snapped him out from his trance. "What's wrong?"

The three others turned silently to face him.

"You seem sad that she's gone," Travis told him with suspicion in his voice.

"Isn't it sad to lose a human soul over this?" he asked in response.

"We are the SOL! Nothing is more important than the SOL. One slave's life is nothing compared to the SOL," he roared back.

"You mean compared to your power driven appetite," Matthew interjected.

They stared back in silence.

"No, we mean to the SOL," Travis said between his teeth.

Faith began in an evil smirk, "Are you with us? Do you even know what we are doing? We have not told you."

"I know enough to know that what you are doing is wrong," he said boldly and with confidence.

"How is ensuring the human race goes on, wrong?" Travis asked.

"You are ensuring the human race is enslaved to you and your offspring," Matthew corrected him. "This is a people, a nation meant to repopulate the surface and rebuild what was so great. The SOL started off as a science experiment, and then became the only way humans were to survive. They, we, have survived. Now it's time to live."

"You suggest we unleash the SOL on the surface to be eaten alive by RMH? What kind of HC members do you think we are?" Faith asked him.

"I know about Level Base," Matthew said. "You are ensuring your slaves will never leave. The whole SOL is a lie and you exile anyone who wants to know the truth into the den of lions that you've created."

"We are trying to protect the SOL!" Travis yelled at him. He turned his head sharply to the right and saw two green beady eyes staring at him at a far distance waiting for something to happen.

"You are trying to protect your seats of power!" Matthew yelled back.

"Matthew, power is what makes the SOL go round. Without it, there would be only anarchy," Hunter whispered to his grandfather.

"No, my grandson, you have much to learn. Leadership creates progress, and power creates strife," he told him.

"No one would follow us if we didn't give them an extra incentive to do so," Travis said.

"By rigging the options: follow us or die? You are tyrants and soulless dictators. You don't care about the SOL. You have humans' blood on your hands. Does it make you feel more powerful to know you killed for your own benefit?" Matthew asked out of breath from arguing.

"Yes, it does," he smiled, and his eyes danced. Pulling a knife from inside his robes, he stabbed Matthew in the stomach, pulled it up and then out. Matthew's eyes stared into Travis' as the agony welled in his eyes.

He gasped for air when he felt a sharp pain in his back. Falling to his knees, he turned his head and saw his grandson holding a bloody blade and smiling with satisfaction on his face.

"You too, my son?" he asked barely audible.

In response to this question, Hunter kicked his grandfather off the hovercraft, turned and left him for dead. Faith looked at him with disgust as the hover craft took off back towards the SOL in the distance. Her pride kept her from acknowledging that he was right.

His blood soaked into the black dirt. The darkness was closing in too fast around him. Matthew's wrinkled old hand went to the Jumyoo he had tucked inside his robes. He injected himself with all that was left. Pulling another bottle from his robes, he drank the hormone imbalancer he had prepared for this occasion. He writhed in the dirt for a little while, and then he finally breathed and became absolutely still as the fierce, cold winds blew his hair around his peaceful face.

Only a few minutes later, he saw out of the corner of his eye, a pair of green beady eyes coming closer. His vision blurry, he knew he had to get his robes off because they still contained his scent. He tried rolling out of it, but his back was too damaged. The RMH grabbed his hood and yanked it shaking Matthew's entire body.

He groaned in anguish and pain. The RMH yanked again, and this time, Matthew, with every strength from within him, raised his arms and slid out of his robe.

He slowly crawled away unnoticed by the RMH. It was gnashing its teeth and ripping the robe trying to find the delicious meat it smelled.

Several feet away, Matthew lay on his stomach breathing with severe difficulty. The blood still ran warm down his back and his insides felt like tiny bombs going off inside of him. He tried reaching out to Michael and the others, but they did not respond.

The cold slowly numbed his pain, but nothing could numb the heartache. His head buried in his arms, he fell asleep letting the Jumyoo do what it was created to do.

The hovercraft pulled back into the SD, and the HC told the gathered crowd that Matthew was a traitor as well. They ordered the SOL back into their LQ and told them each one would be seen individually by the HP to discuss any issues they had with today's events.

Faith turned and when she put her glasses up to her eyes, she saw two green eyes and a red robe dangling from its mouth. Smiling, she turned back around to face her slaves. She told the other six HC members that Matthew was dead through her BIS.

They all smirked thinking they had done it again: gotten away with murder.

Brent and the other HPs were told to go to their offices. Owen appeared in the computer imaging system in each HP office when they arrived.

"You have a very important job that you will be solely responsible for. If you do not perform to the highest of your ability and complete this job, then your fate will be the same as Mary of Generation 43," he said without stumbling. A list of instructions appeared on the screen. Brent hacked into Melinda and ran the program code Mary had created for this event. The Historian now saw whatever Brent wanted him to see. The first round of individuals came, and none other than Brent's wife stepped inside his office. The HC knew they were chosen and bred to be genetically superior. It was a test for Brent and Violet, but they had a plan, a year in the making.

He gave her Thioxilline, and attached the SBIS. He went into her memory and copied itself into another part of her brain, and deleted the original. He woke her up, and whispered in her ear, "You have all of your memory, but you'll remember the past few hours as a couple of years ago. That's why it won't make sense to you seeing her exiled and then conversing with her in the DQ years later. Do you remember the plan? That was what I supposed to do."

"I know Brent," she whispered rubbing her head. Owen stepped inside his office.

"Ah, I see you are doing well. May I take a look?" Owen asked Brent.

"I just woke her with adrenaline as the document said. It would be dangerous for me to immediately inject her with Thioxilline again," Brent informed him.

"No it won't," Owen protested. "I will do it myself," he said as he grabbed the nearest syringe and put it up to her neck. Brent slapped it out of his hand, "That's adrenaline!" he yelled. "Do you want to kill her?"

"Brent of Generation 43, calm down. It was a simple mistake. I apologize," Owen said as he turned around and filled a syringe with Thioxilline. "Now Violet of Generation 43, this will not hurt," he told her.

"But my head is hurting so bad already," she breathlessly told him as her eyes drunkenly followed the syringe in his hand.

"Calm my child. It will not be that bad," he said as he injected her. He placed the SBIS upon her head, and took the hand interface equipment in his hands. Brent stepped to the side and behind him.

If Matthew is exiled as well, who is going to look after us? He thought to himself. *Should I continue with the plan?*

He picked up a syringe of Thioxilline, and injected Owen in the neck just as he was viewing her wake up but before Brent told her she had all of her memory.

He locked his office door. He let Violet sleep. He put the SBIS on Owen and went through his memory to see if his thoughts were being recorded as well via his BIS. After a few minutes of searching, he found out that Matthew was dead, a message sent from HC member Faith. Brent's heart sank.

"No, No, No, No," he whispered to himself. He looked to his wife, and whispered, "She will not die in vain." He erased Owen's memory of the past few moments and took the SBIS and placed it on her and erased her memory of him telling her she had all her memory to the point where Owen entered. He replaced the hand interface equipment on Owen. He unlocked his door, knelt down beside him, and started yelling, "Owen! Owen!" He finally came to, and Brent was bent over him checking his pulse.

"What happened?" he asked as he reached for the back of his head.

"Something happened: my guess is that there was a short in the circuit. You looked like you were jolted and then you fell backwards and hit your head," Brent told him. "Violet is fine. Her vitals are normal. Are you alright? How do you feel?"

"I am alright," he struggled to stand up and Brent tried to help him, but Owen thrust his hand away. "Good job, Brent of Generation 43. Continue on," he said as wobbled out the door. After the door shut, Brent went to the computer and inputted the scenario into the Historian's eyes. Walking over to Violet, he unhooked all the equipment, and stroked her hand and her cheek until she woke.

"Did he do anything?" she asked still groggy from the medicine.

"No, all your memory is still there," he smiled. He leaned down and kissed her on her forehead.

"I need to tell you something," he told her. She looked up at him with wary eyes. "Matthew was exiled this morning. Faith saw him die."

"What are we going to do?" Violet asked.

"Should we all die in vain? We are helpless without Matthew," Brent said.

"I'm not letting Mary die alone on the surface," Violet insisted.

"Would you rather have all of us die on the surface?" Brent asked.

"I would rather be able to sleep at night knowing I didn't let my best friend die for nothing. Brent, I have chosen what I want for me. Like Mary said, you have to choose your own life and what you want to be remembered for when you die," Violet told him. "I'm following through with our plan. We are genetically superior. We can do this with or without Matthew."

"If that is what you want, I want it also," Brent whispered as he helped her sit up.

"What about the others? They are not all assigned to me. Their memories will be erased. Matthew was the one who was supposed to give them their memories back. Is it just going to be you and me following through with the plan?" Brent asked her.

"If that's the way it will turn out, then yes," she responded with no blink in her eye.

"Alright, Vi," he responded. He escorted her out and the next person came in.

It was Josh of Generation 43, an engineer. Instead of telling him he needed a DNA-R and DNA-B because he was the surface, he asked him a question as he would ask all of his patients that day: "Do you want to remember what happened today?" Most of them, including Josh, answered "Yes".

If they answered yes, he told them they could never repeat what he was about to tell them to anyone. He went over to the hidden safe, deactivated the protective shield and it appeared in the wall. He pulled out the transmitter he extracted from Mary's leg.

He began by saying, "The SOL is not what it seems. Mary was the first to find this out. Every one of us is injected with one of these transmitters at birth, so that the Historian can keep track of us: where we are, who we are talking to, the surroundings of our environment. He can look into your life at any time of any day." By this time, the person sitting on the bed looked utterly shocked. "She took hers out, or rather I did because she asked me to. She then was taken by the HC and her memory was supposed to be erased. However, Matthew decided it was time for someone to know. He left her memory intact and implanted her with a modified transmitter, so he could help her learn more. That is probably why he was left on the surface as well." Then Brent would ask, "Do you want me to continue, or do you want me to erase your memory of events you've learned today?"

All of them would say, "Continue, please!"

He would tell them of the HC's plan to keep them all as slaves. He told them of the one so long ago and how history was repeating itself. He told them about the erased work done by previous generations. He told them of the clones on Level Base, and their purpose in their plan.

At this point, they would ask, "What are we supposed to do? Follow Mary to our deaths?"

He answered them by telling of Ana of Generation 39's plan. Then he told them of their plan to retake the SOL and discontinue the cloning of the RMH. He would tell them that since Matthew is no longer with them, it changed things. Their plan would take longer to complete, but it would be completed nonetheless. He asked them if they wanted to live for the freedom Mary described.

Most of them said yes, but a few answered no, that their life was better here as a slave than on the surface with nothing. However, they promised they would not tell anyone of their plan, and left acting like they had a headache.

Brent only erased two memories out of the thirty-seven SOL dwellers he saw that day. Out of the thirty-five that kept their memories, thirty-one wanted out of their slavery.

Violet exited the HP office and ran into Michael. She whispered into his ear, "Matthew is dead. Turn around and go back to your LQ if you want to keep your memories."

Michael looked down and off into the distance at the news. He stared into Violet's eyes. He was thinking about whether or not he should. He began to walk toward the HP office.

Violet suddenly grabbed his arm and yanked him back. Her eyes told him everything. She whispered under her breath, "We are all in this together. Don't give up and leave Mary to die."

He pulled his arm away, and glared at her. He knew she was right, but the pain in his body and in his heart needed his pride so he could get through the night. Without saying a word, he sulked silently back to his LQ.

Violet followed him at a distance. She told Katy and Rhome who were coming off the transporter. They all turned and rode the transporter back to Level Three. Michael was already in his LQ. The three of them whispered amongst themselves.

"What do we do?" Katy asked.

"We go on as planned," Violet answered.

"But how, with Matthew gone and Michael out of it?" Rhome asked.

"We will figure out a way," Violet said. "First, we cannot do anything for Matthew. He is gone. Michael, we can help. Rhome, go and talk to him," Violet ordered.

"I don't know what to say," Rhome confessed.

"Fine, I'll go," Violet said. "Katy, you are the BI expert. Find a way to send in a bot that will send Brent a message saying to cover our tracks for now. He is in the system. He can create a scenario that we all went to see him for our...DNA-R and B," she said as she rolled her eyes.

"Alright, I'm on it," Katy said as she turned and walked towards the transporter.

"Rhome, do you remember that hormone imbalancer creation Mary told us about a long time ago?" Violet asked.

"Yes," Rhome said as someone passed by and nodded.

"Did Matthew send the instructions to you for you to make it?"

"Yes," Rhome replied. "I'm on it." He turned to leave. She grabbed his shoulder.

"Remember, we only have three days," she told him.

"I know," he said as he peered back over his shoulder.

Violet released him, and went and knocked on Michael's door. In silence, the door opened. Michael sat on the sleeping cot holding a bottle of Jumyoo in his hands. Seeing this, Violet quickly stepped inside, shut and locked the LQ door.

"Michael, I am so sorry," she began as she turned to face him. He just looked blankly at the floor. She walked up to him and gently took the Jumyoo from his hands. "What are you doing with this?" she asked.

"Trying to make the pain go away," he replied.

"It can't heal heartache," she said as she touched his shoulder.

"I know. I just can't believe I let her be taken like that," he said as his face grimaced.

"You will find her. We just need to follow through with this plan that you helped us come up with," Violet urged him. "I know it's hard, but this was the plan."

"Matthew's dead. How is this supposed to work now?" Michael asked. "We can't even talk to each other without someone going in and overriding the system and hoping the Historian is not watching us in real time."

"No, but that's where we just have to have a little faith," Violet responded.

"A little faith has gotten us nowhere!" Michael yelled at her.

"Michael! A little faith has gotten us progress with which success will follow if we go through with our plan!" She yelled back.

A knock came at the door. "Computer, who is at the door?" Michael asked.

"Rachel of Generation 43 and Blake of Generation 43," the computer responded.

"Open the door," he commanded. Rachel and Blake slid in.

"We could hear you from out there," Rachel said. After some moments of awkward silence, she continued, "We received word that Matthew is no longer with us."

"Yes, it's true," Violet said.

"Well for some good news: Rhome is working on the hormone imbalancers. Katy is working on the bots. I received the chemical formula for paralysis from Rhome while he was working in CD, and have finished a weapon to disburse it," Rachel informed them.

"And I am almost done working on a portable device to help us recreate the Jumyoo when we go to the surface," Blake inputted.

"Has anyone talked to Jenna and Shawn?" Violet asked.

"Shawn just finished with the formula for visual manipulation, and now he is working on expanding on Michael's invention of the OXYmass," Rachel responded.

"What is Jenna doing?" Michael piped in.

"Jenna is trying to recreate a portable SD shell. She has made a lot of progress, but it still not complete," Blake replied. After a few moments of pause, he continued, "All of Mary's records are in the archives Matthew kept. One of us is going to have to go in and obtain them to distribute."

"I will go," Michael said.

"But Michael, you are working on creating the Jumyoo in a pill form. When will you go?" Rachel said. "It is hard enough to work when we can in the hour of sleep."

"I can. I will. I have the best access point to the LOH," Michael said as he looked to the wall.

"Is all the Jumyoo and past work in there?" Blake asked.

"Yes, and Brent has copies in his safe," Michael responded. "Who will stay and fulfill Matthew's job?" he asked after another few moments of silence.

No one responded. "We will figure it out when the time comes," Violet replied.

"Violet, what are you doing?" Blake asked her changing the subject.

"Right now, I'm trying to figure out why we are so behind. I thought everything was supposed to be done when Mary went to the surface. We have three days, three days!" she sighed. "I," she began as she breathed out, "have created all the topical maps we need, and also took Mary's plans and expanded on them to create a fortress and other things we'll need for our life on the surface."

"Well, it sounds to me that everything is in order just a day or two behind. We can do this," Rachel said.

"But Mary is up there in the dark by herself. Everything should be done!" Violet yelled at her.

"Violet breathe. Everyone just take an extra dose of Jumyoo tonight, and we will work until the wakeup call. Rhome is making the hormone imbalancer as we speak, and Brent can cover us from his office," Rachel said.

"Tell the others," Violet ordered as she took in a deep breath. Rachel nodded, and turned to leave. She stopped and placed her hand on Michael's other shoulder.

"Michael, we will find her. We will find her in time," she whispered to him.

Rachel and Blake turned and swiftly left Michael's LQ. Violet looked at him. "Don't do anything stupid," she said as she smiled. He looked up and half-heartedly smiled back. She left him alone. He went over to the computer in the wall and used his last RQ tokens for the day. The darkness encased him as he lay on his sleeping cot shedding tears of guilt.

***

The cold winds whipped about him as he lay on the ground. Hours, maybe even days had passed. Matthew looked up groggily. In the distance he saw the illumination of the SD.

"It must be a workday," he grumbled under his breath. He felt his stomach and the crusty blood where the open wound once was. He tried to stand but fell blindly back into the black dirt. The blood in his fingers almost quit circulating. He couldn't feel his face, not even stinging pin pricks. He began to crawl towards the light, and tried to send signals to the others that he was still alive.

Reaching the huge dome, he pulled himself up and opened the SD door. Slipping through the crowd, he fell into the transporter. "Level Base," he told it as he sat in the corner with his back helplessly leaned against the transporter wall. He could see their thoughts now.

I am alive. I have already made plans to set up my quarters on Level Base. Everything is already there, he told them. Overriding the access point through his BIS, Matthew entered Level Base. In pitch blackness he found his way to the back room in the corner, which he had created specifically for this occasion. The lights turned on, and he saw to his dismay, the clones were gone. In their place were tiny fetuses growing again. The container labeled Damingin still had the crack in it from when Mary first discovered him.

They've released the clones, Matthew informed the others.

Michael was on the surface when he received this transmission. He looked up and into the darkness of the surface. "Mary," he mouthed. Matthew read his thoughts, and responded, *Michael, it is not yet time. She will be fine. We need to protect what we already have. Stay here and we will follow the plan. Have patience, my son, patience. I have everything down here in Level Base. I am filing Mary's records as we speak. Finish your mission, Michael.*

Michael stepped back towards his work station, and looked back at his work: an equation he had already figured out ages ago.

Chapter 7

A PRECARIOUS ENCOUNTER

Travis violently shoved Mary off the hovercraft. "Die here, like the rest," he snarled at her.

"I will survive, and I will free the SOL from you," Mary snapped back.

"Try your best. You'll be dead by tonight," Travis snickered.

Mary saw Matthew, in the back of the hovercraft, drop a few things on the ground.

I'm leaving a few things that will help you survive. Search for the Statue of Liberty. Remember your mission: build a dwelling for those leaving the SOL in the future.

Thank you, Matthew. Please don't take too long rallying the others, Mary pleaded.

The light coming from beneath the hovercraft began to dim as the craft traveled further and further away. Mary tried to run after it and kick it, but she missed and fell to her knee. Travis laughed his bold laugh. Hunter's eyes pierced through the darkness.

"You can't keep them as slaves forever!" she yelled with all her might.

"We have and we will, Mary of Generation 43!" Travis yelled back as Mary stood up and watched the hovercraft vanish into a small pin prick on the horizon. Alone in blackness, the cold winds whipped around her face, and the warmth in her hands disappeared.

She dropped to the ground trying to feel for the items Matthew dropped. Darkness encased her. She finally found the spot where the items lay. There was what felt like an atom gun and holder, her workbag and light pin. She flicked the light pin on, and it brightly illuminated her surroundings. Holding the light pin in her mouth, she quickly adjusted the holder to where it would strap to her leg and after rummaging through her workbag, she attached it to the inside of her uniform.

She surveyed the land. Nothingness was all around her, so she began to walk in the opposite direction of the hovercraft like Matthew had told her to. *Dead ahead,* he instructed, *dwelled the Statue of Liberty.*

After seemingly hours of endless walking, she came to a place unlike she had ever seen before. A great wall of bones, mud, and stone stood in front of her. There were gaps in between and through the wall like someone or something had broken through at many different points. Swallowing her fear, she firmly placed her hand on her atom gun, and hoisted herself into one of the holes.

Crawling deeper into the crusted like substance, the blackness seemed to go on and on. She held on to her light pin for dear life as she shined it in front of her.

She heard a noise and snapped her head to the left. A half decayed skull silently screamed at her from within the grave that it lay. Her light cast shadows upon its once living face.

"It's dead," she whispered to herself as she calmed her breathing and removed her hand from her mouth. Facing the unknown, she kept crawling forward, until she came to the end of the small tunnel. She heard rustling up above and turned and shined the light up in the air, but all there she could see were old and forgotten weapons dangling over the edge of the wall. Her heart pounded faster, as she slowly turned back around to an empty wasteland.

"Nothing to hide behind, and nothing to take cover with," she softly said as she dimmed her light and slowly made her way through the dirt and mud.

Hours upon hours passed until she could finally look into the distance with her light pin and saw tall towers that at least once stood tall and were now bent over from the atrophy of time.

"Dead ahead," she whispered to herself. Taking a deep breath, she started in on the old city. She lowered her light even more thinking that maybe the RMH are attracted to light or that it would give away her position. "Don't stray from the path," she chattered through her teeth. Coldness began to sink into her face, but her uniform kept her body warm. She could barely make out the air she exhaled. The community was eerily quiet and dead. She saw something green come into sight at the far end of her light pin's reach. She jumped to hide behind a piece of building that had fallen centuries ago and turned out her light. Calming down her breathing, she realized it was pitch black.

Ana could not have survived through this, Mary thought. *How am I going to?* To calm her nerves, she began coming up with all the ways she could survive. *I am genetically superior. I have to live. I have my atom gun. I have a light pin. Maybe the RMH don't like the light. Maybe they will run away from me because I have a light. Maybe they will run toward me because I have something they have never seen before. I am small. I am fast. I can outrun them. If I do get attacked, I can just use my atom gun. I've never shot an atom gun, but hopefully it will work.* She worked up enough courage to come out from behind the fallen piece of building. She turned her light pin to low and began to walk. *It's just dead ahead,* she thought reassuringly.

She heard a noise come from behind her.

She ran.

She slowed down once she reached another pathway and turned around pointing her light pin down the narrow passageway situated between two tall towers: nothing to be seen.

She lightly laughed at her being frightened so easily, but a pair of green beady eyes greeted her as she turned around. The RMH growled at her as it reached around Mary's neck and squeezed. The hard calloused flesh was even more horrible than she remembered in her lessons from the SOL so long ago. Panicking, Mary swung her left arm to jab at its eyes, but its third hand caught it just as she touched the soft green of its eyes. It blinked and stared her dead in the face. Its breath smelled of rotted flesh. Its teeth were sharpened and ready to devour something delicious.

Mary reached for her atom gun, but the RMH grabbed her arm and bit into the meaty flesh of her bicep.

Yelling in pain, Mary shocked the RMH enough to where it was enough to shake her left hand loose. She took her light pin and jabbed it into its neck.

Everything immediately disappeared into darkness except its glowing green eyes and the light pin's illumination coming from within the RMH's neck.

It howled in pain as its warm black blood sprayed onto Mary's face. It let go of her and she stumbled backwards gripping her crippled arm.

She pulled the atom gun from its holder with her good limb, aimed at its still glowing eyes and pulled the trigger as he lunged for her. She heard a whirring sound and then felt a zap in her arm. She saw the glowing eyes disappear into the darkness. A deep thud resounded in the ground.

She walked over to the light pin still illuminating from within the RMH's neck and pulled it out. She wiped off the blood with the dirt from the ground next to the place where the RMH's head should have been.

The adrenaline rushing through her body numbed her senses. Bleeding profusely, she didn't know what to do but stare at it. She kept walking.

"Dead ahead," she told herself over and over again. The light pin swung in her hand as she walked: the light bouncing with every step.

She began to feel dizzy and remembered her crippled arm.

"Stupid," she said referring to herself. She remembered her workbag, pulled it out and injected a dose of Jumyoo into her arm. She heard a noise come from the distance. She began to briskly walk away as another pair of beady eyes came forth from an adjacent passageway. It started towards her but then tripped over the dead body. Mary ran as fast as she could holding her bloody arm as she ran.

She got to high ground, pulled her atom gun from its holder, and turned around only to see nothing behind her. She shined her light pin back down onto the old city and could barely witness two RMH shadows fighting over the dead body.

She sighed a sigh of relief and continued on through the old city hiding behind every mound, corner or piece of metal or building she could find keeping her light low and to the ground.

Matthew, why didn't you give me the ability to see in the dark? She thought to him, but realizing he was probably too far away by now to be connected. *Why didn't we wait until I could get the visual manipulation serum? I thought that was the plan.*

Continuing forward, her arm numbed. The coldness began to sink to the inner depths of her head. The darkness commenced to take away her sanity.

"Michael, there are plenty of RMH here. The HC didn't lie to us about their number. I miss you, Michael. Matthew, take care of him please," Mary whispered to herself as she trudged on. "There's nothing here. Matthew lied to me," Mary said a little louder. She stopped suddenly and shot her light pin through the darkness all around her. "There is nothing here," she said a little louder than the last time. She had lost her sense of direction.

She felt alone and utterly helpless. She patted her atom gun. *Well not utterly helpless*, she thought.

"Which way was I going?" she asked herself. She shined the light on the ground around her, and assumed that the footprints in the dirt were hers. She continued on in the way they were traveling. Her head twitched from the cold. *The ground just won't stay still*, Mary thought. *If only the ground would stay still, I would be able to find the Statue of Liberty.* Mary's senses didn't tell her she needed another dose of Jumyoo to stay alive. She had lost blood in abundance and the air was getting thinner and dirtier. Mary coughed for the first time in her life. *I'm dying,* she told herself as she reached for her chest.

It had been four days since the hovercraft left her there to die. Four days without sleep or food or water draining the usefulness of the Jumyoo.

"Who's there?" she yelled out shining her light pin crazily around. Two green beady eyes were watching her from a distance hidden and out of Mary's line of sight.

"Show yourself!" She yelled out again. The red blood still dripped from her arm because the uniform was keeping her blood warm, inhibiting it from clotting. Her neck still aching from her attack prevented her from being able to turn her head completely. Her breath dissipated in front of her. "It's so…cold," she murmured through vibrating breaths.

Pressing on, she came to a building half in the ground. She clumsily stepped inside the long broken glass window. A table stood right there by the window, broken like everything else in this world. Mary sat down and leaned back against it. Her vision blurred. Her head bobbed. Her mind spaced in and out. Then in her left eye she could barely make out a thought process being sent to her.

Take Jumyoo. Take another dose of Jumyoo.

She pulled the workbag from inside her uniform and stabbed herself with the Jumyoo filled syringe. Then her eyes closed, and she passed out with the light pin shining forth from inside the ancient, abandoned office building.

She awoke to a RMH licking the blood off her arm with its long, green snake like tongue.

She screamed and grabbed her atom gun as its hands reached for her throat. She pulled the trigger, heard a whirring sound, and as he landed on top of the gun, she felt a zap in her arm. She witnessed the target of the aim, its chest, dissolve into a million pieces. It fell on her crushing her ribs. Mary couldn't breathe. She didn't know if it was the horrid stench of the RMH or its blood in the air or just from the sheer weight of the being. From the light of her light pin, she saw a brown and red mist hovering overhead.

Her arm stuck out through the hole the atom gun had created. Its face was so close. *It is not human,* she thought. *The HC was right. They are not human anymore.*

Using her bad arm, she pushed it up and off of her with several grunts and heaves. She had to slide her other arm out from underneath. Her light pin was dimming.

Being fully conscious, she took another dose of Jumyoo, and left her victim, knowing other RMH would smell the death and come running.

"I have to find this Statue of Liberty soon," she whispered to herself, "or I will be dead in a few days." She looked at the atom gun. "So few charges left," she reluctantly told herself. As she was walking, she suddenly stepped onto nothingness and fell down. She screamed, and grabbed for anything to keep from sliding down into whatever lay beneath. A metal pipe stuck out and she, by luck, grabbed it.

Hanging by this one metal pipe, she felt her holder loosen from the friction between her uniform and the dirt she had just slid down. She grabbed the atom gun from it with her bad arm.

She tried to dig her feet into the side of the wall. She held the light pin between her ring and pinky finger as she grasped the metal pipe with the same hand. She was losing grip of the light pin. The dirt kept sliding out from underneath her feet. She heard a noise.

"Not now," she whispered hopelessly. But as she listened more closely, she realized it was coming from below. She situated the handle of the atom gun in her mouth, grabbed the light pin from her hand and shone it down in to the pit. Only it wasn't a pit. It was an open tunnel with rushing water in it. She had never heard the sound of rushing water before, but somehow, she instinctively knew what it was.

Up ahead an old bridge still existed. "How do I get up from here to get to the bridge to go across?" Hanging in the air, she suddenly had an idea. Aiming the atom gun at the dirt in the wall, she thought about it again, but went ahead and pulled the trigger. The dirt in the wall dissipated into the air. A hole existed now. She swung her legs up into it and was able to crawl her way to the top.

She walked along the edge of the drop off towards the longstanding bridge. As she got closer, the more unsure she became of her chances of making it across. It was only supported by old cable wires and crumbling concrete. There were holes and cracks and missing pieces. The bridge that once stood tall now slouched and sighed, standing only with the support of the wind. She shined her light down the bridge's passageway. *Dead ahead,* she thought to herself.

She began to make her way across one slow, cautious step at a time. She noticed the bridge began to slant the further she went. All of the sudden her foot slipped and she fell. She lost grip of her light pin. She tried to catch it as it rolled down and off the side of the bridge. Her arm stuck through the old railing reaching down into the darkness. She watched the light in the water move farther and farther away.

Not believing what just happened, she blinked and held her breath in the complete darkness with her hand still outstretched toward the water below. She heard the rail creak. Tears ran down her face and followed the same path as her light pin.

She cautiously pushed herself up to the, what she figured to be, the center of the bridge's passageway. There she began to crawl towards the other end. Her hands reaching out and patting the ground before she placed her weight on it. Her eyes weren't adjusting to the darkness. She was blind prey.

She prayed to the God the SOL told her about, the one she had read about in the sacred text. *Please let me find it. Please let me get there. Please help the rest of the SOL to have an easier journey than me when they come. Please let…*her prayer cut off by a large thud several feet in front of her.

She looked up and saw two green beady eyes staring down at her. She reached for her atom gun, but it lunged on her too quickly. Its long nails pierced her chest.

"AHHHHHHHH!!!" Mary screamed in agony. It ripped open her uniform. She whacked it upside the head with her good arm. She could feel its nails slide out of her body as it fell.

Mary was lost in the darkness. She was on her feet now, but kept low to the ground, breathing heavily, holding her aching chest feeling the warm blood seep out of her body. She held onto her workbag and stuffed it deeper inside her uniform. Her eyes opened wide, but it would have been the same if her eyes were closed.

She heard something behind her. She turned quickly, but it was too late, the RMH had already jumped on her. Good for Mary, the bridge slanted and when she fell, she was able to kick him up and off of her. He started to slide down the bridge. All of the sudden, Mary felt an immense pain in her leg; the RMH had taken hold of her. Mary felt the bridge go out from underneath her. She reached up and grabbed something.

She was hanging in the air with an RMH attached to her leg. It began climbing up her body. *Where's my gun? Where's my weapon?* Mary began to panic. She kicked the RMH in the head. That slowed him down, but he was so heavy. She reached up with her bad arm and felt something; it was her gun half off the bridge. She grabbed it and aimed it down at the green beady eyes and pulled the trigger. The RMH had grabbed the gun. She heard the whirring sound. The RMH yanked her arm out of socket before she felt the zap.

Falling, the dead RMH took the gun with him as he slid off her arm and fell to the rushing water down below.

The pain was too much. It hurt to breathe. Mary didn't know how she was going to get back up on the bridge.

Her aching arms, her bleeding chest, her throbbing legs made it difficult to keep hanging on. Her only good limb was the arm that was hanging on to the - whatever it was that was keeping her from plummeting to a watery death.

She heard a large CRRREEEEEAAAAAKKKKK and felt whatever it was she was holding on to start to give way.

If you are there, help me. Don't let me die here.

Then she felt herself drop even though she was still holding on for dear life. She wasn't going straight down though; it was like she was swinging, but falling all at the same time. She closed her eyes, and then felt her body hit a wall. The air knocked itself out of her lungs, but no matter what, her hand was glued to the thing she was holding on to. Finally she realized she was on the other side of the bridge. She smiled as tears of joy, relief, anxiety, etc. fell down her face. She also realized it must have been the railing she was grabbing on to because she didn't slide off like if it had been a cable. She swung her arm up and grabbed on to the same rail she was holding on to with her other arm. The pain was excruciating. Mary let out the breath she had been holding along with a moan in pain. Her face winced as she dug her feet into the side of the wall, and began hoisting herself up along the railing.

She finally reached the top and threw her body up over the edge and groaned in pain writhing on her back as she wormed her way to a more firm place in the ground. Her chest rose and fell, rose and fell. She grabbed inside her uniform and pulled out the Jumyoo. She gave herself a large dose and replaced it within her uniform.

She lay there blinking back the welling tears. She was alive for now. She was weaponless and blind and crippled. She now possessed only one useful object, the Jumyoo.

Her feet dangled over the edge. *Sleep and eat!* Benjamin's words came to her. She pulled out her workbag again and gave herself another dose of Jumyoo. She figured by now, she'd be almost out of that as well. She could hear her heartbeat still beating strong and powerful just as it was bred to be. She rolled over and pulled herself along the ground with her good arm. She found a crevice in the ground and rolled inside. The cold didn't reach her as much in there. Before she knew it, she was asleep.

She awoke with a start. The fire dream had come to her again and it had warmed her body. Darkness surrounded her and her heat beat faster. She had forgotten where she was. Then it slowly came back to her.

Surveying around her, she looked for any green eyes. There were none. She silently thanked God, fate, destiny, good fortune, luck, and whatever else that came to mind. Inching forward, she found she was able to stand again. The Jumyoo was working and working quickly.

She stumbled through darkness. She felt as if she was climbing a steep hill. Breathing heavily, she pulled herself up to more darkness.

At least it's leveled out, she thought.

She stopped suddenly and sharply turned her head to the left. She held her breath.

Not again, she thought while turning her body to face the sounds coming toward her. Her breathing shaky, she placed her right hand on her thigh and felt an empty atom gun holder. She closed her eyes. There was no change in her surroundings. She opened them and saw six pairs of beady eyes approaching her. They began to come faster and faster. She held out her hand and leaned forward on her left foot.

She didn't know what else to do except yell "STOP!!!" She yelled it at the top of her lungs. They kept coming at her. *I am going to die this time.*

"STOP!!!!" She yelled again. *I have to stay alive. I must stay alive.*

She balled her right hand into a fist as the adrenaline rushed to her head. She felt something slither up her arm. She jumped back and swung her balled hand. Missing her target, she was helpless in the blackness.

"STOP!!" she yelled into the darkness surrounding her. The eyes were so close. She let out her breath she had been holding and quickly swallowed another. She could feel the warmth of their breath on her face and neck. She swung again, but one of them caught her good arm and broke it. Mary yelled in pain and dropped to the floor. "Please leave me in peace!!!" Mary yelled out again as one seized her leg. *I am going to die,* she thought desperately.

A hard, raspy voice grumbled, "Who are you?"

She stared this RMH in the eyes, not believing that they were able to speak.

"Answer me or die!" the voice roared.

Mary answered in a shaky voice, "I..am Mary...of the SOL...I left...I found out what they were doing to you."

She felt a hand around her throat. "Why should we believe you? Your kind takes us and mutilates our bodies. Your kind wants us all dead. I remember when your kind tried to act as if they wanted to help us. You lie. We are human. What are you?"

"I am human also," Mary responded with a weak voice as her toes barely touched the Earth.

"LIAR!" They all yelled in unison. "You are not human! You are weak and fragile and easy to break." The RMH brought Mary so close to him that she could see its harsh face from the illumination of his eyes.

"We are. A little over a thousand years ago, there was a nuclear war. There were one hundred human babies put in underground place to ensure the human's survival. They thought everyone was going to die, but you survived. I didn't know you still maintained your humanity. They lied to us."

"Just as you are lying to me," the RMH growled.

Mary felt its nails dig into her throat. Her warm blood began to slightly ooze from her warm flesh.

"No," Mary said as she gasped for the dirty air that enveloped her. "Your ancestors were like me." She tried to pry away the hand that held her. She could hear the others grunt.

"They told me that your kind travels alone," Mary said trying to tell them the obvious difference between what she was witnessing and what she was told. She felt its nails dig deeper into her throat.

"No, only the ones who want to kill us travel alone. They are deserters and ruthless," it grumbled. "Just like you. You are pathetic. We knew you were coming from when you first entered our territory. We spared you then because we were unsure of your intentions, but I see now, that you want to infiltrate our headquarters." It began to laugh a course and deep laugh at the helpless thing that it held its his hand which squeezed harder around Mary's neck.

"Please Ana wants me here," Mary said with her last available breath.

The RMH abruptly quit laughing and dropped Mary. She hit her head on the ground. Seeing nothing, she closed her eyes and passed out in a growing puddle of her own warm blood.

***

Mary's eyes slowly opened. Her vision distorted. She slowly blinked for a few moments trying to make out her surroundings. She could feel her chest heave and fall. Tilting her head to the side, she felt an immense pain shoot through her body. She moaned a little. A light came on from somewhere, and an old lady was seated to her left.

"So you are the one," the old lady whispered to herself. "Most would be dead by exsanguination. My Ben must have done a good job breeding you," she proudly said as she stroked her lamed left arm.

Mary couldn't put all the pieces together. She grabbed for her workbag.

"I already gave you my last dose of Jumyoo. You need to save yours."

"Ana?" Mary could only mouth her name.

"Yes, I am the forgotten Ana. I have been busy at work here rebuilding some of the old world with the other humans getting ready for the war that will partake in these desert fields."

"Other humans?" Mary asked in weak, fragile voice.

"You know them as the RMH, but they are very human. They survive. They fight and die for the things they love," She said as she stood up. "Just as we do…or did," she whispered in Mary's ear. Ana patted her shoulder. "Get some sleep and heal. I'll explain tomorrow."

So many things were running through Mary's head. *Matthew, where are you?* She thought missing her old friend. Somewhere far away and 900 feet below ground, Matthew received a partially processed thought. He could barely interpret it. *I am here Mary preparing the SOL. Be strong. Do not fail. You will not be alone. Michael and the others are on their way to you.* Matthew closed his eyes and opened them. Sitting on the HP table, Tara of Generation 43 looked up to him.

"Do you know what you must do?" Matthew asked him.

"I do," she responded.

Matthew injected the serum into her neck.

Mary awoke with a start.

"What's wrong?" Ana asked her.

"I had that dream again," Mary said. Her heart burned within her chest.

"The one about the fire?" she asked her.

"Yes, how did you know?" Mary said sitting up without any pain.

"You can take off your bandages now," Ana said and then to answer her question she replied, "I told Ben to make you have those dreams after you read a book from the Library of History. Is that what they are still calling it?"

"But how?" Mary asked ignoring her seemingly rhetorical question.

"He just put it into your genes to respond that way when you were exposed to anything from the Library of History," Ana explained.

"What do they mean?" Mary asked.

"Isn't it obvious?" Ana asked in response.

Mary stared blankly back at this aged woman.

"You are so young with so much left to learn," Ana shook her head and sat down next to Mary. "The SOL controls the fire that you and the scientists use. It is only there to aid in your learning and creation of objects. The fire there is small and can't do much damage. I saw the fires of the 1990s. They were large and uncontrolled by man. They did what they wanted. They broke free. Yes, much was dead after the fire died itself, but it left a new beginning for something else to grow in behind it. Something old is reborn."

"But that doesn't explain why I saw my friends, my family burning in the fire and not dying. That doesn't explain why this dark figure comes in and laughs at my pitiful attempts to save them. That doesn't explain why he always says 'Show me why they are worth saving' and walks away. That doesn't explain why I always wake up frightened with my chest wanting to explode," Mary retorted.

"Ah yes, but it does," Ana looked upon Mary with the wisdom she would never know. Ana put her arm on her shoulder, looked deep into her eyes. "But it does," she repeated. Ana left Mary alone with her thoughts.

"How is she?" Trangin asked Ana in his usual low, grumbling voice as she walked outside the Lady's crown into the darkness.

"She will be fine, Trangin," Ana answered him looking into his green eyes. "She has much to learn, but physically she will be fine."

"I forgot about her. It had been so long since you told us another was coming," Trangin said again. "I'm sorry, Ana, for almost killing her."

"You didn't almost kill her," Ana laughed a little to herself. "She was bred to be strong and resilient. When she is sleeping, I will take you in and you can see all the wounds she doesn't have any more. Her arm is almost like new. She is a bright one, too. She created the Jumyoo," Ana said with a prideful tone.

"Ah did she bring more?" Trangin asked his leader.

"Just what she was able to make. There is still a little left for us to try to recreate it. Have Jinmogen and the others returned with the equipment I asked for?"

"He is my youngest son, and the others are the sons and daughters of the twelve who protect you. They will return," Trangin said with a prideful tone in his harsh and old voice.

"I'm not questioning if they will return, Trangin. I am simply asking if they have returned," Ana said peacefully.

"No, Ana. They have not returned," Trangin said with his head slanted down.

"Mary is here now. Have Briscogi start phase II," Ana ordered.

Trangin, now old but still with the strength of four men, nodded. She lifted his chin and looked into his green illuminating eyes.

"Be proud of your children, Trangin. They will free you and their offspring just as Mary's offspring will free the SOL. Then we may be able to live peacefully alongside one another," Ana patted his shoulder. They sat in the darkness, one blind in the darkness, the other not. They knew they needed each other if their plan of old was to succeed.

Chapter 8
THE ORIGINS OF THE PACT

"You will not be able to suppress us any longer!" Ana exclaimed as she stood on the edge of the hovercraft facing the Head Council.

Mark of Generation 38 threw a punch at her, knocking his fist into the side of her face.

Ana tumbled off the hovercraft clutching her jaw. As she lay in the dirt, the cold winds blew against her.

She lifted her angry eyes to them.

"For six years, you betrayed our laws. Now you deserve to die," Mark of Generation 38 told her.

Matthew stood in the back and dropped a bottle of Jumyoo, a light pin, and an atom gun onto the ground. Ana was already bleeding from the punch she received from the HC member. Her hair falling in front of her face, she spat at them.

"Pathetic," the HC member said. Matthew looked at her and nodded, signaling he would carry on her plan back in the SOL.

The hovercraft left her there to die. All she could see was the pitch blackness that enclosed her. Ana crawled over to where the items lay.

She gave herself a dose that took up half the bottle and put the rest inside her uniform. She carried the atom gun in one hand and the light pin in the other. She began to run in the opposite direction of the hovercraft.

I'm not going to die. I will show you even if I die before its time, Ana thought to herself. *Right foot, Left foot, right foot, left foot,* she repeated to herself. *Come on Jumyoo, make me stronger; make my muscles young again. Make me run for longer. Make my lungs work harder.* She came to an old city. She didn't slow down, but just kept on running. Breathing heavy, heart racing, she knew she couldn't withstand an RMH attack without using more of her precious stash of

Jumyoo. Her knees began to ache. With every pound on the dirt, her feet felt more and more brittle. She had been running for two days.

She came to an old bridge. She fell to her knees. She couldn't go on. Her heart wanted to explode. She couldn't catch her breath. She fell to one hand, the other placed on her chest gripping her uniform. She wasn't aware of the green beady eyes coming towards her from behind.

Soon they surrounded her as she was coughing and trying to breathe in the thin, dirty air.

"Patience, Gringin," the RMH said to his brother: the last part of his name was said with a low growl deep in his throat. "We don't kill. We wait till they are already dead."

Ana looked up and with short breaths, she shined her dimming light pin on them. Shielding their eyes, they growled at her.

She raised her atom gun. "Leave me alone," she said gasping for air. Then she collapsed and blacked out.

The twelve young RMH looked at her wondering if she was dead or not. Trangin knelt down and wrapped his hand around her neck. "I feel a slight pulse. It's still alive," he announced to the group.

"What do we do with it?" Gringin asked his younger brother.

"We will take it to our cave and wait until it dies," Trangin answered. With one arm, he picked her up and threw her over his shoulder. Grab that thing!" he ordered Rhetti pointing to the atom gun. He picked up the light pin and flicked it off.

Rhetti retorted, "It was using it like a weapon. Are we sure we want to take it with us? What if it wakes up and kills us?"

"It is almost dead. It will not have the strength to even wake up," Trangin said in his deep, raspy voice.

Rhetti growled a low gurgle in the back of her throat. She picked it up. They all jumped, hopped, ran across the bridge toward their dwelling. A single RMH stood at the other side.

"Cross only if you give me the meat you carry or die," he growled at Trangin. Then he saw the others appear behind him. Trangin watched him as he cowered back into the crevice he called a cave. They all marched by the single RMH, glaring at him, disgusted that he dare threaten their fearless leader. They took the hill of dirt with five long strides.

Then in the distance, there it was, home sweet home. Trangin proudly carried Ana on his shoulder. His cousins and alliances growled in respect as he walked in with the others behind him. He threw her on the floor.

"What is it?" a young RMH asked poking at Ana's arm.

"I'm not sure, but it is not dead yet," Trangin announced to the gathering crowd.

"I have seen this before," Trangin's great grandfather spoke quietly in the back. The crowd made way for him to come closer to the thing. "When I was young, younger than you Trangin, one of these came and wore this exact thing," he said in a hard, aged voice pointing to Ana's uniform.

"Can we eat it?" Napti asked.

"It said he was human," he continued. They all looked upon him in disbelief, "He said more would be coming, but I never saw one again until now."

"What were they coming for?" Trangin asked.

"They were escaping. He told us this estranged story, but some of our kind went to help his people. They never came back."

"Then we should kill this one for what its ancestors did to our people!" Therti yelled and picked Ana up by the leg.

"No, he said it was those that were holding him and his people enslaved. I fear this one probably escaped as well."

Therti let go of her leg. "Then what do we do with it?" she asked in a cold hard voice.

"We give it life, and eat something else. I want to know what happened to our allies so long ago," the old RMH suggested.

"Why don't we eat you, old man!" a voice shouted out. At this Trangin jumped on top of the statue lady's withered nose, growled loudly and beat his chest.

"Show yourself!" he bellowed into the crowd.

"We're hungry, and you've brought us nothing to eat," a young RMH stepped forth.

"We don't eat our own kind," Gringin told him.

The young RMH flashed his sharp teeth.

Trangin jumped off the statue and ran towards him. "We took you in as one of us. Leave if you don't honor our code," Trangin growled as he got in his face.

"I will be full tonight," he sneered back. He turned and left the large group. He headed back towards the bridge, toward the city.

"He is a deserter!" Trangin yelled.

They all turned their backs to him as he sulked further and further away into the darkness.

Ana moaned and rolled over on her back.

Gringin knelt down and stared at this creature in the face mesmerized by the oddity of its features.

Trangin made his way back over to Ana. He looked at his great grandfather and asked in his usual husky voice, "Do you think she escaped or was one of the ones holding the rest as slaves? She was carrying that," he said pointing to the atom gun Rhetti still had in her hand. "And this," he said showing the light pin.

Rhetti threw it down. "It was defending itself," she said in its defense.

Ana's eyes slowly opened to the blackness that was around her. Gringin growled low in his throat. Ana gasped at the sound and froze. Trangin knelt down on the other side.

"Where did you come from?" he snarled at her.

"Who's there?" Ana asked in a small weak voice.

"Answer me you pitiful creature!" Trangin asked again louder and more forcefully.

"I am from the SOL," Ana replied helplessly.

"Why are you here?" Gringin asked.

"I discovered the truth about our world, and the Head Council sentenced me to death on the surface."

Trangin looked at his great grandfather for guidance.

"Why do you carry a weapon?" he asked in the gentlest voice he could muster.

"There are others who know and are silent for the time being. It is part of the plan. One of those gave it to me to protect myself, to stay alive," Ana answered.

"Why must you stay alive?" Trangin asked now curious about this strange race.

"There is another coming. I must stay alive and start what needs to be done," Ana answered. Her head hurt from being dropped and thrown so many times.

"What are you to do?" Gringin asked.

"Show your faces!" Ana screamed out in fear at the green glowing eyes surrounding her.

Gringin and Trangin looked at each other, then back at her.

"She's blind," Gringin assumed out loud.

"I'm not blind. Where is there light?" Ana retorted.

"What is light?" Gringin asked.

"Light so I can see," Ana said not sure how to describe light.

"No light," Trangin answered in a deep, unsympathetic voice.

"Where am I?" she asked knowing she was at the mercy of RMH.

"You are amongst the Ayngin tribe," Trangin said with pride.

"You are not like the RMH I have read about," Ana said to herself.

Napti cocked her head to the side hearing what she had said. "Who are the RMH?" she asked in a curious tone.

"That is the name the SOL gives you."

"Us? What are you weakling?" she snapped back.

"I am human," Ana responded.

"We are human too!" Napti yelled at her.

Trangin's great grandfather said in a gentle voice, "This is what the other said. They don't believe we are human. They think we are ravaging, selfish beings whose only law is the survival of the fittest."

Gringin looked up at him. "Yet sometimes we are just that," he said remembering back to the thousands he'd seen roaming by themselves killing whatever lies in their path. Ana put her hand to her head.

Trangin had knelt there quietly thinking about the things Ana had just conveyed.

"What is this plan you speak of?" he asked her.

It was too late. Ana's eyes rolled back and she passed out; the air was too thin. Gringin slid his hands underneath her head and legs. There he felt something hard and smooth on the back of Ana's head. "There is something on her head," he announced to Trangin as he picked her up. Trangin held her head in his hand.

"I don't know what this is, but I don't trust it or her," he said and let her head drop. "It is female?" he turned to his great grandfather.

"I would guess yes, she is female. The other I saw a long time ago was male. It looks different than him."

Gringin took her inside the statue's head which was warmer and what was called their cave. He laid her down on his dirt mound.

Linati, his mate, followed him inside. "What are you doing?" she asked.

"It is so small and weak. It can't survive here," he responded.

"Then we will have something to eat," she said.

"I don't think we should let it die. To me, it sounds like there is a race somewhere dying or needing help."

"What are they to you?"

"I don't know," he said as he slouched his already slouched shoulders. "Yes, I do," he said.

Linati approached her mate and rubbed his arm. "Yegi died because of me," he blurted out.

"Don't think of that. She was cut off from the tribe," she consoled him.

"Yegi was my sister," Gringin stood tall. "We left our old cave, and I thought she was with us. It was my responsibility to make sure she was with us."

"Gringin, that was years ago. Yegi is gone," Linati frankly said.

"This thing could be like Yegi, alone and fighting to survive, to find someone, to find something. But no one took care of Yegi. She died alone and in pain and fear."

"How do you know this thing is like Yegi?"

"I don't. It could be lying, but I will take care of it. It will be my responsibility if it is lying or telling the truth," Gringin announced as Trangin walked in.

"Gringin, my eldest brother, are you really taking responsibility for this thing?" he asked unsure of his intentions.

Linati let his arm drop and slowly walked over to the odd creature.

"I think we have to do something Trangin. It is a living thing. It isn't dead. I don't think it wants to die right now. It has something it has to do. It's still breathing. Look at it," he said pointing to Ana. "Its chest is fighting to breathe." Ana's chest struggled to inflate and harshly fell time and time again.

Linati glanced at the creature. "It does seem it wants to stay alive. It has something worth fighting for," she quietly inputted supporting her mate.

Trangin's great grandfather descended into their cave. "The human male that came so long ago said he had found something worth living for and dying for. He said he was exiled from his home for his knowledge of things unknown. He told us the ones who held him captive were cowards, not wanting the people to know the truth. He said he was discovered after he created his plan, but those who wanted to know truth would have to seek it. When he died years later, he said his life would not have been in vain. He didn't struggle to survive. He gave up his last breath with a hope in his people. This one," he said as he hobbled over to Ana, "wants to live for the same reason that man died. I assume she has a plan. She knows her life won't be in vain either."

"When the others didn't come back, what happened to him?"

"We questioned him, but he was so sorry. He told us it would be dangerous, but we didn't listen. We went there without a plan, without knowing how strong they really were. We looked at him, so weak and fragile thinking it wouldn't be that hard to free his people. Those who went never came back not because of this creature, but because of our premature actions without having any knowledge of the enemy."

Linati reached down with her third hand and brushed the hair from Ana's head. With her other hands she folded its arms.

After Trangin's great grandfather finished speaking, Linati turned to the others, stood up and said with a firm tone, "Then I suggest that we make a plan and help her people."

Trangin walked past Gringin and faced Linati. "Help it, but always assume it's lying to survive." He looked down at Ana with wary eyes. The others peered in from above.

"Trangin, what does it eat?" Linati asked. Trangin turned to his great grandfather for this answer.

"The man ate what we ate, but he had to build something called a fire to turn it brown so that he could eat it," the old RMH said to Linati.

Gringin interjected, "Then we need to go find some food to feed our tribe."

Trangin shot him an evil look. Linati agreed and said she would stay with the creature while the rest went to look for food. Gringin subtly nodded his head in appreciation.

The hunting party left, and Linati shooed the others away. Trangin's great grandfather was the only one to remain. He clumsily sat down by the dirt mound. Linati sat beside the creature.

"I don't know what Gringin will do if this creature dies. He will blame himself just as he blames himself for Yegi," Linati confided in him.

"I know these creatures need warmth to stay alive. Take some of the tribe and find some wood to bring back here. I will stay and make sure no one harms her," he assured Linati.

Linati nodded her head, and took the hill with one jump. She peered down at the creature and went on her way.

"In my old age, I have seen much," he said to the sleeping creature. "I have had many years to think about what happened so long ago. I can't help but think what a waste of life. You need to live so we can know what is going on in this world in which you live," he said as he looked at Ana's still closed eyes and long, hard breaths. "I want to know why they keep you captive."

Ana twitched in her sleep. "You need to live," he told her again. He gently leaned his old and tired back against the dirt mound and fell asleep.

***

Linati woke the old man with the sound of her dropping all different sizes of wood on the dirt and muddy ground in front of him.

"We found these. Is it enough?" she asked him.

"It looks like it," he responded as his hard leathery eyelids blinked once or twice.

"What do we do with it?"

He bent over the wood. "The man made this fire by digging a little hole and placing a piece of wood on top," he said as he dug a little hole. With his nails he carved out a placeholder for the second piece of wood. "Now you spin the wood quickly with your hands until the wood puts forth fire. Then you slowly add the other pieces of wood to make it last longer," he told her as he sat back.

She put her three hands on the piece of wood, and held the other piece down with her feet. Her strength rivaled that of three men of the old world. She spun it so hard and quickly that smoke came up instantaneously.

Linati jumped back in shock. "What is that?" she asked.

"The thing that comes before the fire," the old man responded. "Keep going, Linati." He hissed as he said the last part of her name.

Linati unsure of what else was going to come, she went back to the wood and began to spin faster. A little orange flame appeared.

Linati stopped as the sudden burst of light hurt her eyes. The old man shielded his eyes and bent over the fire and lightly blew into the dug hole. The fire grew a little with every gentle blow. He sat back again.

"Do we put her in it?" Linati asked.

"No, we move her by it. Do you feel the heat coming from it?"

"No," Linati responded. Her skin was too calloused by the cold to feel the warmth of the fire.

"Get another piece of wood and break it into smaller pieces and throw it in the hole," he ordered her. She did as she was told and then picked Ana up and placed her near the fire.

She sat back down next to her. "She seems to be breathing better," she observed aloud.

"So it seems," he answered.

"What's wrong with her?" Linati asked.

"I don't know, but just as we need sleep to heal, she needs it too," he said wisely.

"How is she human?" Linati asked.

"The male from long ago said there was a war. At that time we all looked like him, but the radiation from the war turned us into us, but some of them were put in an underground cave to live. He said they lied to him about us and our way of life."

"What are they telling them?" Linati asked with a curious undertone.

"That we are savage and selfish. We travel alone with no conscious. We are ravage animals playing the game of the survival of the fittest. They kill us and take us to their underground cave to show them how disgusting we are and how dangerous we are. They use us to scare his people into submission. Those who went to help his people went to talk with the leaders to show we are not that way, but as I've said before, they never came back."

Overhearing their conversation, Ana whispered into the dark, "They clone your kind and raise them to be that way, then let them loose on the surface."

It had been three days since she had fallen asleep.

"They intentionally set murderers and ravage beasts loose on the surface to validate the stories they tell us," she continued as her voice dwindled. Linati and the old RMH turned their eyes toward her. Ana saw the green pierce through the darkness and the light of the fire bounce off of their dark, ashen skin.

"But the real ones, you, are not like that at all. I would be dead and you would be full," Ana whispered again. She coughed a pitiful cough. "It's so dark here," she murmured as she gazed into the small fire.

"They clone us?" Linati asked. "What is clone?"

"They take and kill you. They extract your DNA and re-birth you. Only, clones don't have a conscience. They don't know right from wrong. Clones don't have souls. They are just machines doing what they are programmed to do," Ana whispered quietly. "They have cloned millions of you. They roam the surface killing off your kind. I guess that's the Head Council's intention. We are on the losing side of this war. I have a plan set in the SOL that will bring them to the surface, but I don't know what I'm going to do once they get here. I need your help."

Linati growled. "We helped your kind ages ago, and we were murdered. Why should we help you now?"

"Because if you don't, it will only be a matter of time until your tribe is wiped out and all those like you are dead," Ana said as she stared into the green eyes that stared back at her. "It might be another hundred years before that happens, but if we don't start now with our plans to counter their attack, it will be too late."

Linati turned to the fire. "How can two species so different work together?"

The old RMH gently spoke in his harsh, rash voice, "Linati, anyone can work together with the same goal in mind."

A large wave of noise came from outside. Many growls and grunts signified Trangin and the hunting party had come back with food.

"Linati go eat and then bring us back some," the old RMH asked Linati.

She nodded and briskly got up and left.

The old RMH turned to face Ana. "I believe your story. Throughout the years, I have seen less and less tribes of men. Instead, they travel alone and are ruthless, just as your Head Council tells you."

"But they have made it that way," Ana protested.

"I believe you just as I believed the man who came before you."

"What man?" Ana asked curiously.

"There was a man who wore the same thing as you, who said he came from a place called the SOL, and who told us of a deranged Head Council. He did not tell us about what they did to our kind. Now we know. Maybe he did not know."

"Will you help me?" Ana asked bluntly.

"I will try my best. There is a greater danger here to our kind as well. I will try to sway the others to believe in you as well," he answered.

"What is your name?" Ana sincerely asked.

"My name is Gringin. Every firstborn son is named after their father and every firstborn daughter is named after their mother. This keeps those who die in memory," he explained. "What do they call you?"

"I am Ana of Generation 39," she responded.

Linati slid down the dirt hill from the entrance with two pieces of meat in her hand. She handed one to Gringin and dropped the other into the fire. She reached in and grabbed it once it browned. The coldness had numbed her nerves. She did not feel the fire burn her skin as she reached in and handed the meat to Ana.

Ana dropped it into the dirt. "It's hot!" she exclaimed. She picked it up with her fingertips and blew on it until it cooled down. She looked at it. Through the light of the fire, she had never seen anything like this in all her life. "What is this?" Ana asked Linati.

"Some animal," she replied. "You have to eat or you will die."

Ana took it with both hands and bit into it. She had to rip the piece in her mouth from the rest of the piece with her teeth. She chomped her food until it was small enough to swallow. She didn't know what it was, but it was good, and she wanted more. She savagely bit into it again and again.

"She's hungry," Gringin said as he entered the cave. He walked up to his mate. "How is she doing?"

"Well. We need to talk. The entire tribe needs to decide on what we are going to do," Linati told her mate. She motioned to the old RMH, "Come, we need to tell the tribe."

All three left the cave while Ana lay near the fire being warmed and full.

They walked round the statue's head and approached Trangin. They told him what the creature had said.

"How can you be sure?"

His great, great grandfather, Gringin, answered him, "Because I believe her just as I believed the one who came to us years ago."

"If you believe it, then I believe it," he said as he turned to rally the tribe.

"Brothers, sisters: days ago I brought to you a creature, a creature who says it is human," he continued in a loud, bellowing and coarse voice, "That creature says her society is ruled by a Head Council who takes our kind and kills us only to remake us but in an evil way. They are the ones roaming the land and killing us slowly when we do not travel in numbers. She says there will be a time coming when we will no longer exist, and the Earth will be overrun by these evil imitations. She suggests we work together to build up our defenses and prepare for a day that we do not wish to see. She says there will be more like her coming but not for years and years. Do we believe her?"

There was silence amongst the tribe. Then Gringin, the old RMH, came forth. "I believe her. I believe in the past, and I believe in the future. A man like her came many years ago before most of you were born. He told us his people were held captive. This woman tells us the same thing only she gives us more of what has happened. I believe her story. We should unite now to save our grandchildren from the brutal and fatal forces that will present themselves in the future. We need to save ourselves from this Head Council. She knows the enemy. We do not. We know the land. She does not. Together we will be victorious!" He raised his old fist in the air in triumph. A loud growl filled the night air in agreement with the old man's words.

"We will let her heal, and then we will plan with her to create our defense against the Head Council," Trangin ordered. His brother Gringin slid away from the crowd and went to Ana's side.

"What is your name?" she asked him as his shadow from the fire fell upon her.

"My name is Gringin," he replied in his usual rough voice.

"You are the firstborn son," she assumed.

"Yes, I am. Ana? Are you the firstborn daughter?" he asked.

"No, where I come from, there is only one child per couple."

"A couple of what?" he asked.

"A couple: two mates," she responded with a smile. She could tell he tensed up with embarrassment as his shoulders rose and hugged his neck. He turned his face toward the ground.

Ana changed the subject. "What did they decide?"

"We are going to help save our people and yours," he replied with his shoulders relaxing. "But you have to heal first. Trangin, our leader will create a plan with you."

Linati entered the cave. "Gringin, let her sleep. She needs to heal. The rest of the tribe is inside full and sleeping. You need to sleep as well. You've been out hunting for days. You will need your strength for tomorrow."

Gringin nodded and he and Linati lay down on the other side of the dirt mound away from the fire.

"Linati?" Ana asked for her.

"Yes Ana?" the darkness responded.

"Is there ever light here?"

"No, the fire is the first time I have ever seen light. It hurts my eyes," she answered.

"Don't worry. The fire is dying anyways. Soon it'll be darkness again," Ana said with the slightest undertone of disappointment.

Ana watched as the fire slowly lingered to its last breaths of life until she closed her eyes and fell into another deep slumber.

Another three days passed when Ana finally woke again. She awakened feeling completely rejuvenated as if she were half her age.

Someone had relit the fire as shadows of the RMH were cast upon the walls of the cave. Linati and Gringin were still there waiting for her to wake up.

"Does your kind sleep long like you?" Gringin asked.

"No, I needed to heal, so that I can live long enough until the next human comes to the surface," she replied not giving away her most valuable and only possession: her half empty bottle of Jumyoo still tucked away beneath her uniform.

"Trangin has gone to find food with some others. When he gets back, he will meet with you to come up with a plan," Gringin informed her.

"Do they know this is a life-long commitment?" she asked referring to the tribe.

"Yes. We told them yesterday while you were sleeping," Gringin responded. "I told them I would protect you," he continued after a moment of silence.

"Protect me from what?" Ana asked.

"From whatever may befall us throughout the years. I assumed complete responsibility of you," he replied.

"Why would you do that?" Ana asked.

"Because I need to," he responded bluntly in his raspy voice.

"Here, we saved some for you." Linati said as she handed her a piece of meat, already browned.

"Thank you," Ana said as her lips quivered. She bit into it.

"Trangin is back!" Someone yelled from within the statue. It echoed all the way up to where Ana, Gringin and Linati stood. A mad rush of RMH dashed out both ends of the statue to meet the hands that have fed them through the years.

Trangin dropped the whatever-it-was on the ground, and headed toward the statue head.

"Trangin!" a voice called out from the crowd. He spun around.

"Who calls me?" he bellowed over the feasting.

"I want to come with you when you talk to Ana," Rhetti requested as she came forth.

He grunted; then motioned her to follow him. Ana saw them enter through the firelight.

Trangin walked straight up to Ana and asked, "What should we do?"

"We need to build up an army. We need to recruit all of your kind, and kill off the clones. Then we need to prepare for my kind to come to the surface. We need to develop a counter weapon against theirs. We need to recreate this," she said as she pulled the bottle of Jumyoo from her uniform.

"What is this?" Trangin asked gently taking the fragile bottle.

"The Japanese created it a millennia ago. They called it Jumyoo. It lengthens your life, heals you, or allows you to go days without food, water and sleep: a very valuable little resource. That little bit is all there is in the world," she answered.

"Hmm. Very rare," Trangin agreed with her. "How do we know who are the cloned humans?"

"I don't know. They are clones. Find the ones that kill without regard for life. Find the ones who been trained to do nothing but kill at all costs. I can't see in this darkness," she said as she looked around at the black shadows cast on the walls. "You will have to be the eyes in the field."

"We can't make those like us band together. Our tribe is shrinking. Some of them think they can survive easier by themselves. They leave and we never see or hear of them again. We need to have something that will keep us banded together for the length of this plan."

"Tell them it is for their survival. Tell them the truth," Ana said a little louder as her hands balled into fists.

"What is the truth?" he asked with distrust in his eyes and voice.

"I told you the truth!" she yelled at him.

He grabbed her around the neck and ran her to into the wall.

"You will not talk to me like that!" he growled at her.

"Trangin!" his brother, Gringin, roared.

"What is it?" Trangin grumbled deep in his throat as his eyes stared straight into Ana's eyes.

"Let her go," he snarled again.

"Who are you to command me?" he glared at his brother as he had walked up beside him.

"Let her go!" he bellowed in Trangin's face. "She is an equal in this matter. We need her if we are to survive!"

Trangin still held on to Ana's neck as Ana's toes barely touched the earth. He watched as she struggled to breathe.

A few moments passed.

"Let her go," Gringin said again with a low growl in the back of his throat.

"No," Trangin said matching the same low growl. The anger teemed in Gringin's face as he lunged toward Trangin knocking his grip off of Ana.

Shrieks of rage filled the space bringing the others to the cave's entrance. Linati pushed her way through the crowd of grunting beasts as rumors started to spread about the origin of the fight.

"Stop! Stop it! Please stop!" were all the words Ana could cry out. Tears ran down her face as she gently held her aching neck. She screamed in pain as the two fighting RMH got close to her and knocked into her leg.

Linati finally got through and yelled in the loudest voice Ana had ever heard, "STOP!!" There was a growling sound in the back of her throat as she looked at the two. Her face paled in the firelight as her fiery green eyes widened and her scowl voided.

Trangin had impaled his brother's side with his fingernails. Blood ran freely into the dirt. Gringin's eyes narrowed in pain. An anguished smile crossed his face.

Gringin held his brother's arm as he spit out the words, "I'm sorry. Trangin, I'm sorry for Yegi." He bowed his head as Trangin placed his other hand on his shoulder and put his forehead to Gringin's. His face winced. He still could not forgive him.

Linati walked over to her mate as the others watched in utter silence. Trangin slowly pulled out his hand. They could hear the slurping noise that Trangin's nails made as they slid out of his brother's body.

Linati grabbed Gringin as he fell to his knees. She cradled his head in her three arms. She moaned in pain as his eyes closed. She cried out again and again.

Trangin fell to his knees with his hand still dripping with his brother's blood. Ana crawled over to the RMH who lay barely alive, and pulled out her precious life-giving Jumyoo. She injected Gringin right in the wound. She had read about serious wounds in the Library of History and how to treat them. She put Linati's hand over the wound and told her to push on it so the blood would clot.

"Does anyone have any cloth? Towels? Linens?" Everyone stared back hopelessly. "Alcohol? Rum? Anything?!?" she yelled in desperation.

Noticing the light, Ana grabbed a piece of wood from the fire. "Hold his arms down!" She yelled at Linati. She removed her hand from Gringin's side, his black blood still running thick, and placed them on his arms to hold him down. Searing his wound, Gringin howled in pain and his muscles contracted. Taking short, quick breaths, his eyes rolled back into his head.

"What are you doing to him!" Linati yelled at Ana.

"I'm trying to save his life!" Ana screamed back.

The wound now looked like a tar pit upon his skin, but Gringin still took in life-giving air and breathed it out. The coolness of the air stung his side. He wanted to bring his hand to cover it, but Linati held him down with her mighty strength. Trangin still looked at the three in a daze, not believing he had almost killed his brother.

"He needs to sleep. His body needs to regenerate. With the serum I gave him, he will live only if he eats and sleeps," she told Linati and the others. Linati nodded and drug him over to the dirt mound. Then she lulled him to sleep with her deep, raspy singing.

The others went to lay down deep within the statue when Trangin's great grandfather shooed them away. He laid his hand to rest on his great grandson's shoulder.

"Trangin, he is your brother. You may see differently on things, and I know you haven't forgiven him yet, but he is your blood. You need each other to survive. You are always too skeptical of good things, and he is always too willing to accept them. Balance is key, Trangin. I hope he survives, or else, the world and our future may be at stake," the old man whispered in Trangin's ear.

At this, Trangin bowed his head, and as bad as he wanted to cry, he could not. The tears simply were not there.

The metal cave walls echoed the rumors back to where Trangin kneeled.

"He killed his own brother." "Why were they fighting?" "Gringin wanted Trangin's place as leader." "Trangin wanted to kill the creature." "They got in a fight over Yegi." "Who's Yegi?" "Yegi was their younger sister who was left behind."

Those were some of the rumors floating among the tribe. Trangin looked up, and saw his only family on the other side of the cave. Gringin's whimpering brought quieting from his mate. Ana sweating from her brow in the coldness, tore strips of her uniform to soak up the burned blood from his body. His great grandfather chanted some sort of old healing song as he placed his hand upon Gringin's head.

Trangin rose to his feet and silently sulked over to Gringin with his hand now stained with his blood.

Hours passed and his wound showed signs of healing, but he still paled in color as time went on.

Still another couple of hours passed and Trangin grabbed Gringin's hand at last. He opened his eyes barely and looked his brother in the eyes as Trangin told him he forgave him for Yegi.

Gringin grinned at Trangin.

"I'm sorry, Gringin. I never meant for this to happen."

"As do I," Gringin mumbled through the pain.

Ana leaned over and injected Gringin with another dose of Jumyoo. "He needs to sleep," she told Trangin.

Trangin's eyes found their way to hers. Their faces were so close they could feel each other's breath on their noses. Linati pushed them away.

"Let him sleep," she whispered.

***

Days passed and finally, Gringin awoke to the sweet aroma of decaying meat. His wound was fully healed and barely visible. He tore into the slab of meat that was set aside for him. The rumors died after his great grandfather went to set the story straight for the rest of the tribe. Trangin hadn't moved from Gringin's side, and Linati still cradled his body in her arms.

"We need to create a plan of action," he said as he chewed and swallowed.

"Gringin, we are basing our entire existence on the story of this creature who calls itself a human," Trangin retorted.

"What if she is right? Do you want your children to be slaughtered like animals?" Gringin snapped back.

"What if she is wrong? Do you want to risk your own life advancing an ulterior motive? What if her Head Council sent her here to gather all of us in one place so they can destroy us?" Trangin uttered.

"She saved my life, Trangin. Why would she want to kill us all but then save my life?" he asked.

"To make us believe her. Why would her Head Council want to kill us just to have more of those clones with no conscience roam the Earth? Where is the motive? They have their underground society. Why do they want us gone?"

"Because they know we would help their kind just like we are helped the man who came when Gringin was young like you, and just like we are helping Ana who came to us a few weeks ago," Gringin answered in a low voice. "They know that if they kill us off, the people who are exiled will indeed die and they can continue to be tyrants and suppress her people's will to live a meaningful life."

"And we live meaningful lives?" Trangin asked in a louder voice. Ana stirred in her sleep.

"Yes," Gringin answered softly.

"Why? All we do is eat, sleep, and hunt, and eat some more and try to survive in this blasted world that our ancestors left to us," Trangin said hopelessly as he threw a hand up in the air, stood up and paced around, head to the ground.

"I see much more in it than that," Gringin said as gently as he could. "We do eat, sleep, hunt, and survive, but we also have someone, our tribe, who protects us and knows our faults, but still loves us. Isn't love what keeps us going? Trying to maintain our humanity when the rest of everyone else just do what they need to survive?"

Trangin bowed his head and breathed deeply. "You're right." Gringin smiled and finished up his slab of meat. "Gringin, whatever Ana gave you is something we are going to need if we have to fight these Head Council pawns. I think I saw one, it attacked us: one against eleven, and it injured Rhetti and Therti before we killed it. They are strong, much stronger than us."

"Are Rhetti and Therti going to be ok?" Gringin asked.

"Yeah, Ana gave them a small dose of that stuff. They're sleeping it off," Trangin replied.

Gringin looked down at his own wound, now just what looked like a small scratch, and placed his hand over it. "How much of it is left?" he asked Trangin.

"Ana said just under a quarter," he answered. They both turned to look at Ana. "Does she know how to create it?"

"I don't know, but even if she did, I doubt she could up here without any of the materials she needs," Gringin said.

"She needed this fire, and we gave it to her. Maybe we could find the materials she needs to recreate it?" Trangin said with a little hope in his voice.

"Maybe," Gringin answered. "We'll ask her when she wakes."

"How are we going to band all of our kind together?" Trangin asked. "They don't listen. We can't provide for all of them. Another one of our tribe left yesterday. We are losing them."

Ana's eyes popped open as she heard Trangin talking to Gringin. Laying on her side with her arm under her head facing the wall, she lay still just listening.

"Trangin, we just need to present a united front. We all need to be on the same page with the same goal. If we have a purpose and can produce some sort of progress, they will stay."

"No one will stay if we can't find food. Our code prohibits us from eating our own kind. All we find when we go out hunting is our kind slaughtered. It's hard to find dead animals."

"Then maybe we will have to start killing our animals if we are to continue to survive," Gringin suggested. Trangin looked upon him in disgust. "Do you have a better solution?" he asked.

Trangin growled low in his throat and leaned his head on his head. "No," he answered.

"I know it goes against everything we stand for, but you did almost kill me, right?" Gringin said with a half laugh.

Trangin just looked at him, and didn't return the laugh. "It was an accident," he muttered as he slouched even lower and looked away from the fire.

An awkward silence filled the air between them. Ana lay with her eyes closed now in deep thought, wondering how they could carry this primal plan out.

"Trangin, I know," Gringin mumbled.

Another silence sat between them.

"Ana was saying something about that stuff. She said it allows you to go days without food and sleep or can heal you or can extend your life," Trangin said excitedly.

"If she can recreate it, then we don't need to hunt for food," Gringin said catching his drift.

Ana lay in the shadows doubting her ability to recreate the Jumyoo without the technology the SOL possessed. Then a thought crossed her mind. Maybe she couldn't recreate it, but maybe there was some Jumyoo still left in the hospitals and homes of the old world. She closed her eyes tight trying to remember everything she read about the old world. An image partially fragmented came into her mind: a map of New York City. She silenced Trangin's and Gringin's conversation, and focused in on this mental image: trying to zoom in and make out the labels next to major buildings to locate the nearest hospital.

She almost had a clear image, when Linati pushed her on the shoulder. "Trangin and Gringin want to talk with you," she muttered through her gaping vampire teeth.

Ana opened her eyes and sat up. Looking at the two brothers, she said, "I think I have a plan." They looked at each other and back, their green eyes fixed on her.

"A plan for what?" Gringin asked.

"A plan to keep everyone satisfied and healed when we fight the cloned RMH!" Ana exclaimed.

"What are the RMH?" Linati asked simultaneously as Trangin asked, "What is this plan?"

"The RMH are the clones of you," Ana answered not wanting to offend her newfound allies. "The plan is that the Jumyoo, this serum," she said holding it in the air, "was found in hospitals, nursing homes, residence homes, first aid kits, anywhere anyone was rich enough to buy it. I don't think I can remake it here, but if we go look for it, maybe there is still some left."

"Do you think it will still work a thousand years later?" Linati asked.

"I don't know, but I believe it is worth a try to at least find it."

"How are we going to test it?" Trangin asked. "I don't want to give our tribe false hope."

"Someone could cut themselves superficially, and inject the serum. If it doesn't work, then it doesn't cause any damage, and if it does, then we are ready to commence our original plan," Ana explained.

"What is our original plan?" Linati asked looking around at the three of them.

"We are going to rally all of our kind that remain and try to fight back against these clones, to retake our territory, and to save ourselves from a brutal genocide," Trangin answered.

"But Trangin, they are clones! Her Head Council will just make more," Linati said pointing at Ana. "We will be fighting against an endless army. How will we win?"

"We will kill them all!" Trangin shouted. "Then her Head Council will have to come up themselves to do their dirty job since their mindless clones do nothing but die!"

"Did you not see the weapon she carried?" Linati asked once again pointing to Ana. "They will slaughter us!" Linati cried out.

"They have superior weapons, but they cannot see in the dark. You know the land, and if all of their clones are dead, then they will have no one, unless, they manipulate the mindless humans that are underneath them to fight their war," Ana inputted.

"What was that, that weapon you carried?" Gringin asked.

"It is an atom gun. If you pull the trigger and once the pulse hits solid matter, it disjoints the molecular bonds, and hence the name, turns whatever it hits into singular unbounded atoms or puts it into a gaseous state," Ana explained.

"What are molecular bonds?" Gringin asked.

"Every person is made up of molecules which are bonded together, and within those molecules are atoms bonded together. It breaks those bonds, so in effect you are dismantled when the pulse from the gun hits you," Ana clarified.

Linati clutched her chest as a disgusted look crossed her face.

Trangin directed the subject of conversation back to the important details. "Where would we find these hospitals, homes, and whatever else you said?"

"I'm not sure. I was trying to remember a map I saw of New York City. It will tell us where the closest nursing homes, hospitals, and clinics are," Ana replied.

"I will assemble our tribe, and we will send out a search party to find this serum," Trangin said as he stood up.

"I will have to go with them. I am the only one who can tell what it looks like," Ana said.

"But you cannot see in the dark," Trangin retorted.

"I can with fire," Ana said as her eyes drifted toward the flame.

"But what will happen if they are attacked and you die? You wouldn't have even seen it coming," Linati said in support of Trangin.

"I will go with her. I vowed to protect her, and I will," Gringin said as he stood up next to his brother.

"You will need your strength, Gringin. They will leave when you are fully healed. Now sleep," Trangin ordered. Gringin half-smiled, and slapped Trangin on the back.

"Whatever you say," Gringin said as he looked at his mildly burned side.

As Gringin went back to sleep with Linati by his side, Ana and Trangin went further into the statue to present their plan of survival to the tribe.

"Ayngin tribe, our kind is in great danger! We risk extinction unless we act now!" Trangin's voice echoed throughout their cave dwelling as Ana stared straight into the blackness filled with glowing green, beady eyes. Trangin pointed to her, and said, "Ana comes to us with help and knowledge to aid in our survival, but we must fight for our survival. She alone cannot save us. We must increase our number. We must find our lifeblood. We must have our purpose. Our purpose is to live and to survive!"

A loud roar of grunts, yells, cries and stomping indicated they agreed.

Trangin continued, "Our children will have to fight once they age. Their children may have to fight as well. This commitment is a life-long commitment. Some of us may die. Some of us may be scattered. Some of us may live without loved ones. I am telling you now, once we start to fight, we either fight until we die or the war is over, or we give up and let your fellow human become extinct. I will not make you fight, but if you choose not to help in anyway, then I ask you to stay out of our way."

A moment of silence filled the blackness that enveloped them. They looked around at their loved ones: brothers, sisters, mothers, fathers, sons, daughters, cousins, friends.

Then out of the crowd, one voice yelled, "I am with you until the end Trangin!"

Another voice followed, "As am I." Another loud uproar came along with it.

Trangin bellowed, "The Ayngin tribe will fight for humankind and ensure the survival of our species!"

The load roar got even louder, and Ana smiled into the darkness.

Trangin continued, "We will rest tonight, and tomorrow we will initiate our war for freedom!" He grabbed Ana's arm to turn her back. They walked to the head of the statue with the roar dying down behind them. A flicker of flame showed itself at the end of the tunnel.

"Do you think they will fight until the end?" Ana whispered to Trangin as they neared where Gringin lay.

"Ayngians will keep to their word," Trangin said proudly as his chest puffed.

"What did the tribe say?" Linati asked eagerly as they entered into the firelight.

"They are in agreement to fight for our survival. We will begin to plan tomorrow," Trangin informed Linati.

Gringin stirred in his sleep, and Linati placed her hand on his arm.

"Do you think this war is something we can win?" She asked unsure of the outcome.

"If we don't, we will die trying," Trangin answered her. "What else can we do?"

"Nothing. We must fight," Linati answered in response. She sat down, and as Trangin and Ana laid down to sleep, she gently placed her other hand upon her stomach. She looked to Gringin, then closed her eyes and tried to sleep.

Chapter 9
THE LONG WAR

The days turned into long weeks. The long weeks turned into longer months. The longer months turned into even longer years.

Every once in a while, Ana and her search team would find a supply of Jumyoo, and thankful it still worked, they used it sparingly. Gringin had gone with her, and he kept his word to protect her. They had also found clothes that still held together and canned food that may or may not still have been good. Ana found a pair of night vision goggles in a store they had dug down to find the entrance. Using their survival techniques and strategic instincts, they stockpiled their findings to carry back to the statue every year. Ana stayed with the other half of the team that continued searching for useful objects. They tracked themselves on where they went and drew a map in the dirt every chance they could to remember it and relay it back to those back home.

Rhetti led one of the teams to find humans of their kind to join their cause. Therti, Napti and Largein led the other teams. Little did they know, but the cloned RMH were recruiting their own kind as well.

Fifteen years later, they all finally returned. Trangin was married to Soonum, from the Nimum tribe. Ana had grown older along with Gringin and the others. Linati pushed forth from the crowd when they arrived.

"Gringin! Gringin!" she shouted.

He turned his head to the side and remembered her familiar voice. "Linati!" he bellowed.

She raced into his arms. Gringin led her by the hand to their old dwelling inside the statue's head. "There is someone I want you to meet!" she exclaimed.

Gringin's confusion made her laugh a little. "Briscogi!" she called. A bumbling little fourteen year old girl raced up to her mother.

"Yes?"

"Briscogi, I want you to meet your father," Linati said as she held his hand.

Gringin felt his insides melt away, and the worries of the present drift into nothingness as he gazed upon his own flesh and blood. "I am Gringin," he introduced himself.

"I know. I am Briscogi," she said. Gringin smiled, and she smiled back.

"Go help welcome the new people," Linati ordered, and Briscogi ran off.

"Why didn't you tell me?" Gringin asked Linati with all the sorrow in the world in his voice.

"I knew that if you found out I was pregnant when you left, you wouldn't have left. Ana needed you," Linati said.

"But I was gone for fifteen years!" Gringin exclaimed as his hand went to his head.

Linati brought his hand down and gently wrapped her fingers around his. "She loves you for what you did, I made sure she knew of her father," Linati explained.

"Why did you name her Briscogi and not Linati?" Gringin questioned her.

"I named her after your mother. Your older sister died young, leaving her name forgotten. It is my way of saying you mean more to me than anything in this world, and I will do anything to support you and our mission to save our kind," Linati firmly said as she squeezed his hands.

Gringin smiled, and caressed her face. "I love you," he whispered in his usual low raspy voice.

Linati smiled and said, "As I love you too." Hand in hand they walked out to meet all the newcomers.

Trangin announced they had quadrupled their original size, and the tribe now consisted of 7,236 committed members. The supply of Jumyoo kept everyone content but not feeling full. The feeling of hunger kept everyone frustrated, but at least no one was starving. The canned food made those who ate it sick, but at least no one died from it.

Ana and her search team found beds, guns, ammunition, clothes, wood, pipes, rope, glass, mirrors, night vision goggles, swords, grenades, hospital syringes and drugs, gauze, first aid kits, engines – very old, but maybe repairable, and other things of the sort.

No one touched the items the transportation team brought back, because no one knew how to use them or what they were for, so they left it sitting there for fifteen years until Ana got back.

She taught them how make concrete to expand the dwelling.

"Trangin!" She shouted out, and he came to her side. "Do you think all of us can fit inside the statue for now?"

"Yes," he said as he laughed.

"We will need to build some sort of fort," she said as she looked around to the city and the bridge. "We will take the fort's edge to the hill where the land drops to the river below."

"Very good," Trangin said nodding. "A place to defend a base of supply," he agreed. "I have an update from the field. We have recruited another tribe, the Yugom tribe, but they want to stay where they are."

"And where is that?" Ana asked.

"In the caves of the mountains," Trangin answered.

Ana tried to remember the map of New England she once saw. "That's great! If we need a counter attack, they will be there. We will need some sort of signal to display if we need help. Have your men come up with something and send a team out there to meet with them," Ana commanded.

"Yes, Ana," he said as he turned to leave.

"Wait, Trangin. One more thing. We need a team, a very large team of every able being, to start building the fort, our base," she said as she looked up to him.

"Yes," he growled as he looked down to her with pride.

They surrounded the statue with twenty foot walls of concrete defining their large territory. They built watch towers, six on each side. Fire would be their signal if they saw anyone coming. They found large pieces of solid steel from the buildings that had partially collapsed and used them for the one gigantic doorway opening up to New York City and closing out its enemies. They built armor and shields. They built wooden spears and metal swords, and Ana taught them how to shoot a gun and how to load it. She trained them to kill.

The lightless day was coming to an end, so Ana wrapped things up with her final class. "The clones will look like lost loved ones, but do not be fooled!" she warned. "They are not your loved ones, but imitations meant to kill you," she told her class for the day. "And what are you going to do to those soulless imitations?"

"Kill them!" they shouted in unison as they raised their right hands showing the pieces of red cloth tied around their arms signifying that they were human.

"Why do we kill them?" Ana yelled.

"To save our children!" they again shouted in unison.

Ana nodded as she said, "Go home, be with your family. Tomorrow, we will fight!"

Trangin and Gringin stood by her side in their armor ready for battle.

"Do you think we are ready?" Gringin asked her while the three of them walked back to the statue head.

"They are motivated. They are skilled. They have a purpose. They have something worth fighting for, and they know that. Yes, I believe we are ready," Ana confidently answered. Trangin nodded in unison.

"What is our first plan of action?" Gringin asked.

"We will send out units to purge the city. Then we will move into the mountains and down the river bank. We will build more concrete walls to define that area as our own. I'm not sure where the SOL is located, but we will find it," Ana paused. "and when we do, God help us. We are not ready to fight my kind. They will win," Ana said as she sighed deeply and held back tears.

"Are you for certain? We outnumber your kind greatly. Already we have 5,000 men in our tribe alone, not including the women and the children. We also have eleven other tribes who are committed to our mission. Our women are ready to fight and are our defenders of this home. We have fighters on both sides, and you said your SOL only has around three hundred? How will they win?" Trangin asked.

"I'm sure though that when that time comes, you and I will be long gone. Hopefully we can teach our children and students how to think and to innovate. That way, they will be able to create some sort of defense against the technology of the SOL," Ana said with a gleam of hope in her eyes. Trangin looked around uneasily, and Gringin's head bowed as she said those words.

"Don't tell the others. It will ruin their morale," she ordered.

"Yes, Ana," they said in unison.

"Go be with your mates tonight," Ana suggested. "It will be a long time until you see them again."

They smiled and Gringin placed his hand on her shoulder, stared into her eyes, and said, "Thank you."

"For what?" she replied to his kindness.

"Thank you for helping us," he said.

She smiled at him, and he left to be with Linati and his daughter, Briscogi.

Ana, still donning the uniform of the SOL underneath the clothes of the old world, stood atop the large dirt mound that helped support the concrete wall. She looked over the edge and saw little roaches roaming about in the city. "Tomorrow, all of you will die," she said to herself. Rhetti had first watch, as she met her coming up to the watch tower.

"Ana, do you think we can win this war?" Rhetti asked her.

"The war will be over with your children or your children's children. It will be up to them how much they want to live. But, the battles that will ensue during our lifetime, we will win," Ana answered.

Rhetti breathed a sigh of relief. "My son was ready to put on his father's armor and go with him tomorrow," she said with a partial laugh.

"He is only seven!" Ana exclaimed.

"Yes, but if the other children are like him, I have no doubt in my mind that we will win the war," Rhetti calmly said as she turned and went to the watch tower. Ana smiled and knew she was doing the right thing.

Once again no sun greeted the morning, just as it hadn't done in the past twenty years, or the past millennia for that matter.

Ana awoke and felt the dirty air through her nostrils and mouth. She looked to her left and there Gringin and Linati lay on their dirt mound. She looked to her right and there Trangin and Soonum lay on their dirt mound. She rolled off her metal spring bed they had found in the hospital.

She went to the statue's opening on the top of the lady's head, and looked out to the mud brick homes she had helped build.

She couldn't help but wonder how many clones inhabited the Earth. The numbers Trangin rattled off the day before seemed large to Ana but her SOL lessons told her there were at least a million, if not more, RMH left roaming the surface.

Was it another lie the SOL fed to her or where there that many more clones?

She suddenly felt a wave of weight fall upon her heart. She had to be strong for Trangin and Gringin and her army. She had to mask the doubt she had in her heart. She needed to believe in the positive outcome. She straightened her spine and rolled her shoulders back as she stared into the darkness around her.

"Today we fight back," she quietly whispered to herself.

"Today we will win," Gringin said as he came up behind her. Trangin followed.

"Today we will claim what is ours," Trangin assured them. They came to the statue's entrance and the three of them looked out onto the army they had built.

"Wake them," Ana ordered. Gringin took out a metal stick they had found and banged it against another scrap of metal hanging on a pole. A loud gong filled the air, and like magic, twenty-four thousand men lined up and faced the statue.

Trangin looked at her, and Ana asked him, "Do you want to say anything? They follow you."

Trangin rebutted her logic, "No, they follow you. They are willing to give their lives for you and your vision which is a better future for all of them. You must say something. You must make them want to fight. You must encourage them and assure them they will be victorious."

Ana took a deep breath.

"Ana, Trangin and I and our families are behind you. We will follow you to the end," Gringin whispered in her ear as a last boost of confidence before Ana began.

Ana turned to look at them, nodded, turned back around with a fire in her eyes, and began. "Men of the tribes who stand before me today, you are the protectors of the future, the avengers of the fallen and the victors of the present. You protect the future for your children. You protect the future of your race. You avenge those that have already fallen for the survival of your species. You avenge those that have been killed by those that were created to annihilate you. You avenge your loved ones lost. You fight with a passion the clones will never know. You fight with a greater might and force that the clones cannot beat. You fight with skill and precision that the clones cannot escape." She looked a few of them in the eyes, and continued in an overly loud bellowing voice, "Today, you will be victorious!"

A loud roar overcame the air that hovered above the fort. No one noticed the spy scrambling back across the old bridge. The four leaders came forth to Ana, Trangin and Gringin along with the signal bearers.

Ana told the leaders, "Today we will go out into the city. We will kill anyone who attacks us. We will look in every building, every crack, every crevice to find any living thing. If it is human, it can join us or stay out of our way. If it is clone, kill it. There are seven of us. The ocean is behind us. We can only go West and spread North and South from there. We will start as one unit and as we go deeper into the city, we'll split up. By the end of today, we will have retaken our territory. Tomorrow, we will build a border. The next day we will move forward from there. I will lead us out."

The others nodded in agreement, turned and went to assemble their battalions.

The women came out clad in armor and bow and arrows and took their places among the walls' watch towers. Linati and Soonum came to the statue's entrance. They had first shift.

"We will watch over you," Linati told Gringin as she gently brushed his face. Soonum did the same to Trangin. They left and made their way through the army camp to the walls.

Ana stepped outside the walls of the Fort of the Lady with an army behind her. She sent her archers to line the bridge near the entrance to make sure the army would have a safe entrance into the city. As they marched across, Ana looked into the daunting old city and thought she saw millions of green beady eyes. She blinked and they were gone. Her mind was playing tricks on her. She held up her hand to signal the troops to halt once they were across the bridge. She observed the eerie stillness in the front of the city. They marched onward as Gringin's battalion followed behind.

The utter silence unnerved Ana's army. She sensed them looking around and up at the buildings with a growing sense that something wasn't quite right. All of a sudden a rain of arrows fell upon Ana and her battalion. She screamed for them to get under cover. Some held their shields overhead. Some darted to the buildings but were met with the strong brute force of the cloned RMH army. Ana cried a yell of war and ran toward the building knowing the others would follow. She jumped into the old building and with her spear stabbed a RMH through the neck and catapulted herself inside. She landed inside and faced another line of RMH. She glanced back across the way. Half her battalion was in the other building, the other half was inside with her. A few lay dead in the street. She saw RMH fall from the rooftops with arrows in their chest.

She pulled out her gun, and let rain an array of fatal bullets into the enemy until it ran out of ammunition.

Pulling out her sword to defend herself, the rest of the ground clones rushed her. They were stronger than her, but she was quicker and more agile. She was sixty years of age, but she looked thirty and felt twenty. A RMH came down with a large cleaver, but Ana twirled underneath him and ran him through the back. As he fell to his knees, another RMH swung a bat-like piece of wood. Ana used the shield to block his blow. The smack sent shockwaves through her shoulder and arm. She countered with a side blow to the neck with her sword. Another threw a dagger to Ana's back, but one of hers blocked it with his shield. The RMH were falling one by one. The humans stood their ground. Gringin's battalion finally got to the place where the clones had rained arrows onto Ana. Linati, Soonum and the others had killed all the RMH archers that were sitting on the rooftops. Gringin's men helped push forward the battle line. They stormed the surrounding buildings and killed all the clones they could find.

Making their way further into the city, another small scrimmage ensued. Ana knew that no matter how powerful Linati and the others were, they could not protect them any longer. They were too far away. Trangin and the other four leaders had split up each going a different way. There were no signals for help. However, the humans came out victorious once again.

They left traces where they had been by leaving dead RMH bodies in their wake. Sometimes one of the resistance would cry out and drop down to their knees and hold in their arms a clone of someone they had lost long ago. Their close friends would have to pull them away and tell them that isn't who they thought it was. The person they knew was dead and this thing was just an imitation meant to trick those who loved the deceased in order to kill them. After friends' consolation, they would rise to their feet, look each one of their friends in the eyes and walk back towards the rest of their battalion.

Ana and Gringin were coming along a split in the way, and she knew they would have to part ways. A full day of fighting quickly brought exhaustion into the physical bodies of the men, but their hearts still burned with passion to avenge their brothers and sisters who had fallen that day and in the past.

They decided to camp out there. Ana was among the first to have watch duty. Armed with bow and arrow and a machine gun, she sat at the top of the building, looking out into the city.

"How many did you lose today?" Gringin asked as he came up to Ana.

"Seven," she answered softly. "You?"

"Four," he gently said.

"So it begins," Ana said as she stared off and up to the black sky.

"What?" Gringin asked perplexed.

"The casualty count," she answered still looking off to the sky. "Do you think the sun will ever shine down on this place again?"

"I hope not. We can't see in the light," Gringin said. Ana looked at him, and a moment of strange silence sat between them. "Eleven isn't a bad number for both of our armies," Gringin continued back on the original subject.

"It is when you are outnumbered," Ana whispered to herself.

"What do you mean? How many of them are there?" he asked with a little shake in is voice.

"I don't know, but we're not even half way through the city and already I estimate we've killed 4000 of them, with just our men. This is just one city. There are twelve tribes from the northeast region. We promised the other tribes we would secure their homeland before we disband. That was the deal, and we already lost eleven!" Ana stopped, looked down, and took a deep breath. "Have we prepared for the burial of our fallen?" Ana said softly as she looked up and into Gringin's eyes.

"Yes," he answered. Another strange silence stood between them. "Ana, this task may seem impossible, but you yourself said, 'we wouldn't win this war in our lifetimes.' We'll never know if our children win or lose, but we all stand behind you because you stand for our kind."

"We have to create something that will kill them off by the masses, and then we have to get to the root of the source, the Head Council. Now that last part, Gringin, is an impossible task. If we don't accomplish that task, we've doomed your race to an eternal war, and if they don't continue to fight back, then they will have doomed themselves to annihilation."

"So what you're telling me is that we can't win either way?" Gringin asked with only a shred of hope still clinging to his heart.

"I set into a motion a way we could win, but it will be generations before it comes to light. Then all we can do is hope that everyone follows through," she said with a sigh.

"Who is everyone?" Gringin asked.

"Those who are not born yet," she responded.

"You put our hope, our only hope in winning this war, in peoples not yet born?" Gringin asked with a deep set growl in the back of his throat.

"What was I supposed to do? It took us twenty years to build an army! How much longer to build weapons that will defeat the technology of the SOL? What would you have me do? Stay quiet, and let your kind die horrific deaths just so some soulless being can take over its likeness to kill the ones who loved them? Stay quiet, so that my kind can continue to kill your kind without even knowing it? Stay quiet, so that eventually your kind is exterminated and my kind is further enslaved to do the work of the Head

Council? What would you have me do?!" she yelled as she threw her hands up in the air.

Gringin stood up in silence. "You at least could have said something before we began all this and let us make our own decision."

"What would you have decided, Gringin?" Ana stared him in the eyes just as he did to her.

"I would have decided to fight," Gringin finally said.

"Should I ask the others also?" Ana inquired.

"No, you shouldn't. They knew. We all knew," Gringin answered. "I think everyone here had someone killed by the RMH. They would have decided the same thing as me."

"How do you know?" Ana asked.

Gringin sighed and looked down from the building from which they were. Across the way, another watchman waved to them. He waved back.

Finally he answered, "I can see it in their eyes."

***

Time stood still for those who were fighting: each day the same. Defending the fort were the wives and children. Some of the RMH snuck in behind the battlefield lines and tried to attack the Fort of the Lady, but the humans were too skilled with bow and arrow. Then the sudden realization that they were running out of supplies to make their arrows began to sink in. They resorted to using other supplies to make small concrete balls to use in sling shots. The children grew and provided the next generation.

Briscogi taught the new children to fight using spear, bow and arrow, sling shot, sword, and with things around them if they were to ever find themselves weaponless.

Ana found herself in that situation. It was the 1,206th battle, and the RMH were learning their fighting styles. Ana presumed that somewhere they were organizing with a leader named Damingin, but she couldn't figure out where they were headquartered.

She lay on the ground, chest heaving, head pounding, arms numbing. She watched as the RMH raised a large piece of metal over its head.

"DIE!!!" it yelled at her as it brought the metal down. Ana rolled out of the way and on to her feet. The RMH swung the metal at her, but she blocked it with her shield knocking her weak body down again. She scrambled out of the way as it tried to kill her. She threw dirt in its eyes. As it stumbled backwards, she picked up a little wood stick and rushed it, only shallowly piercing it through the ribs. Crying out in pain, it grabbed Ana's hair and head butted her. Ana staggered in place, her vision blurry and distorted. Losing her balance, she fell down and blacked out.

Out of the corner of his eye, Gringin saw Ana go down. He quickly killed the RMH he was fighting with a single wave of his blade and rushed over to help her. The RMH picked Ana up by the throat.

"You pathetic human," it growled between its teeth. Then it fell to its knees: a sword pierced through his back. Gringin caught Ana as she fell from the RMH's grip. He gently laid her down out of harm's way under a nearby log in the field.

Sword in hand, he stood up. Turning around, he rushed another RMH. It spun to face him; Gringin halted mid-run. There in front of him stood his long held guilt and source of rage against the clones.

"Yegi?" he asked breathlessly. A sudden immense shooting pain shocked his body. He looked down and coming forth from his chest was a spear head. He glanced up with blood starting to trickle from his mouth. Falling to his knees, Yegi approached him and whispered into his ear, "I'm not Yegi." Then it laughed an evil laugh as it ran him through with its sword.

He gasped for air. Then he looked deep into its eyes as he struggled to stand up.

"You're dying stupid human; stop trying to live. Just lie down and die," it haughtily laughed at him.

He grinned and suddenly stabbed Yegi's clone through the heart, and whispered in its ear before he forced its head into the ground, "Humans die standing up."

He painfully stood up long enough to watch it writhe in the dirt and die with its eyes open to him as he hovered above it. Then he looked around as his vision blurred the images he saw together. He saw his brothers, some falling and some pushing forward. Then gradually, the noises of war silenced, the smell of death disappeared, and the beat of his heart ceased. For the final time, his eyes closed to the darkness. His lifeless body collapsed and fell to the blood-stained, dirty ground.

Hours passed and the RMH finally retreated. Ana's eyes opened to darkness. She felt around her and found her night vision goggles. Putting them on, she saw the dead clone beside her. Wondering how it got that way, she looked up and surveyed her surroundings. The silence was frightening. An immense shooting and throbbing pain found itself in the core of her head. She reached up and felt blood on her forehead and on her lip.

Sitting up, she looked around for her men. As far as she could see, there were only bodies lying on the ground. A light fog had overcome the field on which they were fighting. She crawled around, looking for someone she knew, searching for someone who was still alive.

She came across Unik, a solider from another tribe. "Help me Ana," he mouthed to her. She pulled out her bottle of Jumyoo and injected him with some.

"Sleep," she said. "I'll come back for you." He nodded and closed his eyes while Ana went to find more survivors.

She only found a handful of her men who were still alive. She kept asking what happened and where were the others, but no one could answer her.

She approached one of her own who lay on his side with a spear in his back. He had the red cloth tied around his wrist to signify he was human. She crawled around to the other side of him and looked at his face. Then, she began to cry.

Placing her hand on his shoulder and her head on his head, she whispered, "Rest now, my friend. Rest now." Then she kissed his cold cheek, and stayed with his body a little while longer. "Rest now, my friend," she repeated as her tears frosted as they fell into the dirty cold ground.

Seven men came forth through the fog calling her and Gringin's name. They held the few Ana had found still alive in their arms. She dried her tears and yelled, "Over here!"

They found her and when they saw Gringin, they fell to their knees. Ana saw Unik with them. They couldn't help but cry out in agony, for one of their fearless leaders lay dead in front of them. "Gringin's dead," they whispered amongst each other.

They were there for a while, taking the spear out of his chest, wiping the blood off of his body, and trying to make his body match his peaceful face.

They carried him back to the place where they were camped. That night, moans and cries took the place of silence.

Ana sat by herself off on a log in the distance away from the camp somewhere remembering back twenty years ago when they decided to stick together instead of split. They had made so much progress since then. They had reached the mountains wiping clones off the face of the planet. They recruited even more tribes and added to their number. Then she remembered all the battles. Whispering to herself as a tear slid down her face, she said, "You saved my life so many times, and the one time you needed me, I was nowhere to be found." A horrific vengeance began to grow in Ana's heart against the clones, the murderous RMH.

The fog became thicker.

She saw six human silhouettes coming toward her from the opposite direction of the camp. Alert, Ana stood up, and placed her right hand on her sword.

"Who is your leader?" she yelled to see if they were friends or foes.

No answer. Ana pulled her sword from its sheath: tip to the ground.

She yelled again at the six figures, "Who are your leaders?"

No answer. She lifted her sword to a defensive position. They were too close. She grabbed a dagger out of her boot and held it in her left hand. She was too far away to call for help. Her shield lie broken back on the battlefield.

"There's no need for weapons, Ana, I presume?" one of them said in a deep husky voice. She looked at their wrists hoping there were strips of red cloth tied round them. There were none.

"Who are you?" Ana said low in the back of her throat. The six began to circle her and the log on which she had been sitting.

"I am Damingin," the one who spoke before said.

"Don't be a coward, come where I can see your face," Ana angrily challenged him.

"Harsh words, Ana," he said coming closer but motioning the others to stay where they were.

"Since all of your leaders are dead, we thought you might want to surrender, that way we won't have to slay you all tomorrow," Damingin said as he touched the tip of her sword. "Sharp," he sarcastically murmured. The others snickered.

"We will not surrender!" Ana yelled at him.

"Are you sure?" he growled showing her an atom gun tied around his waist. "You know we are just teasing you with this little scrimmage. We could kill all of you tonight, if we wanted." He paused. "Are you sure you don't want to admit defeat?"

Ana silenced her tongue as her face burned with hatred.

"Then I'm afraid we will have to kill you tomorrow," he said as he turned around.

"No. I will kill all of your army tomorrow, and I will build a wall with their bodies outlining the territories that we've won back from you!" Ana maliciously snarled.

He stopped and slightly peered over his shoulder. "I would like to see you try," he said as he motioned the others to leave with him.

"You will and you will see your army fall!" she called after him. He flicked his hand in the air as to say 'Go ahead and try.'

Anger seamed into Ana's face as she spun around and ran back to camp. Everyone looked hopeless, helpless, and defeated. They barely looked up as she ran through to Gringin's body.

She stood up on the large rock on which he was laid, and bellowed, "Armies of men! My brothers and sisters, I can't make the pain go away. The love and respect you had for Gringin is the same love and respect I had for him. He was a great leader, friend, and protector. Today we lost a great hero! Tomorrow we will avenge his death! Tomorrow we will unleash a hell never known before amongst his murderers!"

The men began to congregate together.

Ana continued, "Tomorrow we will slay the army of the enemy! Tomorrow we will build a wall with their bodies. Tomorrow they will see the territory we have won. Tomorrow they will brutally see at their dying breath that the humans are victorious!"

A loud roar filled the fog that enveloped the camp. Ana looked at them all as far as she could see, and raised her sword in the air.

"FOR GRINGIN!" she yelled.

"FOR GRINGIN!" her army yelled back.

She jumped off the rock, and four signal bearers lifted Gringin up and placed him into the grave they had dug.

Ana laid the only flag they had to symbolize their race on Gringin's face.

They began to cover him with earth.

Later, they all slept for the bloody day ahead. Ana knew they were all older and tired from fighting. She worried about the atom gun. They had run out of ammunition long ago, and had resorted to swords and arrows.

"No one should have to fight this long," she whispered to her lost friend as she closed her eyes to a restless sleep.

Eight hours later, she awoke to the same dark, blacken clouds. A northern watchman was sending a signal to Ana. A large army was coming their way:

not certain if friend or foe. Ana prayed it was friend since Damingin and his army were south of them.

Another signal came. Ana eagerly watched the signal bearer from across the way. They are friend. Ana ran across the camp and down the hill to meet them.

Briscogi was leading another army.

"Briscogi?" Ana gasped.

"Yes, Ana. We thought you could use some help," she smiled.

"I'm so glad to see you!" she exclaimed as she hugged her long ago friend. "Who is left back home?" Ana said out of breath.

"The next generation and my best student, my little brother, is teaching them everything you taught me," Briscogi responded.

"Little brother?" Ana asked confused.

"Gringin was born five months after you left twenty years ago," she replied.

"Did Gringin know?" Ana asked with a deep weight set upon her heart.

"No, Linati didn't want him to know until he came back. She made sure he knew of his father, just as with me," Briscogi answered.

"Where is Linati?" Ana asked looking for her amongst the army and trying to change the subject, she did not want to give her the bad news when she had a smile on her face.

"My mother died yesterday," Briscogi said. "We got word this morning."

"How?" Ana asked with her heart filling with sorrow.

"I don't know. They said she just grabbed her chest and fell over," Briscogi responded with her eyes downcast. "Where is Gringin?" she asked after a moment of silence.

Ana pulled her aside. "He died yesterday in battle."

Briscogi withdrew her eyes from Ana to the hill and saw the lone watchman. Blinking, she replied, "Then I suppose we will be avenging his death today?"

"Yes. If I die as well, you are to build the wall with the bodies of the RMH."

"Twenty years later and we finally accomplish what we were supposed to accomplish in one day. My father missed it by one day," she said.

Ana motioned to the army to follow them as they began walking up and over the hill.

"Have you any word from the others?" Ana asked.

"Trangin secured the northern front. They are building the wall as we speak. Agnu finally beat the last RMH in his area and is connecting his wall to Trangin's. Hirn is securing the western front with Yiwi. As of when I left, they were making preparations to build a wall."

"And Juio?" Ana asked as they reached the top of the hill.

"Juio died last year. Giurn took his place. They are fifty miles from here securing the southwest border. They haven't started a wall yet. We haven't heard from you in the past two years so we came to find you and resupply you with troops, food, and Jumyoo for the wounded."

"Thank you. I believe we will need your help on this day," Ana said remembering her vow she made to Damingin the night before.

"Where are your wounded?" Briscogi asked.

"On the second hill on the right," Ana said as she pointed her in the correct direction.

Briscogi turned around and motioned for the Jumyoo carriers to go to where the wounded were.

"How many men do you have? How long have you been marching? Do you and your army need rest?" Ana asked.

"I have thirteen thousand with me. Rhetti took another seven to help Giurn. We've only been up for two hours, we are ready when you are ready," Briscogi said with the same loyalty in her voice as her father.

"Go into camp and rest awhile. I'll take the first wave out. Come out when all your men have had two hours to rest," Ana ordered.

"Yes Ana," Briscogi answered. "Give the order," she told the nearby signal bearer.

Ana went to rustle up her troops and lead them out to victory.

Standing on the rock, she bellowed, "Today…we will avenge our brothers, our sisters, and all those who have died fighting for our race to continue to exist."

Her army began to breathe harder as their nostrils flared.

"Today…we have been joined with our brothers and sisters from home. Today…we will fight with our hearts ablaze. Today…we are invincible. Today…we will be victorious. Today…is the day that our enemy will fall!" she yelled with all her might into the crowd.

"Today they will fall!" her army roared back to her.

She raised her sword, turned, jumped off the rock and began to march toward their enemy's camp. Ten thousand soldiers loyally followed her. She glanced to her right. It just didn't seem the same without her friend next to her, but she continued onward unwavering in her step.

The cold breeze slightly sneaked in through Ana's old and worn uniform. Her body ached and her mind tired. She could feel the muscles in her arm holding her sword up start to shake, but she still kept her sword lifted high for her men and women who were fighting for their survival. The fog was lifting, as was the morale of the soldiers for this last battle.

In the distance she could make out several silhouettes. She lowered her sword. She stopped as the few silhouettes she saw blend into a dark line. Turning to her men, she knew they had found the headquarters of the enemy. She stared in the eyes of the men who made up the first line.

Raising her sword high, she yelled, "For Gringin!", turned and ran toward the enemy. Yells of war came behind her, and the ground shook as ten thousand men rushed into battle only to find they were severely outnumbered.

Ana swung high her sword and used her dagger for close attacks. Jumping in the midst of these imitations, she found her senses numbing in the cold. Sweat poured from her brow. She made a path for the others to follow. She didn't care if she killed them quick like she had in the past. She just wanted them to die for taking away her beloved friend. Hacking through the crowd, she glanced up and saw six silhouettes standing above on the hill.

"Damingin," she growled. He shot his atom gun into his own army as he looked in her direction with a large half smirked grin on his smug face.

Rushing toward the next RMH, she swung, and it was dead. She felt this new energy in her body and in her mind. This hatred for these disgusting things that want to take life away made her unstoppable. She saw one of her brothers go down, she raced toward the RMH, but it was too late as it stabbed him with a pointed stick over and over again. She jumped and plowed into the murderer with her dagger stabbing over and over again just as it had done to her fellow human. She comforted another fallen brother and bandaged his wounds. She gave him a dose of her Jumyoo hoping it would work. He fell asleep. She gently laid his head on the ground.

She crawled over to one of her men barely alive. She gave him some of her Jumyoo as well. She looked up and around, they were surrounded by their own.

She whispered to him, "Not a human dies today." He nodded and she pulled him on the other side of a log half buried in the ground. "I'll come back for you," she assured. "Sleep," she commanded.

She leapt over the log and ran toward the battle line.

Hours passed and the humans looked like the victors. Ana ran up the hill with her army. Damingin and the others were nowhere to be found, but on the other side of the hill lay another army of RMH.

She turned to her friends, her men, and looked each of them in the eyes in an unspoken agreement. Racing down the hill, they clashed into the front of the line. The few archers with arrows left sent soaring deadly darts into the air. In the distance, she could see the mountains.

Giurn and her army came up over the hilltop slaying the last RMH until they saw the massive army that lay on the other side. Giurn held her gun high and rushed the enemy with what was left of her army behind her. Ana saw six figures standing at the mouth of a cave. "Cowards!" she yelled and stabbed a RMH in the chest. Gunfire could be heard in the rising fog, then the clash of metal to metal.

She picked up a broken spear and threw with a thundering force into the enemy. They had them cornered. Giurn ran to Ana.

"You think we're putting a dent in their plans?" she asked with an out of breath laugh.

"Yes," Ana responded just as she killed another one. Giurn shot an arrow that whizzed past her helmet. A RMH in front of Ana fell, dead. "Thanks," she told Giurn.

"You going after Damingin?" Giurn asked her as she shot another fatal arrow.

"Yeah," Ana responded as she struck down another one.

"I'm going with you," Giurn told her. Ana nodded and they pushed forward into the enemy's dwindling front line never looking back.

Cutting into the heart of the RMH stronghold, they split Damingin's army in two. She saw he and the five others turn and run into the mountains.

"What are they afraid of?" Giurn asked sarcastically as they began to climb up the mountainside. Soon more of their men began to follow them as the enemy ground troops began to fade away.

Swinging up to the cliff, Ana hunched over and peered into the cave. Giurn followed her.

"It could be a trap," Ana warned. "They could have more hidden within the caves just as they had more hidden on the other side of the hill."

"I agree," she said in a low voice. Standing up, they looked like guardians into the cave's entrance. Their men began to appear behind them as they walked into the deep.

Peering around every corner and rock, they made their way deeper into the cave.

All of the sudden, Giurn heard a whizzing noise, then felt a deep thud within her stomach. Looking down, she saw an arrow extruding from her armor. She fell to her knees and Ana did the same while lunging at her to pull her behind a large rock. "Get down!" she yelled to the men behind her, then looked back to Giurn.

"It's not so bad," Giurn said staring at her wound and the blood on her hand.

"I'm going to pull it out. You apply pressure. I'll give you the rest of my Jumyoo," Ana said as she grasped the arrow.

"No, your life is more important than mine. I have a feeling you might need it within the hour. I'm fine. Go," Giurn whispered as she broke the arrow. Ana was left with the arrow's back in her hand. Ana looked deep into her eyes. "Go," she repeated.

"I'll come back for you," Ana said. "No one dies today." Ana put her hand on her shoulder. Giurn did the same.

"Go," she said again. Ana nodded and slid away behind the next available rock. The foul stench of clone came from within.

She picked up a smaller rock and sent it hurling. The echo of its land pulsated through the cave. Then she heard Giurn's voice behind her, "Go, I'll cover for you." Ana got up and ran as arrows went flying by. She pulled her dagger from her belt, leapt over a rock and landed on an archer's face. Looking up, she saw a sword coming down at her. Quickly, she rolled away and the sword hit the dead archer instead. Throwing her dagger, she killed the swordsman.

"Two down, four to go," she haughtily whispered to herself as she pulled the dagger from its neck and continued downward into the cave taking great, powerful strides full of confidence, revenge and abhorrence.

One lunged at her from behind a tall rock shooting surges from his atom gun at her. Ana held up her sword as the tip disintegrated into thin air. She grabbed a rock and hurled it at the next surge as she leapt forward. The rock disappeared into thin air, and as soon it was no more, so was the RMH with a broken sword and dagger running him through.

Ana picked up the atom gun and saw there were only two charges left. She had three more clones left to kill. Throwing away her now useless sword, she carried forward deeper inside the mountain, fearless and alone, atom gun in her right hand and dagger in her left. Her heart burdened with vengeance and her mind clouded by hatred. She had never felt her heart beat so much at once. She felt invincible as her breathing was calm and sweat ceased to pour from her brow. Her eyes narrowed and her stride lengthened.

She came to the very back of the cave in the mountain. She shot her atom gun towards the two guards that blocked the entrance of the small room while she was situated behind a rock. One surge took off one guard's leg. The second surge took out the chest of the other. The legless guard moaned and yelled in pain as his nails scratched the rock underneath him.

"Damingin," she whispered to herself, "today will be your last day and you will know that the humans will forever be victorious as the last of your army lies thrashing in pain in front of you." Ana quietly snuck around the rock and peered inside the back room over the half dead guard. There he was, standing facing the back wall, the dead end of the cave. He narrowed his eyes and smirked as he heard the fatal stab of his last guard.

"Oh the fearless Ana, the brave and courageous leader of man has come to kill me," he said as he turned to face her. She raised her dagger to throw with deadly force. "Except I shall not be the one to die," he growled as he pulled his atom gun from his belt and pulled the trigger. An intense and sudden, deep pain settled itself into what was left of Ana's shoulder just as she released the dagger that sailed into Damingin's chest. He looked down unwilling to notice the fact that he had been stabbed. The first time in forty years had he ever been wounded. He stumbled over to her as she lay looking blankly up at the cave's rocks hanging overhead. He knocked off her goggles and her vision went black. Damingin found her Jumyoo and used the rest of it on himself. He threw it away as Ana heard it in the distance smash against the cave walls. He slid out the dagger and let it fall as he clutched his chest and wiped the blood from his mouth. He sat down and leaned back against the rock, closed his eyes and tried to let the Jumyoo take over.

It seemed like hours passed as Ana drifted in and out of consciousness. Briscogi peered into the long tunnel as she stood at the entrance of the cave.

"Has anyone gone in after them?" she asked the men who still stood guard.

"Giurn and Ana went in a long time ago. We found Giurn half alive. She wasn't speaking clearly, but we sent troops around the mountain to find if any caves lead out the other way. They were in too deep for us to go in after them. We gave word to start finding the wounded, piling the dead RMH and burying our dead soldiers," Unik said as he pointed back down toward the battlefield.

Briscogi asked, "So no one went in to help Ana?"

"No," Unik said as he turned his eyes to the rocky ground.

Briscogi grabbed her blood-stained sword and flew down the tunnel as several others followed her. At the point when she came across the dead archer, she told half the men to stay put and guard this point in the cave. They went down a little further and came across the slaughtered sentry and she told the rest of her men to do the same. Only she and two others ventured forward.

They came to the back room in the cave and saw the two dead guards as they approached from behind the large rock.

Briscogi peered into the room and saw Ana laying on the floor and Damingin leaning against the back wall. She thought they were both dead. The three entered the room and went to Ana's side. Briscogi gave all of her Jumyoo to Ana and wrapped up her shoulder in the cloth she wore around her waist. Then they heard a whirring sound, looked back and saw the atom gun held in Damingin's hand. Briscogi looked to her left and saw that both of her soldiers lay dead in front her. She braced herself to leap out of the way when she saw him pull the trigger again, but this time, the gun just clicked. Her gaze upon him deepened as her eyes filled with rage. She picked up one of her fellow man's swords and walked with pride and strength in her step towards him.

"Those men were my friends," she whispered to him. "They will be the last of mankind you will ever murder," she growled as she walked closer with the two swords out on either side of her.

She crossed them and put the edges at his neck.

"You might have won today, human, but we are the RMH, and we will all be reborn. You cannot win; you can only die. Then we will kill your children, every...single...one of them!" Damingin yelled as he clutched his mortal wound. He glared at Briscogi with abhorrence in his eyes.

"Mankind's children will be ready for you and your creators," Briscogi snarled. "They will do to them, just as I do to you." With that, she pulled her swords apart as hard as she could as beads of sweat formed on her forehead. A thud and a roll signified the great Damingin was dead. She went over, picked up his head and walked back to Ana who struggled to sit up.

"Ana, here you are," Briscogi said as she put on her goggles for her. She fell back down as Briscogi caught her head before it hit the floor.

"I'm still alive?" Ana asked still light-headed and out of her sense of reality.

"Yes, Ana. Sleep for a little while. Gain your strength back," Briscogi answered her as she watched Ana's eyes close and her body still.

Hours passed. Ana woke to find her human soldiers dead at her side. "Damingin killed them," Briscogi said to her.

"I thought I killed Damingin," Ana said as she struggled to stand.

"We thought you did too. That is why we turned our backs to him. It was my fault. I should have made sure he was dead first," Briscogi said as she folded the hands of one of her friends. She bowed her head and closed his eyes. "I'm so sorry," she whispered.

Ana glanced in the direction of Damingin, "You killed him?"

"Yes," Briscogi answered.

"Thank you," Ana whispered to her. "Are you ready to build that wall?"

"Let's go build that wall," she replied.

Ana smiled, picked herself up and followed Briscogi out, but before they went into the line sight of their men, Briscogi handed Ana Damingin's head. "They follow you," she said.

"Briscogi, I'm getting old and I am wounded beyond repair," she said looking to her shoulder. "You will be the next leader of this army after I am gone. You and the offspring of the SOL will finish what was started. The men need to tell stories about you. They need to know the truth," Ana responded as she handed the head back to her.

"As you wish, my leader," Briscogi responded and took the head back.

They approached the first wave of guards and Ana told them to gather the dead and bring them outside to be buried.

They stepped outside the cave and Briscogi held high the head of Damingin. A roar of victory came over and up the mountain to the ears of Briscogi and Ana. The men who were on the same ledge as they, kneeled in reverence of their victorious leaders.

"We have won. We have won!" Briscogi shouted at the top of her lungs. "We have won this war. We are alive. Our brothers and sisters have not fallen in vain. They are here with us in spirit and in victory, for without them, for without their courage and selflessness, we would not be here, standing, alive and triumphant! This war is for those who have fallen by our side! This war is for those not yet born! This war has been for our survival!" Briscogi yelled as she thrust her sword upwards piercing the blackness as a small trickle of light gleamed on the blade.

Ana looked up and saw something she had never witnessed before and thought she would never witness in her lifetime: a small glimmer of the moon's shining light. Though as soon as it had appeared, it vanished with the cold winds. She smiled and looked out amongst the thousands of humans that were before her. *A good world can come again*, she thought as her eyes danced in the darkness.

***

They spent the next years burying their dead and building a massive wall that separated the human territory from the clones or the clones that would come in the future as they were all dead at that point in time; if only the plan had come into effect a little sooner.

Ana had estimated based on her knowledge from the Library of History that the humans controlled what was Eastern Canada in the old world to the Rocky Mountains and as far south as the northern border of Tennessee.

The next generation was born and learning to fight and think and learn. The found the old school of the old world, an institute of technology. They dug their way in and transferred everything back to the Fort of the Lady.

Ana lay in her hospital bed. Her left arm was practically useless. She had laid there many months seeing if the Jumyoo would regrow the top part of her shoulder, but sadly it only took the pain away. She had her arm wrapped up against the bottom of her ribcage.

In those months she dreamt of Benjamin. She would wake up with tears on her face. She longed to be with him. She felt the guilt well up inside of her as she realized this is the same pain she made Linati and the others endure. She hid her emotional agony from her friends and loyal soldiers. She was still a great leader, though now Briscogi had taken on her war leader persona. She taught the children everything she knew from engineering to information to mechanics to history to survival and to friendship, faith and loyalty.

"Those," she told her students, "were the only real things worth dying for: friendship, faith, and loyalty. You can't touch them, hold them or see them, but you can live them, feel them, and witness them. Those virtues keep you human. Those virtues are what the ones of great died for, so that you could have the opportunity to know them."

One young girl in the back raised her hand. Ana nodded toward her, and she asked, "Where do you come from? You do not look like the rest of us. You don't even look similar. Are you human as well?"

Ana smiled and nodded. "We are all human. The clones are the RMH. The reason many of you only have one parent whether it be your mother or your father is because they died. They died fighting for those virtues and for you. I come from a place called the SOL," she began. She told them the long ago story behind their present. She told them of her great and mighty friend, Gringin. She told them of the present itself. She told them of the future they would have.

"Why do they want to kill us?" Jinmogen asked.

"They want to wipe out your species so that they can keep their power in the SOL. They knew you would help us if we tried to escape. The RMH will not," Ana answered him.

"So we are helping you or us?" Nthati asked.

"We are one in the same. We may look different, but we are both human. We are helping us," Ana asked.

"So my father died five weeks ago killing more RMH. I thought you said you beat them?" Nthati asked.

"The SOL creates the clones, which we call the RMH, to be disposable. They have given them all atom guns now, and we have had to adapt to different warfare techniques. They broke through the walls we have built and now rampage the city. We are doing our best to keep them out and repair the walls, but they will keep coming. That is why you will be the end of this war. You will be the ones who destroy their creators," Ana prophesied.

"Why don't they just come kill us themselves?" Nthati asked as her eyes narrowed.

"Because they are cowards! They don't want to bloody their hands with us. They don't deem us worthy enough to do so," Yrenik yelled in the class. Ana quieted the class' roar.

"Why do you want to kill your own kind?" Jinmogen asked once all was quiet again.

"The leaders are not of my kind. The slaves they hold in their own stupidity are of my kind," she somewhat laughed at the irony in the situation. "The leaders quit being of my kind when they neglected human life and favored power. They are not of my kind because they worship greed and authority. They can torment my people because they believe that is what is best for them. The tormenting is unending because their consciences fail to realize the oppression they are creating for the ones under their powerful thumb. At least, the clones sleep and their murderous rages have their breaks. The Head Council would kill an entire race of their brothers and sisters to sacrifice for their god of power and not think twice about it. No, I do not think that is what God wants. Though, I have seen myself grow weary from the hate and vengeance I've held in my heart for so many years. I have worshipped the god of hate to give me strength, and look where I am now," she said motioning to her shoulder. "Worship the God of justice," she advised. "And he will not steer you wrong. Fight for what is good, and fight back against what is evil. With that, you cannot go wrong. However, you must know what is right and what is wrong. You must have the right motives when you do what you must do, or you will turn into something you can't recognize and end up dead inside," she said as she looked off into the far distance.

"I think that would be worse than actually dying," Jinmogen whispered.

Ana heard him despite his subtleness. "Wisdom has been bestowed upon you, young Jinmogen," Ana whispered back.

She smiled upon Trangin's young son. Her eyes, her now gray eyes, tired and old, had forgotten how to beam at the whisper of hope. They had forgotten that day so long ago when they witnessed her friend lying dead in the cold winter dirt.

Chapter 10

JOURNEY OF THE OTHERS

For their last day in the SOL, Matthew sent this message to the nine that remained: *Brent and Violet will have to stay behind for a while longer. They will join the rest of you on the surface once their work is complete.*

He opened his eyes. "Ana, your plan will succeed," he promised the ghost in his memory.

He glanced back over his shoulder towards the rapidly growing RMH babies inside their containers. The large metal door that led into his secret sanctuary was only slightly cracked open. He leaned forward onto his clasped hands. The shadows from the single light that hung overhead fell on his face.

He was receiving a message from Brent and Violet: *Why must we stay? We have already finished our parts of the plan.*

He responded, *Because there is more that needs to be done. When everyone is dismissed to the DQ, sneak away to Level Base. I will make sure no one knows.*

Brent looked at his wife. "What more is there?" he whispered.

"I don't know," she said as the bell rang to dismiss everyone to the DQ. They each drank the hormone imbalancer. They had adapted to the initial side effects, and swallowed it all at once with a deep breath. Slumping away from the crowd, they entered the transporter. Matthew was in control of it and programmed it to go to Level Base without detection. The doors opened wide into the cloning facility.

Stumbling through the dark, they approached Damingin's container. Its green eyes glared at them as they walked past. Stepping into the dimly lit room, Matthew did not notice them. They tapped on his shoulder, and he looked up but then back down to his work.

"Matthew," Brent said.

"Brent is that you?" Matthew whispered into the darkness.

"Yes, Violet and I have come," he responded.

"Why did you take the hormone imbalancer? Now it will be harder to do what I need to do," Matthew grouchily murmured.

"We are sorry. We didn't want anyone to see us enter the transporter," Violet innocently said.

"I need you to lie down on the HP bed," he curtly told Violet.

"Yes, Matthew," she responded as she went and lay down. He came back with a spider gadget, and Violet's eyes widened at the sight of it.

"What is that, Matthew?" Brent asked as he gently grabbed his arm.

"It is a biopsic extractor," he replied. "I am going to extract her fetus," he scholarly said.

"Her fetus?" Brent asked. "She's not pregnant."

"Yes, she is. She cannot survive the trek with the pregnancy," he explained.

"You are going to take my baby?" Violet asked as she covered her stomach with her hand, and began to sit up.

"It's a fetus. Your baby will be born, but just not by you. I will take the fetus, care for it externally, and he will be born here."

"What for?" Brent asked as his grip tightened.

"It's a boy?" Violet asked not fully comprehending the situation.

"Because there is a 99.8% probability that Violet will not survive the surface conditions if she is with child. She is the weakest one of the ten we created," his voice tightened with Brent's grip.

"Are you saying we are experiments?" Brent asked with no response in return. "Our baby will not become an experiment, one of those!" Brent yelled at him as he kicked the door open allowing a visual of the RMH babies suspended in a red nurturing juice with tubes coming out of them.

"Don't you realize? You are all experiments! Every single one of you!" Matthew responded and jerked his arm away. Nostrils flared, Brent and Matthew stood staring each other down.

"You are not taking our child," Brent boldly declared. "Violet, we are leaving."

Matthew quickly pulled a syringe from inside his robes and inserted Thioxilline into Brent's neck. Brent stumbled backwards as his vision blurred. Matthew watched as he fell to the ground. Violet jumped off the table, but Matthew cornered her as she tried to escape. "I did not want to do this," Matthew told Violet as he approached her.

"Why are you doing this to me, to us?" Violet asked as she stepped back. "You said we were capable of things that the others weren't. Why can't I keep my child? There has to be something that I can take or do to have him with me. My little boy should be with me," Violet whispered as the tears glazed over her eyes.

"All the simulations say you will die, and I made a promise a long time ago," Matthew told her with tears welling in his eyes also. All of the sudden someone stepped out from behind the darkness, grabbed Violet and injected her with Thioxilline. She went limp in the stranger's arms.

"Benjamin, be careful with her," Matthew said as he laid her on the HP bed.

"Yes, Matthew," a young Benjamin responded. "Before we start," he said as Matthew was adjusting the spider gadget on her lower abdomen. "I need to know something."

"What is it that you need to know?" Matthew responded as he readied the computer imaging system.

"Why…why did you clone me?" Benjamin asked.

"You asked to be cloned. When you left to find Ana, you asked to be cloned and for me to not tell you of her," Matthew said as he looked up and into his eyes. "Which I apologize now for mentioning her."

"Ana?" he asked.

"Ana, your wife, the one who put all of this in motion," Matthew answered.

"Where did you get the fetus for me?"

"I took it from your parent's reproductive file. All of the SOL's reproductive cells are harvested at birth. Then when it is time for the next generation to begin, the woman goes into the HP for a DNA-R, and is injected with her and her mate's reproductive cells; thus a fetus is formed."

"Then how is she with child?" Benjamin asked.

"These are the chosen ones you helped create. Their genes are superior and their reproductive cells regrew once the original ones were harvested for filing," Matthew explained.

"Why can't we just use the filed reproductive cells for the fetus?" Benjamin asked.

"Because the baby will die when she journeys across the surface to meet the others, and also because the filings are with Hunter now in Level Five. I am unable to access them. They aren't data that you can hack in and download, but physical objects. It is too risky to try and obtain them."

"How do you know she and the baby will die?" Benjamin asked.

"Extremely cold winds, hard terrain, and lack of nourishment, even the Jumyoo can't help with nourishment of a fetus. Violet is the weakest one of the ten you created. You can even tell by her eyes. She will get sick, and her baby will get sick. They both will die. She needs the nourishment that the baby will take from her to live. They need her on the surface, and we need her to reproduce otherwise our genetic line is undone," Matthew explained. "Which is why in the near future, you will need to go to Level Five and obtain the filings for Michael and Mary, just in case Mary dies, we will have their reproductive cells to create their offspring."

"Why don't we just create offspring for them?" Benjamin asked.

"We shouldn't play God, Benjamin. We just had to in order for the people of the SOL to get out of their bondage. That was in the past."

"What are we doing now?"

"Playing God," Matthew said as he shook his head as he stroked Violet's cheek.

"How do you know she will die?" Benjamin asked again.

"Because she has lived before. Don't you remember?" Matthew said as he looked up again at him.

"No," he replied.

"Oh yes, that was clone number two," Matthew said. "Your parent clone wanted to make sure they, meaning these beings, would be able to survive on the surface and reproduce. You put several copies of them into those containers and then impregnated them. Then you subjected them to the conditions of the trek. Every time, thirteen times, Violet and her baby died and the others' lived. No matter what you did, you couldn't get the right DNA sequence to save them. We need all of them to live and reproduce so that we can have a chance to win this war!" Matthew finished the procedure. "So you see, Benjamin, because of us, she and her baby will not die, if we take her baby now."

Looking into the spider gadget, he could barely make out the tiny fetus. "Isn't it beautiful?" He quickly placed the fetus into an external container, and using the computer imaging system, he connected all the nutrients he would need to grow. "We will not accelerate his growth," Matthew explained as he looked down at the tiny human.

"We are recreating them again?" Benjamin asked.

"No, we aren't creating anyone. We are nurturing their offspring," Matthew said. "Where is our transportation bot?"

"Right here. I will activate it," Benjamin replied as Matthew walked over and injected the extraction spot in Violet with Jumyoo.

"Help me put her in," Matthew said as he curled his arm under her head. Benjamin picked her up and gently placed her inside, moving a strand of her hair out of her face. A metal divider slid over her and rotated her onto her side. "Now for the other," Matthew said. Benjamin picked Brent's top half up and tried slinging him into the transporter bot. Several minutes later, Benjamin finally got Brent into the bot as sweat began to bead on his forehead.

"Alright, send them back, my boy," Matthew said as he turned to work on the DNA creations. Benjamin punched in the LQ number and hit the enter button on the control panel. The container closed and turned upright. It rolled out of the room and into the transporter.

A few hours later, Brent's eyes slowly opened to darkness. "Violet?" he called out. "Violet?" he called out again louder when no response greeted him.

"I'm here," she said through the tears. "I think we are in some type of container. I've been trying to figure out how to open it."

"Vi, it's on a timer. We have five seconds left," Brent told her as he looked up to a small timing device counting down the milliseconds.

The top slid up and the metal divider slid back into place. Brent pulled himself out and rolled out onto the floor. He helped Violet out. Then the transporter bot closed, stood up vertically and rolled out back down the corridor. As the door shut, Brent walked over to his wife who was seated on their sleeping cot.

"I can't…he won't...respond to me," she began to cry as she was trying to contact Matthew. All Brent could do was hold onto Violet as the tears of pain violently came forth from her blue-gray eyes.

Violet, I am sorry that I took your baby, but it was for your own good. You will never know what I mean by that, but I am asking you to have a little faith in me, Matthew sent to her.

Violet screamed and stood up and ran over to the mirror. "Get out of my head!" she shouted.

Brent ran to her as she collapsed on the floor just as he received a similar message. He held her head to his chest as he kneeled on the floor. She grabbed around his waist and yelled as loud as the pain she felt inside.

The others have already left. Brent, I took the liberty to make copies of the work done by the ten of you. Please leave your copies in your office safe. The next HP will find it there. When Violet fully heals, you will need the visual manipulation injection and the hormone imbalancer. Make her sleep and the Jumyoo will heal her by the end of the next workday. You will need to come down to Level Base for the visual manipulation injection, Matthew told Brent.

If you care so much about us, why would you put us through this? Brent asked him ignoring the instructions.

I ran multiple simulations, and found Violet and your son would not survive during the journey you make to find the others. I am allowing the baby to grow here, so that it can live. You may never understand, but know, I did this so that our plan may succeed, Matthew explained to him.

"The plan?" Brent whispered to himself as if it didn't matter anymore

Make her sleep, Matthew ordered changing the subject. *Make her sleep or she will not heal in time. She will die if she does not heal in time.* Matthew added for emphasis. *Give her another dose of Jumyoo in six hours.*

Brent picked her up and carried her to the sleeping cot. "Violet," he said, "we are going to need sleep," he murmured in a low voice.

"Sleep? Our baby is gone, and you want me to sleep?" Violet asked as she turned away from him. Brent looked up and there on the counter beside him was a Thioxilline syringe.

I knew she wouldn't go to sleep by herself, Matthew told him as he read his thoughts.

"Vi, we need to sleep. You need to heal," he said as noticed a small amount of blood starting to seep in through her uniform. "You are tearing the extraction spot. You cannot get sick, Violet," he pleaded. She touched her stomach. "I'm going to give us something to help us sleep, alright Vi?" She didn't respond, but just lay looking at the closed door. He gave her a dose and found there was enough for one more person.

I knew you wouldn't be able to sleep either, Matthew said as Brent understood his notion. He went and lay next to his wife who was fighting to stay awake. He injected himself in the neck and threw it towards the wall.

"I love you," Violet whispered through her soft lips.

"I will always love you Vi," Brent whispered back just before his vision failed him, and his eyes closed to his beautiful wife.

***

"Do you know why Brent and Vi are staying?" Katy asked as they stepped into the SPR-E.

"No, none of us do," Rhome whispered to her.

Matthew appeared behind them with a syringe in his hand.

Shawn noticed him. "Why are Brent and Violet staying?" he asked.

"I need them to carry on something for me since the Head Council believes me to dead," he responded. "I have with me here the visual manipulation serum. It will hurt, but you will be able to see in the darkness."

Blake stepped forward, and sat down on the holographic projector table.

"You must keep your eyes open," Matthew said as he attached a nerve scanner to each of Blake's temples. The scanners let out an audible beep, and Matthew inserted the visual manipulation serum into the scanner. Blake's mouth grimaced in pain, but his vision became intensely vivid. "Keep your eyes open," Matthew told him.

"Everything looks like there is a bright light shining on it," Blake responded as he balled his hands into fists to try and control the intense burning he felt in his eyes. He didn't know his eyes were turning red and watering from the burn.

"A few more seconds," Matthew told him as he watched the counter on the nerve scanner.

He unhooked the scanners, and said to Blake, "You can close your eyes now."

"Ah, that hurt," Blake said as he closed his eyes, bent his head down and brought his hand up to rub the side of his head.

"Did Mary receive this?" Katy asked as she sat down.

"No, it wasn't complete yet," he shot a glaring look to Shawn. "I thought it was. It was both our faults."

"So Mary is alone on the surface, blind in the dark?" Katy asked.

"Yes," Matthew responded. "I can still somewhat see her thoughts. She is alive," he told them as he placed the nerve scanners on Katy's temples.

"Blake, what do you see?" Rachel asked him.

"Everything just seems so much brighter than usual," he responded. "And you have a red tint to you," he added. "All of you do,"

"This serum takes what little light unseen by the naked eye and enhances it several times so that you will be able to see in the dark. It also allows you to see heat traces. That is why you see the red tint in the people and active machines here."

"Why the machines?" Rachel asked.

"Because the machines produce heat when they run," Matthew answered her as he removed the scanners and told Katy she could close her eyes.

"It's so bright," she whispered.

"How long does this last?" Jenna asked.

"As long as your optic nerves are intact with your eye," Shawn answered, and Matthew nodded in agreement.

After all of them had their vision altered, Matthew handed Michael the equipment and serum. "Mary and your offspring, when the time comes, will need this as well. Keep it in a safe place. I have more for Brent and Violet," Matthew told him.

Michael nodded. The others entered the elevator, but Matthew caught Michael by the arm and whispered in his ear, "She is alive, and you will find her. You were bred to protect her, but you fell in love with her yourself."

Michael smiled and looked back toward the old man. "Good luck," he told him.

"Hurry, Mary needs you. Don't slow your trek for Brent and Violet. They will find you," Matthew advised the group as they all stood within the elevator. "Good luck, and may God be with you," Matthew told them as the doors slid shut.

The transporter doors opened to darkness, but the seven stepped out into a world lit by the tiny moon glimmers that survived past the black clouds.

As they came to the SD's large doors, they looked back at the life they were leaving behind.

Shawn started to laugh. "Look what some idiot left up here," he said as he pointed to a cargo hover craft.

"Why is it outside the SD?" Jenna asked.

"To transport the clones?" Rachel responded in more of a question than a declaration.

"Well, it's ours now," Rhome said as he hopped up into it.

"Do you think they'll know?" Katy asked.

"No, they obviously left it up here to be taken. They won't know if we took it or the clones," Rhome answered as he shook his head.

"Go on in," Blake told the others as he stood at the step. Michael and Shawn heaved their work packs into the cargo area and stepped inside.

"What are these?" Shawn said as he held up an atom gun looking in disbelief and curiosity at Michael.

"I think the more important question is why are they here and why would the Head Council leave such advanced weaponry with the clones?" Michael responded to him.

Rachel poked her head in. "What is this?" she asked as Katy threw in her work pack. "Did Matthew leave this here for us? Or did the HC leave this here for the clones?" Rachel asked before her first question could be answered.

"I hope and pray Matthew left this here for us," Shawn said.

"Is everyone on?" Rhome asked behind him. "Because I'm leaving!" he yelled as he pushed the accelerator button. The thrust of movement sent them all flying backwards.

"What are you doing?!?!" Blake yelled at Rhome as he pulled himself up.

"Look behind you!" Rhome yelled back. Blake stuck his head out and around the cargo hold and saw six RMH following close behind, and four more coming from each side. "Go faster! Go faster!" Blake yelled at him.

"It won't go any faster! It's a cargo hover, it's not meant for speed!" Rhome yelled back.

Michael uncovered thousands of atom guns in the floor compartments of the cargo hold. Breathing escaped them all for a moment. "Grab one and start shooting!" He yelled the order. A large thud appeared on the side of the cargo hold, and Michael felt the craft sway to the side. "We can't tip over," he told them as he ran to the other side of the cargo hold and felt the craft level out. "Hold me while I go out the top!" he yelled to Shawn. He pushed open one of the glass windows on top of the hold, and hoisted himself up. Shawn grabbed his legs.

Leaning over the side, he pulled the trigger as a massive hand came to greet his face. The headless RMH fell off the side of the cargo hold as Michael began to bleed on his cheek and forehead. He turned on his stomach and hooked his feet under the window for leverage. He just began shooting at anything that moved nearby.

"Pass me a gun, Michael. They are catching up to us!" Blake shouted. Michael threw him a gun; Blake caught it and immediately shot a RMH that was poised to jump in the control pit. Katy busted out another window on the side and began shooting. Jenna was exchanging used guns for charged guns. Rachel used one of her five paralysis bombs and launched into the densest area of RMH. Immediately they fell.

But on the other side of the cargo, a RMH jumped on the top of the cargo hold just as Michael ran out of charges, and picked him up by the neck. Throwing him off, he jumped inside only to meet the whirring sound of an atom gun.

"Go back! Michael's not here!" Shawn yelled to Rhome.

"What do you mean he's not here?" Rhome yelled back.

"Go back! Turn around!" Shawn yelled again as the hover craft began to make its wide circle.

The RMH surrounded Michael, and one viciously picked him up with one of his strong arms. "You fight bravely. Too bad you must die," he told him as he maliciously squeezed his face. Michael yelled in pain, just as an atom charge hit his captor's head. A wave of atom charges made their way into the group of RMH.

"Come on Michael! Get up!" Blake yelled to him as the others held off the RMH. He rolled over as fast as he could. He tried running to the hover craft, but his arm was broken and his leg hurt too much to run. Blake jumped off the hover craft and came to his aid. "Come on! I got you," he told him as he hooked Michael's arm over his head. "Rhome! Open the door!" he yelled as the little half door began to open to the ground, and they ran and hopped in.

"Get us out of here!" Michael yelled.

"Don't have to tell me twice," Rhome said as the door closed, and he pushed the accelerator button. Blake dug into his work pack, and pulled out some Jumyoo. "Here take this!" he yelled to Michael as he stood back up and began defending the craft.

"They are relentless!" Shawn said as he was trying to push the craft to go faster. An hour had passed and the RMH were still on their tail. A dark and daunting wall appeared in the distance, and the RMH began to back off as they neared it.

"They are giving up!" Shawn said as he pulled his head back inside the hold. "Give me another gun! We've got some ones who still think they can take us!" he told Rachel.

But before he could pull the trigger, the RMH he was aiming at fell dead with a stick coming out of its chest. Then another fell.

"Blake, are you throwing sticks at them?" he yelled over the craft's propulsion system.

"No, but they are," he answered as he pointed ahead.

In front of them stood a long line of RMH hurling spears at the RMH who were chasing the craft. The last of the chasers retreated, and Rhome slowed the craft to a stop in front of the line of RMH that stood before them.

Blake pointed the atom gun at the one who stepped forward.

"We mean you no harm. Come with us. We have been awaiting your arrival for a hundred years," she said in a loud voice set in the back of her throat.

"Who are you, and why do you want to help us?" Rhome asked.

Briscogi stopped and peered over her shoulder. "You will know in time," she said as she motioned her men.

"What are they doing?" Blake asked as they came closer.

"Put the gun down, Blake," Michael said as he noticed Blake panicking. Rhome also noticed Blake's spastic side to side movements of his eyes and head, and put his hand on the gun to lower it. He pulled it away, and whispered, "They scared off the hostile RMH. Maybe they are a different breed, or some clones who found a conscience. Either way, we have no other way to find Mary. We have to trust them at this point."

They were roping up the hover craft. Then they shot arrows up into the sky where the ropes were attached.

"Please come with me," an RMH told them. They all exited leaving their work packs behind in the cargo craft. He came to the wall, and started crawling through a hole. The others followed him. It was dark and disgusting filled with bones and a dank stench filled their nostrils. Reaching the other side, everything looked the same, except they could see an outline of an old city in the far off distance. Then they heard a clanking noise as they looked up and the hover craft floating in the air slowly descending to the ground below.

"Who are you?" Michael asked as he put his weight on his good leg.

"We are the humans. I am Mungerin of the Ayngin tribe. This is my first time outside the fortress walls," he told them as he kept walking.

All of the sudden, Briscogi stepped in front of him. "Put them in the cargo hold. We can't risk having them die," she ordered him.

Mungerin nodded his head, and turned to them. "Briscogi has spoken. Go to the cargo hold."

Two of the soldiers opened the doors and found the dead clone inside. They ripped him out and stood him on stake facing a hole in the wall. Katy shuttered at the sight.

A loud clang of the doors signaled they were all inside.

"What are they going to do with us?" Jenna asked the others in a low voice afraid their conversation would be heard. The hover craft's propulsion system turned on, and they moved forward.

"They haven't killed us," Katy said, "but they killed their own kind to save us."

"Maybe there is a civil war going on," Blake suggested. "And they need us to win."

"How do they even know us?" Rhome asked.

"Mary," Michael said. "That is the only way they knew we were coming."

The others nodded in agreement. "That means she's alive, Michael," Jenna said as she touched his shoulder.

"I know," Michael said as he smiled a smile of relief.

All of the sudden, a roar came about outside the craft. Rachel looked out of the window and saw a small scrimmage ensuing.

A large group of RMH came up over broken pieces of the old world shooting atom guns at them. The seven's escort was falling quickly. Rhome pulled an atom gun from beneath the floor and began shooting out of the small window.

The doors opened and Mungerin shouted, "Hand me a gun!" Rachel tossed him one and another. He threw the second to Briscogi.

"Come on!" she shouted to her men.

They felt the hover craft sink to the ground and the propulsion system crackle and then snap. Rhome tried jumping out of the cargo hold to help fight when one of the soldiers pushed him back in and yelled to them all, "Stay here and keep your heads down! Hand me some more guns!"

Rachel slid him three as the hover craft titled and banged against the hard ground beneath. Little holes began appearing on the cargo hold's walls.

Katy's breathing became frantic. "We are all going to die! We're going to die!" she yelled as the hover craft began tilting from side to side touching the ground and bouncing in the air from a faulty propulsion system. Rhome crawled over to her and yelled at her, "We are in the middle of a war. They are protecting us! Keep your head down and we will make it out alive! Do you hear me?" She nodded. "Good, hand me another gun," he told her.

Finally the fighting died down. They brought their wounded to the cargo hold and laid them there. Closing the doors, the escort half pulled, half pushed the cargo craft along. Michael pulled out his Jumyoo and tried giving it to the nearest RMH, but the RMH refused saying, "Your life is more valuable than mine."

"But you are wounded. I will survive without it," he told the soldier, and went ahead and injected him anyway. The others began following his actions. Rhome looked out the small window and told the nearest soldier, "We are able to walk, and we should help transport the craft. Let those who are unable to pull to sit in here instead of us," referring to the soldier next to him to limped along.

Briscogi overheard his request and came up alongside the craft. "No," she replied. "If we are attacked again, I do not want you in a vulnerable position."

"But look at your men and women; they are hurting," Rhome said.

"No," Briscogi said again. "We are all soldiers. We know what we must do, and we must get you back to the fortress alive and not badly wounded. We are glad you brought a craft for us to carry you in."

"But..." Rhome began again.

"No," Briscogi answered as she moved forward. "We are almost home!" she told the others as she ran to the front of her squad.

Trudging up the hill, they came to the peak. Looking they saw a gigantic statue of a lady laid sideways in the ground. The element she held in her hand now broken off and lay in the dirt by what was left of her face. Her arm jutted into the sky reaching and reaching for something. A light came from within this lady's crown. They all ventured forth towards the mighty fortress that had been built up and around the lady of liberty.

Entering through the gigantic gates, a loud cheer of its inhabitants greeted them. A loud voice growled from above, "Briscogi, where are they?"

"They are in the cargo hold. They have brought weaponry and other aid to help our fight for our freedom!" she yelled to the crowd.

The doors opened and the wounded were brought out first and taken inside the statue. Michael peered out through one of the small holes in the cargo wall. "I don't see Mary," he whispered to the others.

Mungerin appeared at the doors' opening. "Come. We all want to see the ones we have waited for."

"Waited for?" Katy whispered to Jenna. Jenna shrugged her shoulders as they were tightening their work packs to their backs. Blake and Michael were the first ones to exit the hold with their work packs firmly planted in their strong arms. They stepped out into the darkness seeing thousands upon thousands of RMH standing and cheering in front of them. The seven lined up in a row facing the crowd. A woman appeared at the top of the hill standing next to the one who bellowed when they first entered.

"We are now complete! With these standing in front of us, we will now be able to win this long war! They bring far superior technology than our enemy, and a willingness to free their people, just as we desire to see our people freed from suffering. We are meant to live for so much more. Don't forget why you are here and what you are fighting for!" Ana yelled at them through the blackness.

A loud roar let itself loose amongst the crowd as Briscogi motioned for her soldiers to escort the seven to the head of the statue. The crowd made way for them as they went to the top of the hill while grunting and hollering for them.

Upon reaching the top, Ana turned them to face the crowd again. "Today we will witness the turning point in this war! Today we will be victorious always!" she yelled and with the roar of agreement behind her she turned and led the seven into the light.

"Mary!" Michael yelled as he saw her lying there in the old hospital bed. Rushing over to her, he scooped his arm under her back and pulled her up to him. Her eyes opened to his wonderful face and smiled.

"You came for me," she whispered as she wrapped her arms around him and laid her head to rest on his shoulder.

Ana felt a sting of pain in her heart. "We have prepared for you," she told the others as she stumbled on her words. She led them further into the lady of liberty. "We sectioned off the inside and each pair of you has their own private space."

"Thank you. I am assuming you are Ana?" Blake asked.

She peered over her shoulder. "Yes," she responded. "I am she."

Mary noticed the rest as they ventured further. "Where's Brent and Vi?" she asked Michael.

"Matthew told us that they needed to stay a while longer to finish some work that came up," he responded. "I just hope they can make it. We were chased the entire way here, but we also were on a hover craft filled with atom guns. I think the HC left it there for the clones."

"We will need to send help to them," Mary thought aloud. "Trangin!" she yelled as he appeared in the entrance way. "Two more are on their way. Please put together an escort team to go find them and bring them back," she requested with an urgency in her eyes as she looked through the dim light in the corner at the dark silhouette in the entrance way.

"Yes, Mary," he responded. "Consider it done!" he growled as he turned and walked away.

***

Brent's eyes opened to witness the beautiful visage of his wife and her black hair sweetly curled around her fair skinned face.

He was receiving a message from Matthew: *Today you will leave after DQ hours. I have added RQ tokens to Violet's cache. Deposit them so she can take the day off. She still needs to heal. Give her more Jumyoo. Then leave for your work day.*

The wakeup call came only seconds after Brent received Matthew's instructions.

Violet slowly opened her eyes.

"Vi, keep sleeping. You need to heal," Brent told her as he injected her with Jumyoo and another small dose of Thioxilline. "I will come back for you when it's time," he told her as her eyes began to close.

He lay down next to her for a few more minutes whispering little thoughts to her sleeping body. Then he got up and went Level Two for the work day.

Is there anything else you need from me? Brent asked Matthew while he walked into his HP office.

Yes I need you to find the deleted memories in the CPU2000 cache. I have other things that require my attention. Then set those memories in a separate file in the Omega account, Matthew responded.

That shouldn't take long to do, Brent said as he smiled cockily.

Oh, but it will my young one. It will. You must search through centuries of deleted files and piece them all together, Matthew told him.

Brent rolled his eyes and shook his head. "Well, I guess I'd better get started," he whispered to himself.

The following hours passed so slowly. At the end of the work day, he had put together only twenty memories. The DQ hour had already passed when Matthew came to him again.

Brent, thank you for what you have done for me. You have helped speed up the progress of this plan. Go back to Violet and give her some more Jumyoo. Wake her and load your work packs. Drink the hormone imbalancer and meet me in the SPR-E, Matthew instructed.

Brent nodded as he slowly exited the system. Matthew read his thoughts.

Both of you will be better off without this child for now. Have a little faith in me, Matthew told him. *You will be reunited with him. I will make sure he knows his mother and father. That, my son, I promise you.*

Brent somewhat smiled and after a few moments of silence, responded, *Thank you.*

He had reached his LQ, and opened the door to find Violet giving herself another dose of Jumyoo and saw the work packs already filled leaning against the wall.

"Vi, you should be resting," Brent said as the door shut behind him.

"I am rested. My extraction wound is completely healed over. I am ready to go and get out of this slavery," Vi said as she stood up from the sleeping cot.

Brent walked over to her, and then just stood there looking into her eyes.

"Did you eat?" he asked her.

"Yes, Brent," she responded as he guided her back down. He sat down next to her. She leaned in and placed her head on his shoulder. "We are going to have to do this alone. Matthew told me that he instructed the others to not slow down and wait for us."

"I know. He told me the same. We can do this though. If anything happens, I will always be there for you," he replied. He gently wrapped his brawny hand around hers.

"I know," she whispered as a smile gracefully appeared on her milky face.

Brent and Violet snuck away to the SPR-E, and met Matthew who then did the visual manipulation procedures on both of them.

"Good luck to both of you," he told them as they entered the elevator.

"Good luck to you, Matthew. You've a lot of work cut out for you," Brent told him.

"I know. I've recruited help. Don't worry, I'll have the entire SOL converted within the next few years," Matthew told him.

Brent smiled. "Don't take too long," he said as Violet looked up to him.

You will soon see why I did what I did, Violet, Matthew told her as he witnessed the hatred in her eyes.

We shall see, Violet responded as she turned her eyes from him.

The elevator doors shut and Brent and Violet found themselves stepping out into the SD.

"I think it's a three-hundred mile trek," Brent told her.

"Don't tell me that," Violet said as she slumped. "I was very optimistic, until you told me that."

Brent laughed sarcastically. "One mile at a time," he said. "One mile at a time."

"Let's start with steps, and then we'll move to miles," Violet suggested. They exited the SD. "Straight ahead," she said as she stepped further into the darkness.

A few days passed and it seemed the further away they trekked from the SOL, the colder the winds became.

"Vi, come on. I see something up ahead," Brent said as he pressed forward. The winds were rushing by with fatal freeze. "Vi!" Brent shouted as he turned and found empty space next to his side. Looking around frantically, he shouted into the darkness, "Violet!!" Then off in the distance, he spotted a silhouette hunched over and then collapsing into the ground. He took off running back towards her. "Violet!" he yelled as he neared. Sliding in the dirt next to her, he grabbed her hand and he bent down over her.

"I'mmmm…so…sorry...I…I…" she chattered between her teeth.

"Vi, come on. There's something right over there. Come on, Vi," Brent told her as he caressed her face.

"I…can't…go…" she said as her lungs couldn't fill up with oxygen. Her eyes rolled back into her head and then closed. Her body still shook with fever.

"Violet!" Brent yelled. He hooked his arm under her neck. "Violet, wake up!" He tried shielding the winds from her pale face. He strapped her work pack on top of his work pack on his back and stuffed their work bags into his uniform. "Alright Vi, we are going to make it," he told her limp body as he picked her up and cradled her like a new born baby.

The wall he saw in the distance was not getting any closer as the hot tinge of fatigue grew in his legs and arms. "I have to get to it," he told himself as looked into his wife's face. He was only a little over a mile away. He screamed as Violet's dead weight was overtaking him. He fell to a knee. "Come on, Vi; we are so close," he told her as he let her gently fall to the ground. He collapsed next to her, his body exhausted. He pulled out his Jumyoo and gave her and himself a dose. "Can't stay out here," he told himself. "I must get her to the others," he said as he looked up to the wall. Out of breath, he picked her up again and tried to walk. He could only manage a few steps, so he began to crawl and pull her along as he talked to himself along the way trying to keep his mind focused on getting her to safety.

He came across ugly disgusting bodies pinned to the ground like flies on a wall. He just began crawling harder looking up from time to time making sure nothing would fall on them from the sky.

An hour passed and he came to the base of the wall. "Vi, we're here," he said as he pulled himself up. The burn in his legs was unbearable, but he pushed through and lifted Violet up into a hole in the wall.

He blocked the hole with his work pack and pushed Violet's hair out of her face. He pulled out their work bags and gave her another dose of Jumyoo.

Her skin was quickly tinting blue. He rolled her onto her side and held onto her while he rubbed her back with both of his hands. Her cold cheek pressed against his.

"Come on, Vi," he whispered to her.

The short, quick breaths she took far apart meant life was still with her, but for how long was the question Brent worried about as he tried to keep her alive.

Her eyes flickered open and close. Then all of sudden, Brent heard something and sharply looked up.

"Michael?" he whispered and heard his words echo down the hole and out into the open darkness.

No answer returned to him except the howling of the winds outside of the tunnel in the wall. He looked to Violet. Her eyes looked sunken and dark. Her lips tinged with a touch of purple and blue. The color completely vanished from her face.

"Vi, stay with me. We are almost there," he whispered to her. He could feel her chest ever so slightly push out against him and then sink back. He could feel the cold air fill the gap between them every time she exhaled, but she was at least still breathing.

He heard the sound again: a loud, crackling sound. "Who's there?" he asked. His voice shrieked from the cold frozen around his vocal chords.

Once again, no answer returned to him.

Brent pulled his atom gun from his work pack. With Violet in one arm and the atom gun aimed toward the entrance of the hole on the other side, he yelled, "Who's there?" This time, he yelled with all the air in his lungs.

"We are here to bring you to the others. Mary sent us to help you," a voice called from the other side. All of the sudden, a hideous face appeared at the other side of the hole. Brent still held his atom gun high. "We are here to help you," he said again. "She looks sick. We must get her to our home," another said as he appeared beside the one who had spoken first. He pointed to Violet.

"Did you say Mary sent you?" Brent asked.

"Yes. The seven others are with her now," one answered him. "We have come to protect you as you travel through the city."

Brent crawled with Violet still in his arms closer to the RMH with his atom gun still in his hand. "What are you protecting us from?" he asked still wary of them.

"The RMH. We are sending some men to the other side to retrieve your work packs. Do not be alarmed if you find someone following you," he answered.

"What?" Brent asked. "Aren't you the RMH?"

Brent heard a growl, and then these words followed, "You know them as the clones. We call them the RMH."

"The clones? I thought everything on the surface was a clone," Brent responded as he stopped and tightened his grip on his atom gun.

"Almost. We are mankind's last stand against them. The gap between our kind and the RMH is widening especially with every wave of clones your Head Council sends to the surface, but we have you and the others now," he explained as Brent began to move forward again. Violet coughed a pitiful little cough. "We need to get her to our home. She will regain her health there. You have chosen a bad time to come. We call this time, the dead time. If you do not have shelter, your chances of surviving are slim."

"Alright," Brent said as he handed Violet to the thing who called itself a man. He cradled her like a baby. She was so small in his arms. The other RMH helped Brent out of the hole. Looking back, he saw two pairs of green eyes coming forth. They carried their work packs.

"My name is Mungerin," he told Brent as he looked up to signal the watchmen.

"I am Brent and this is my wife, Violet," Brent responded to the uncanny introduction.

"Let's move then, Brent. It looks like she doesn't have much time," Mungerin told him and nodded his head forward to signal to the other twenty soldiers with him to begin to head back.

After a day and a half of trekking, they came to the bridge. A light shone forth from the statue's head, and immediately a hope filled Brent. He looked to his wife tightly carried in Mungerin's arm and smiled. They had made it to their new home.

The gigantic gates opened and a welcome befell them. Instantly, the crowds lifted their heads and made way for them to the head of the statue at the top of the hill.

Chapter 11
THE SOL'S VOYAGE

Josh of Generation 43 awoke next to his wife as she gently stroked his forehead and blonde hair. Her brown eyes looked down upon him with love and care.

"Josh, do you feel well now?" Tara asked him.

"No, I have a pounding headache," he responded groggily.

"I know. I had the same headache," Tara whispered to him as she held his cheek. He reached and wrapped his fingers around the back of her neck. He felt the BIS there, and smiled. "Matthew may be a wonderful savior for us all, but his gentleness in handling procedures should be improved," she laughed.

Josh smiled. "Yes, I agree," he replied as he closed his eyes to try and soften his headache. "How much longer until the wakeup call sounds?"

"Three hours," Tara responded.

"That doesn't leave much time to do what we must do," he told her.

"Sleep now, Josh. We can do it the next work day," she said as she lay down beside him. He smiled and turned on his side to pull her closer to him. She kissed his forehead. "All I can think about is poor Mary," she confided to her husband.

"I think about the others. She is the lucky one. She got out. She's the reason why we were led to the truth," Josh responded.

"Do you think it is strange that three to four days after Mary was exiled, all of her friends vanish from the SOL?" she asked. "I know the HC says that they sent all of them on an expedition to test the soil outside the SD, but I thought it was strange," Tara said before Josh had a chance to answer her question. "They've never done that before."

"I think they left because they needed to leave," Josh replied after a few moments of private thought. "I mean, if they took you away from me and I didn't have my memory erased, I would leave too. I would take as many people that were willing to go and try to find you."

Tara sweetly kissed him. "I don't know if I could have made the sacrifice Mary did, though."

"What do you mean?" Josh asked.

"I don't know if I could let them leave me in the cold and in the darkness just so that the SOL might come to their senses and realize the truth. She probably died for all of us to have a chance at living free from the HC. Then that poor woman, Ana, had no chance of survival. No one went after her. I just don't know if I could give my life so people could have a choice to live with freedom or to live with oppression," Tara whispered.

"But I'm glad she did what she did," Josh whispered back.

Tara smiled and sweetly said as she tiredly closed her eyes, "Me too."

It only seemed like minutes later when the wakeup call sounded. Their eyes opened, and they just laid there wishing life was different. Then remembering what they needed to do, they jumped from their sleeping cot. On the counter, Josh noticed several tablets situated there. "So these are it," he said to himself as Tara walked up behind him. Sitting next to the tablets, there laid two little vials of hormone imbalancer. Josh grabbed them and handed one to Tara. "I'm ready when you are," he said as he brought the vile to his lips.

"I'm ready," she told him as she drank hers down, and Josh did the same. A sharp pain found itself in their left eyes. Matthew coached them through the effects of the hormone imbalancer, and finally, the pain subsided.

You are very ambitious, he told them. *I already inputted that you are on your way to your work stations. You are free to carry out our plan,* he told them. *Do you remember what I told you?*

Yes, we do, Josh replied to him as he witnessed Tara nod in agreement.

Then, do what you must do, he told them.

"I will go to the DQ first, I suppose," Josh told Tara. "No one is there."

"Great, I will head to the RQ. No one is there either," Tara said.

Josh slid into the DQ down the hall and waved to his wife who kept towards the transporter. He found the wall panel in the back and deactivated the protective shield. He logged into Omega 7 and uploaded the tablet into the DQ database. A screen displayed requiring user interaction saying these words:

PULL THE PANEL BACK ONTO THE WALL AND TELL NO ONE OF THESE CONTENTS.
THIS RECORDING IS FOR YOUR EYES ONLY.

VERIFICATION THAT THESE CONTENTS WILL NOT BE GIVEN TO THE HEAD COUNCIL

YES, I VERIFY
NO, I DO NOT VERIFY

Then images of the day when Mary was sentenced to the surface rapidly flashed on the projection wall based on the memories Brent and Matthew recovered. Following these images were images of Mary rapidly flashed by explaining what happened in the past and the plan is for the future. The message UPLOAD COMPLETE popped up on the screen. "That was easy," he told himself.

Don't forget to program the file, Matthew told him.

"Yes, of course," he said. "Nothing's easy." *Matthew, how long will it take for someone to find this?* He asked.

Well, since we do not have the liberty to be public about this, then it will be whenever someone happens upon it.

That could be years, Josh responded.

Yes, I know.

Will we be going to the surface any time soon? Josh asked.

I don't know. That is up to the ten that are already there. It could be months or a few years, Matthew replied.

What? How can you be sure? Josh thought to him as a look of panic overtook his face.

Have a little faith, Matthew responded. *Most of the SOL must be on our side when the time comes.*

We must wait years before we can leave this place of tyranny? Josh asked with sorrow in his heart.

Yes, but isn't it worth the wait? Matthew responded with another question.

I suppose, he replied.

He left the tablet there in the wall and quickly went to his next destination.

***

Five months passed. Most of the SOL knew about Ana, Mary and the one who came before them. Only one hundred sixty of the SOL's inhabitants wore the old BIS to connect them to Matthew. The others knew but did not want to leave their life of slavery because they were afraid of the unknown.

Matthew sat in his back room office looking out to the growing RMH in their containers. Five months gone, and he could not think of a way to destroy the cloning facility without jeopardizing everything they all had worked for. The stress of it all kept him up at night, made him go a little insane, and allowed him to forget to take Jumyoo. He got up and walked over to the set of containers that held Brent and Violet's eight month old fetus almost ready to be born. Smiling, he whispered to a little boy, "You look like your father. You have the same pointy nose as Brent." The little boy twitched in his coma. He leaned against the container. He felt weak. His legs barely held him up. He looked past him to two others: a brother and sister in the containers behind him. "Now you two look more like your mother, Mary with the pouty lips," he said as he smiled with a heavy heart. "You had better get along. You two be nice to your cousin here," he said as he patted the container he leaned against.

"Matthew, we have another who has uploaded the file from the RQ, Andrew of Generation 43," Benjamin gently said as he looked to his wise mentor.

"Good. Good," he said as kept looking at the human he had created. His lungs felt weak. They barely provided him enough oxygen to keep his thought processes intact. Benjamin ambled over to Matthew. "If Andrew wants to know the truth, do you want to do the procedure?" Matthew asked Benjamin.

"Yes," Benjamin replied.

"Good," Matthew said again. "Look how old they are becoming," Matthew said referring to the humans in the containers after a few moments of pause.

"Yes," Benjamin replied. A beep sounded in the corner. Benjamin went to investigate. "Matthew, the brain functions on this one are increasing. I think she might be coming out of her coma."

"That is impossible," Matthew said as he shuffled over to the young girl. "Well, it is not impossible, but very unlikely," he whispered as he looked at the data output readings. "Give her a small dose of Thioxilline," he ordered Benjamin.

"Yes, Matthew," he responded as he inputted the dosage amount into the computer. "Brain functions are slowing," he read off the newly run report.

"Good," Matthew replied.

"Matthew, will the Mary and Violet know their own children when they see them?" Benjamin asked.

"Probably not, but in their brain interfacing sequence, I have made sure the children know who their parents are. When they go to the surface, they will be able to tell them what has happened here," Matthew answered.

"What if the ten are already dead?" Benjamin asked.

"They are not. I can still see some fragmented thought processes from them," Matthew said as he looked up toward the surface. "But if we cannot figure out how to stop the cloning of the RMH, they will be overrun." Matthew pounded his fist into his hand and turned around to gaze upon the monstrous beings while his nostrils flared. "Phase I went about seamlessly. Phase II is being completed as we speak, but Phase III...Phase III is the one I cannot figure out how to accomplish," Matthew told himself as he shook his head as his vision blurred a little bit.

"Maybe I can help?" Benjamin suggested.

"No, No," Matthew said. "Your knowledge is not great enough yet."

"Why don't we just go cut off their oxygen and nutrients supply?" Benjamin proposed.

"Because the HC will see a pattern when all 400,000 of their minions die at once. Then they will come here to investigate and find us. Then what good will it do if we are all dead including these?" he said pointing to the three humans behind him. "In seven months, these RMH will set foot on the surface."

"We have until then to figure something out," Benjamin assumed.

"It is hard to destroy something that you are using," Matthew wisely said as he put his hand on the glass container that held the young girl. At that moment, Matthew grabbed his chest and fell over.

Benjamin rushed to him and knelt down yelling, "Matthew! Matthew!" He felt for his pulse, but he could not feel it. He ran back to the backroom and grabbed the cardiac medical equipment. He sat the cardiothoracic spider bug on top of his chest and turned it on. Little legs came out of the device and inserted themselves into Matthew's chest. The imaging system turned on and Benjamin saw where the legs were going. One shocked his heart and another pierced his lung to insert oxygen. No response from Matthew body. Benjamin ran back to the backroom again and came back carrying a large syringe of Jumyoo. He injected Matthew in the left arm. "Come on, Matthew. You need to live!" Benjamin kept saying over and over again. Another shock and another wave of oxygen came, but there was still no response from Matthew's body.

Eighteen minutes passed, and Matthew lay dead on the floor of Level Base. Benjamin told the cardiothoracic bug to run a diagnostic of Matthew's heart and lungs. The report was displayed on the screen Benjamin held in his hands. He reviewed it and came upon the conclusion. "Cause of Death:

Natural – Sudden Cardiac Death," Benjamin read off of the report. He put his head in his hand and rubbed his temples as he threw the screen on the floor beside him. "What am I supposed to do now?" he whispered to himself. "I need to finish Phase III, but first things first," he said as he looked to his old mentor and friend. He went and activated a transportation bot. Then after extracting all the information from Matthew's BIS, he gently placed Matthew inside and walked with it to the burial place in the Floor of Rest. It was the hour of sleep, so no one witnessed him placing Matthew in one of the burial tubes. Then he watched as his mentor's body burned and his ashes pushed into the soil that surrounded the SOL. With a tear in his eye, he quickly turned and left that place.

Sitting alone in the backroom of Level Base, he rummaged through his thoughts. He needed to carry out what Matthew was doing. He needed to connect everyone who was with them in the SOL. He needed to take Matthew's place, but how, was the question. He decided to transfer everything that was on Matthew's BIS to his BIS, and hoped he wouldn't die from the massive amount of information that would be downloaded to his brain. He logged into the Omega 7 account and had Melinda begin the data transfer once he lay down on the HP bed. He injected himself with a full bottle of Jumyoo. The data transfer started. His body violently shook and salivated foam began to excrete from the sides of his mouth. His eyes rolled back in his head and his heart rate rapidly increased. He screamed in agony. He hands stiffened and his knees buckled.

Then it was all over. He breathed as his body weakened and his mind raced. His head pounded and his muscles ached. But the new amount of information that he now possessed was so great. However his body tired, he needed rest. His eyes slowly closed, and he slept.

Benjamin's eyes opened to Melinda standing in the corner. "Log out of Omega 7," Benjamin told her. Her head twitched and then she disappeared. He sat up holding his head. Dizziness overcame him and he fell back down. He moaned in discomfort. He thought of an idea Matthew had a long, long time ago. He would mix human and RMH DNA. Matthew decided against it, because he didn't want to mix the bloodlines.

"I am mixing human DNA so that the RMH can have more human attributes and the other clones can kill them off since they won't recognize them," Benjamin thought aloud. "Or better yet, what if I change the brain interfacing sequence so that they help humans," he said as his eyes lit up. He scrambled over to the computer to all of the RMH clones, and accessed their brain interfacing sequence. He altered their drives and passions, so that their brain would recognize traits such as mercy, love, kindness, and peace. "Five months of hate and killing imprints might not let these new sequences take control of their brains," Benjamin told himself as his shoulders slumped. "Well, at least, if they ever see these things take place, they will know what to associate them with. Maybe these new sequences will give them a conscience," he rationalized. "Hopefully, Mary and the others will be given a fighting chance with these alterations."

Chapter 12
MAN'S CREATION

"That year Michael died." She paused. "We've lost so many since then," Mary began as she spoke to the next generation, those who didn't have to worry about war or fighting or tyranny, murder or untimely death.

"When did he die?" a young ten year old asked.

"In the year 3111, he died," Mary said as she looked off into the distance and rubbed her hands together. She quit taking the Jumyoo when she didn't need it to survive or heal from battle. She lived only because the others needed her to give her knowledge to the young, but she did not want to live.

She could feel the pain in her fingers and joints. Her eyesight was failing, and her breathing was lessening. The cold breeze swept by her face. It was less cold than she remembered, and her grimace of pain fell into a frown of sadness. Someone came in through the doors of the haven she had helped create so long ago. The moonlight shined through the black clouds.

She remembered back to her encounter with Benjamin of Generation 39 on the Floor of Rest. She couldn't understand why he had wanted to die, but now as she has lived over half a century without the man she still holds close to her heart, she comprehends the feeling.

There were still nights when she awoke with tears on her face whispering the words, "You will always live with me."

"How did he die?" a young voice she recognized asked.

Turning from her daze, she made out her beautiful great grandson's face. Touching his cheek, she smiled at him. He was perfect in every single way because he was bred to be that way; nothing left to chance.

"Your great grandfather died a hero," she began as she looked upon her great grandson's beaming face and smiling blue eyes, remembering back to that horrible night of battle.

***

Trangin, Ana, Mary, Michael, Rhome, Katy, Violet, Brent, Jenna, Shawn, Rachel and Blake all stood around a metal table within the lady of liberty. They had gotten a message from the border troops that a second wave of clones had been let loose. The first wave retreated into the mountains somewhere. The humans feared they were waiting for the second wave to come, and now they had.

"Why didn't the SOL destroy the cloning facility?" Ana asked with an old, tired and worn-out voice.

"Ask them," Trangin said as he pointed an old knobby finger at Mary.

"I don't understand. Matthew was in Level Base. Why didn't he sabotage the place?" Michael asked.

"Matthew got you all here, didn't he? He has his reasons," Ana defended him as she sat down, fatigued with standing for so long. "Have a little faith in him."

"What are we supposed to do now?" Katy asked. "We have twice as many clones to kill."

"We killed four times as many clones that there are today," Trangin haughtily said.

"But we lost a lot of good men and women as well," Ana whispered.

"But now we have the technology of the SOL with us," Violet inputted.

"What makes you think the SOL hasn't advanced their technology since you got here?" Trangin asked.

"Because the SOL's progress is erased after every fifty years," Violet responded. "And we aren't there to make their progress for them."

Mary put her hand on her barely pregnant round belly, "Either way, we were all bred to be the best, and the best is what we have," she told them. "We have added so many advancements to already advanced plans that we created."

"So, unless they have another round of geniuses working for the HC, I don't see how their technology would better ours," Katy said supporting her friends.

"I agree," Violet said. "But we always have to assume the worst."

"I will start the young on mass producing another batch of the atom gun," Brent told them.

"I fear we will need them in abundance," Ana said. "The first wave didn't come in strong, so we will have a lot to kill in a short amount of time."

"I know. I already created an expansion charge on the gun. It can now shoot fifty-five charges instead of five," Brent said as he laughed at the old technology. A breeze came in through some cracks in the walls of the statue and made the single light about the table sway back and forth.

Trangin shielded his eyes. "Why did you put that light up anyway? You all can see in the dark like the rest of us," he complained.

"We can see in both light and dark. It just reminds us of a better time," Violet said as she looked up to it. The holographic generator on the table laid out the land and Violet inputted their current situation.

Jenna explained, "We are the red dots; they are the blue dots. We utilized the old world's satellite system and are tracking movements. However, we don't know who is who. We are just assuming that the ones on our side of the fence are humans."

"That's not a very good assumption," Trangin growled under his breath.

"I know. That is why someone must watch and see if any of the people begin clashing. Then we will know, and we can send troops to help," Shawn explained.

"We can also monitor our destroyer team's movements," Violet added.

"We believe this is them," Jenna explained. "There is this big square thing about thirty miles from them. Do you see?" she asked pointing to a small gray square on the map. "We believe that is the SOL."

"They are closer than what I thought," Mary whispered.

"Do you think we sent enough?" Michael asked.

"Yes, the SOL can't have more than three hundred inhabitants. Most of them are clueless to what is going on," Violet answered.

"I think it will be an easy fight. We gave them detailed maps of the SOL and their mission is easy: destroy the cloning facility and bring out those who wear the sign, the BIS" Jenna explained.

"Easier said than done," Trangin told them. "But my son, Jinmogen, leads them, and he will accomplish this mission."

"We know. That is why we sent him to lead it," Violet put in.

Trangin boast a smile of pride, and looked to his old friend, Ana, who smiled back.

A horn was heard outside. "We have a messenger," Trangin said aloud.

Outside, a group of young soldiers stopped the six outsiders before they entered the gate of the haven. They noticed the red strips of cloth tied around the messenger's wrists.

"Where are you from, and what is your business here?" Ranjin asked.

"I am from the Yregin tribe, and my name is Jinre. I have come from commander Mungerin with a message only for the twelve," the outsider began.

Ranjin tilted his head and looked him up and down with his eyes. He looked up at the watchmen who were aiming their atom guns at them.

"They will need to stay out here," Ranjin said to the others that were with him with his hand up signaling to the watchmen to be alert.

"Very well," he smiled coldly.

Ranjin snapped his fingers and two soldiers appeared at the door. "I will escort you to them," he told the stranger.

As they neared the head of the statue, ten guards surrounded it.

"I will leave you here. I will be waiting for you to come back," Ranjin told him as he pointed to the door.

As he approached the entrance, one of the guards came forth and told him, "We will need to hold all of your weaponry out here."

The messenger took out his sword, dagger and throwing spears, and handed them to the guard.

"We will need your arrows as well," the guard said. He unhooked the sling and handed it to him as well.

"Do you have an atom gun?" the guard asked.

"It's useless; I used all the charges coming here," he replied as he tossed it to him with an unsettling smile.

"I will introduce you, and see when they have time to see you," another guard told him as he slipped inside.

"Twelve of great, there is a messenger here. His name is Jinre. He says he comes from Mungerin's army with a message for you only," the guard said.

"Mungerin?" Katy asked.

"Yes," the guard replied.

The twelve looked at each other. "Our head general of the west?" Katy asked Violet.

"Yes, that is the only Mungerin I know," Violet answered.

"Why wouldn't he send Empgin, his messenger?" Brent asked. They looked at the holographic map. "Here is Mungerin's army," Brent said as he pointed a large mass of people in the west.

"They don't appear to be fighting," Katy added.

"What if that is the enemy, and they are all dead?" Violet asked.

"The messenger says the message is only for the twelve," the guard said interrupting their conversation as he looked to Soonum and some of Trangin's children as they sat around the circle of the twelve.

Trangin looked to his wife and nodded. She got up and gently touched his arm and he looked upon her with love as she turned her face from him and said to the children, "Follow me. We will go, and leave them be."

Six children slowly rose and bid farewell to their father. Soonum led them out, and then turned to the adolescents. "You too," she said. Soonum came to Mary as she handed her twin baby boys, David and Mark. Mary nodded to Soonum thanking her for taking them. Trangin's adolescent children slowly followed Soonum out, and the door shut behind them.

"Bring him in," Trangin growled to the guard. He turned and then the outsider entered. Ana gasped. Mary yelled, "Guards!" Michael reached for the atom gun under the table. Trangin growled a deep growl and pulled out his atom gun, but it was too late. The stranger pulled another atom gun from inside his breast plate. Three times he pulled the trigger starting in a wave from left to right. The first pulse hit Trangin square in the chest. The second pulse hit Ana in the shoulder as she tried catching Trangin as he fell. The third pulse was meant for Mary. He would have kept firing except Rhome had stabbed him in the back with a spear, and Brent lobbed off his hand with a sword. Michael had shot him with an atom pulse in the shoulder. He had taken a stance in front of Mary as he shot. Michael's arm dropped and he heard his gun hit the floor. He still stood as he looked down to see a hole in the right part of his chest. Then he felt Mary's hands come around him as he fell to the floor.

Rachel and Katy rushed to Ana because there was nothing they could do for Trangin; he was already dead. Ana's left arm was detached. They tried to stop the bleeding and were pumping her full of Jumyoo. Violet and Blake went to Michael and were doing the same thing.

A deep and horrible voice appeared in the room. An old and scarred Damingin growled in the back of his throat as he laughed, "You will all die!"

Then he laid his head back and died with a wicked little smile on his lips. His black blood slowly ran down and down, further into the lady of liberty.

"Michael!" Mary yelled at him as his eyes rolled back and forth. "Michael, stay with me. Stay with me!" She didn't hear the horns going off around the perimeter of the fortress walls or see the mass movement of little red dots rapidly approach their haven on the holographic map. She didn't notice that the light overhead went out.

She cradled his head in her arms as the others were injecting him with Jumyoo. Beside her, Ana died as she whispered something Katy could not make out. The horns were blowing too loudly.

"Ana!" Katy yelled at her. The life was gone from her old gray eyes. Katy sat up and looked around at the bloody room. Rachel hit her hard on her shoulder, and yelled, "She's dead, Katy. Come on! Snap out of it. We are under attack!" as she pulled her up by her arm.

Katy and Rachel left her, grabbed their communicators and left their meeting place inside the lady of liberty. Brent and Rhome were already outside giving orders and conducting a counter attack and defense stance.

"Come on Michael, you can do this. Stay with us," Violet kept saying. She grabbed a heat blade and seared off his wound. His lips were turning blue. Mary couldn't see straight as her tears welled in her eyes. She caressed his face. All she could do was repeat his name in a whisper, "Michael. Michael. Michael."

Violet leaned back. There was nothing more she could do. Blake had already stood up.

"I'm sorry," she whispered to herself as Blake grabbed her wrist and pulled her away from their friend. They ran out of the meeting room to try and save what they had worked so hard to build.

Violet stopped at the door, peered back at all the death, and then with a deep breath went into battle with a hard set revenge in her eyes.

Mary didn't take her eyes off of Michael. He was becoming so pale, so quickly.

He didn't move.

She wanted him to move, to give her something that would let her know everything would be alright.

Her tears fell on his face, and he looked up to her. He could barely breathe. His chest only slightly rose. He reached his hand to his unborn child as he locked eyes with his beautiful wife, and whispered, "My heart lives with you."

"Michael, no," she pleaded with fate.

"Stay," she pleaded with him.

"I love you," she kissed his cold lips.

"I love you," she whispered.

Then as soon as his eyes closed shortly after, the same cold winds that breezed her face, also took the spirit of the one she loved away.

***

"I need more troops on the left flank!" Brent yelled into his communicator. "Mary! Mary!" he yelled on a different channel. Mary didn't hear it as she held onto Michael instead.

Violet ran up to him. "Michael's dead. So are Ana and Trangin. On the map, there are enemy lines all around us except to the east," Violet told him. "I've got an experimental weapon I've been working on. I'm going to use it," she said as she ran off toward the armory building.

"I need those catapults to be throwing atom pulses!" he yelled into the communicator as he nodded to his wife. "Secure the gate! Don't let them in!" Pieces of their concrete fort were blowing up all around him. Holes presented themselves as RMH crawled in.

"Signal the other tribes!" Shawn yelled into his communicator from the other side of the fort. But there was no fire lit in the watch tower on the far side of the fort. "Where is the signal?" Brent yelled back to him. No response came as his eyes widened watching the tower disintegrate into nothingness and its top fall down within itself. "Violet!" He screamed as she was running towards the tower to the armory. She couldn't hear him. Pulling her atom gun from its sling, she made a path to her beloved experimental boom launcher. "Shawn! Get out of there!" Brent yelled. "Violet! Stop! We need to regroup within the fort!" Brent yelled into the communicator. There was no response from Shawn. "Brent, I'm almost there. I can see it," a rough and scratchy signal came back from Violet.

"We need to regroup!" Blake transmitted. "They've overrun us. We need to fall back to the statue!" Rhome transmitted on all channels.

"There are no defenses at the statue. Pull back to the inner fort and hold!" Brent ordered as he shot a quick and sweat beaded look toward the fallen tower.

Mary looked up to the communicator sitting on the table listening to that last communication, then up at the lightless light swaying in the wind. Gently, she laid Michael's head on the floor and kissed his forehead. "For you and our children," she whispered. She grabbed the communicator, the light, the holographic map generator, and the atom gun that lay next to Michael. Emptying the atom cartridge and taking apart the generator, and piecing together the light components, she carried her creation outside and then proceeded to calmly climb to the top of the statue with a pole and a heavy emptiness set in her heart. She rammed the pole into the statue's head. She slammed the base of the communicator onto the pole. She wedged the light components on top. She thrust the cartridge into the bottom. Then as she looked out into the RMH army that was overrunning the fort, she realized no words were necessary for what she was about to do. She shoved the generator into the side and holographic pulsed light shone out like a star in the darkest of nights.

Brent yelled in his communicator, "Kill them now! Now's your chance!" He tried to turn around to see what it was, but even that light hurt his eyes. Atom pulses were flying in one direction only. The RMH couldn't even see where they shooting, much less what direction.

"Enemy is retreating," a scratchy voice responded.

"Good to hear your voice again, Shawn," Brent replied.

"Got separated from the communicator when that atom pulse hit."

Then all of the sudden, Brent saw Violet running up to the top of the wall with a huge piece of metal weaponry. Once at the top, she knelt toward the enemy, hoisted her weapon over her shoulder and pulled the trigger. An immense wave of light shone out in a broad array, and then a loud whirring sound that somewhat deafened everyone near there resounded in the ground. Following the whirring sound, a thunderous zap came knocking Violet down to the ground. She peered up over the top of the wall and saw the enemy no more. Smiling ear to ear, she took off running toward the other end of the fort dodging atom pulses and arrows to take out that portion of the enemy as well. Brent smiled too.

***

Jinmogen and his team crouched at the entrance of the SOL covered by the darkness. He turned to those that followed him, and said, "Today we free their people and destroy the cloning facility and Head Council." Sounds of growls filled the air above them. "Let's go!" he said as he opened the doors of the SD. They silently crept to the elevator, and lowered themselves to the SOL. They entered into the SPR; all was dark. "This is their hour of sleep. They are all on Level Three," he told them as he led the way to the transporter. They went in groups and like ghosts snuck their way into the LQ of the inhabitants of the SOL. They woke each person by putting their hand over their mouths and showed them a holographic image of Mary. They felt the back of their heads. If there was no BIS, they offered that they come with them to freedom. If there was a BIS, they told them they were sent by Mary to gather them.

"I am so glad you've finally come. Matthew was right. He knew someone would be coming to take us. I just didn't expect that someone to be an RMH," Josh whispered as he and Tara grabbed their Jumyoo and workbags to follow Jinmogen out.

"We are not RMH!" Jinmogen said as he pushed him against the wall. "The devils that kill us are RMH," he told him as he backed off.

"Then what are you?" Josh asked.

"I am human, as are you," he replied. "Can you get us to Level Base?" Jinmogen harshly whispered to change the subject and stay on mission.

"Yes, I can," Josh replied as he thought to Benjamin. *The RMH are here. They've come to take us to Mary. They need into Level Base. Please override the system.*

The RMH? Benjamin asked. *The clones?*

No, they are the original RMH. My guess is that they have sided with Mary and the others against the clones, Josh explained.

Alright, go the transporter, and I will have it take you to Level Base, Benjamin responded.

"Follow me," Josh told Jinmogen and his team. They entered the transporter and Level Base appeared before their eyes.

"This is sin," Jinmogen said as he saw little RMH fetuses growing in the containers. Benjamin appeared in the back.

"Yes, it is. I don't know how to make it stop. I've just been altering their brain interfacing sequences, so that maybe they will learn in time that killing is wrong," Benjamin said as he touched a glass container. "The last wave that went out was altered."

"Well we've come to destroy this facility," Jinmogen answered him.

"Go ahead," Benjamin said. "I'm done with it," as he held three young children's' hands. "These are the children of the ten who went to the surface three years ago. Take them to their parents," Benjamin ordered.

"Yes, of course," Jinmogen said. "Get what you need, and then follow Kinhion to Level One." He then ordered Yit and three others to go to Level Zero, find the six HC members and kill them. "Tell me if you run into any trouble," Jinmogen said holding up his communicator. Benjamin appeared holding his workbag. They followed Kinhion out leaving Jinmogen and seven others. "Ready?" he asked.

"Ready as I'll ever be," one replied.

"Give it war, boys!" he yelled as they begin to raid the facility with atom charges. Fifty-five charges to a gun, and each used two guns to take out the facility. Nothing but dust in the air remained. They turned to leave, and entered the transporter. They met up with Yit and the three others on Level Zero.

"Mission accomplished," Yit said as he stepped into the transporter swinging his atom gun on his finger. They entered the SPR and found all the SOL members still there.

"Why haven't you left yet?" Jinmogen asked.

"We are receiving visual manipulation, so we will be able to see on the surface," Tara answered him. "There are two hundred of us, so it will take a while," she explained.

"Take up the ones who have already received it," Jinmogen ordered. He seemed harsh on the outside, but on the inside, he smiled because he knew that their world, both these SOL inhabitants and his own, would forever be changed. The SOL would be used as a laboratory to recreate the old world and offer technology and aid in the war to lead them to victory and a better future.

They made their way back to the fort. As soon as he came over the hill, hurt filled his eyes. His beloved home had been attacked. They entered the gates with guns pointed in their faces. "I am Jinmogen, son of Trangin, one of the twelve. Let us enter!" Jinmogen firmly told the young soldier. "I bring the members of the SOL. We have destroyed the cloning facility. Let us enter," he told him again. Finally, the scared soldier lowered his weapon and allowed them to enter. Jinmogen saw Brent standing in the midst of the fort, and approached him.

"Jinmogen, I'm sorry," Brent said when he saw him.

"Sorry, for what?" Jinmogen asked.

Brent closed his eyes. "I thought you knew," he whispered as he looked up to the meeting place. Jinmogen looked to him then up at the meeting place then back at Brent. He took off running towards the statue's head. He burst open the door and there laid directly in front of him was Mary sitting next to Michael staring at the wall rocking back and forth, preparing her speech, talking to herself. Next, he saw Ana laying on the floor dead, and then he fell on his knees. He struggled to crawl over to his father. Letting out such a yell of anguish, it shook the metal room that encased them. Benjamin appeared at the doorway. He felt a hand on his shoulder.

Katy whispered in his ear, "I'm sorry, Benjamin. Ana is dead."

Benjamin walked in and looked upon this old, dead woman. "I never knew her," he responded with no pain in his eyes. Then he said politely, "Though I am sorry she is gone." He looked over to Michael. "Ironic. We made their offspring assuming Mary would be the one to die," he whispered to himself. "I guess not all things go according to plan." Then he turned and left without saying anymore.

Katy watched him leave speechless. Then her attention went to all the death in the room. "This wasn't worth it," she whispered to herself. "Not anymore."

Mary watched Benjamin walk out of the room. She recognized him from her first encounter with the LOH. "I have to speak with the people," she said more to herself than to anyone else in the room.

"Mary, I am so sorry," Katy said as she knelt down to her friend. Mary stared off at the corner hearing Jinmogen's cries and feeling the same cries in her soul.

"We must go on, so that they do not die in vain," Mary said as she touched Michael's cold but tenderly folded hands. "The army does not know that they are dead yet, and I will have to tell them."

"I can do it for you," Katy offered as she placed her hand on Mary's shoulder.

"It is my responsibility. I was chosen to lead; I was created for this, this very moment. This is not your burden," Mary told her as she stood up. Walking outside the room, the darkness had set in again. Her light weapon only had fifty pulses. She looked down over the ridge and into the inner fort and saw the surface humans, afraid and paranoid of another attack, and she saw the humans from the SOL, confused and wanting to go back.

They saw her and pointed. "Look it's Mary!" They exclaimed. "Mary, what do we do? Where do we go?"

"SILENCE!" Mary yelled into the crowd. The eight remaining leaders joined behind her just before she began to speak facing into the darkness daring fate to come what may. The cold whisper of the wind breezed her face, and she could faintly hear the words, "My heart lives with you." Then she knew he was there with her in that moment, and she began to speak with a force and passion she never before had possessed. "Victory!" she yelled with an extended breath as raised her atom gun into the air, and the surface humans let out a wave of thunderous shrieking that shook the entire fort. "We have earned victory my friends and brothers and sisters. We have defended our homeland. We have survived and kept what is human alive! We have earned the right to live this life! To breath this air! To walk this ground!" She paused as the roar grew louder, and then died down as her pause grew longer. "The SOL's cloning facility has been destroyed and is under our control." Another roar arose from the crowd. "It will be used for developing, advancing and building our new life here once the war is ended. It will also aid us in ending the war in our favor." The clang of metal to show support of this initiative sounded from below. "We have come a long way from Ana and Trangin's time. We have lost many good women and men, soldiers, mothers, fathers, sons and daughters, friends and loved ones. Today is no different. There has been much sacrifice, much trial, much tribulation, and yet we have overcome. I come to you with grave information: our leaders, the mighty Trangin, the wise Ana, and the brave Michael have been killed." Complete silence filled the inner fort. No one spoke. No metal clanged. Not even the humans from the SOL made a noise. "There is a time to…" Mary began, but a messenger came running up to the inner fort's gates.

"My name is Empgin," he called out, as he saw the atom guns begin to point towards him. "I am General Mungerin's messenger." The guards threw him on the ground and stripped him of his weapons and armor leaving him naked.

"He has no weapons," the guard told the others.

"What is your message?" the guard asked as four other guards still pointed their atom guns at Empgin.

"My message is only for the twelve from General Mungerin," Empgin said. "I wear the band of the humans. Why do you treat me with such disrespect?" He asked holding up his arm.

"Don't move, or we will shoot," the guard told him. "Do you not see what has happened here? Do you not see our walls? It all started with a messenger who had a red band and a message for the twelve, and now three of…"

"Shut up…" the first guard told him. "He could be here just getting information. Don't say anything else."

"I am Empgin!" he yelled.

"What is your message?" the guard asked him.

"It is only for the twelve," Empgin replied. Brent and Blake came up to him.

"It is Empgin," Brent told the guard. They released him and helped him stand. "What is the message Empgin?"

"I must only tell you and the others," Empgin said as he looked around at the crumbling walls of the Fort of the Lady.

"Come with us," Brent said as they all walked up to the statue's head. Empgin saw the three of the twelve lying dead on the floor, and fell to his knees.

"Now there are only nine," Empgin said as his head hung in sorrow.

"What is your message?" Brent said again as the nine circled the table in front of him.

"We were attacked two days ago. We couldn't hold them off. They left us in shambles. There were too many of them. They are headed here," Empgin said.

"You are too late," Mary said. "What kept you? Why did it take you so long to get here?" Mary asked through clenched teeth.

"I went to the tribes in the mountains first to tell them. Kindin leads them. They are half a day's march behind me. They are coming to help," Empgin said as he closed his eyes.

"We survived here. What is left of the RMH is retreating into the plains. They should have met Kindin's army by now," Rachel said as she wiped the dusty dirt from her cheek. Mary turned to look at Michael lying peacefully on the floor, then to Ana and Trangin.

"Where is the map so we can see what's going on?" Katy asked.

"I used it to make the light pulse," Mary said as she pointed upwards. Blake went out and retrieved Mary's creation. "I think I can put it back together," she said when he came in.

In five minutes, the holographic map was functioning.

"Here is Kindin's army," Jenna said pointing to a mass of red dots. "It looks like the RMH are retreating," she said as red dots were running away to the south.

"How do you know that is not Kindin?" Shawn said. "We made that mistake last time: assuming who was who."

"Kindin's army wouldn't retreat to the south; he would retreat back to the mountains," Jenna argued.

"We need to regroup and bury our dead," Mary said. "Empgin, go find out if Kindin's army is where we think he is. If he is, tell him to go back to the mountains to keep their homes safe, and watch for our signal of light. Then we will meet once we have tended to our wounded and uplifted our soldiers' morale. If not, try not to get killed and come back to tell us as quickly as you can."

Brent nodded in agreement as he looked to his brother. "It will be several days until we are ready to fight again. Many of ours are wounded. We will wait for your return."

Empgin stood up and nodded. "I'm sorry. If only I had come sooner."

"Go, so we know what our position is and what we need to do for our next movements," Mary said with her eyes downcast.

"Yes, Mary," he said and left.

"If that is Kindin, then we can stay here for a while. The cloning facility was destroyed. The RMH have nowhere to go," Jenna said.

"I want to kill them," Mary said with tears forming in her eyes. "They all deserve to die."

"Another day, Mary," Violet said as she took her arm.

Nine hours passed as the inhabitants of the Fort of the Lady buried their dead and tended their wounded. Empgin returned. "They wait for your signal," he told them.

Mary walked outside and stood in front of the fresh dirt mound. "It's almost over," she whispered.

***

After that last battle which had been intricately planned by the RMH, spies slipped into the human population, and had been living there for a month or so. Most of the spies were found out and killed, all except for one. Seeing how they lived and what they fought for made him question himself. Mary called the humans together, and as she looked out upon them, she gently smiled especially at her very young son and daughter, Laura and Nathan, who reminded her so much of Michael. Benjamin had created them in the SOL. She loved them as they stood there with their tiny hands holding onto the fingers of their uncle, but there was something missing in her heart.

"Peoples of men and women, we have sacrificed so much for peace, life, happiness and love. We have fought bravely for those who have been killed in this long, long war, but those who have died live on in those who love them," Mary began. Briscogi looked to her brother standing beside her, and smiled. "The RMH population is dwindling. They have no replacements to take the place of their dead. I believe this war is coming to an end, and we will have won our survival. We know where they are headquartered in the plains beyond the city, and we will march out to meet them face to face. We will end this war tomorrow! For those we have lost, we will end this war, and we will end it victoriously!" she yelled as she raised her atom gun in the air. A loud roar of agreement followed. "Sleep well tonight," she bid her fellow humans as she turned to go into her dwelling telling a solider to go give the light signal to Kindin.

"Mary, are you going to go out with us?" Violet asked as she was inside waiting for her to enter, motioning to her belly.

"Why wouldn't I?" Mary asked as she picked up the Jumyoo pill. A few moments of silence passed between them.

"I miss him too," Violet said referring to Michael. Mary looked towards her and said nothing.

"Mary, you don't want to endanger the baby," Violet said just as Katy entered, and said, "Mary, an RMH was found amongst us. He says he is tired of fighting."

"Bring him to the top of the hill," Mary ordered as she put her Jumyoo pill back on the counter. She didn't want to take it anyways. "So what, Violet? We are in control of the SOL. If I die, Benjamin can go engineer our offspring."

Katy stood still as the deepening silence grew tense and hostile. "That is my niece or nephew. You are not going with us," Violet retorted. "Michael didn't die to let you walk into your death."

"Michael died killing Damingin; he just stepped in front of me to do it. I lead everyone here, Violet. I am the person they look up to now that Ana is gone. I have to be there. Michael died to give our children a better life, one where we could at least have a chance to rebuild the old world and grow to what our ancient ancestors would have wanted us to become. If I die, I die for the same reason," Mary said as she held Violet's hands in her own. "Katy please go tell the guards to bring the RMH to the top of the hill."

"Alright Mary," Katy responded as she gave her friend a hug, then ran out and told the guards. Mary, Violet and the RMH reached the hill at the same time.

"Why don't you want to fight anymore? Is it because you have heard of your imminent defeat upon daybreak?" Mary assumingly asked him.

"No," the RMH hissed. "I could have gone back and told them. We would have been ready for you."

"So you are a traitor," Brent said as he stepped forward.

"No," the RMH hissed again. "I just don't see why I am fighting. Why am I killing you? We are alike. We are the same. Why am I killing my brothers and sisters?"

"We are nothing alike. You are a soulless imitation, nothing but a disgusting clone," Jinmogen growled at him as he raised his atom gun towards him.

The RMH closed his eyes, and said, "At least I die with a clean conscience." Jinmogen was about to pull the trigger when Mary stepped in between the gun and the RMH.

"Mary, step aside. Let me kill this one before he kills us," Jinmogen told her.

"You will not order me," Mary firmly told Jinmogen. She turned to the RMH and got in his face. His green eyes looked up to her. "How do you know what a clean conscience is?" she asked him.

"I don't know what it is, but there has been rumor among our army that some of us just walk straight into battle unarmed because they want to die with a clean conscience, so that they can give back to those that they have killed," the RMH said.

"A clean conscience means you can sleep when the hour of sleep befalls you," Mary retorted. "You have killed so many of us for nothing. Do you sleep at night?" she asked him.

"No," he replied. "I can't."

"What do they call you?" Mary asked.

"10542," he responded.

"I am asking for your name, soldier," Mary told him. "Not your unit number."

"They call me 10542. That is my name," he stated. "My friends call me Ten-Two," he said more in a raspy whisper.

"You have friends?" Jinmogen asked.

"Yes, we do. Our mentors do not though. They don't care whether we live or die. I don't know if they were born that way or if it is years of war that made them so callous. If it's the war, I don't want to fight anymore," Ten-Two said.

"Then don't," Mary suggested. "Go and tell your friends who feel the same way as you to not fight tomorrow, and we will spare you."

"Mary," Brent said as he pulled her aside. "He is the enemy. We can't trust him," Brent whispered to her as his eyes were glued to the RMH.

Jinmogen whispered in the conversation as well. "I agree, Mary," he said. "Last time we trusted one of these, my father was murdered as well as Ana and your mate, Michael."

Mary's heart stung at remembering what happened that fateful day not that long ago. "Nevertheless, we are supposed to have a little faith right?" she asked wanting their approval.

"No, Mary," Brent said. "He was my brother, and because of what happened, I will never trust that thing or anything like it."

"Benjamin said he made the second wave of clones more human," Mary protested.

"That thing will never be human," Jinmogen declared.

"Would you kill someone who wants to die for things they've done?" Mary asked.

"Depends on who the someone is," Jinmogen answered.

"Your father would be ashamed," Mary said. The hurt in Jinmogen's eyes turned to rage.

"You do not speak of my father. He would be proud of me. I have gotten us to where we are today," Jinmogen said as he puffed his chest.

"You?" Mary asked. "No, my young friend, you are mistaken. Ana, Benjamin, and Matthew have gotten us to where we are today."

"My father killed the RMH, so that you could come here. My uncle died making an easy path for you," Jinmogen rebutted.

Brent jutted in, "Enough. What are we to do about the RMH?"

Mary said, "I suggest letting the clone go back to his army. We are smart. There are only a few of them left. We can see where they are, anywhere they are. We will adapt our plan."

Jinmogen's rage burned within him. "I say we kill it now," he snarled.

"Where is your faith?" Mary asked.

"I have no faith in war," Jinmogen answered.

Briscogi appeared behind Jinmogen as she placed her hand on his shoulder. "Jinmogen, I know where you are coming from. When they killed my father, I wanted to kill every last one of them, and then I did. I killed every last one of them, even Damingin. It didn't bring Gringin back to me though. I didn't believe Ana when she said the war wasn't over. I didn't believe that another from the SOL would come, much less than two hundred. Ana told me it was because I didn't have any faith in the things she said."

"This woman isn't Ana," Jinmogen obviously pointed out.

"I know, Jinmogen, but sometimes we have to go with our gut. Out of all the RMH I have fought with and conversed with before I killed them, none of them ever talked of friends or conscience," Briscogi said. "Maybe he could save some lives, some of our lives tomorrow. If not, we adapt. We always do."

After a few moments, Jinmogen harshly growled, "Do what you want," and turned and left the group.

Brent went up to Ten-Two, and told him, "Go back to your army, gather those who feel as you do, and stay out of our way when we come to end this war." The guards let go of his arms, and Ten-Two stood up.

"Thank you for your mercy," he said as he nodded to Mary. "I will not fail you."

"Then go," Mary said. "And do what you must do to have a clean conscience."

The crowd barely split as he made his way to the entrance of the gigantic fort. Many spit on him, and pushed his shoulder. He didn't fight back. Five guards escorted him to the gate and cruelly bid him farewell as he exited.

Ten-Two ran back to his base. The leader, Damingin, wanted to speak with him. All were around, mentors and soldiers alike. "What are their plans?" Damingin hissed.

"They are going to kill all of us," Ten-Two said.

A short pause of silence lived for a few moments until a deafening ring of laughter filled the air.

"They think they can kill us?" Damingin asked. "You pitiful fool, get out of my sight."

"Yes, Damingin," Ten-Two said as he bowed and walked away to his group.

"What did they really say?" one of his friends, Six-Eight, asked.

"They said they were going to kill us," Ten-Two replied. "I'm not going to fight tomorrow. They said if I don't fight, they would spare me. I overheard some of their conversation. They said that maybe I could save some lives," he told them.

"If we don't fight, do you think they would spare us as well?" Nine-Nine asked.

"I don't know," he replied.

"Why do they want to kill us? Why are we even fighting?" Three-One asked.

"They said because we killed them," Ten-Two explained. "Long before we were born. You know, they called me a soulless imitation, a clone," he said looking confused.

"A clone? What is a clone?" Three-One asked.

"I don't know. A soulless imitation?" Ten-Two answered.

"Well I am going to show them I am not a soulless imitation," Three-One said. "I don't want to fight with them anymore. I don't think it's right."

"Gather the rest of us who feel that way. We will kill all who don't, and then when the enemy greets us tomorrow, we won't have something to prove to them," Ten-Two told the eight that surrounded him.

That night, three hundred RMH went through their own camp and slaughtered the rest of their army. They didn't kill Damingin though. They tied him to a wooden pole they stuck in the ground at the forefront of the battlefield. He thrashed about, calling them all cowards and traitors until the small glimmers of light shone through the blackness. Then over the hill, the enemy appeared. The RMH lowered their weapons and put them on the ground. They all knelt down except Ten-Two who walked out to meet the enemy.

"What are you doing?" Brent told him as twelve of them approached to meet him in the middle. Ranjin, Briscogi, and Jinmogen now took the place of Trangin, Ana, and Michael.

"I and the others who believe as I do have gone through our camp and killed anyone who still wanted to kill you. Our leader, Damingin, is there," he said as he pointed behind him to a furious RMH tied to a pole. "He is the only one alive who still wants to kill you even though he is severely outnumbered. I suppose the army follows me now," Ten-Two told them.

Mary looked to Jinmogen. "A little faith goes a long way," she whispered to him.

"Yes, Mary," he responded. They all walked to where Damingin was as their army approached closer with every step the twelve took. The RMH army was still kneeling. Mary looked upon his face, and a rage filled her eyes. "You killed my mate," she said using the vocabulary of the surface humans.

"No, I didn't," Damingin said. "But we did plan on that happening. The old Damingin was getting old, so we let him infiltrate your headquarters. He was supposed to kill all of you."

Mary bit her lip as her brows bunched in hatred.

"We don't see why we are in this war. Why are we killing them?" Ten-Two asked.

"Because they are not like us," Damingin growled.

"Look at them. We are like them," Ten-Two said.

Minutes passed waiting for Damingin to say something and finally, he responded, "Yes, you are right. I can see it now."

"Then are you with us?" Ten-Two asked.

"Yes, I am," Damingin responded. Ten-Two motioned for some of his men to untie him. As soon as they let him loose, he grabbed a dagger hidden in his chest strap and lunged for Mary. Ten-Two jumped in front of her as Jinmogen had no problem pulling the trigger to his atom gun. A squishy sound resounded through the air as the dagger penetrated Ten-Two's chest and a shrill zap hummed as an atom pulse hit Damingin square in the head.

Mary caught Ten-Two as he fell, and immediately whipped out her Jumyoo and gave it to him. "It will be alright," she told him as he struggled to breathe. She pulled off the linen around her waist and applied pressure to his deep wound. She slowly pulled the dagger from his chest as he moaned in pain. "Thank you, Ten-Two," she whispered to him.

"Only to save the one who showed me mercy," he whispered back.

"You will not die today," she promised him.

"Don't promise things that won't happen," he said as blood trickled from his mouth. She crushed a pill and sprinkled it into his wound. Brent knelt down beside her and told Ten-Two to sleep.

"Have a little faith," Mary whispered to him.

"What's faith?" he whispered as he struggled to breathe again.

"Believing something will happen when you cannot see it," she explained. She caressed his face. "You see, I have faith that God will not let another die in my arms, especially another, who saved my life," she whispered as a tear slid from her eye. "And you, who has brought an end to this centuries' long war."

Ten-Two half-heartedly smiled. "I'm so sorry," he told her.

"Sleep now; let us take care of you," she gently commanded him. His eyes, little by little, closed in the shallow night.

Chapter 13
BLACK BLOSSOM

Recorded 4.11.3207

Today I went outside as I know my health is failing. I saw something in the distance as I walked to the door of the haven we had created so long ago. Michael has now been gone for ninety-six years, three months and three days. Every day seems longer without him. The years seem like passing dreams.

Yet, I have learned to live and carry out our plans we made together without him. I now have passed on those plans to our descendants, and my place has now come to teach the younger ones all that I know. The others, my friends, have kept me living. I sometimes think back to the last night I spent with him. He held onto me around my waist, pressing his stomach against mine to feel our child move within me. I remember back to the last night we were together in the SOL: the way he took me in his arms. We broke the rules. Sacrifice, we told each other, so our children could grow up knowing the truth. Sacrifice, I tell myself now, so our family could live.

I came to the haven's door which now encompassed the bridge and entire city and gazed in the desolate distance; I could see nothing but darkness. Benjamin could recreate the human's reproductive cells using a device he created while he lived alone in the backroom of Level Base. The humans multiplied after that.

Looking back across the decades, I wonder, was it all worth it?

At first, a dark and daunting haze overcame my mind, but yet, somehow, I felt enlightened. I had been blessed in my life. Every scar on my body and every healed bone is a vivid memory that makes up the moments of my life. They have made my body the stronger and my mind the quicker. My BIS was still attached to my head, sending signals into the unknown.

Outside this haven that I have placed myself in, there is so much to learn and so much to experience; there is so much unknown. However, at 121 years of age, my life is coming to an end, and that I know. I do not want to live here any longer.

Then when I see and understand all that has happened, I finally answer, 'Yes, it was worth it.' My children are free to learn what they desire. My children's children do not have to fight for the breath of life. They are not restrained and enslaved to a life of meaningless torture under the thumb of a head council. Truth and knowledge are their friends, and freedom is their brother.

I gave the last of my Jumyoo to my youngest daughter Arianna, the last child of Michael's. The last child I bore from my womb. Our children are working to recreate the old world. Ana's plan did succeed, but there was so much sacrifice. Arianna is a beautiful woman, and takes Jumyoo with every meal. She is ninety-five years of age, but she looks like I did when I was only twenty-five: bright blue eyes, long black hair, muscled, toned body, and most importantly, she possesses a quick mind. Her mind is quicker than mine ever was. I know she is a great leader along with our other children.

Our children will not have to worry about war-fare or death at any sudden moment. They will not have to live in fear. I know Michael would have loved to know that.

The surface humans are still good friends of the humans from the SOL. They live in the mountains and we in the plains. They awake when the moon specks glow through the night clouds, and we when the tiny sun shimmers through the ominous day clouds. They have become distant allies. I pray that nothing ever will change that fact, but we are humans, all of us. One thing I've noticed throughout the years and observed throughout the world's history, is that humans have their own free will and subject others to the consequences of their actions.

I fear that one day, and I pray that, that day is centuries in the future, there will be a war between the two humans. I believe we will win when the time comes. Matthew did well in creating our offspring. I do not think they will be the ones to declare war. They are too advanced for petty discrimination.

I opened the door and stepped outside our haven. I breathed in the horrid air and immediately started coughing. Then as I opened my eyes, I saw something I had never seen before in my life, but something I had dreamed about night after night after endless night: a fiery sunrise.

It was very faint, just small red and orange glimmers hovering above the earth, but it gave me hope that this world we had created up on this surface was not the end. In that moment, Michael was there with me.

I closed the door behind me, and I stepped closer to that magnificent yellow rising out of the horizon. I spread out my arms as I felt something I have never felt before: the sun's affectionate rays upon my aged skin. I became warm and all my dreams couldn't compare to this moment. I walked towards this sun, this giver of energy and warmth, this announcer of the coming day, and I kept walking.

I finally stopped and opened my eyes. Before me there was a tree, a very small tree. I fell to my knees. I was right: the God who created all these things can once again create the same beautiful world that mankind took away.

Life was able to go on in the midst of struggle, survival, and heartache, just like the rest of us, I suppose.

I looked up and into the horizon and saw a human silhouette walking towards me followed by another and another. I stood up, and they started waving to me. I came closer. They all wore the now dirty, aged uniforms of the SOL. The ones that remained couldn't function without the guidance of the HC, so they left but were unwilling to come to our haven. However, one by one, they would come when they found themselves lost and without hope.

***

"Follow me," Mary said as they came into hearing range. One was hurt, probably attacked by a RMH, the so few that still remain. Not all of the ones there that day when the war ended really wanted to stop killing. They became deserters and stole loads of the precious Jumyoo before they took off.

"We need water. We hiked all night. We need to find this haven everyone speaks of," one man said.

"Our home is not far from here," Mary told them. "There they will give you water and rest." Mary led them to the haven, opened the door and signaled for the watchmen to blow the horn.

Mary thought back to when the horn symbolized something was wrong, and now it symbolized a lost people had found their way to a new life.

Men and women came out from their dwellings and eagerly helped them: gave them water, bandaged their wounds. Others began building the newcomers a dwelling place.

Mary asked the apparent leader, "Did you find anything on your way here?"

"Lots of rotting bones and dust," he replied.

"I was afraid of that," Mary whispered.

"However, I did find this," he said as he pulled out a pink little thing from his work pack.

Mary gasped in awe. "May I?" she asked.

"Yes," he said as he handed it to her. "What is it?"

"It is a flower," Mary responded. She had only seen pictures.

"What is that?"

"A symbol of rebirth," she answered. She sometimes forgot that not everyone knew the things she knew. She must explain it to them in words they understand or show them, and even then, some do not understand, or even want to learn.

She kept a record in the lady of liberty, writing down and drawing what she has seen on the walls. It became the museum and place of learning. She knew that when she died, there would be a great loss of knowledge. She tried to pass on what she knew to her children, grandchildren, and great grandchildren.

The door closed and the warmth of the sun vanished. Mary turned around, peered out and imagined a new world, one not destroyed by the splitting of atoms.

"Mother, come back inside! It's not good for you to be up all the time," Arianna told her mother as she came out to see what all the commotion was about.

"I'll come inside in a moment," she responded. Mary's youngest great grandson ran up to her, hugged her and looked up at her with his big blue eyes; eyes that Michael possessed.

"Mary, come inside," he pleaded.

"Not yet, my love," she said as she smiled down at him. "I have a question for you. Do you see all these people?" Mary asked him while scanning the entire fortress.

"Yes," he responded to such a silly question.

"One day, Samuel, you will lead these people into the knowledge that made this world great. One day, Samuel, you will build a better world than I have built for these people. And one day, Samuel, you will learn what has happened. Never be afraid to learn."

"Alright, Mary," he responded. Then he turned and ran off to play with the other children.

"Ma'am...Ma'am," the man she had spoken with earlier said.

"Yes?" she responded.

"His leg, look at it! It's bent, and he can't move it. An RMH attacked us and he grabbed him first. What do we do?" he asked her.

"His leg appears to be broken," Mary said as she cocked an eyebrow. She had seen too many broken bones and hearts and bodies.

"Do you have an HP here?" he asked snapping her out of her thoughts of the past.

"Yes, several," Mary answered and politely smiled at him. She motioned Brent's great granddaughter, Eva. "Her name means life," she told the man. "She gives it back to the people every day. She is the best HP we have."

Eva came to Mary and immediately noticed the wounded leg. She scanned it and gave him Thioxilline and Jumyoo. She set his leg and bandaged it. Then she hardened the linens with a click of her machine.

Others' daughters stood by watching. One day, Mary thought, we will have a University just like in the old world.

"Watch and learn. Listen and learn. Do and learn. That is what we do here. It is how we pass on our knowledge," Mary told the young man.

After a few moments of silence, she asked him, "When were you attacked?"

"Almost seventy-two hours ago. We killed the thing. We got him down and I took a rock to its head. I never knew I could kill something. It was such a rush though. Tyler had to grab my hand. He said, 'It's dead, Richard. It's dead.' That's when I noticed that pink thing next to its head, so I picked it up."

"The flower," Mary acknowledged. "So it's RMH blood that has stained it then."

"I suppose," he said.

Mary began to cough and became weak at the knees. Richard, the man she was talking to, stood there and did nothing. He watched her with those brown eyes. She put her hand to her mouth and felt wetness. Blood ran down her fingers. Richard's eyes danced. A slight smile curled into his lips. Mary knew that smile. It's the same smile that appeared on the lips of Hunter, the Historian, after the Head Council sentenced her to the surface.

"Help me," she whispered to him.

He stood there. She became afraid of what he would do when she was gone. He is the one of the killers she have read about. Putting him on the surface let his inner demon come out. There are no restraints up here, and that is why he stood there watching her die with a grin on his face.

"Mother!" Arianna yelled.

At the sound of another's voice, he put her arm around his neck and helped her stand up.

"Let's get you inside!" my daughter said as she came running up to me.

"Can you help me?" she asked Richard.

"Affirmative," he responded.

As Mary lay on the cot, she knew her time was coming. Arianna leaned over her patting her forehead with a cold linen cloth.

"Arianna, listen to me. Don't trust anyone. Don't trust Richard or the newcomers. They don't mean well. I'm afraid of what I see in them," Mary warned her daughter.

"Yes, mother," Arianna responded.

"Arianna, I have kept records of my life and my experiences. Please read them and learn. Don't make the same mistakes as I have made. Don't be a prisoner within these walls. Find out the unknown. Make this world better. Knowledge is the most important possession you can own. Don't rent it out occasionally. Live it, breathe it, learn it, apply it and never ever stop acquiring it. Be a glutton for knowledge. It will keep you alive," Mary advised.

"I will, mother." Mary could see the tears swell in her eyes.

"Don't cry because I will be gone; cry because these people are ignorant and do not understand. You will teach them all you know. Don't let your knowledge die with you as it is dying with me," Mary said.

"Mother, you gave me life. You gave everyone here a chance at life, at living life. How can you say they are ignorant? And how can you say your knowledge is dying with you? You have given us everything," Arianna protested.

"No, I have taught, but they do not want to learn. I speak, and they do not listen. Ari, they are arrogant and ignorant. The SOL made them believe that they know everything. They don't. They barely have scratched the surface! I have left behind the things that they need to know, but all my knowledge that has brought me true happiness is going to die as a fire dies after its climax.

I…" Mary began to feel the wetness slither out of the side of her mouth as her chest violently shook.

"Mother quit! You're making yourself cough again," Arianna pleaded.

"Ari, I'm going to die whether it's tonight or in the morning. I want to tell you something. Come closer." She leaned in with her misty eyes gazing into her mother's. "Always look to the future and plan for it. Always remember the past and learn from it. You have given three lives in your short lifetime. You, you be the one to give everyone a chance at not a normal life, but a great life. Pass on what I have taught you. I have given you enough knowledge to live a great life and to lead these people who are searching for something. They do not know what they need, but I do because I have it. Teach with all your might, Arianna, and maybe, just maybe they will come to their senses and open their minds to the glory of the knowledge that God has given us to search for and have eternally," Mary uttered.

"I don't think I can do this without you, Mother. You have always been my guiding light. I have always come to you with everything, and you have always had an answer," Arianna said.

Mary chuckled a little. "Ask deeper questions, Arianna, and you will find, I don't know all the answers. I wasted some of my years not exploring to find more knowledge. I wasted some of my time not attaining the unattainable. Yes, my goal is impossible, but you can and the people outside can finish it. Reference the walls and my journals, for that is where I will live on in the people. I will live on through you. I will always be your guiding light. My heart lives with you. Just look to the sky, the sun, the moon, and the stars: when these appear again in the sky know that the time is coming that you will need to be prepared."

"What do you mean?" she asked.

"Look outside."

She walked to the door of the dwelling and stepped outside. She held open the door and the light flooded in.

"Is that the sun, mother?"

"Yes, yes it is," Mary replied.

Her eyes began to well with hopeful tears.

"With this emergence of the sun comes new opportunities. You will lead these people to a new beginning. There is something your father and I never told you. The hand of fire is a part of the statue of liberty. Buried there, we, all ten of us, placed a metal chest for the next big event that would take place. There is a large rock placed there over the site. I want you to find that rock. I want you to dig and recover what's inside."

"Mary, I've never met my father," Arianna said.

"Yes, I know, but he is with me, and so you have met him," Mary responded.

"What's inside the chest, mother?" Arianna asked as she smiled at her mother's response.

"Go see," she told her. "I want you to have all the knowledge that you can. Something is going to happen, Ari. I don't know what, but I have this horrible feeling that it will be bad. Don't trust the newcomers. Build up your defenses. Gather the best people that you can trust, Rhome's family, Blake's, Shawn's and Brent's. Keep them with you at all times. Know that they are the ones who will defend you when the time comes. Get the knowledge you need to build the things that will protect you," Mary told her daughter.

"Mother, I'm scared," Arianna whispered.

"Ari, go to the rock. Find it, learn it, use it and save this haven," Mary said. "Find the surface humans and use our old alliances. The people here didn't believe me when I told them what that woman told me, so long ago. They have done nothing to prevent the past from happening again. Irony always finds itself present in the end," Mary said hopelessly as she smiled a despairing smile. "I tired myself with useless words, but you, you need to prepare for what is to come," she told herself.

"Mother, I will. I promise, I will," she responded. Mary knew then that she had hope in the future, and that the things that have happened in the past and the lives that were lost were not all in vain. She did not leave them to be buried alive in their graves.

Mary began to cough some more, this time more violently. Her eyesight almost instantly dimmed. It was getting harder to breathe.

"Mother, tell me…tell me…one more time," she pleaded.

"I can't, Ari. I…love you. My heart lives with you, and that's where…I'll be."

"Mother, I need you," she said as she pushed her mother's beautiful silver hair out of her face.

She was crying.

Chapter 14
THE SOUL LIVES ON

Recorded 4.12.3207

I remember her lying there, with this blood stained flower in her hand. She had wanted so much a pure flower, but she failed to realize that nothing is perfect. Everything has its stains and secrets.

The SOL knew that and tried to prevent the idea of imperfection from imbedding itself into the minds of its inhabitants. She was one of the few who understood the human's inner nature, but she was pure in heart, body and soul. She did not let that inner nature overtake her unlike certain others who read those stories and did not take them as lessons but as models.

Sleep overtook her that night.

I stroked her long beautiful silver hair and pushed it behind her ear. Watching her chest struggle to rise and then violently drop over and over again kept me awake praying that once again her lungs wouldn't fail her.

I still had so much to tell her, so many things I needed to know, and a multitude of questions left unanswered.

Time passed so slowly that night.

I thought the day would never come.

Then again, I'm not so sure I wanted the day to come.

On every one hundredth count, I dipped the cloth in water, and once again placed it across her forehead. I looked across the room and visualized her sitting at the table recording her story, her knowledge for us to learn and use to build the better life she always dreamed of.

She embedded her story into my heart, and her only wish was for me to carry it on and protect the things she had saved.

I don't know why I told her I never knew my father. I knew him because she made him alive to me. I wish I could go back a few hours and take back what I said. I saw the hurt in her eyes when I blurted that phrase out. My older brothers, David and Mark, would tell me stories of our father.

'Even though, he is no longer here,' they would say. 'He watched over us and made sure we lived on.' I would always beam, and then they would tell me, 'He died saving you and mother.' I would hide back tears, smile, excuse myself, and then run to mother. She always was there when I needed her.

However, this time and onward, I fear it will be different. I'm not sure if I'm ready to let my mother go, but then again, my mother was not ready to let my father go. She went on and did great things despite her being alone. Thus, I know I can go on because she is in my spirit.

I know it will be difficult and many will die for this place, but if it still stands in the end, I will have done my job and my duty to my mother. I don't know what she's talking about, but I believe her: that another war is coming. I don't know when or where it will take place, but I need to start plans for preparation now. I will follow her blindly.

She has never been wrong and has always led me to a better tomorrow even if it meant a bad today. I will do as she told me. I will lead the others. I will share with the others the knowledge that I have and the knowledge that my mother has given me, so that they too might realize the sacrifice she had given to this safe haven for those who were exiled or have run away from the SOL. There is no other place these people can call home, and that is why we must protect it against all odds.

I know there is a Library of History in the SOL, but it is so far away. However, I know that we have a Library of History of our own close by available to everyone who wishes to learn.

I remember having this revelation after she passed. She died not knowing what would become of us, but even then she had faith that I would follow her still.

I remember her hand twitched in the tranquility of the night and snapped me from my trance.

She began to cough again. This time these coughs were weak as if her lungs were slowly being depleted of the oxygen she needed to survive. She put her hand to her mouth. The blood wouldn't stop coming.

I used the cloth on her forehead to catch the blood. She grabbed my wrist. Her blood warmed the top of my hand as it oozed through my fingers and on the underneath to my palm. I stroked her forehead with a strip of cold linen; that is all I could think of to do.

She finally quit. She could barely breathe. I witnessed the same struggle to inhale and the too quick exhale as before. The cloth drenched in her blood dripped red water on to the floor. I placed it in the water bowl and used the other towel to clean up the blood.

Her blood on my hand will always be in my memory because that is when I realized that I knew her time was coming almost imminently.

"Mother, I love you," I said instinctively after I washed the blood from my hand.

Somehow the questions left unanswered didn't seem so important to me anymore, but the love she had for me did. I looked over through the open door into one of the sleeping rooms and saw my husband holding our grandson as they slept. And on the floor our other two sleeping grandchildren lay.

They will never fathom the love my mother had for them. That is why I must love them the way she loved me, so that they might one day realize the true love she had for everyone who calls her their own.

She coughed one more time. I held her hand up to my cheek and gently wrapped my other hand around her wrist. I looked deeply into her fading blue eyes as she struggled to say these words:

"I believe…I believe…in a better world…one where God is at the center…making things…as they ought to be."

And then she breathed her last as a gentle cold breeze swept by my face and touched my tears as they softly fell.

I delicately closed her eyes.

I wept bitterly as I leaned into her chest, and tried to hear or more wished to hear her heartbeat at least once more. I heard nothing.

I sat back up and folded her small yet strong hands over that blood-stained flower, for that is what she lived to see: the perfection life once possessed, knowing she would never witness it until the end. She lived for the purity of knowledge and died wanting more.

My husband woke up as the morning sunrise filtered through our dwelling's windows and door cracks. He looked at me, and I shook my head. He knew then.

He woke our grandchildren and then went to the other sleeping rooms and woke my three boys and their families. They all came to me. Kneeling down, the tears welled in their eyes. My husband came to my side, put his hand on my shoulder, his forehead to the back of my neck and gently whispered, "I'm so sorry, Ari."

"Is she really gone, grandmother?" Samuel asked me with his child-like innocence as he came and sat in my lap.

"No," I told him. "She's going to be here in your heart," I said as I pointed to his chest. "She'll be right there. She'll be with you as long as you keep her there."

He smiled up at me.

"Then, I'll keep her there forever." His blue eyes danced as his grandmother's once did.

My siblings, David, Mark, Laura and Nathan came in through the door, and their shadows touched her. They came closer, kneeled, and bowed their heads. I could see the tears in their eyes. Then they turned and swiftly left. My three boys and their families whispered sweet thoughts and memories.

"You'll be with us forever in our hearts," they said.

***

Arianna and her family walked outside the dwelling. The people had gathered. She looked at them. They bowed their heads paying their respects.

Her husband and sons went back inside, brought Mary out, and set her on the altar the people had prepared during the night. Then everyone kneeled.

"She was the fourth who died of the twelve who had built this sanctuary, this haven of rest and peace. The first three died so long ago. She gave hope to all those who broke the rules of the SOL. She preached that life was once great, ruled by the goodness of the heart. She prophesied that we could recreate that same great life. That dream is what she lived for, and that dream is why she kept on living," Arianna said as she spoke out to the grieving people.

"She was a natural leader. She possessed a great knowledge, a knowledge we will never know," she continued and paused holding back her tears as she witnessed all were crying.

A mighty silence swept the people as their fearless savior lay dead before them. The children were even silent.

"It's not too late…to learn…to grow…to become the dream my mother had when she first discovered this lady of liberty, this lady of freedom," Arianna began again as she looked into the near distance and saw the flame, the hand of fire, of which her mother had spoken.

The people looked up, and the sunlight from the sunrise danced in their eyes and on their faces.

"Out of the darkness, a flicker of light, hope and newness is born. The year is 3207. My mother was a great woman. I live on to tell her tale to those who might listen and learn."

ABOUT THE AUTHOR

Lauren Lee enchanted herself with worlds that may or may not come to be, and wrote short stories and novels in her early years about underwater societies and life after death using her preacher's sermons as inspiration for her writing. Continuing into adulthood, Lauren writes stories about possible unknown worlds with underlying themes and parallels of Christian struggles in life and the continual fight and sacrifice for good.

Lauren grew up in Fort Worth, Texas, attended Texas A&M University, and earned her Bachelors of Business Administration in Accounting and her Masters of Science in Management Information Systems in 2011. She resides in Dallas, Texas with her Yorkshire Terrier, Rascal.

For a preview of Lauren Lee's upcoming books or more information, please visit: www.laurenlee-online.com

CPSIA information can be obtained at www.ICGtesting.com
Printed in the USA
LVOW011628111111

254579LV00026B/52/P

9 781461 126638